The Bond Series

Book 2

THE WAR BOND

Keylee Hargis

The Bond Series Book 2

THE WAR BOND

ISBN: 978-1-7359207-2-6

First Edition: 2021

Printed in the United States.

For Taylor, who always supported me through my rough paths in writing. Even when I thought I was stuck completely; you were there to give me that final push of encouragement.

PACK TERRITORIES

CHAPTER ONE

—◇—

—Before Christian and Scarlett—
Octavia

I groaned, feeling that annoying tug my heart gave in my chest. Being cheated on sucks.

"You'll get over it, girly," Lesley encouraged, her lips tugging up into a sympathetic and slightly sad smile.

I stared up at her with a slight glare and this itchy feeling at the back of my throat as I grumbled out, "I'm lying in a bathtub eating ice cream. I'm never going to get over this."

"Why are you in the bathtub again?" She asked, crossing her arms over her chest.

I bit the inside of my cheek sheepishly, trying hard to rack my brain for the right words to convey how I somehow ended up torturing myself in the confinements of this measly bathtub. Puffing out a sigh and shrugging, I leveled Lesley with the best nonchalant stare I could muster.

"I was taking off my jewelry and saw the earrings Josh bought me. The thought of him made me want to cry and drown my sorrows in a bowl of Ben and Jerry's, so I ended up grabbing a blanket and pillow and slept in the tub," and for maybe a bit of dramatics, I shoved a spoonful of ice cream into my mouth.

"Sorry." She mumbled, covering her mouth to shield her obvious snicker. I rolled my eyes, pulling the blanket tighter around me in embarrassment.

"It's not funny," I grumbled, my mouth full of ice cream.

Then, like a flipped switch, Lesley threw her arms up and smiled wide. Her face lit up, and her mouth started moving so fast, I barely had time to process about the words coming tumbling out. "I didn't just come over to get your mind off of that jerk. Today is your birthday! You're turning twenty-one, and we need to celebrate. You need to forget about Josh."

I groaned for what felt like the billionth time that day, numbly mumbling, "It's not that easy."

"I know you loved him, but you can do so much better. No guy would cheat on you if he were truly devoted to you." I avoided eye contact after hearing her very true words. She was right. Of course, she was right.

"I know. It's just hard, ok, Lesley? I shifted at a young age and never found my mate. I just thought that maybe he was the one, that I shouldn't have even continued to look for a mate when he was supposed to take me as his. I just thought... " I trailed off, feeling the stinging of tears at the corners of my eyes.

"You are a strong she-wolf who doesn't let people bring you down. *Get your butt up!* We are going out for your birthday, and I'm not taking no for an answer!" I whined once more, sinking further into my blankets, the ice cream I was eating cradled close to my chest protectively. She unabashedly walked over and snatched the soft blankets off of me, and yanked my bowl out of my hands.

"Up," she ordered.

I stared at her, wondering if I could mentally make it through tonight. I didn't want to celebrate my birthday. I just wanted to be alone with my ice cream and blankets.

"Now, Octavia. What happened to that girl who didn't take crap from anyone? You're going to bounce back, but you need to let your girls help you do that. Please, get up."

After a minute of deliberation, I finally stood, my legs wobbling as I got out of the bathtub.

"I just texted the girls, and they are on their way. All of us are going out tonight, so get ready, or I will force you, and it won't be pretty."

I rolled my eyes. "Ok! Goddess, stop staring at me like you're going to kill me."

It didn't take long before I heard the yells of excitement as the girls walked into my house. I was pulled to the living room as they started putting different things on me and giggling excitedly.

"This is ridiculous," I stated, my lips pursed to keep me from laughing as I stood in the center of my living room. The girls all circled me, each sporting a more cynical smile than the first.

"I am not wearing a tiara!" I tried to take it off, but they stopped me.

"You look cute." Allison grinned, her dainty fingers coming up to fix the bejeweled crown that currently sat atop my head with the number twenty-one on the front of it.

"Girls, please." I laughed, playfully swatting away her hands.

"Nope, girls night!" my good friend, Liza, chirped.

As I looked at my best friends Lesley, Allison, Rebecca, Liza, and Morgan, I thought maybe this night wouldn't be so bad. Allison laughed while Rebecca and Liza giggled, and Morgan hollered out an enthusiastic howl followed by, "Alpha Ryker sent out a mind link yesterday. Everyone has to be out of the human territory by midnight, but I say we go to The Wolf Cave." My eyes widened.

"But, the wolf cave is-"

"The biggest club on human territory, which Alpha Ryker himself owns, so we'll be fine. If we're in his club, why would it matter if we're on human territory? Wolves will be all over that place. Don't be a party pooper, 'Tavia." Liza finished for me, giving me one of her usual so-what looks. I felt my hands fiddling with one another, and the thought of getting in trouble made the hairs on the back of my neck stand—from fear or excitement, I couldn't really tell.

"Fine, but if we get caught, it's on you!"

"Let's go!" Lesley snatched my keys from my hand, and we all quickly followed her out, the sound of heels against the floor echoing behind us.

The Wolf Cave was a short drive from my house, but we still made the best of it with singing and dancing in the car, and slowly but surely, Josh was nothing but a faint whisper in my mind.

When we finally did pull up at the club and went in, overplayed pop music was blaring, bodies were grinding, people were drinking who knows what, and I was regretting ever coming.

The Wolf Cave is the place to go for wolves because they have a drink called 'wolf's venom,' which is the only thing that gets us even remotely drunk. It probably could kill a human if they had too much. Normal human drinks don't do much for our wolves, but a bottle of tequila is a different story.

We all got into the club, and immediately Morgan and Allison were off getting us all drinks. Rebecca and Liza were instantly bombarded by two handsome twins twice their sizes, and Lesley had stayed by my side the further we got into the club. Still, as soon as we made it to an open seat, her nerves were visible to everyone around us.

She would tuck a stray lock of hair behind her ear or mess with her sparkly blouse, her gaze shifting to her right every few seconds the whole time. Lesley was the more innocent one in the group with the biggest heart. She felt it in her bones not to leave my side.

I leaned forward. "You can go. I don't mind!"

She jumped, her head shooting in my direction so that she could stare at me in surprise. "What do you mean?!" She yelled back. "I'm not going anywhere!"

I chuckled to myself, my eyes traveling to where her eyes had just been. There was a tall, dark, and handsome wolf eyeing her. I looked back at her with a brow raised in mock arrogance. She giggled and rolled her eyes, but that nervousness still hadn't left her.

"Are you sure?" She looked hesitant, like she didn't want to leave me in case I tried seeking out another tub of Ben and Jerry's.

I smiled reassuringly at her and pushed her in his direction. "Just go! I'll be fine! I promise! I'll meet with you all later. Now go have some fun, girl!" Lesley threw her head back with giddy laughter, her bare legs pulling her towards the man.

Morgan and Allison walked up to me, offering me a shot just minutes after Lesley's departure. I took it, holding it in my hands as they shot me pleading eyes.

"I'll take it in a minute! Go dance! I just need to get my mind straight first." I lied. They frowned but gave me a small nod, leaving me be.

Many would say I had terrible friends since they left me, but that wasn't the case in my eyes. It was our normal thing. Usually, I was the one first to run off to get myself into whatever trouble I could manage. Birthday or not, I wasn't in the mood tonight.

Time ticked by, and it had only been about an hour since we had arrived. I remained in the same spot, bored out of my mind. I tried to encourage myself to get up and have fun, but it was useless. My heart still ached with each beat of the music around me. Nobody, not even a single guy, had come up to talk with me, buy me a drink, or ask me for a dance.

Did I even want that to happen?

Looking at my watch, I waited, trying desperately to keep my mind sedated for just a little bit longer. I couldn't stand being in this club anymore. I felt like I was about to implode with all the emotions suddenly taking me over with each passing minute. I had also lost track of all the girls, and that hadn't helped my mood in the slightest, either.

When the clock finally struck twelve, the song 'The Big Bad Wolf' came on, and everyone let out a howl. I refrained, not really getting into the whole howling thing. My mood was too sour.

"Care to dance?" I jumped at the sound of an unfamiliar drawl coming from a guy I hadn't even noticed walk up to me.

I gave him a half-hearted once over. I just wanted all of this to be over so that I could go home and get back to wallowing in my own post-breakup pain.

"No thanks," I replied. He looked surprised but nodded and walked off to find his next victim.

As soon as his back was to me, it hit me. Why had I turned down an attractive guy who had asked for a dance? Wasn't I whining about it before?

I could let loose now! *I needed to let loose now.*

Huffing, I threw back the shot the girls had given me when we first arrived and stood up, heading towards the bar.

"Wolf's venom, line 'em up," I said, slapping down a twenty. The bartender grinned, walking to a box. He unlocked it and pulled out four tubes, sitting them in front of me.

"Eyes," he demanded—it was the law. I flashed him my wolf's eye color, and he nodded, pouring the solution into shot glasses.

I took a deep breath and started drinking them one by one. The taste was bitter and burned my throat like pure acid. When I downed the last one, my taste buds were numbed, and I could feel my toes curling in excitement for more. I motioned for another one, and the bartender raised a brow.

"Slow your roll. What has gotten you so worked up?" The bartender asked, holding his hands out as if he was going to steady me.

"I'm paying you to get me drunk, not for me to tell you my life story," I shot back. He held his hands up more in defense this time.

"Just asking. Wolf's venom is dangerous on second doses—even for a wolf." I groaned, shaking my head.

"I got cheated on," I admitted, slouching on the bar stool in defeat.

"Yikes. I'm sorry to hear that... here." He reached under the counter and pulled out a half-full bottle of tequila, sliding it towards me.

"Take it. It's on the house. Be safe." My eyes lit up as I snatched the bottle, muttering my thanks before trudging back to my safe place on the couch.

I spotted Allison dancing with a guy about halfway and smiled.

"Allison!" I yelled, and she turned towards me as I held up the bottle, already feeling the buzz coming.

"Yeah!" She yelled. "Get drunk! Screw that little—" she was cut short when the power shut off and small gasps broke out.

The hair on the back of my neck stood as unease filtered through my body. I blinked, letting my wolf eyes glow to see around the room.

Allison looked around nervously as she walked closer to me, leaving the guy she was previously with. Though, when a tart smell hit my nose, I kicked into gear. *Wolfsbane.*

"Allison, we have to go," I whispered and grabbed her arm.

"I smell it, too," She mumbled, letting me lead her away. I cursed inwardly, noticing her stumble behind me because of her drunken state.

"It has to be hunters." I halted, looking around for the others.

"The girls..." She trailed off worriedly.

"Girls, where are you?" I asked through our mindlink.

"We got out of there. I got the others; you need to find Allison and get out!" Liza's voice drifted through my head.

I snatched Allison's small frame up wedding style since she was stumbling around like a hippy on acid. Using my wolf speed, I started to push through people towards the exit. As I was almost there, something stung my thigh, and I tripped forward, laying out across the floor with Allison.

The lights switched back on, and I looked down, seeing blood oozing from my outer thigh. My teeth gritted together as it burned and bubbled.

"Oh, my Goddess," Allison said and went to put her hand on it, but I shoved her away.

"It's wolfsbane. Don't touch it." I stuttered out. The wolf's venom I had previously shot back was seeping through my system, along with this poison. My buzz was turning into nothing good.

As I looked around, that's when I noticed we were the only wolves that had stayed past midnight. Goddess, why did I let them talk me into this? *I knew it would do us no good.*

When my body locked up due to the wolfsbane, panic seeped through me. I tried to push my mindlink beyond its capability to reach Alpha

Ryker. My eyes stung with tears as I forced my mental capacity to reach him, but it was useless. He was too far up in rank.

"Are you stupid? Get out of here!" I yelled at Allison as the number of humans started to lower. The hunters would get to us soon.

"Not without you!" She screamed, desperately trying to pull me up.

"I'm dead weight. I can't feel my legs, Allison. You need to just go. If they were able to shoot me, they're near."

As I heard the sound of boots walking around the hard concrete, I knew I couldn't have spoken truer words.

"Well, well, well," A woman with combat boots in all black walked up in front of us, her tongue rolling over her white teeth in an almost sick fascination. "We have two pups in distress." She grinned, causing me to let out a snarl.

"Oh, I'm so terrified, someone help me," she cried in mock terror.

"Stay back," Allison growled.

"Well, I'm the one with the wolfsbane bullets, and you're a buzzed wolf. Who's really going to win this?" She raised her gun and fired a bullet at Allison, but as it spiraled towards her, it stopped an inch before her face. A monstrous hand held it in its palm.

My eyes trailed up the leather-clad arm of the catcher, over his shoulder, and onto his face. As I looked at his angular jaw and piercing blue eyes, my blood froze. Alpha Ryker. He came.

And he looked pissed.

"You come into my club, you threaten my pack, and you wound my member. How rude." Alpha Ryker threw the useless bullet to the side, the light clang of metal hitting the floor.

He stepped towards the girl with a predatory look in his eyes. "Are you really that stupid to mess with the Power Pack? We have that name for a reason." He asked, his eyes flashing his wolf's startling purple eyes, the color of power and dominance.

"I am not scared of you." She snapped, her hands tightening around her gun.

He grinned almost cynically, folding his arms. "How patriotic," He mocked.

She fired a bullet at him, but he stepped to the side with impossible speed. Gritting his teeth together, he charged for her. She tried to fight back as he smacked the gun out of her hands, but it was a battle she was destined to lose. Within seconds had her by the neck, raising her off the ground as her legs kicked in the air. If possible, my muscles tensed further.

"You messed with the wrong Alpha." He growled and threw his head forward, knocking into her own. He let her drop to the ground, completely unconscious.

"Take her and question her. I don't care what you have to do to get answers. Her friends are around here somewhere. Find them, too. No one leaves!" Alpha Ryker snapped at the members he had brought with him. They all hustled as soon as he was done giving out orders while he just leaned over the girl's body. If I didn't know anybody, I would have said he looked quite pleased with himself.

Then, clenching his jaw, Alpha Ryker slowly looked towards us, making my heart stop.

"What part of get off human territory by twelve do you not understand?" He snapped.

Goddess, stay with me.

CHAPTER TWO

⸻ ◊ ⸻

Octavia

Getting scorned by your alpha isn't what it's worth. It's quite terrifying, really. As I sat on a bed, a doctor attempted to remove the bullet from my flesh.

"Ow!" I screamed as he dug deeper with the tweezers.

Alpha Ryker stood beside me. "Stop yelling," He ordered, and I glared lethal daggers his way.

"I don't know if you noticed... but it hurts!"

"You should have thought about that before staying past twelve. Octavia, you deliberately disobeyed me."

"Who are you... Mufasa?" I gritted through clenched teeth as the doctor pulled another bullet fragment out.

"Watch your tone." He ordered, his eyes flashing a threatening purple.

My retort was cut off when the curtain opened, revealing Allison. Though, the man—no, the boy—that stood next to her had my heart shattering all over again. It was Josh. They stared at Alpha Ryker, looking starstruck as if they couldn't believe he was here in their presence.

"Definitely not. Get out," I growled at Josh.

"He was just worried," Allison tried to explain.

"How dare you bring him back he- OW!" I threw my head back onto the pillow. There was an IV in my arm that was supposed to fight the wolfsbane, but it wasn't helping. My red-hot fever was making me cranky.

Alpha Ryker's hand sat on my shoulder. "Breathe," he murmured and turned his attention towards Josh and Allison.

"Why are you here?" He asked firmly.

"I came to see her, alpha." He stated, bowing his head.

"Really now? That was obvious. She clearly doesn't want you here, so I'm going to ask you again, why are you here?"

"Hurry up!" I yelled at the doctor as he took his precious time with those damn tweezers. I'll have to remember to apologize later, but for now, it can wait.

"I was worried," Josh replied, his eyes cast south.

"Worried because I could have died and the last thing you did was cheat on me. Good times." I mocked, feeling drops of sweat glide down my forehead.

Alpha Ryker made a surprised face. "I can't do teen drama," he mumbled and crossed his bulging arms against his broad chest. "Allison, I told you to wait in my office, did I not?"

"Yes, sir, but he-"

"I don't care what your excuse is. Go back there and wait like you were told. Josh, go home." I grinned, and Ryker looked at me, causing my grin to falter slightly.

"Don't think you're off the hook because you got shot. I'm here to make sure you don't kill him," he said, pointing at the sweating doctor. "You'll have your punishment. You do know that people who go against my orders are usually put in the cells, right?" My eyes widened.

"Please don't," I almost whispered.

"We'll see. Do tell me the other friends you stayed with. You and Allison are not the only ones receiving a punishment." he replied, turning to look at the two idiots still standing by the door. "Are you stupid? Go! Do I need to say it in Italian?" they bowed their heads walking off, and he sighed, shaking his head as he ran a hand through his black, curly hair.

"Teens."

✳✳✳

"How could you be so careless?" My mom questioned as she cut up some vegetables for dinner.

"I came over to your house to tell you what happened, not to be scorned again. Alpha Ryker took care of that."

"Tone." I rolled my eyes, sitting on a barstool as she placed her knife on the counter, resting her hands on her hips. "Well... what's your punishment?"

"I have to clean the packhouse for the month," I shrugged, knowing it could have been far worse.

"That's not going to be fun."

"It's better than a cell."

"That is very true." She wiped her hands on her apron but gave me a sideways glance. "Did your...you know... *other side* get out?" she trailed off.

I looked away, shaking my head. "I didn't lose control. She didn't get out, I promise." I mumbled.

"Well, that's good. You need to keep her locked away. She's nothing but trouble." she confirmed, and soon my dad walked in, pulling from my thoughts of the dangerous beast that lurked within me.

"Look what came in the mail." He smiled and handed my mom a gold envelope. I refrained from rolling my eyes at my father. We didn't have the best relationship.

Her eyes widened as she opened it carefully, and a hand was brought to her mouth.

I cocked an eyebrow and looked at her expectantly. "Well, are you going to tell us what it is?"

"The alpha king has found his mate." She explained, her face still showing tremendous shock.

"No fair. I was hoping I was his mate. Is it a note telling me he's sorry that he chose someone else?" I joked, and my mom rolled her eyes.

"This is for a ball, you goofball. He's introducing her. Alpha Ryker must have sent us this." She stated excitedly.

"Why send it to us?"

"Because your dad is head gamma."

Right, the head warrior in training our men. I wanted to roll my eyes at the thought. I had enough of him training me as a kid. The horrible memories made me sick to my stomach. He saw me as nothing but an abomination—a woman with a secret no one could know about.

"Do we all have to go?" I asked, ripping away from my thoughts.

"Of course, if you get invited to this, it's an order. It's King Christian, Octavia. You don't turn him down. We'll have to find you a gown."

"Fine by me."

"How exciting." she chirped like a kid on Christmas. "We'll go after dinner!"

Once dinner was over, she quickly forced me out the door and into her car as we drove to the nearest dress shop. Not long after that, my mother had me trying on dress after dress until she found one that amazed her.

"Mom, I can't breathe," I choked out as she tightened the corset of the dress.

"Good." I rolled my eyes at her response.

She spun me around and brought her hands up to cover her mouth. "You look beautiful." I couldn't help but smile as I turned to look in the mirror.

"I feel beautiful." Which is something I don't feel often.

As I looked closely, my eyes were dull and dark bags sat beneath them staring right back at me. I finally realized that I had to let go of Josh and learn to move on and start a new life without him. Sometimes you just have to raise two middle fingers to the world and keep walking—even if you feel like everything around you is burning down.

I've gone through too much as a kid and teen not to be happy for the time being.

Tomorrow was the night of the big ball, and for some reason, I felt so excited. It could be the fact that it was of a new era with a new queen. It could be the fact that we were invited to a royal ball, for the best of the best. Who knows, but I was going to make the best of it. I knew that.

"We're buying it. Come on!" Mom laughed, urging me to change.

CHAPTER THREE

❖

Octavia

The ball was too packed for my comfort. My parents were far more excited than I was, I believe. My mom immediately went off once she saw someone she knew leaving my father and me in the dust. Then my father eventually left me to talk to other head gammas.

What a great way to start a night, alone and nervous. I huffed, picking up my dress as I walked, instantly regretting getting such a puffy dress.

As I walked by people, I saw a drink bar and headed over. A girl maybe around my age stood there looking rather nervous. I chuckled softly, knowing I felt the same. She was absolutely gorgeous as she stood in her gold dress. Her fiery, red hair was curled to perfection, making even me jealous.

"She must be some lucky girl," I said to her, trying to make conversation, and a smile appeared on her face as I grabbed something off the bar.

"She is..."

"Do you think she's stuck up or in it for the money?" I asked, sipping my drink, watching her eyes widen.

"No! I- I mean, I would hope not." She was quick to spit out, sipping her drink with a nervous look. I let out a small laugh.

"I know. I want our Queen to be devoted to us wolves and him, of course. A happy King and Queen make us a happy kingdom." She stared at me with an emotion I couldn't quite grasp.

"She will be. I promise." I turned to look at her with a raised brow.

"One can only hope. I'm Octavia," I stuck out my hand.

"Call me Scarlett." She replied while shaking it.

"Rings a bell," I mumbled. "Have we met?"

She shook her head. "No, I don't believe so. What pack are you from?"

"Oh, Power pack, Alpha Ryker." She nodded and saw the alpha talking amongst others across the room with curious eyes.

"He saved my life not too long ago. There was a shooting." I said as I pulled up my dress a little to show her my bullet wound from the other night. "Luckily, he showed up on time. He's an excellent Alpha."

"Oh, my Goddess." She said, and I nodded, dropping the end of my dress.

"The hunters are getting bad. I heard the King met with Alpha Mason, which can only mean war." The thought worried me.

She looked like she was about to speak when her eyes drifted to someone as the crowd separated easily. No one other than the king walked towards us, causing me almost to leap forward and bow at his feet. I went to reach out and smack Scarlett on the arm to tell her to straighten her posture and bow her head, but before I could, he called out to her.

"Ready, babe?" Scarlett smiled, nodding.

"Yes." She mumbled softly, glancing at me.

It took me a minute to process what just happened, and my eyes slowly widened. *Oh no.* I basically just accused my queen of being a gold digger.

"I promise, I will not let you down." She stated as he pulled her away.

I brought a shaky hand to cover my mouth. "What the hell just happened?" I mumbled. I glanced down at my drink and decided to tip it back, gulping it down to lighten the embarrassment with a buzz.

"Needed that." I nodded to myself and headed off to the crowd of people watching as Scarlett, and the King stood at the top of the steps.

The music was being softened, and chatter died down.

King Christian gave a sappy but heartfelt speech about her, and soon they were off to greet more people.

I watched from afar as they laughed and smiled, moving from person to person. They were amazing together—anyone with eyes could see how in love they already are. I wanted that. I wanted a mate.

Josh floated through my mind, and I sighed. That relationship was basically a lost cause.

"I see you haven't caused any cat fights yet." I heard a flirtatious voice say, and I rolled my eyes, turning to see Alpha Ryker.

"Alpha," I said with a bow of my head, and he smirked, messing with the cuff links to his expensive suit.

"Call me Ryker. I think we're past formalities, don't you?" I couldn't help but let out a small laugh at that.

"Thanks again, for the other night," I smiled, and his expression turned serious.

"Of course. I would have done it for any of my pack members. Just be more careful next time, ok?"

"I will, alpha. You know, I didn't even want to go—" my words stopped as a scent caught my attention. It smelled amazing. Like pine and cinnamon.

"Weird question, but have you been around anyone in particular tonight?" I asked, my mind in a haze. I took a step forward, and he cocked an eyebrow while giving me a questionable look as to why I was coming so close to him.

"We're at a ball, love. I've been around everyone." he awkwardly took a step away from me.

"No, it's... it's this scent." my eyes darted around, my heartbeat quickening, and I closed my eyes, trying to focus on it. There were too many scents to get a distinct direction as to where it was coming from.

I opened my eyes, and Ryker stared at me with curious eyes. "Is it a mouthwatering scent? Like you would do anything to follow it? Hell, you'd buy a candle that smelled like that?" He questioned, and I shrugged.

"I guess."

"Has your wolf howled with joy yet?"

"No... but she's fidgety."

"Well, Octavia, most likely... your mate is in the room," Ryker explained, and my posture immediately straightened.

No way. Minutes ago, I was just wishing I would find my mate, and here I am, catching his scent. I whipped around, trying to narrow down the direction it was coming from.

"Eager, are we?" Ryker snickered.

This can't be happening. The scent was becoming distant, and I panicked, trying to follow after it. I left Ryker in the dust, dodging around people left and right.

"Excuse me!" I yelled, still trying to fit through the crowd of people, but they would barely budge.

"Move!" A powerful voice boomed, and everyone scattered out of my way.

Ryker took my hand. "Point me in the direction." I nodded to our left, and he started walking that way. I mentally thanked him as people scattered from our path.

My mom made eye contact with me, and her eyes widened, locking on our conjoined hands.

"What did you do now?" she mindlinked, and I rolled my eyes.

"I'll tell you later. It's not important right now."

"Wait," I stressed, and he halted as I looked around. The scent was almost overbearing in this area.

A whiff of the delightful scent hit me, and I turned in that direction. My eyes locked on a man in front of me and my wolf started jumping around eagerly. As if he caught my scent, he turned from his conversation. When his eyes connected with mine, my wolf let out a howl of joy.

I couldn't help but look him over. He had a strong, sharp jawline, and his short dark hair had a slight curl to it. As my eyes roamed his face, I noticed a subtle five o'clock shadow. Finally, I looked back at his chocolate brown eyes.

This beautiful man was no other than Mason Cage.

My wolf was now howling with joy, and my hands started to shake as the words effortlessly fell from our lips. "Mate."

His eyes zeroed in on mine and Ryker's conjoined hands and the most ferocious growl I've heard ripped through his chest, silencing some people around him.

Alpha Mason is my mate.

CHAPTER FOUR

◆─◇─◆

Octavia

There was a time where I imagined finding my mate. He would run up to me, pull me in his arms, and spin me around. We would laugh and smile and would run off together. Though, that was no reality... this was.

Mason reached us and pulled me from Ryker's grasp within seconds.

"Hello, Mason." Ryker grinned, obviously amused.

"I wouldn't with the snarky comments," Mason growled out.

"I just helped you find your mate! You should be happy. Turn that frown upside down, friend." Ryker joked, and I questioned if he was really that stupid. With the look on Alpha Mason's face, he wasn't here to joke around.

"Let's go. We need to talk." Mason ordered, giving me a small glance. I gave him a small nod, not liking where this seemed to be heading.

"Wait," Ryker called out.

We turned, looking at him curiously.

"I was wondering, how did you not sniff your mate out? Shouldn't you have found her and not the other way around? Unless you didn't want to find her..." Ryker smirked, looking accomplished.

"Enough," Mason spoke through clenched teeth and turned back towards me. "Ignore him. He just wants to stir up nothing but trouble. Come on," he motioned me to follow him once more.

Though, my feet didn't move. I felt like a bullet just went through my chest. As much as I hated to admit it, Alpha Ryker was right. Alpha Mason should have found me first. He is an alpha, of course. His senses are ten times better than mine could ever be.

"Alphas normally have better senses, so it's weird that you didn't find her first," Ryker mocked a thinking face, confirming my suspicion.

"Don't listen to him, just, please... I want to talk." Mason tried to urge me to come with him, but I cocked an eyebrow.

"Maybe I don't want to." he looked surprised by my objection, and Ryker laughed.

"Whoops." he winked, walking off through the crowd.

"You sensed me first, didn't you?" I folded my arms, and he looked away. "Just say the words," I whispered.

"I'm not rejecting you," He was quick to say, and I rolled my eyes.

"Well, it sure seems like you are. That's why you want to talk, isn't it? To take me back to some room for you to give me some crappy story on why you don't want a mate, and that's why you didn't come to look for me?" I scoffed, looking him over in disgust.

"Cut the attitude."

"No, I think I have a right to be upset, Alpha." I mocked.

He grabbed me by the arm and pulled me through the crowd. I tried my best to put up a fight, but it was no use. He was too strong and too determined. I gave up as we finally made it out of the ballroom and down a hallway to some door, and he ushered me in, slamming it behind him.

I turned away from him in anger, trying my best to cool down before I could feel the horrible side of me to try and emerge. With my anger spiking, she became aware of my surroundings with eagerness.

"Sit."

My head snapped to the side, glaring at him through glossy eyes. "I'm not your pet dog."

He pulled at his hair in frustration and motioned to a chair in the room. "Please, just freaking sit."

I cursed him, taking a seat on the couch only to watch him pace back and forth.

"You're going to burn a hole in the carpet," I pointed out, and he closed his eyes—most likely to try to calm himself down and not rip my head off.

"I don't need a mate." he finally opened his eyes, giving me a tired stare.

I couldn't help but laugh. "I got that much, which is why I said what I said earlier. This," I motioned to the room and him bringing me here, "was pointless." I went to stand up, but he stopped me from doing so.

"Would you let me finish? I don't want a mate because I don't need you sharing the weight I carry on my shoulders. I have enemies, I have to always be on guard, and I can't be distracted."

"Mason, mates are supposed to be there to help with that, to comfort you."

"You'll just be a distraction." He shook his head in disagreement.

"You're incurable," I mumbled, standing to my feet, but he blocked the door.

Cursing once more, I yelled, "Mason! Just let me leave already!"

"Wait."

"For what? Why don't you do us both a favor and reject me? Stringing this out will only be a mess." I explained, and he looked almost hurt.

"I'm not going to reject you. I've already told you that."

"Oh, sorry, I forgot you had to look good for your people. I'll just be the person on the side unable to move on and find love and be miserable all the time." He shook his head.

"That's not true."

"Do you even hear yourself right now? You just said you didn't want a mate! I'm not going to sit here miserable. Yes, I know if I die, you die because if anyone's mate dies, it'll drive the other insane and most likely to death, but don't worry. I'll wear shoulder pads and knee pads at all times." I once again tried to move past him, but he grabbed me and spun me to where my back was against the door.

"Please, don't try to leave. Let me finish."

"You don't want a mate, yet you don't want to reject me. Do you hear how insane that sounds? It's either you reject me and let me go, or you try this out and see where it goes. It's not that hard."

He rolled his eyes and almost growled. "It's not that easy either. I can't... I can't have a mate right now. Not with what all is going on. Do you want to know why I didn't come to you first? Because I saw you, and I was hoping that once I dealt with some things and got some enemies off my back that I would find you again in hopes to start something real. I can't let you get hurt... I won't. That's why I don't want to reject you. There's plenty of time. I just need to figure my crap out."

I looked away from his intense stare not knowing how to reply to that. What am I supposed to say? Yes, let me be with you and be put as a potential target for enemies? I'll just reject you myself? Truth is, this is the part no one ever prepares you for. They get you all excited about finding your mate, yet they never tell you what to expect after that.

"You'll never leave your title," I mumbled, and he looked at me in confusion.

"What?"

"Your title will always be associated with you, Mason. You're always going to be the Alpha of War until you're old. That means you're always going to have enemies. We've met—our wolves have identified as mates. It's too late. I'll be in heat soon, and the mate bond has already started. It's a risk I would have to take as your mate, but I'm okay with that. I want a shot at happiness, but the question is… do you?"

His eyes never left mine as he took in what I said. I could see him having an internal battle with himself, but he finally nodded. "I do." he cursed, looking up. "I didn't want it to go this way. I just thought…" he shook his head.

"You thought what?"

"It doesn't matter. The bond has started now. There's no going back. You have to realize that however this goes, I'll constantly be protective over you and worried. You don't understand the threats that have been made against me lately or what's to come."

Taking a deep breath, I raised a shaky hand and boldly rested it against his cheek. "I wouldn't expect anything less. It means you care."

"Ok then." A breath I didn't know I was holding left me.

"Now, are you going to ask me my name or?" He let out a small laugh.

"What is your name?"

"Octavia Knight."

"Pretty name…"

"Now, can I go back to the ball we are supposed to be attending? My mother is probably worried sick. We didn't exactly have a smooth transition from that room to here." I mused.

"Yes, but after, I want you to come back to my pack with me. I can have someone retrieve your things from your house, but the full moon is only a few days away."

"Isn't that too soon? I mean… I barely know you."

"Not when your heat starts and the full moon is at its peak. I need to be there with you. Plus, as I said, the enemies…"

I stared at him silently for a moment. His eyes never left mine, and I couldn't help but wonder what was behind them. He constantly puts on a face of apathy, so it's hard even to imagine what he would be thinking. Would he share that with me? Will he continually be closed off around me? Millions of questions filled my mind until they slowly started to worry me.

What scared me most is that people like me… they don't get a happy ending.

CHAPTER FIVE

◆◇◆

Octavia

I stared out the window of the car. Mason was silent beside me as we drove to his pack. My parents barely even batted an eye when I told them I was Mason's mate and had to leave. They practically shoved me into the car with him. In my eyes, I felt as if they were relieved to wash their hands of me.

"Being mated to an alpha is amazing, go!" my mother had told me. *How lovely.*

I questioned everything. Why him? I had dreamed of this moment and played it over in my head a million times and never once had thought it would be like this. I never thought that my mate would be someone in power—the Alpha of War at that. The thought alone scared me. *People in power never sit well with me.*

There really was no happily ever after.

Glancing over at Mason, I saw him looking through papers in a folder.

"What's that?" I asked, trying to make conversations.

"Papers."

I deadpanned at him. "Really? I thought they were sheets of ice, my bad." I snarkily replied.

He sighed deeply. "It's pack work. These are some papers that Alpha Christian gave me to look over." He flipped one over, and I curiously leaned closer to get a better look at it.

"About the war?" He glanced at me curiously.

"How do you know about that?"

"It's been passed around. Plus, Alpha Christian only really meets with you if it's important, and he usually brings all alphas together for meetings. He only met with you, the Alpha of War, which can only mean there's an upcoming war. Common sense, honestly."

"Well, yes. The hunters are getting bad again. They're starting to take wolves hostage." This caught my attention.

"What? Why?"

"I'm guessing for experimenting. The last wolf that went missing, that we know of, was about two weeks ago. Her name was Aurora, and she was from my pack."

"They're just asking for a war." I scoffed, and he nodded.

He didn't say anything else as he vigorously looked over his papers. Once it grew quiet again, I shook my head, turning to look back out the window. *I guess this is my new life.*

The War Pack was just as terrifying as the stories I was told.

A huge electric fence was the first thing you saw of the pack. Barbed wire was laid across the top, giving it a threatening look. Guards were lined up along the fence, armed and ready. Their uniforms were a deep black with the pack's symbol—a wolf locked within a cage.

When the guards noticed Alpha Mason's car, one nodded to someone in a watchtower. Then, the loud creaking was heard as the gates started to unlock and sweep open.

I sat in shock as we drove through, and I saw the large prisons. It was just like the stories I'd learned. The prisons were all to the right of the pack, and guards ventured around everywhere to ensure there was no trouble lurking around. At first, I thought there would be no homey feeling to this pack, but as we drove deeper into the pack, away from the prisons, the place lightened up some.

More houses were spread out, and there were four large pack houses located close to one another. Pack houses are where teens or small families could stay. It was kind of like an apartment building in the human towns. Stores and markets were here and there, and the more I thought about it, this place was almost bigger than my old pack.

When the car slowed, I looked out as we went through another set of gates, and at the end of the driveway stood a tall mansion—which could only be Mason's.

He finally looked up from his work, noticing we were here, looking rather pleased. He quickly gathered his work together, threw open the car door once we stopped, and quickly made his exit. My eyes widened at this quickness, and I tried my best to exit as quickly as he did.

Why is he so fast? I scurried behind him up the steps as two men opened two large, mahogany doors, and Mason waltzed right through them. When I finally made it into his house, I was just in time to see a girl throw herself into Mason's arms, and he laughed, *he actually laughed,* spinning her around.

My wolf scratched to be let loose, but I remained calm. Now isn't the time to get all territorial. I barely know the man and just hours before… I was ready to let him reject me.

"Um… who's this?" The girl asked, finally turning to me.

"This is Octavia, a friend." he smiled at her.

At that point, my wolf was ready to rip him to shreds, not even caring about the girl who he had an arm around. I let out a humorless laugh shaking my head.

The girl gave Mason a curious glance, almost as if she didn't believe his own words. I offered a small smile to her, trying my best to seem polite. Though, when Mason finally looked at me, his eyes said it all: *I'm sorry.*

"I'm going to go… somewhere… that's not here," I mumbled, walking off down a hall.

"Octavia, wait!" Mason called out.

I huffed in annoyance, pausing as I headed down the hall. He jogged up next to me and gave me a solemn look.

"Don't," I grumbled, not having the energy to argue again.

"It's not what you're thinking." He was quick to state, and I folded my arms.

"Mason, I really don't care. We just met. You don't have to explain anything to me. Though, it would have been nice to hear you somewhat acknowledge me as your mate."

"It was my sister. She just got back from her honeymoon with her husband."

I shrugged once more, still trying to act like I didn't care, but he rolled his eyes.

"You can drop the tough girl act, ok? Act your age. I'm trying to make this work here, I-" I cut him off. *Act my age?* I was way more mature than he was. At least I would have the courage to tell my own sibling he was my mate.

"Make what work, exactly? Our *friendship*?" The stab was immature, sure, but I couldn't help but say it.

"My sister has the biggest mouth ever, so If I would have told her... she would have told everyone. I need time."

"I don't need time. I know what I want! I want a mate, Mason! Not a coward." A growl rumbled in his chest.

"You don't understand. Hop off your pedestal for a minute and stop thinking about yourself." he snarled, turning his back to me before retreating down the hall.

"Yet you seem to be doing the same thing," I spoke barely above a whisper. "I need my friends," I said to myself and decided to explore the mansion to think about everything.

After walking around for a while, my sadness turned to anger, and I found a random room to get mad in. I yelled. I cursed. I kicked things. At that point, I didn't care. I didn't deserve this. I wanted a mate to show off to the world. I wanted everyone to know that I was experiencing the dream that everyone wanted. Call me selfish, but I don't care.

"Why me?" I sobbed out, feeling exhausted as I collapsed onto the bed behind me. The familiar stinging of the wound in my leg brought me from my pity party, causing me to wince.

I pulled up my dress, seeing the wound slowly leaking the red crimson color I hated to see. Marvelous, I ripped the stitches. I closed my eyes, taking in a deep breath, and stood up when something crunched underneath my foot. My eyes snapped open as I looked down.

"Is this part of an alarm clock?" I mumbled, squatting down, and sure enough, it was.

Whoever broke this did not like waking up, that's for sure.

CHAPTER SIX

───◆◇◆───

Octavia

I walked throughout the halls of the mansion in the hope of finding someone to bandage this now open wound. There has to be an infirmary or something around here somewhere.

I turned a corner, abruptly smashing into someone. I looked up seeing a guy maybe a little younger than Mason.

"I'm so sorry," he stressed, moving aside.

"No, I'm sorry. I wasn't looking where I was going," I let out a nervous laugh. The man held an air of authority to him. My wolf could practically feel it swarming around him, and everyone knew that me and authority don't go well together.

"It's no problem. I haven't seen you around here. Are you new around these parts?" He asked, and I nodded.

"Just moved. I'm Mason's..." I trailed off, so badly wanting to shout that I was his mate, but if he was trying so hard to hide it, then I knew there was a reason. "I'm just a friend." the man nodded, raising his brows a bit.

"Mason didn't mention a new friend around here." Of course, he didn't.

"But any friend of Mason's is a friend of mine... I'm Alaric, his beta." That explains the authority. Alaric was his second in command.

"Octavia," I stuck out my hand awkwardly, and he let out a small laugh, shaking it.

"You wouldn't know where a girl could get a wound bandaged around here, would you?" He raised a brow with a small smile.

"Well, I've been in more fights than I can count on one hand, so I had to learn." He joked.

"What a troublemaker." I teased.

"Oh, totally. Mason just loves it." he chuckled, nodding his head in the direction I came from. "I'll walk you there."

He led me down a hall into a small room that looked to be a small examining room. He patted a chair. "Sit down. I can patch you up. What happened? And may I ask why you're wearing a ball gown?"

I snorted. "Mason wanted me to come back to the pack to... catch up, and I didn't have time to change. Now, the wound is from a bullet wound. I just ripped the stitches. It's healing fine, but the stitches help the healing process, so I'd rather just patch it up again then to let my wolf do all the work alone."

"Understandable, it's an easy fix. Why did you get shot?" he asked as I lifted my dress a little as he squatted down to examine it.

My cheeks warmed at the thought. "Um, my friends convinced me to stay at one of Alpha Ryker's clubs past midnight, and hunters showed up."

"Goodness. You're lucky to be alive. You should listen to your alpha's rules," he mumbled, turning to grab some medical supplies.

"I know. I felt terrible after, but don't worry… he chewed me out for it. He's the one that saved us that night."

"He may be a pain in the ass half the time, but he's a great alpha."

I nodded my head in agreement. "He truly is." I was gonna miss his quirky pack meetings and the funny speeches he gave at them.

"So how do you know Mason again?" he started to clean the wound, removing any old stitches.

"Family friend."

"Oh… well, that's nice, he's had it rough, which I'm sure you know. It's good to know he has someone there in his corner.

"Yeah…"

We continued chatting as he fixed up my wound. Turns out he's actually pretty cool.

"No way!" I laughed out as he told me a story about him and Mason as a kid. "That's hilarious." He laughed with me, shrugging. Unfortunately, our conversation was disrupted when the door opened and in walked the devil himself.

"Hey, man," Alaric said to Mason.

"Getting cozy, are we?" Mason asked, looking at me, and I squinted my eyes at him.

"Quite." I mocked.

"I've been looking everywhere for you, Octavia."

"That would be my fault. I was chatting her up after I helped her fix her wound. She just ripped a few stitches." Alaric explained, and Mason's features softened.

"Why didn't you come to find me? I would have helped you. How did you even rip them?"

"Don't know." I lied, looking away from him. "And I didn't want to bother you. It wasn't a big deal."

"Alaric, can you go check the perimeter and make sure the guards have everything locked up for the night?"

"For sure, man. I'll see you around?" He asked, looking at me, and I smiled.

"I'm counting on it." Ha, *take that, Mason.*

After Alaric left, Mason gave me a tight look.

"What'd I do now?" I asked, and he rolled his eyes.

"You know you could have come to find me. Believe it or not, I already care about you. I don't want you hurting. And really? You could flirt with anyone, but you choose not only my beta but my best friend?"

"That is truly my fault... I didn't think you had any friends." I teased, earning a low growl, and I sat back satisfied.

"Come, it's late, and we have to leave early to go meet Alpha Christian tomorrow morning since all the alphas are meeting. You need to sleep." He practically ordered, and I rolled my eyes.

"I already found a room."

"Where?"

"Hall B, I think."

"That is for community service members and staff, so you get an actual room. No room for discussion." He turned, walking out the door.

I huffed, getting up. *I really want out of this dress.* I bickered with him all the way up to my new room. Well... it was really me just yelling nonsense at him about how he could have at least gotten me some clothes for tonight until my things were here.

"I have nothing to even sleep in." I finished my rant as we stopped at a door. He opened it and motioned for me to go in.

The room looked more amazing to sleep in than the previous one I had been in, but I wasn't going to tell him that. Instead, I gave him a small thanks and turned towards my bed as he left.

I reached behind me to untie this stupid dress' corset. The top of the dress finally came loose, and I went to fully pull it off when I heard my door open. I let out a small shriek, holding my dress to my chest as I looked at Mason with furious eyes.

"It's called knocking!" I growled out.

He looked amused, and before I realized it, something hit my face causing me to yelp in shock. Looking down, a shirt fell into my hands.

"Goodnight." I couldn't help but notice the small smirk on his face as he shut the door behind him.

He had given me his shirt to sleep in.

***

I had woken up to find a bag of clothes to change into, which I was grateful for. Though, it wasn't long before Mason came to tell me it was time to go.

The car ride was dreadful since Mason apparently didn't know how to make conversation, so I stared out the window until we had arrived at the King's palace. Mason was escorted to their meeting, and I was told to explore. The palace was something I never thought I'd get to see in person, and I was glad I actually came today. It was beautiful. Outside was even better. I made my way out to the garden when I noticed someone sitting on a bench. I noticed the bright red hair and let out a small laugh. *Scarlett.*

"Well, look what we have here." She turned, slightly startled at my words, but her expression instantly changed.

"Octavia!" She beamed as she made her way to me.

"Queen Scarlett," I bowed my head to show my respect.

She giggled. "I think we're much past formalities. Call me Scarlett."

"I did kind of accuse you of being a gold digger and didn't know you were the queen at the time. Sorry about that," I spoke sheepishly.

She waved me off. "Oh, it's fine. I'm sure others have said much worse about me. What brings you to the Royal pack?"

"It's rather shocking, actually," I said, and she motioned me over to the bench she previously was sitting on.

"Spill." She smiled ear to ear. I was happy she was so kind. I didn't have any friends in this new life at the moment, and it was nice to talk to someone about this—to someone who would understand, so I told her everything.

We talked for a bit, and her words helped some. She was such a kind woman, someone who I would be glad to call a best friend if we get the chance to get closer. Our topic changed course when she revealed that she had been marked. After some jokes about it, I pouted.

"I'm jealous."

"Don't be. We had a huge fight today. He keeps himself so calm and collected and won't even argue back. It makes me mad."

"Well, he is the king, after all. He's probably mastered it over the years. He's like a God to people; he has to remain calm and collected. Sometimes that's what us wolves have to look to." I tried to explain, at least how I saw it.

"I guess you're right."

"Do you want to get out of here?" I asked as an idea popped into my head, and her eyes lit up as she nodded.

"Well, I'll have to tell Christian, but I'm sure he won't mind."

***

"Absolutely not." Christian and Mason snapped at the same time.

"What? Why not?" Scarlett whined as we pouted. "Please?! You can send a guard with us! We just want to go to the mall."

Christian looked down, thinking about it. My eyes widened slightly, hoping he'd give in at Scarlett's plea.

"You're not actually considering this, are you?" Mason stated, his eyes wide in disbelief.

"Boys, just let the girls have fun. Don't be a party pooper." Alpha Ryker said with a smug grin.

"Do you want your teeth knocked out because I can manage that?" Mason snapped.

"Please try." Ryker mocked, leaning his arms on the table in a challenging way.

"I'm starting to question if you're both nine years old? Sit down and act your age before I knock both of your teeth out." Alpha Jackson snapped, annoyed and looked at them with a glare to say, 'try me'.

After a minute of arguing between the Alphas, and some much-needed input from Alpha Jackson, Christian sighed in defeat.

"Okay, I'll send my guard Luke with you. I trust him."

I felt as if I would burst at the seams. I was actually getting to go out with a new friend! This was going to be so much fun.

I looked over to Mason, whose eyes softened. "If anything happens, you call me immediately, all right?" Mason softly spoke, and my heart confused me by doing a little flip in my chest.

"Of course."

CHAPTER SEVEN

Octavia

It was safe to say, Christian was going to *hate* me after we got back. The day started casually. We went to the mall, shopped around, then I got the text from Liza. *Come to my party*, she had asked. I don't know if it was the fear of missing out or the fact I missed all my friends from back home, but I was determined to go.

On the other hand, Scarlett was petrified as I snuck us out of the bathroom window at the mall and ditched our guard. I could tell she was worried about what Christian would think, just as I was worried what this would do to my relationship with Mason, but I just wanted to get away. I needed space to breathe.

Now, as I stood in front of the huge house that the party was at, I felt all the commotion we went through to get here was worth it. I had our new dresses we bought laid over my arm, and I glanced over at Scarlett, who gulped, looking at her dead cell phone, and nervously stuck it in her pocket. "We have hunters tied up in the trunk of our car down the road," she mumbled, realization kicking in.

"I know. They should have stayed away from us, to begin with. We'll worry about them later. Now is the time to let loose and have fun."

"We left the mall, ditched our guard, fought hunters after we were stupid enough to run out of gas, and now we're at a party. We're dead, Octavia."

"We'll deal with the consequences later. Let's go inside and change and then live in the moment before our worlds come crashing back down."

An angel and a devil, that's the pair we were. Unfortunately, I seemed to be a bad influence in this case.

We entered the house, sidestepping people to get to a nearby bathroom to change. It didn't take long before we were looking in the mirror at our appearance. "See? It's going to be fine." I tried my best to encourage.

Scarlett didn't look convinced. She looked as if she was going to throw up at any minute. "Let's just go. There's no turning back now." She groaned.

We left the bathroom, and I was on the lookout for Liza and finally saw her from afar.

"Liza!" I squealed.

"Tav!" she called out, walking over to us, her eyes alight with excitement. "Who's this?" Liza asked as she looked at Scarlett.

"This is my new and best friend, Scarlett. Look, we have to keep our eyes on her. She's a golden prize. Anything happens to her, and we're dead."

"Hey!" Scarlett protested. I giggled, shooting her a wink.

"Wait, Scarlett... as in..?"

"She's the King's mate!"

Liza's eyes widened, and she quickly bowed her head. "I'm so sorry, your majesty. Please let me know if you need anything."

"Please, just call me Scarlett. No formal introductions necessary. Just think of me as one of you girls!"

"I'd be honored!" She grinned and linked each of her arms with one of ours.

"Where have you been lately?" Liza questioned me.

"Uh, she's been crashing with me for a while. I met her at the ball and just wanted to get to know her. Make a new friend, you know?" Scarlett covered.

I was grateful for that. I couldn't exactly say I was mated to Alpha Mason, nor that I moved fully just yet. What was I supposed to say when I had no idea what Mason and I were going to be? If it would even work out?

Liza seemed to understand, and before I knew it, we were handed drinks laced with wolf's venom.

And that's where our night went to crap.

It was like it happened all too fast. First, the scream and the music being cut off, Scarlett arguing with some girl who was just wanting attention, and then Derek Merrington, some mannerless boy, stepping in only to get himself into a mess I know he wished he hadn't.

Why did he have to push Scarlett?! Why couldn't he have just left it alone?

It was like slow motion as I was dragged out of the house with Scarlett, Mason gripping my arm tightly as Christian ushered Scarlett into a car in front of us. "Christian, I'm sorry." she cried out.

"I don't want to hear it," he mumbled. "Do you realize what you've done?" He slammed their car door with great force.

I flinched at the thought, my heart beating furiously in my chest. *We got someone banished from their pack—their home.*

Mason guided me to a black SUV behind the car Scarlett had gotten into and opened the passenger door. "Get in."

"Mason…"

"Don't. We'll talk in a few."

Goddess, save me from what was about to happen.

CHAPTER EIGHT

———◆◇◆———

Octavia

I was more than scared, to be frank. The look of irritation and disappointment on both Christian and Mason's faces was something no one wanted to witness. Scarlett held onto me tightly, fearing what was to come. Mason could hardly look at me as he paced around Christian's office.

"I cannot even begin to describe how angry I am," Christian growled, folding his arms and leaning against the front of his desk.

"You don't have to. It's okay," I spoke, clearly not thinking my words over as Mason's eyes narrowed at me.

"No smart remarks while we're talking either," he snapped, sending me a glare.

"What made you lie to us? Was it something we did?" Christian asked, a look of confusion prominent on his face.

"We were sick of doing nothing all the time! I love spending time with you, Christian, but sometimes I'm going to want to spend time with my friends too. I want to go to places and stop staring at the walls of this palace. I know what we did was stupid and childish, but sometimes you have to let me breathe," Scarlett confessed, and he sighed, pinching the bridge of his nose.

"Let you breathe? I'm sorry that we're in the middle of a war and I can't let you go party and get drunk with your so-called 'friends'. It's not safe! You're about to be Queen, Scarlett. Do you know what this could do to your reputation?!"

I looked down, knowing this was all my fault and yet she hasn't blamed a thing on me. She should have... I was nothing but the problem in this scenario. I didn't take her seriously. She's about to be my queen, and I led her into a situation that could have gotten her hurt or even killed.

"Nothing's safe anymore! As far as my reputation goes, I don't care. I'm not going to be some Queen stuck in this palace fearing the unknown and letting you do everything while I sit idly by."

"You could've gotten hurt. Hell, you almost did! Be grateful I was there in time."

I wanted to tell her to quit arguing, for us just to leave and let them calm down, but her next words made me wish I would have spoken sooner.

"Please, I could have handled him just. Just like I handled that hunter." I tightened my grip on her arm, knowing I just went pale.

"What did you just say?" Mason gritted out.

"Mason! Did I ever tell you how great your new haircut lo—"

"Answer me, now."

"We may or may not have run out of gas, so we decided to walk to the Power Pack. Then hunters showed up. They're currently tied up inside our trunk," she mumbled.

"I cannot believe this!" Christian snarled, standing up.

"Whose idea was this?" Mason asked.

"Mine," I confessed sheepishly. "Though, if that guard weren't with us in the first place, then maybe we would have stayed and wouldn't have felt the need to go against the rules," I added, not caring how this went anymore. We were already done for.

"Would you really have stayed?" Mason questioned.

"Probably not... but it's the thought that counts," I shot back.

"This... this is why I never wanted a mate! I don't want to have to babysit someone! If you die, I die! So, now I will have to worry you're not trying to do something stupid constantly. You're an immature teen, Octavia! Grow up. I don't even know why the Goddess paired me with you." Mason finally snapped.

"Hey! Back off!" Scarlett snarled as I looked down to blink away the tears stinging at my eyes. "And here I was telling her you were such a great guy, Mason, but I was wrong. You're a jerk."

I tuned out the rest of their conversation as I realized this was my new life. A life with guards and never being able to do anything freely. I was no longer some girl in a pack. I was the mate to the Alpha of War. I had more to think about and a new reputation to uphold.

I was brought from my thoughts as Scarlett started to pull me up from the couch.

"Where do you think you two are going? We're not done talking!" Mason snarled, taking a step towards us.

"I don't want to disrespect you, Mason, but I'm not exactly calm at the moment myself. Let us go, and we can all talk when we've all collected ourselves. If there's one thing that you need to know about me, it's that I stand up for the ones I care about, no matter what."

I looked at Scarlett, a feeling of happiness coursing through me as she effortlessly took up for me. "What you said to your mate was hurtful, and I think you really need to dwell on that before she comes back to you with a rejection of the mate bond." Mason slowly looked at me, and I had to look away, not realizing that I also had the power to reject him if I wanted to.

Do I?

"Come on. Let's just go." I told her softly.

We left the room with heavy hearts. I knew she didn't like speaking to Christian or Mason that way, but she did make valid points. Although, we were most definitely in the wrong.

Scarlett and I had a great talk over some ice cream, which made me feel a lot better than she realized. After we said what needed to be said and agreed that we needed to apologize for our actions tonight, I told her I was heading to bed. Little did she know, I left and went straight to the bar downstairs.

I threw back a shot of tequila, liking the burn it sent down my throat.

"You're Mason's mate, right?" I heard and turned to see a guy sit next to me.

"Sadly," I sighed.

"I'm Axel." He told me before motioning for the bartender, and he slid Axel a beer.

"Regular?" I mused.

"Beta. Christian's beta, to be exact." I nodded at his response. I'd need a beer every night if I had to work for the king too.

"I'm assuming that's how you know I'm Mason's mate? Not many know. Apparently, it's a secret that is to never get out."

"Yes, I'm close with Christian. If you want my opinion, though, I don't think Mason is doing it to hide you. He's just trying to protect you. Maybe you should try to get to know him a little better, and it would all make sense."

"I've tried. He won't budge."

"Have you, though? Truly." He asked, and I sighed.

"Maybe not to the best of my abilities."

"Then that's what you need to work on. Arguing with each other will get you nowhere. Trust me, I know."

"So, you know why he's so closed off? Why can't you just tell me? I mean, I know the stories that he's this powerful Alpha who has brought pain to all his enemies and all that. You know, the stories people like to tell as you sit around a fire at night."

Axel let out a small laugh. "I think people hype those stories up a lot more than you would think, but it's not my story to tell. He'll tell you when the time is right, and I can guarantee you that you'll see him in a new light and understand his protective ways towards you soon enough."

I looked down at my empty shot glass, hoping Axel was right. "Bartender, another, please." I mocked, causing Axel to snort.

"Do you think drinking is the answer to all this?"

"For now, I do," I grumbled, grabbing the new shot and throwing it back.

An hour later, I was drunk and telling Axel my whole life story, while he watched me with amused eyes.

"And, and he dared to tell me I need a babysitter." I hiccupped out.

"How rude of him." Axel teased, and I rolled my eyes, letting my head fall against the bar with a groan.

"I need to go to bed."

"That you do…"

I started to stand from the stool but stumbled, and he caught me quickly.

"I don't know what's wrong with me," I pouted, trying to straighten my posture.

"You're drunk." Axel chuckled.

"Don't tell Mason," I whispered, my eyes wide.

"I don't think that's necessary."

"Why not?" I placed a hand on my hip.

"Because you can't stand straight without wobbling."

"I'm screwed," I whined.

"Come on, let's go find Mason." He swept me up bridal style.

"I can't face him like this, Axel. He already hates me."

"I highly doubt that. If it will make you feel better, just act asleep or something," he suggested.

"Got it," I confirmed. I was going to make this my best act yet, so I started making fake snoring noises.

"Not like that," He mused, chuckling softly.

"Sorry. I thought that would really sell it." he shook his head at me as he continued to carry me through the quiet halls of the palace.

Axel walked us into Christian's office, and I remained quiet as I smelt his familiar scent.

"Alpha Christian, Alpha Mason." he greeted.

"Is she okay?" Mason's voice filled with worry.

"Yeah, she's just passed out drunk, I believe. I went to grab a beer from the bar and saw her." It was all a lie, but I mentally thanked him for doing this for me.

"I got her. Thank you, Axel."

"Of course, sir." I felt myself moving, but when it felt like sparks danced down my body, all the way to my toes, I knew I was in Mason's arms.

"I'll get her to bed," Mason replied, already walking away.

I curled more to his chest, feeling a sudden sleep coming on.

"I know you're not asleep." He pointed out, and I couldn't help but smile.

"I know, but look where it ended me. The only place I want to be right now."

He stayed quiet for a few until I heard him sigh. "One day. I promise. One day, I'll tell you everything." I started to doze off, but I do remember a kiss being placed on the top of my head.

CHAPTER NINE

◆◇◆

Octavia

It had been days since we left Scarlett and Christian. Christian, I think, didn't like me so much anymore. I knew that was coming, but it still hurt seeing the look he gave me as we said our goodbyes—one of distaste. Maybe he'd come around, Scarlett said he would, but I honestly wasn't sure. The real bumming part was that it had also been days since Mason had spoken to me. After my night with tequila, he didn't say much or talk about what happened. The only thing that hasn't left my mind is his last words to me that night.

I wished for the day he'd open up to me, but as Axel said, he'll tell me when the time is right. Now here I laid in bed staring at the ceiling, questioning fate. I never understood why people said we were cursed. I figured it was because we were cursed to worship the moon. I'm sure that was the original reason, but I had a different look. *We were cursed to have to depend on someone else for happiness.*

I could kill to be normal. Love who I want, be with who I want, and not have to worry one bit. Though, I wasn't normal. Not in the slightest. Maybe that's why the Goddess paired Mason and me together. Neither one of us is normal. We both have constricting pasts that are hard to talk about—secrets we don't want to get out.

Pulling myself from my thoughts, I reached towards my nightstand as I heard my phone go off. Picking it up, I smiled at the caller ID. Liza's face lit the screen, and I eagerly accepted the video call. She met me with a raised brow.

"Hello? Care to explain what the hell happened at my party?"

I let out a snort, shaking my head. "Gosh, Liza, there is so much to tell. I can't right now, but soon, I'll tell you everything."

She pouted. "I was so ready for some tea to be spilled."

I giggled. "In due time…"

"Well, are you still at The Royal Pack with Scarlett? When are you coming home? I miss you." My heart clenched at her confession. Remembering the lie Scarlett spilled to cover for me, I had to go along with it.

"I don't know when I'll be coming home, honestly… As I said, a lot is going on that I can't discuss right now."

"Well, you did look close with Alpha Mason after he came to your rescue. Is that part of the reason?"

I pursed my lips. "Something like that."

"Oh, my Goddess! Are you seeing him?" she screeched, causing a small laugh to escape me.

"It's complicated. I don't know what's happening between us if I am to be honest."

She frowned. "I'm sorry to hear that. Look, I know it seems amazing to be hanging around an alpha, but you both have mates out there somewhere. Don't get too close to him, ok? I don't want you getting your heart broken. Alphas are more prone to finding their mates, or so I've heard."

I felt terrible omitting the truth. I so badly wanted to shout at her that he was my mate and I had finally found him, but I refrained. She'd know soon enough. I just had to wait a little longer.

"Yeah, I know, Liza. I'm being careful, I promise."

"Well, good. At least give me some details if you're sneaking around with the big, bad alpha." She teased. "Is he a good kisser?"

"I… don't know yet. Haven't gotten that far."

"What?! You mean to tell me you haven't even kissed the man yet? Hop on that while you can, girlfriend!"

I belched out a laugh, holding my stomach. "I'll tell you if I ever do."

"Oh, you better." She grinned.

Looking at the time, I groaned. "It's late. I need to go to bed."

"Me, too. I have to get up early. I'm meeting the girls for breakfast tomorrow. We all miss you terribly."

I bit the inside of my cheek, a pang of homesickness hitting me. "Same here. Night, Liza. I love you."

"Love you, too, 'Tavia. Keep me updated about that hunk of an alpha." I grinned, nodding before I ended the call.

Staring up at the ceiling after our talk, I frowned. My life felt like a mess. "This blows," I mumbled, tossing the covers off me.

I was wide awake, knowing I wouldn't get any sleep with the questions and thoughts wracking my brain at the moment. I walked into my bathroom and splashed some water on my face. Looking up in the mirror, I sighed.

"What is wrong with you?" I asked my reflection. "Why does no one want you?"

The dark circles under my eyes seemed as if they never wanted to leave, my pale skin looked as if I hadn't seen the sun in days, and I felt like I was slowly crumbling piece by piece.

I shook my head at myself, leaving my small pity party and went to turn on my ceiling fan. *It was terribly hot in here.* Though, my eyes widened at the thought. I walked to my window quickly and looked up.

"Oh, goddess," I mumbled, seeing the full moon staring down at me. *One word, one painful night: heat.*

The moon was almost at its peak, and I had maybe ten minutes to prepare. Thinking quickly, I ran to the bathroom and turned on the water in the tub as cold as it could get. I walked over to my purse, opened it, and took out some pain tablets tossing them back. I frantically tried to remember the steps my mother taught me as a kid.

My scent… right. I walked to the bed, snatching a blanket off of it and stuffed the crack under the door leading into the hall.

Though, I felt the first wave of heat hit me as I made my way into the bathroom. I groaned as I latched onto the bathroom counter to balance myself. It felt like mere cramps at the moment, but I knew it was about to get much worse. I took in a deep breath, standing upright, and closed the door before locking it. I took a towel to stuff the crack under the door as I did earlier. That way, no one would be able to smell my scent. *Unmated males did not need to get a hold of it.*

I stepped into the water, not bothering to remove my clothes. I tried to control my breathing as I felt the pain start to rise. My mom had prepared me for this moment for a long time. She told me what would happen when one meets their mate and how you always needed to be ready. I was now mentally thanking her.

I saw the clouds disperse from around the moon through the bathroom window next to the tub and sighed. I can do this. I can do this. "I do not have to rely on a man to take care of me." I encouraged myself. "I'm strong, I'm brave, I—"

A painful stab shot through me, and I gasped out in pain, reaching over to snatch a nearby rag and stuffed it into my mouth. A painful scream ripped through me right after, somewhat muffled by the material lodged between my teeth.

Tears leaked down my face, and at the same time, the water was starting to leak over the edge of the tub. I was too weak to turn it off.

I froze when I felt the familiar tapping in my mind. She was begging to be released, to help me in any way she could, but I knew she wouldn't do anything but harm those around me. I was losing the battle, though, seeing black veins crawl up my arms.

"NO!" I screamed out, the rag falling from my mouth as I tried to force her down. *I can't let her out.*

That side of me could never be released again. The beast inside me… she was nothing but a haunting past. One that I wish I could forget. One that will forever be trapped somewhere far deep within my mind.

I tried to think positively, but my mind kept drifting to Mason and how badly I needed his comfort right now. Though, I was brought from my thoughts as a loud pounding sounded on the bedroom door. I was too weak to reply, and my eyes grew weak. Slowly, the black veins faded.

It hurts so much.

I heard a crash, and soon the bathroom door was kicked open, pieces of wood flying everywhere. Mason's worried eyes met mine, and I let out a sob.

"Mason, it hurts."

He cut the water off and, in seconds, stepped into the tub, causing water to slosh over. He moved behind me so I could rest between his legs, my body falling against his chest. I didn't care at that moment how he had been treating me. I tried to tell myself I could do this alone but obviously couldn't.

I held onto his hands tightly and could hear his soft heartbeat, the complete opposite of my harsh beating one, and finally felt the pain cease for a moment.

"I'm so sorry," I said to him, tears falling as pain coursed through me once more.

"You have nothing to apologize for," he mumbled, sitting his chin on the top of my head.

"I… I'm a brat who is immature and can't do anything right. I'm sorry for how I've been acting towards you, not knowing your story, I just—"

"Octavia, we're both at fault. This isn't going to be easy between us, but we'll work around it. Just forget about all that right now. We need to focus on you."

"Why? Why can't you just... be with me?" I finally asked him, the pain starting to disperse as he rubbed my sides gently.

"Because... people who get close to me always die." He admitted, causing my jaw to drop slightly.

"What?"

Mason sighed, raising a hand to wipe my tears. "There are some things you don't understand. I don't trust anything until this war is over. I'll be damned if I let her take my mate too." I gave him a confused look.

"Her? Who's her?"

He looked like he didn't want to talk about the subject, but nonetheless, he started explaining. "Megan. She is one of the best hunters there is. She is the reason behind this war. She is the reason my father and mother are dead, the reason I watched my baby brother die in my arms, Octavia. I only got to my sister in time. I couldn't save all of them, and I hate myself every day for that."

"I'm so sorry, Mason," he looked like he was about to reply, but my yelp from another wave of pain stopped him. Mason looked pained as he watched me cry out, clutching onto him tightly. He wrapped his arms around my waist, hugging me to try and give me all the contact I could get.

"I can't do this." I cried out.

"It will be over soon; you can do this. If you're the same woman that took down two hunters, you can do it." I let out a strangled laugh.

Finally, when the wave of pain passed, I looked up at him, taking the painless moment to try and talk to him. "I don't care about the consequences, Mason. I'm your mate. We make things better for each other. You're letting her win as she watches you suffer in a life of misery. Let me make you happy. Let's make each other happy." my hand was now resting on his cheek.

Mason didn't reply as he stared at me, an empty look in his eyes that made me wonder if he could ever feel happy again as long as she was walking this earth.

I tried to delve further. "Forget this cold image of you. Stop living in the life people make for you. That's never fun. Life is about taking a risk, sometimes you get hurt, but that's the risk you take." He looked deep in thought, and I was about to take my hand away when he grabbed it, stopping me.

I groaned as more pain hit, and I closed my eyes. It wasn't as bad now, but it still hurt like hell. I stared at Mason with pleading eyes. I don't know what I wanted at the moment, but I knew I needed him.

"To hell with it." He mumbled as one of his hands grabbed the back of my head and pulled me to him, crashing his lips onto mine. The second our lips met, the pain vanished.

Mason turned me to face him completely, my legs straddling his lap. Instinctively, I laced my fingers through his hair as he held onto my hips tightly. He pulled back just centimeters from my lips, a finger moving to push a piece of hair out of my face as he looked at me intensely. My eyes pleaded with him. Don't stop. *Please don't stop just yet.* At this moment, it was just us. No pain. No worries. Just us strengthening as mates. I could feel it in my chest.

Cautiously, I leaned back forward and placed my lips on his once more. His response was hesitant, unlike before. I could practically feel the gears turning in his head as he pondered his choice. It was as if it pained him to do this, which I hated.

I pulled back a frown present on my face. "We don't have to do this," I mumbled. "You're not in the right mindset."

I went to move away, but his hands gripped my hips, holding me in place. As he stared at me, my chest rose and fell heavily. *Do something,* I wanted to yell. Pain started to spike again, and I winced, shifting uncomfortably. One of his hands snaked around my back as his eyes flashed a deep red. He hauled me back up fully on his lap, his mouth clashing against mine once more. He kissed me as if he was starving. After a minute of tortuous kissing, he wrapped his hands under my thighs, effortlessly standing up with me. Stepping out of the tub, he sat me on the bathroom counter, his mouth leaving mine for a second as he reached back to grab his soaked shirt, pulling it over his head.

I braced my hands behind me, taking in his well-defined chest. Scars covered parts of his chest like art. When he stepped closer, I trailed a finger over one, looking up at him with curious eyes. Then my hand moved to the back of his neck and pulled his mouth back down to mine.

Mason let out a small groan as I tugged on his hair, nipping at his bottom lip. His lips left mine as his tongue and teeth dragged down my neck and onto the spot where he would mark me. I couldn't help the gasp that left me as he nipped at the spot, earning a low rumble in his chest as I wrapped my legs around his waist. Pulling me off the counter, he spun us around and walked from the bathroom.

Our mouths met once more as he walked us near the bed. Laying me down softly against it, pulled back. He hovered over me with a lustful look in his eyes. He blinked once. Twice. Slowly, the red color faded, and his beautiful brown ones were back. As if noticing his loss of control, he shook his head.

"I shouldn't have let it get this far. I have to stop. I'm sorry." He apologized, giving me one last kiss. "My control is slipping by the second," he explained, his eyes flickering from his normal brown to red as he fought his wolf down.

"It's ok…"

He moved to sit beside me, giving me a small smile. "Considering your eyes are a bright yellow, I'd say you are losing your control as well." He teased gently.

I quickly looked away in embarrassment, blinking furiously to shove my wolf away. I sat up, slightly fidgety at what just happened between us. What do I even say? My heat was now slowed down. The bond had strengthened and, in response, satisfied the heat torture for the time being.

"Thank you," I mumbled, rubbing my sides gently. The ache was still there, but it was bearable now.

He leaned over, pressing one last kiss to my forehead with closed eyes. His forehead rested against mine after, and he flashed me a small smile. "You're like an enchantress. I want nothing more than to continue this, but I don't want to because of the effects of your heat pressuring us into it. I want this to be because we want to, not because we feel we have to."

"I agree." I nodded.

"Let's get changed," he mumbled, standing up.

I got off the bed and walked into my closet. Resting my back against the door, I let out a strangled breath. Wow. I took a few moments to calm myself and then changed. When I walked back into the room, I didn't expect Mason to be back in here. However, he sat against the headboard with fresh clothes.

"Come here," he opened his arms.

My heart flipped in my chest, and I walked over to him, climbing in the bed. I crawled into his embrace, resting there with tired eyes.

CHAPTER TEN

◆◇◆

Octavia

That next morning, I had woken up alone. As I laid in bed that morning, I couldn't get the feel of his lips on mine out of my mind. Last night went better than I thought it would have. I saw a side of Mason I had so desperately been pining for. I was glad he stayed with me last night and comforted me through the final phases of heat, but a small part of me wished I would have woken up in his arms, a silly thought maybe.

I had tried calling Liza multiple times to fill her in, but her phone went to voicemail each time. Maybe it was for the best. What was I supposed to tell her? That we randomly had a heated moment together? I couldn't exactly tell her I went into heat. Maybe I could say we went out, and it turned into something more? Lies. I just needed to tell her the truth. She wouldn't tell a soul. I trusted her with my life. Tomorrow, I would come clean.

Currently, I found myself wandering through the kitchen, my stomach grumbling and my body aching. I was reaching for the fridge when a voice spoke, startling me.

"Can I help you?"

My head snapped to the side, seeing an older woman with an apron around her waist, flour smeared on it.

"I'm sorry, I didn't mean to frighten you." The woman laughed.

"Oh, that's okay. I just thought I was the only one in here," I smiled. "I was just looking for some breakfast."

"In the dining hall, there is a buffet set up with a lot of food ready to be eaten. I can show you there if you'd like." I smiled at her offer.

"Thank you. I'd appreciate that...?"

"Cheryl, I'm the head chef here. And you are...?"

"Octavia, I'm a friend of Alpha Mason's."

"Perfect, he is in there as well."

My wolf perked up at that. Will he go back to his normal self? Or will he actually want to talk to me?

"Here you go. Have a wonderful day, Octavia." She opened a door, and I saw a few people sitting around eating, I assume higher-up people in the pack with the luxury of staying in the Alpha's mansion. In the very back, Mason, his sister, and Alaric sat at an elegant table laughing together.

I thanked her, making my way in. As if noticing my presence, his head turned, and our eyes met. Not knowing what to do, I shifted my gaze away from him and started walking towards the table lined with food. My stomach growled in anticipation.

I made myself a plate, his eyes burning into me. I walked over to a vacant table and sat down. Nervously, I began eating. Was I supposed to go sit with them? I mean, he didn't tell me to. Hell, he wasn't even around when I woke up. No note to explain either. Though, as I shoved a spoonful of yogurt into my mouth, I wanted the ground to open up and swallow me as I heard footsteps approaching.

"Good morning, Octavia." His husky voice broke the silence around me.

"Good morning, Mason."

"Can I speak to you?" His eyes looked around, "Alone." I nodded scooting back from the table, and stood.

"Where to?" I mumbled, eyeing the food that I so desperately wanted to scarf down.

"My office," He gave me no time to reply as he spun on his heels, hands behind his back, walking towards the door I just came through.

Looking around, I snatched my plate of food and followed after him. My heart picked up its speed with every step. I had a feeling I knew what was about to happen. Once we made it into his office, I sat down on the couch next to the door as millions of thoughts ran through my mind.

As I bit into a piece of bacon, he looked at me amused and let out a small laugh. Ok, so he's in a decent mood. Maybe this isn't a farewell talk.

"How did you sleep? Are you feeling ok?"

Confused by his new change of mood, I nodded. "I slept great. Thanks to you,"

He smiled, looking satisfied as he leaned against the front of his desk. Though, I didn't like the look he had on his face as he thought his next words over.

"Look-" he started to speak, but I beat him to it.

"If you say last night was a mistake, I might actually knock your teeth in." I rushed out.

His eyes flashed from red to brown, making me gulp at his intense glare. "Do you really think that low of me?"

He took my lack of response as his answer, running his hands through his hair agitated. "I was going to say that last night I told you some things that I have never told anyone. So I would really appreciate you keeping them between us." He started. "And, I don't think last night was a mistake. Honestly? It's the happiest I've felt in a while, and that's saying something." My heart tugged at his confession.

"Mason, I'd never tell anyone what you told me. I promise you that."

"But..."

I wanted to curse at the word. *Nothing good ever comes after the word but.*

I looked away, not wanting him to see the panic that washed over me.

A finger was placed under my chin, making me look up at him. "Please don't do that. Don't start thinking the worst. I'm not going anywhere, but for right now, we need to keep this between us. Like I already explained, I have enemies who wouldn't think twice before coming after you. Please just give me some time to get a plan together before I announce our bond."

"I'm a big girl, Mason. I understand your precaution, but you're always going to have enemies. You're the alpha of war. That isn't going to change. Trust me when I say that I can take care of myself." I frowned.

He crouched down in front of me, cupping the sides of my face. "I'm your mate, Octavia. It's my job to worry about you. We're keeping low for a bit, and that's final. Nothing will change between us." He finished, placing a kiss on my forehead, and my eyes fluttered shut at the contact.

It was at that moment that I knew I had to let my selfish needs go. I knew he was just looking out for me, and after what he told me last night, I knew this was a big step for him.

"Ok," I nodded.

"I thought I was going to have to try a lot harder than that," He teased.

I scoffed, giving him a playful shove. "Don't test me."

His chest vibrated with laughter as he stood up, offering me a hand. I took it, setting my plate aside, letting him pull me from the couch as he pulled me to his chest, wrapping an arm around my waist. I couldn't help but smile at how much he changed overnight.

"I have a meeting in a few minutes. Do as you please for a while, and I'll come and find you after. We can get some dinner if you like."

"That sounds nice." I grinned, placing my hands on his chest as I leaned up, kissing his cheek. "Thank you for trying." I nearly whispered.

He looked slightly shocked by my words but gave me a breathtaking smile in response. Pulling out of his grasp, I felt my wolf whine in protest. I had to force myself to walk away from him, but I wanted nothing more than to just lay in his arms for a few minutes longer. I grabbed my plate of food and made my way to the door. As I opened it, he called out my name.

"Yeah?" His back was to me as he looked down at some papers on his desk.

"Don't wander off anywhere and get yourself in a mess," He mused, and I let out a small laugh.

"Tempting." Before he could reply, I quickly shut the door behind me, a bright smile on my face as I walked down the hallway.

***

He didn't tell me to stay out of the bar; which is where I currently sat. Looking around, I was surprised to see a lot of people here. I guess this was where people went in the pack on their lunch break? I figured they would all come at night.

"Abusing alcohol, I see." I turned and saw Alaric, Mason's beta, who was smirking.

"Are you stalking me, beta?"

"Hm. Tempting, but the world doesn't revolve around you, I'm afraid." He sat down next to me. His previous humored expression was replaced with a grumpy one.

"Someone has got you in a mood," I leaned in closer, resting my chin on my fists. "Do tell."

"I just found my girlfriend in bed with another guy," He spilled, and my eyes widened.

"Oh, Goddess!" I turned towards the bartender in a bewildered state. "We're going to need some tequila over here!" I turned back to face a bummed-looking Alaric. "Mate?"

"Thankfully, no."

"Well, that's good. If it makes you feel any better, I was cheated on too. I laid in the bathtub with a blanket and ice cream for days." I grimaced at the thought. It all seemed too silly looking back.

That was a low point for me, that's for sure.

"I might just have to try that." He mocked, and the bartender sat out glasses about to pour us some shots.

"Oh, no, honey," I snorted, taking the bottle from him, and his eyes widened. "Buzz off. We've had a long day." I grumbled.

The man looked at his watch. "It's one o'clock in the afternoon?"

"Scratch that... long life." I corrected with a teasing smile while putting the bottle to my mouth.

Alaric took money from his wallet and gave it to the puzzled bartender. "Ignore her." He waved him off.

"Here." I slid the bottle over.

"I came for a beer... and here I am drinking tequila."

"Hey, if you don't want any—" I went to take it back, but he pushed my hands away.

"Hey, hey, hey. I paid for this. I'm drinking it." He grimaced as he poured some into his mouth.

"See? Feeling better already." I mused, and he cocked an eyebrow.

"If this taste good to you, you're surely an alcoholic, Octavia."

I pondered on the statement. "Probably," I replied truthfully as I took the bottle back.

He went silent, and I watched as his eyes glazed over, his pupils dilating. *I know someone getting a mindlink when I see one.* I'm also pretty certain who that someone is.

"Mason is wondering where you are," He spoke, confirming my thoughts.

"Tell him I'm taking a long, mind-clearing walk,"

"I told him you were with me at the bar. He said to keep an eye on you." Alaric snickered, taking the bottle away from me. "He also said not to let you drink too much. Something about you not being able to handle it."

I scoffed and mock-gasped. "How rude. *True*, but rude."

After a minute of hesitation, he asked, "Are you like his girlfriend or something?"

"Not quite. Now we have half a bottle of tequila to finish, and I don't know about you, but I don't like letting money go to waste."

***

It was safe to say Alaric didn't like wasting money either. The empty tequila bottle sat on the table before us, and we both were too buzzed to care.

"And Josh was such a baby!" I laughed out.

We had moved to a booth and were both having a hard time sitting up straight with the amount of alcohol in our systems.

"Really? How?"

"Dude, he would hit his toe on a corner and tear up. I felt like the man in the relationship half the time." I coughed out a laugh once more, and Alaric gave me a stern look.

"Corners can kill your toes, man." I burst out laughing.

He couldn't help but join in, but I panicked when the laughter died out and our eyes locked.

I suddenly regretted sitting so close to him as he leaned in, and my breath hitched. "What are you doing?"

"I was going to kiss you," He said, sounding confused.

"I can't," I turned my head and heard him sigh.

"Why?" He asked.

"Because one, I'm not a rebound." I mused. "And two, I have my eye on someone. I may be intoxicated, but I'm always loyal." I drawled out and slumped against Alaric's chest. "You can do better than me anyway," I added, and he sighed, wrapping an arm around my shoulder.

"I don't know what to do, honestly." I looked up at him with a slight frown.

"She was stupid. It was her loss. Who knows... maybe your mate is right around the corner waiting with open arms." I countered, and he gave me a goofy grin.

"Maybe."

I felt my wolf perk up as I heard the bell above the door ding. My body froze as I realized who it was. I glanced over, knowing who just walked in. When his eyes met mine, my heart jumped. Mason's eyes zeroed in on me, laying against Alaric's chest, and his fists clenched.

Oh crap.

CHAPTER ELEVEN

─◆◇◆─

Octavia

I gulped, watching him take long, slow strides towards us. I wasn't doing anything wrong, but I felt like I just killed someone by the way he was looking at us. Bringing myself together, I looked over at a confused Alaric.

"You need to go," I spoke in a frantic tone.

"What?" I stood to pull him to his feet.

"Go! For your own good, you idiot! *Go!* Backdoor." He looked towards Mason marching towards us across the bar. When he looked back at me, I knew he'd finally put the pieces together.

"I'll see you later." He mumbled and took off towards the back door.

Mason went to brush past me, but I stopped him by placing my hands on his chest. He was heavily breathing as his gaze was locked on his target ahead.

"Don't start with me." Mason snapped and forcefully brushed past me, headed towards the back exit.

I ran after him like a lost puppy. What is his deal?!

"Stop being immature!" I yelled once we made it outside as I rushed to keep up with him. I once again maneuvered myself in front of him, cupping his face gently so he would look at me.

"What are you doing, Mason?" I asked.

"What am I doing?" He let out a humorless laugh. "*What am I doing*, Octavia?! I'm going to bash his teeth in," he growled.

"No, you aren't. Stopping acting like this. You don't have the right!"

"Really? Because my beta was all over my mate! I think I have the right to be pissed." I scoffed and pushed him backward.

"The fact that you actually think I'd do that sickens me. He's a friend and nothing more. He didn't even know we were mates. Alaric had no rules to go by, and that, *my dear mate*, is *your* fault."

"What you forgot is that betas and alphas have a strong bond. I can peek into his mind whenever I like and see what he's doing. You actually think I'd leave you alone with an unmated male? Absolutely not."

"Why the hell are you peeking around in his mind, Mason?! I get mindlinking to make sure all is good, but that is going too far. Do you not trust me?"

"That's the thing. I trust you both unconditionally, but I will never not worry about you. I was just simply checking in to make sure everything was fine, and then I saw him leaning in to kiss you. I'm so furious I don't even know how to put it into words." His eyes shined a bright red as his anger started rising.

"You need to calm down. Maybe if you had pried into his life more, you would have seen that I pushed him away and even said I was loyal to someone else. That someone being you. He didn't know we were mates, so how was he supposed to know that kissing me wasn't ok? He caught his girlfriend in bed with another guy, so we drank a bit. Sue me."

"I'm done with this conversation," He shook his head, starting to walk away, and I pointed my finger at him angrily.

"No! You don't get to be jealous and act like an ass and then walk away from me. You got hurt. I understand, but there is no need to be! You can't run away from this with your tail tucked between your legs. You can trust my loyalty to you, Mason. He didn't mean any harm. If you had told him the truth from the start, none of that would have happened." I let out a breath of air I didn't know I was holding, waiting for him to reply, but there was none. He stared at me with an unreadable expression.

I looked away, trying to find the words to show him how this was no one's fault, and there was nothing to be mad over, but I couldn't find the right words that didn't involve cussing him out. Finally, I closed my eyes, letting myself calm down. Arguing will get us nowhere.

"Look, Mason, we're mates, and we have to talk things over. We both always try to fix our problems by going in guns blazing and yelling. We have to stop this dance of one step forward and two steps back. I can't physically and emotionally take it anymore. If you want to be mad over something that didn't even happen, then so be it, but just know I'd never do something like that to you. Alaric wouldn't either. He's your best friend, after all. Explain our bond to him. Let him tell his side, but don't try to fix a problem with your fists."

After a minute, he let out a sigh, knowing I was right. "You're right. I'm sorry." He mumbled.

"Thank you for acknowledging that. It's ok. Now, can we please go get the dinner you promised me?" I smiled, and his grumpy mood slowly started to change as he sported a half-smile.

"Lead the way," he motioned before him.

"Yeah, I actually have no idea where anything is here besides the bar," I spoke sheepishly, and he belched out a laugh.

"You need to stop drinking."

I raised my hands in defense. "Honestly, it's not like I do it to drown out my sorrows or anything. I simply like to have a relaxing drink, and sometimes I just take one drink and then everything is a blur, and then I have to ask myself how I got into that situation and—" his hand grabbed hold of my wrist, gently jerking me to him.

I stared up at him with wide eyes. "You talk too much," he joked, placing a soft kiss on my lips that made my toes curl. He pulled back, pressing a kiss on my forehead. "But I'm definitely monitoring your drinking from now on." he mused. "If you have to ask yourself how you get into situations of why you were so drunk… I don't think alcohol is the one at fault."

My cheeks warmed. "Yeah, you're probably right."

He nodded. "Sometimes I am."

"You're right about that. *Sometimes*." I mocked, and he gave me a playful shove.

"Come on. I'm hungry." He laced our fingers together and tried to start walking forward, but I smirked, tugging him back to me. He gave me a confused look.

"I think I need one more kiss to motivate me to walk." I shrugged innocently.

He pursed his lips. "You're ridiculous."

"No… I don't think so." I flashed him a million-dollar smile.

Slowly, he inched closer to me, and his pointer finger and thumb grasped my chin, tilting my head up. His eyes didn't leave mine as he moved closer to my lips. He paused, giving me a small wink, and finally closed the gap. His hands moved to grab my waist, pulling me closer and my arms instinctively wrapped around his neck. The kiss was slow and torturous, but I loved every second of it.

We pulled apart, smiles on our faces. When he rested his forehead against mine, his eyes held unspoken words. I raised a brow, wondering why he was looking at me like that.

"If you want to go public with this, we can. I'll tell everyone in the pack, but I need you to promise me you will do as I say, and you will let me do what is in your best interest. You're right, I will always have enemies, but I will also always do anything in my power to protect you. Do you understand that?" I stared agape.

Speechless, I quickly nodded, my hold on him tightening.

"Good. You may not like it, but if you leave the house, you take me, Alaric, or a guard with you. I would just feel better, even though you should be safe inside the pack walls. You never know." I smiled.

"Deal." His eyes widened.

"I was sure you were going to fight me on that." I laughed, letting my arms drop from his neck and grabbed his hand, lacing my fingers through his.

"You met me halfway, and that's all I could ask for, Mason."

He smiled, giving me one more kiss. "Now, dinner?"

I nodded. "I'm starved."

***

When we headed home later that night, one of the maids rushed to take his jacket with a smile.

"Thank you." He told her, to which she replied with an 'always sir' but the look in her eyes made me squint my own.

She definitely had a thing for him, but I couldn't really blame the woman. He was a sight to see. An Adonis himself.

"Come," He held out his hand for me, and the maid's mouth dropped at his actions causing me to grin as I eagerly grabbed hold of it.

Once we were upstairs, we stopped in front of my room, and I bit my lip.

"I guess this is where we depart." I slightly frowned as I reached for the door handle, but he shook his head.

"Stay with me tonight."

"What?"

"You heard me. Stay with me tonight."

I thought about it but knew that if I wanted to get closer to him, I had to. Plus, the last time I fell asleep in his arms, it was a blissful sleep. "Fine, but no funny business." I mused.

"I would never." He smirked and took my hand in his once more and headed towards his room.

The whole top floor was his. Up here was his office, room, and some other things an alpha needs to do his job. Though, his room was a sight to see. My jaw dropped as I looked it over. It was huge.

"This is where you sleep?" I spat out.

"Yes." He snickered at my shocked state.

The room had a dark color scheme, but this was Mason we're talking about, so it wasn't surprising. There was a huge king-sized bed right in the center of the room. The whole wall to the left side was glass windows looking out to an amazing view. He grabbed a remote and pushed a button, and curtains swept over the glassed window blocking any outside viewers.

I let out a whistle. "You alphas must have it set."

He let out a snort as he switched on a lamp. "Something like that."

A door was open that led into a master bathroom that looked just as nice and big. There was a small seating area, and then a huge flatscreen was on the wall directed towards the bed.

"I'm going to take a quick shower." He mentioned, heading towards his closet.

"Yeah, I need one too. I guess I should have stayed downstairs and done that first." I replied with a nervous laugh.

Why was I all fidgety all of a sudden?

"Just use mine. I'll wait."

"Mason, I'm fine with walking to my room. It's not a big deal."

"I insist." He reminded me, and I looked towards his bathroom and the huge shower looking more inviting by the second.

"Ok, fine."

"Towels are next to the shower on the rack, along with some washcloths. Help yourself to anything you need. There is also some body wash under the sink that you may like better than mine."

"Thank you," I smiled, walking into the bathroom and quickly shut the door behind me. My back rested against the door as I took in the whole room. This was about to be a *really* nice shower.

Though, as I got lost in the many jets and steaming hot water, I realized that I didn't have a single item of clothing to change into. I mentally facepalmed. He probably wanted that to happen.

After I finished up, I wrapped a towel around my body and opened the door peeking out.

"Psst." I said to Mason, who sat on the bed watching TV, and he looked over amused.

"Why are we whispering?" he whispered back.

"I don't have clothes..." I spoke awkwardly, opened the door, and watched as his eyes trailed over me as I stood in nothing but a towel.

"I uh..." He shook his head quickly, and I smirked.

"Cat got your tongue?"

"I wouldn't start teasing," He stood from his spot.

"I can go grab you some. What do you want?"

"I can go get them." Him having to grab my underwear and a bra didn't sit well with me.

"In a towel? I think not." I sighed, growling a little.

"Fine. Dresser, top far left drawer, reach in and grab one of each. Just grab any t-shirt from the drawer underneath the first one." He seemed to think it over, taking in the information.

"Got it," He confirmed and walked towards the door.

"He definitely does not have it," I mumbled as he walked out.

CHAPTER TWELVE

$\diamond$

Mason

As I walked into Octavia's room, I couldn't help but snicker. Was she really that nervous for me to grab her clothes?

Stopping in front of the dresser, I pursed my lips. "Top far left... or was it right?" I mumbled.

Damn.

Going with the right, I pulled the drawer open and froze. *Now I see why she was so nervous.*

"This is interesting," I mumbled, looking at the drawer.

Why does a girl have so many pairs? Yeah... I should have just let her do this. Which pair does she want? Red? Black? Goddess, Mason, she said to not look. Grab some and go.

Shrugging, I grabbed a red pair and shut the drawer. I do have to admit that I didn't think she had such lingerie, let alone so much of it. As I turned to leave, I remembered something else.

A t-shirt, she had told me.

A thought crossed my mind, and I grinned, leaving the room. I headed back to my room and walked in, seeing her sitting on the edge of the bed. I could have laughed at the scene before me. She sat with a towel wrapped around her, awkwardly staring at the TV before her.

"Here," I grinned, chucking them to her and walking to my closet.

"What the hell?" She nearly screeched, causing me to halt.

"What?" I turned to look back at her, her face looking mortified.

"I said the left drawer! Not the right, Mason. Oh, my Goddess, do you ever listen?" She mumbled, covering her face with her hands.

"What's wrong?" I laughed.

"This is lingerie! Left is just bras and underwear. This is what I didn't want you to see." She nearly whispered, peeking up at me, a red tint covering her cheeks.

"Octavia, it's fine," I laughed.

"Did you at least get me a shirt?" She groaned.

"Damn." I faked innocence.

"Mason!"

"Just wear one of mine," I smirked, walking into the closet and grabbing one.

I tossed it to her, but she couldn't help but smile as she retreated into the bathroom. By the time she came back out, I was laying on the bed and looked over. My shirt nearly came to her knees, causing me to belch out a laugh.

"I still can't believe you did that." She sighed, crawling in next to me. I opened my arms, and she crawled to me, wrapping her arms around me and laying her head on my chest. I closed my arms around her, feeling content as my wolf hummed in delight at her closeness.

"Don't worry. I didn't mind. It sure got my mind going to different places." I teased.

"Stop!" She swatted at my chest, causing me to laugh again.

"You are something else." I watched as her eyes fluttered shut.

"Tired?" I asked.

"Extremely." I leaned over, switching off the TV.

"So am I," She broke free of my grasp and rolled over, staring up at the ceiling.

"What are you thinking about?"

"How I'll never get used to this." She replied, turning to face me. She trailed a finger across my jawline, sporting a soft smile. "But that's a good thing. I wouldn't change a thing."

"Me either," I mumbled, placing a kiss on the base of her neck. "I'm going to shower real quick. Don't miss me too much." I teased.

"I'll try not to."

Octavia

I woke up to faint yelling. Quickly sitting up, I looked around frantically.

"Find them! No... I don't care. If they aren't back in their cells by tomorrow morning, you will be taking their spots—that's if my wolf spares you." Mason growled out, ending the call by slamming his phone against the wall to his right.

I looked at his tense stance by the window. The curtains were open, and he was looking out, breathing heavily. I moved to the side to try and see what he was looking at. I froze when I saw no lights from the prisons that were miles away from us. The buildings looked tiny from where we were, but you couldn't miss the huge lights and gated fence.

"Mason?" He looked over to me, and his features relaxed a bit.

"It's ok, Octavia. Go back to bed."

"No, you're upset. What's wrong?" I pushed the covers away, motioning for him to come back over to me.

Reluctantly, he made his way towards me and sat back down on the bed. Repeating his motions from earlier tonight, I offered a half-smile and opened my arms. He let out a small laugh, moving closer to me. As he sat on the edge of the bed, I sat behind him with my arms around his waist and my chin resting on his shoulder. He rested his hands on my thighs, leaning back into me as he started to calm down.

"C block in one of the prisons apparently malfunctioned. The cells were all opened. Prisoners were escaping, and luckily, our defense team got a lot subdued. Some are still missing. All prisons are on mandatory lockdown, as you can see."

"Do you think it was planned?" I asked.

"Definitely. Those prisons have been running perfectly for years. Not once has that happened. A guard had to get close with someone." He pinched the bridge of his nose, too stressed for his own good.

I rubbed my hand over his shoulders, trying to calm him down. Even in the dark, I saw the red eyes trying to emerge as he turned his head, glancing back at me.

"Don't let him have control. Calm down." I reminded him gently.

"I know," he nodded. "Go back to sleep. Everything should be fine in the morning." I let out a yawn and nodded as we moved to lay back down.

"Goodnight, Mason,"

"Goodnight, Octavia."

***

The next morning after we woke, Mason was whisked away with a day of meetings to figure out what happened at the prison. With the look he had on his face when he left, I feel sorry for whoever is on the other side of that conversation.

My morning, though, was not interesting in the slightest. I showered, ate some breakfast, and waited for what seemed like hours for Mason to get back, but he never showed like I thought he would. Now, I was lounging around in his bed, watching some TV show that was playing.

My show was quickly stopped, and a blaring noise broke out, and I grabbed my ears.

"This is your news broadcast system. As you know, on May twenty-fifth, a war had been declared upon by King Christian and Alpha Mason against the hunters of America. This is an update to inform you of new upcoming news...." I sat up, wanting to hear what had happened and if there had been any success, but the door to Mason's room was thrown open, and the door hit the wall with a crack.

I stared at Mason with wide eyes, completely frozen. "Uh…"

"What are you doing here?" He growled out, marching towards his closet.

"Excuse me? Nope. Your attitude is here," I raised one hand high up. "And I'm going to need you to bring it down here." I motioned with my hands, and he rolled his eyes.

"I'm sorry. I'm just fed up at the moment. It was her. She let the prisoners loose. I don't even know how she got to the pack." He growled, clenching his fists. "They broadcasted all that to tell everyone about the prison break, and it makes me look like a weak alpha." He seemed distant as he spoke and started rambling on about something.

"Mason, look at me." I was in front of him quickly and cupped his face, so he was staring at me.

"Megan? Was she who let the prisoners loose?" I asked, ignoring the red that surfaced in his eyes.

"I'm worried." He finally looked at me with no barrier hiding his emotions. His eyes glistened with tears.

"What?" I stuttered out.

"I think she knows that I found my mate. She hasn't taunted me in months, and now, when you come along, she strikes again. I can't lose you."

"Mason, you're not going to lose me. I'm right here." He sighed, resting his forehead against mine with closed eyes.

"I called Christian to send out more guards with my men. It's really happening. I can't take it anymore. This is the first war in hundreds of years." He pulled back, giving me a serious look. "We sent troops out a little bit after the ball, but now we're doubling them, preparing them, and sending them to the fronts. These hunters... I've never seen anything like it. They have weapons that can simply take a wolf out with one blow."

Fear surrounded me.

If Mason is this worried... we're all screwed. A ringing noise brought us from our thoughts, and I let go of Mason. I grabbed my phone off the nightstand and looked at the caller ID. Lesley? I haven't heard from her in weeks.

Excited, I walked into the bathroom to block out the noise of the TV.

"Hey, girl!" I chirped. Instead of her bubbly response, I heard sobs on the other end.

"She's dead!" She sobbed out.

"W-who?" My voice became shaky.

"Liza is dead! She was in a car accident because of those damn hunters! They shot her, Octavia. They have no remorse for anyone! No one is safe." She screamed, and my heart dropped. It was like slow motion as the phone fell from my hands as I covered my mouth in shock.

I looked around, mouth wide open as the news sat in. No... she can't be. I just saw her not too long ago. I... I just spoke with her the other night! *She was fine.* My bottom lip trembled at the thought of never seeing her again. My chest hurt, and I clawed at it, trying to stop the feeling as tears brimmed my eyes. My phone dinged, and I slowly reached down to pick it up.

Then I saw the pictures. The wrecked car. A bullet hole through the window shield. The paramedics. A crying scream left me as the hard truth set in. My legs gave out as I went to drop to my knees.

"Octavia!" Mason yelled, catching me before I hit the ground. He slowly lowered us to the ground as sobs shook my body.

"Octavia," his voice was strained. "I need you to look at me. What happened?" He cupped my cheeks, forcing me to look at him.

"Liza's dead! My best friend is dead, and those hunters killed her! I... what... what do we do?" I cried out, clutching his shirt.

He looked at me with shock and helplessness. Then he just pulled me to his chest, not letting me see any other emotion. "I'll kill them all." I heard him say barely above a whisper.

I felt the familiar tight pull in my chest and the tapping within my mind. I gritted my teeth together; this is not the time for this bullshit! Worriedly, I shakily stood to my feet. I couldn't let Mason see me like this. Confused by my sudden mood change, he stood, and I was quick to turn him, his back to the mirror, as I threw my arms around his neck. He rested his head in the crook of my neck, but what he didn't see was the black veins trying to crawl up my arms. I looked in the mirror, hating myself for what I saw.

My eyes were not their normal color. The color was frightening—a reminder of the creature that lurked within me. One that so desperately wanted to get out and release hell on earth for those who harmed my best friend, who was, at one point, the light of my life.

My friend is dead.

Liza is gone.

And those who played a part in this *will* pay. Even if it cost me my life to make it happen. I looked at myself, knowing what was deep inside me was staring back at me. Slowly, I nodded at it.

You win.

CHAPTER THIRTEEN

---◆---

Octavia

Mason stood beside me, his arm wrapped around my waist, as people gave their speeches. It didn't seem real. Liza's body was hidden behind the cover of the casket. The accident was so bad they couldn't even do an open casket funeral. *She didn't deserve this.*

"Octavia," A voice called, and I looked up, seeing it was my turn. Taking a deep breath, Mason kissed the top of my head and let me go.

I walked to the front of the room. All eyes were on me as I shakily pulled out the speech. I took a deep, shaky breath and begun.

"Hello, I am Octavia Knight, a close friend of Liza's. Liza was..." I paused, looking at the letter, and shook my head, trying to hold back my tears. After a minute, I crumbled the letter up.

"She wouldn't want this from a paper. She would want something from the heart, so that's what I'm going to do." I looked back up, seeing the small smiles of our friends. Lesley gave me an encouraging nod.

"Liza was the girl everyone wanted to be, but she didn't flaunt it. She was the person who was there when you needed someone—no matter if you were friends or not. She always threw excitement into the mix of things and always spiced things up. There was never a dull moment when she was around. She taught me to stand up for myself and not to let anyone walk over me. She is someone who I strive to be today: an intelligent, strong, and brave woman.

"Although I'm sure she'd wring my neck for being so sentimental, I can't help but want you all to know how amazing she was. She was kind and caring. She lit up whatever room she walked into, and she was the type of person to do whatever you asked of her if you needed the help. She was also the person that you wanted to make memories with." I let out a small laugh.

"There was this time when we were maybe fifteen or sixteen, and she wanted to sneak out. I was never the one to do stuff so easily, but she just had a way of convincing people to do anything." Everyone let out a small laugh knowing it was true.

"That night, she popped off the screen to her window. We had no clue where we would go. Nevertheless, we left the house and walked down the road. She complained that her feet hurt, and it was the stupidest idea she had yet, so we turned around and headed back. When we got back to the house, her screen window had been screwed shut, and the window was closed. Liza was always the one to say she was never scared, but that night her dad waited outside for us with crossed arms. I think that was the most terrified I had ever seen her." Again, soft chuckles were heard throughout the crowd. I looked over at her dad, who placed a hand on his heart, tears brimming in his eyes.

"The point is, she always had us doing something. Never were we just sitting around. The second I admitted I was bored, she was scheming away. I've had so many memories with her, and they will forever be with me. It's terrifying to know that she won't be around to make more, but I know she's in a better place and probably convincing the Goddess above to do something scandalous." I couldn't help but let out a small laugh with everyone.

I looked up, placing a hand on my heart. "I love you, Liza." With that, I walked back to Mason, who smiled at me. When I reached him, he opened his arms as I covered my mouth to shield my cries.

***

I stared out the window of the car as we headed back home. Everything just seems fuzzy.

"How about we do something and get your mind off things?" Mason asked me.

"I would be very grateful for that, thank you." I smiled, and he grabbed my hand, bringing it to his lips. "Thank you for being with me today as well."

"Anything for you, ba-" His head shot up abruptly.

"Get down!" he yelled, and soon I was tackled onto the seat as his body covered mine, shielding me from the shots fired through the windows. I gasped, looking over to see the driver's head drop forward against the steering wheel and the car slowly roll to a stop.

"We just can't get a break, can we?" Mason snarled. "Stay down." He whispered into my ear. Moving off me, he raised his leg and kicked the door. It flew off the hinges and hit the road with a crack.

"Be careful." I bit my lip nervously as he emerged from the car. He flashed me a grin, his eyes flashing red and disappeared from my view. I heard grunting and shots being fired.

A loud roar sounded, and I leaned up a little, peeking through the window. A pitch-black wolf stood tall. Bloody bodies were laid across the ground, and only three men remained. Mason's wolf was massive. I watched as he growled, raising his head high in a warning. His eyes are what gave him away. They were red as ever. *A crimson red.* I tilted my head to the side, confused at the slight color change.

He lunged forward, taking no time to go after the men. His jaw locked onto a man's shoulder as he screamed in pain. His mouth moved up, latching onto the man's jugular and instantly ripped it backward. I forced myself to look away.

I bit my nails, a terrible habit, waiting for this to all be over. Though, when I felt the tight pull in my chest again, I knew it wasn't. My senses instantly changed, and I heard footsteps approaching, but before I could react, a hand latched onto my ankle, yanking me from the car. Spinning in whoever's grasp, a man pointed a gun at me with a sadistic grin.

"Two birds, one stone." He mumbled and was about to pull the trigger, but it was like my body had no control of itself when my hands reached out lightning fast, snatching the gun, breaking it in half. The man stared at me, startled.

"You... your eyes are—" He didn't get to finish as a flash of grey tackled him. I turned my head, flinching when I heard tearing and ripping.

I waited before I saw a gray wolf walk near me, looking around in precaution. Mason's wolf walked over, covered in blood. They seemed to be communicating by mindlinking, and I watched Mason giving a deep nod. Most likely thanking the wolf for saving me.

When the wolf looked at me, I couldn't help but laugh when I realized the eyes and the wolfish grin he gave me. Damn, *now drinks are on me this time.* Alaric walked to me and checked me over as Mason walked around, making sure it was clear.

"I'm fine," I laughed, shoving him away, and he gave a wolfish snort. "Idiot," I added.

Mason walked over to me and squatted down.

"What?" I asked.

This would be so much easier if we could mindlink. Alaric pushed me forward with his snout, and I looked at Mason, whose head motioned towards his back.

"You want me to get on you? *Ha!* No thanks." He growled, meaning he was not taking no for an answer. I knew we were a couple of hours out from the pack, and this would be easier, but I was a wolf too!

"I can shift." I reminded him and started to pull my shirt off when Mason let out a horrid growl.

"You can't be serious?" he just stared at me like I was stupid.

He didn't want me to shift because I wouldn't have clothes to change back into.

"I can change behind the car, shift, and grab my clothes with my mouth. Problem solved." He shook his head no, and Alaric nudged me towards Mason once more.

"You are unbelievable." I groaned, and Mason let out an annoyed puff of air and stood up, quickly walking over. I felt him lick my arm, and I jolted back in disgust.

"Ew! Wolf slobber, hello? What the hell?" I mumbled but soon looked down, and my eyes widened as blood dripped from my arm.

I wouldn't be able to run on all fours. Oh. *Oh!*

"Oh, shit! I've been shot!" I yelled as it finally set in.

I couldn't help but start to panic as I rambled on how I was going to lose my arm. Mason and Alaric eventually got fed up, and both roared, shutting me up instantly. Mason lowered himself onto the ground, and I quickly walked over, swinging a leg over and sat gripping his fur tight with one hand as he took off with incredible speed.

CHAPTER FOURTEEN

---◆◇◆---

Octavia

I let out a yelp as I felt the familiar dig in my arm. This part is never fun.

"Calm down," Mason ordered as the sweating doctor used tweezers to retrieve the bullet lodged in my arm.

I quickly grabbed Mason by the top of his shirt with my free arm, yanking him down to eye level. "Listen, buddy, this is the second time I have been—ah!" I closed my eyes, taking a deep breath, "This is the second time I've been shot this year, and I'm *not* a happy camper!" I growled out. "So, unless you want my fist down your throat. Shut. *Up*." I snapped and pushed him away from me.

I could tell by the way he gritted his jaw that I pissed him off with my threat, but he knew I would deliver it, given my circumstance. I looked back at the doctor, finally seeing the tweezers leave with the bullet.

"It's not a wolfsbane bullet. She'll be fine now that it's out." He told Mason, who nodded.

"Much better," I muttered, sighing in relief.

The doctor cleaned the wound and wrapped a bandage around it.

"You'll heal in no time. Just don't strain your arm for a day or two."

"Thanks, but I've been through this before," I patted the doctor on the shoulder, hopping off the bed.

"Let's get you to bed." Mason held his hand out of me, and I took it.

"Sorry for being a brat." I laced my fingers through his.

He chuckled. "I'll let it slide since you just got shot but use that attitude with me again…" he leaned next to my ear, "And I'll just have to put you in your place." He playfully nipped at my ear, causing goosebumps to shoot over my entire body.

I stood bewildered as he snickered, pulling me out of the room with him.

When we finally entered his bedroom, I let out a yawn. I was exhausted. It had been a long day, one that would stay with me for a while. I walked into Mason's closet, grabbing one of his t-shirts and looked back at him, holding it up.

"Can I wear this?"

"Of course. I'm guessing you're staying in here today?" he smiled, almost childlike.

I let out a snort. "If you don't mind. I think I sleep better when you're near."

"Of course, I don't mind. I'd have to agree." He walked to me, wrapping his arms around my waist and pulled me to him. "Are you okay?"

I looked away from his intense stare. "No, but I will be in due time. I just wished I had more time with her. I got so caught up in my new life here. I didn't even bother to reach out to her and explain it all. What if… what if she just… thought I forgot about her?" my bottom lip quivered.

"I doubt she did, Octavia. After that party, I'm sure Liza put the pieces together. Life takes us for weird turns, and sometimes we don't know what to expect, but she wouldn't want you to beat yourself up over this."

"Yeah, I know. I'm going to get changed."

"Ok." He leaned forward, placing a kiss on my forehead, causing my eyes to flutter shut. He then placed one kiss on each eyelid before leaving his closet.

I turned, pulling my clothes off and pulled on the huge t-shirt. Mason came in after I was done and changed as well. When he got in bed, he opened his arms, and I crawled in, laying my head on his chest. After a minute, I turned in his grasp and faced away from him. I couldn't help but reach over and grab my phone off the nightstand.

I went to my messages and clicked Liza's name reading through them, and smiling at her quirkiness I loved so much. I missed her so much. I hated this feeling. Those hunters were going to pay.

I felt Mason's arms wrap around me once more as he pulled me to his chest. He took the phone from my hands and leaned over to place it back on the nightstand.

"She wouldn't want you to keep beating yourself up." He reminded me.

"I know. It just doesn't seem real, you know?" I felt him nod.

"When my brother died. It seemed so… fake. I didn't know how to cope. It was weird him not running up to my room every morning jumping onto my bed to wake me. Christmas was so bland without him, too, but I learned I had to move on and think positive thoughts. They wouldn't want this." My heart clenched as he spoke. I turned towards him, completely forgetting that all this may bring up old memories for him too.

There was barely enough light peeking behind the curtains, so I could only see the outline of his face. I trailed a finger over his cheekbone.

"I'm sorry. I know that must have been hard on you and still is. I couldn't imagine losing my family like that." I nearly whispered. His hand came up to mine that laid against his cheek, and he grabbed it, bringing it to his lips, placing a soft kiss on it.

"Don't be sorry. It was a long time ago. It's what they would have wanted me to do. Besides, I still have Braelyn. That's my sister." I nodded and smiled up at him.

"What?" he grinned.

"I'm happy with you," I confessed.

"I'm happy too, babe." He leaned in to kiss me but stopped when his phone started ringing.

"You have got to be kidding me." He growled out, and I couldn't help but laugh.

He sighed, letting go of me and rolled over to his nightstand and grabbed it, answering.

"What?" I shook my head, rolling my eyes at his informal way of things. "How? Christian, whoa, slow down! Hey! Calm down, explain slowly." Christian? My eyes widened as I sat up.

"What's wrong? Is it Scarlett?!" I frantically asked, and Mason shook his head at me.

"Yeah... ok, I'll let her know." He hung up the phone, frowning. "The sectors were attacked. Many have died. This stays between us, I don't know if she told you or not, but she was from the sectors. That's where her family is."

"Oh no, are they ok?"

"They're MIA as of right now." He said, and I stood up.

"I have to go be with Scarlett. She needs a friend. Please." He thought about it for a moment and nodded.

"We'll get dressed and be on our way. Come on."

***

After a long drive, we finally reached their pack. Christian was quick to tell me where Scarlett was, and I was on my way to find her. I walked through the field and smiled as I saw her sitting by herself. She turned as I approached, and I saw tears in her eyes.

"Oh, girly," I said, sitting next to her, pulling her to me.

"I came right as soon as I heard," I said softly.

"I'm so sick of crying." She mumbled.

"Sometimes it's best to get it all out. It eats at you if you don't."

She seemed to be in thought, and I sighed, looking away. So much shit has happened these past days. I felt as if the world was against us. It probably was.

"I have to act like a queen, and queens don't cry. Some people lost much more than I did tonight. I don't even know whether my family is really dead." She said as I played with her hair.

"With what you told me about your mother, I'm sure those hunters ran in the opposite direction as they saw that flip-flop come off. I'm sure she's fine."

She let out a small, sad laugh. "One can only hope," she mumbled, wiping my tears. "Never mind me, how are you?"

I sighed, laying down looking up at the sky, and she mimicked my actions. I wanted to tell her about Liza, not knowing if she knew already or not, but I refrained. She didn't need more pain added to her day, so I settled with talking about Mason and me.

We talked for a while, and it was nice to see her cheer up. I prayed to the Goddess they quickly found her family. She's such a sweet woman and didn't deserve this. After a few minutes of chatting, we heard footsteps approaching.

"Scarlett!" We heard, and Scarlett sat up quickly, seeing Christian running towards us.

We stood to our feet as he reached her.

"What's wrong?" she questioned with worried eyes, but his smile made me sigh in relief.

"They found them. They're alright." A smile burst across her face as she jumped up, hugging Christian while wrapping her legs around his waist. He chuckled and hugged her to him.

"I told you. You don't mess with a Hispanic woman and her flip-flops." I said, causing them both to laugh.

"Let's go!"

I watched their figures retreat, and I sighed, standing up and dusted myself off. I walked across the field and saw Mason talking to Christian's beta by the palace backdoors. Making my way to them, I smiled at Axel.

"Hey, babe." Mason spoke as I wrapped my arms around him. "Everything go well?"

"They found her parents, so yes."

"I heard." He replied as I looked around.

"I feel like I'm intruding." I blurted out, and Axel looked at me questionably.

"Why? You're the queen's good friend. You're welcome here anytime." Mason nodded in agreement.

"I don't know... something just feels off."

"Are you wanting to stay longer? Christian said we can stay here since we've been driving all night." Mason asked.

"No... I think she needs time with her family. She kind of rushed off. I mean, I would too, but you could tell she really wants time with them. I don't wanna make her feel as if she has to sacrifice her time with them just because I'm here. Unless you're too tired, I'm ready when you are."

"Understandable. Well, if you're ready, then I am too." He turned to Christian's beta. "I'll see you around, Axel. Tell Chris to get those papers to me."

"Will do, sir."

As we walked towards the car, Mason threw an arm around my shoulder. "You're a good friend driving all this way to make sure she's ok."

"Well, I'd want someone to do the same for me. Everyone needs a best friend in their corner. I'm just glad everything is ok. Hearing that definitely made my week better."

CHAPTER FIFTEEN

—◆—

Octavia

After leaving The Royal Pack and heading to our own home, it was easy to say that Mason and I were exhausted and fell asleep the minute we returned. Later, I woke up to an empty bed. I assumed Mason had some meetings to attend. I wondered when I would sit on those, but I doubt it would be any time soon since I wasn't sworn in as Luna yet.

Throwing the covers off me, I stood and headed to the bathroom. I took a long, peaceful shower—just letting the hot water run over me as I thought about everything recently. They say not to take life for granted, you never know what it may throw at you, and I realized just how true that was. With everything that has happened, I feared for the future.

The hunters were getting braver each day, so what's to say they won't try something large again? What was next? Ransacking a pack? Burning down The Royal Palace? What statement would they try to make? The stress of all of this made my head hurt. Mentally, my mind was weakening, and I knew that if I didn't get it under control, I wouldn't be able to hold back the beast inside me for much longer.

It was winning the internal battle with myself, and it knew it. I almost wanted to let her out freely. Maybe then she could get more justice than I ever could. Though, what would Mason think of me? It would most definitely be the end of me… because people like me don't survive once that secret gets out. My head would be on a stake in a heartbeat.

I shuddered at the thought, turning the water to the shower off and got out, drying myself off. I wrapped a towel around me and quickly hurried down to my room to change. Mason would lose it if he knew I was running around the halls in just a towel. I giggled at the thought. Once I had some fresh clothes on, I set off to try and find the man of the hour.

Stopping in front of his office, I knocked but got no response. His scent wasn't recent, either. That's odd. He's always in his office.

Where would a guy go to let off steam? I snickered, shaking my head and headed down the stairs and saw Alaric walking by.

"Hey, loser, care to show me where Mason is? Perhaps the gym?" I asked, and he stopped in his tracks, turning to look at me.

"Yes… you need to go to the gym." I gasped.

"Kidding." He winked and motioned for me to follow him.

We walked down a couple of halls and soon came to a door.

"He's inside. Knock yourself out." I thanked him and grabbed the knob, opening it. I came to a halt taking in the situation. Mason was holding onto the top of a door frame, easily doing pull-ups. Dear Goddess, please help me.

"What's up, babe?" he dropped down from the frame and dusted his hands off, walking to me, but I held my hands out.

"You're shirtless, sweaty, and I'm freshly showered." I grinned, and he let out a playful growl, jerking me towards him and pressing his lips to mine.

"Mason," I grumbled as he let out a small chuckle and pulled away.

"What are you doing here?" he asked, and I felt my cheeks heat up.

"I woke up, and you weren't there. I was just wondering where you went." He smiled down at me.

"Missing me already?" he teased, circling his arms around my waist.

"I didn't know you were working out. Sorry to interrupt."

"Don't be. I haven't in a while and figured I'd let you sleep in while I got in a quick one." he brought up his hand, moving a strand of hair that fell in front of my face. "Feel free to join me."

I grimaced. "No thanks, I'll stick to watching Netflix all day and snacking."

"That's such a healthy habit." He mused.

"Oh, I know."

He laughed, pressing one last kiss on my forehead before letting me go and walked over to pick up some weights. I couldn't help but stare as his muscles rippled when he lifted them.

"Do you want to do something today?" he asked, letting out a puff of air as he worked his biceps.

I gulped, looking away to keep my dirty thoughts at bay. "I would love to… if it doesn't involve working out."

"Anything you want, babe."

"What about a movie night?" I batted my eyes at him as his nose scrunched up. "Oh, come on. You can't hate movie nights. Plus, you said anything I wanted!"

"I don't feel like watching romantic comedies."

I scoffed. "You hurt me." I placed my hand over my heart. "I want horror. You know? Blood, guts, serial killers. That's my shit." He belched out a laugh, placing the weights back down.

"I knew there was some reason we were mates."

"Duh." I winked, walking over to him. I stood on my tiptoes. "Kiss before I go?"

He leaned down but moved his head before our lips met and walked around me, letting out a devilish laugh at my shocked state.

"That was so rude."

"You're the one that was complaining about me being all sweaty."

He turned his back to me, moving onto another workout machine, and I raised a brow. Smirking, I ran and jumped onto his back, causing him to stumble forward. "I'm sure we'll both be sweaty together at one point, so I guess I should get used to it," I said right next to his ear, hearing his breathing hitch slightly as he went completely still.

In a swift movement, he maneuvered us to where my legs were wrapped around his waist, and he stared into my eyes with an intense look. "Well… In that case," He leaned forward, but my hand came up, covering his mouth.

"I'll let you do your exercises. Goddess knows I don't want to." I teased and untangled myself from him, putting space between us before I turned and headed towards the door.

"Funny," He grumbled.

"I'm quite the comedian." I shrugged, grabbing the door handle.

"I'll be up soon. We can do a movie night. Do as you please until then." He replied but was quick to speak up again. "Scratch that, anything *but* the bar!" he added, and I laughed, closing the door behind me.

As I walked down the hall, I heard a crash of glass shattering and small curses. Curiously, I walked around a corner and saw Mason's sister cleaning up broken glass.

"Need some help?" I questioned, and she smiled, looking up at me.

"If you don't mind."

I squatted down, helping pick up the shards of the glistening pieces. "Can I ask what happened?"

"Well, I'm clumsy as they come. I had this vase cleaned and went to put it back on the mantle here but tripped over my own feet."

I snorted. "Sounds like me." She grinned up at me sheepishly.

"I'm Braelyn." She stuck out her free hand, and I shook it.

"Octavia."

"Mason's mate, right?" My eyes widened.

"Please, everyone in the pack knows." She giggled and stood. We started walking with the broken glass and came to a trash can, tossing it in.

"How?"

She raised a brow. "Who do you think?"

"Alaric?" she laughed and nodded.

"Snitch. Didn't even let Mason get to it first." I muttered, and we turned, heading into the main foyer.

She looked like she was in thought before she finally turned and looked at me. "Would you like to go do something for a little bit? I'd love to get to know you more."

"Uh, yeah, sure! I'd love to, but I'd have to be back before it gets dark. Mason and I are having a movie night." I grinned.

"Awe, you guys are so cute. You're lucky. I could never get him to do a movie night."

I waved her off. "It took some convincing. Horror movies apparently grab his attention."

"Not shocking." Braelyn giggled before humming. "Well, what do you wanna do?"

"Oh, I don't care. I'd love just to get out for a bit."

"Do you like ice cream?" She asked.

"No, girl, I love it."

A huge smile spread across her face. "Awesome, me too, come on!"

It didn't take long before we were walking down the street towards an ice cream shop that she declared had the best flavors. As I chatted with her, I noticed her bubbly personality. She was a kind woman that wasn't hard to figure out. Mason seemed happy that I was hanging with her. I could tell she meant a lot to him. Before we left, I told him where we were going. He basically rushed me out the door, telling me to have fun. Either he was excited I was trying to get to know his sister or something is up. *Both were as equally scary.*

Packs usually had everything you would need. Shops, malls, and restaurants, which was nice. It was so we didn't have to go onto human territory, and if we had to, it was always best to go during the day. Although human territory is smaller now, they still had some fun things to do, but speaking most of them hated the supernatural kind, it was best to stay away. Hunters tend to protect them—as if we were going to come and destroy everything they worked to build. It was sad that we had that impression, but I couldn't blame the situation because of our ancestors who tried to take everything from them.

"So, what is your favorite ice cream?" Braelyn brought me from my thoughts as we walked into the shop.

"Probably cookies and cream. What about you?" she thought about it then shrugged.

"I like a lot, to be honest, but if I had to pick... probably cookie dough."

"Oh, that's a yummy one too."

"What can I get for ya?" The cashier grinned, leaning on the counter, and I watched as he studied us.

"I'll take cookie dough, and she'll have cookies and cream," Braelyn answered.

"Bowl or cone?"

"Bowl?" she asked me, and I nodded.

"Both in a bowl."

"Six twenty-one." I went to grab money from my purse, but she'd already handed him a ten.

"Here you go, can I get you anything else, maybe my phone number?" he tried to act smoothly, but Braelyn and I glanced at one another before bursting out laughing.

"We'll pass. Just the ice cream." Braelyn told him, snatching our bowls off the counters, and I had to cover my mouth to stifle my laughter.

We hurried out of the shop, losing it in laughter. "Dude, I'm pretty sure he's like... seventeen or something." She laughed out loud.

"Teenage boys scare me." I giggled, spooning dessert into my mouth.

"Can you imagine if Mason would have been with you?" she asked, and I shook my head.

"Oh, the boy wouldn't have it in him to even dare to try."

"True. You should tell Mason just to see his reaction. I tell my husband all the time just to get him worked up. It's quite funny."

"I'll have to pass on that. Mason gets so jealous he'd probably march down here to scare the poor boy. I'll spare him."

"Yeah, you're right. Probably for the best." She playfully bumped my shoulder with hers.

We decided to walk around the pack while we ate. She wanted to show me some of her favorite shopping spots and the best places to eat at. It was nice talking to someone other than Mason or Alaric. As much as I loved the two's company, I needed some girl time.

"So, how long have you and Mason known each other?" She asked.

"It hasn't been long, but it feels like I've known him all my life," I confessed, and her eyes widened.

"Wow, I guess that's the thing with mates, though. He is your other half, after all. So that day you showed up, that was your first time here?" I nodded.

"He met me at the ball, and after we talked, I came here. I would have gone into heat soon. A mateless heat is ten times more painful, so it was best I come here."

"Understandable. What's that like? Heat, I mean. If you don't mind me asking, of course."

"Heat is... literal hell. It feels like you have acid running through your veins that feels like the flames of fire scorching your body. Then when the moon is high, you get these needle-like stabbing pains in your sides, but when your mate touches you... it almost stops. The pain dulls, and their touch suddenly becomes a drug you feel that you can't survive without. Everyone knows heat is to speed the mating process up, but we wanted to take it slow. So, he held me all night until it was over."

"Goddess, I am so glad I didn't have to go through that." She ran a hand through her hair. "After I met my husband, Dylan, I didn't care to wait and find my mate. In my eyes, I already had. He is everything I've ever wanted and treats me well."

"I'm happy for you," I smiled. "Sometimes you find your other half without the help of the Goddess."

"That is very true. So, when do you think Mason is going to mark you?" She questioned, scooping some ice cream into her mouth.

"Oh uh... we haven't talked about it."

Marking your mate was an intimate act that strengthened your bond like no other. You could mindlink, feel each other's emotions, and it seemed nice, but I didn't know if Mason was ready for something like that. I knew I'd need to take baby steps with him.

"Do you want to be marked?"

"I mean... yeah. The thing is... does he want to mark me?" she scoffed at my question.

"Oh, please, any male wants to mark their mate. Especially to warn away other men. Alphas are even more territorial than the normal wolf. Comes with the title."

"Oh, don't I know. He nearly killed Alaric." She looked at me, amused.

"I know, he told me. He understood, though. He just wished Mason would have told him. I think he was more embarrassed than upset. I mean, he is Mason's best friend after all."

"Dang, he never can shut up," I grumbled. "But yeah, I wish I could have told him too, but Mason was so scared of me getting known as his mate and then getting a target on my back. I think he knew that no matter what, it would always be like that, so we agreed to it."

"Well, that's good." She stopped walking and turned to me. "As much as I would love to keep walking and talking, Mason is asking me where you are." I rolled my eyes, watching as her eyes glazed over mindlinking him.

"He's done with his tasks for the day and is ready for his mate to return." She giggled. I leaned forward, hugging her goodbye. "I'll see you later. I hope we can do this again soon."

"Of course, come find me whenever."

***

"Honey, I'm home!" I called out jokingly as I walked into our room, and Mason walked out of the closet in a t-shirt and sweatpants. *Seeing him look so casual will never get old.*

"Perfect timing, honey." He mocked.

"Please tell me you got the most gruesome movies ready for us?"

"The bloodiest, goriest, and most terrifying of all." He declared, walking over, and I laughed as he pulled me towards him.

"You just got basic horror movies, didn't you?"

"Yep." I playfully pushed him away and shrugged off my jacket.

"Well, at least tell me they're good."

"Octavia, I didn't pick boring ones. I'm a guy, you know."

I gasped, placing a hand on my chest. "You are? Why, I had no idea!"

He rolled his eyes walking over to the shelf by the tv and pointed. "Look for yourself." I walked over and skimmed through them.

"I'm impressed, Alpha."

"I'll show you alpha," He growled, and I shook my head at him.

"You have a dirty mind." He shrugged, brushing past me.

"The dirtiest." I laughed and grabbed a movie off the shelf.

"We are totally watching this one first." I held up the movie, my eyes wide with excitement.

"Why that one?" he asked, amused while moving to sit on the edge of the bed.

"Are you kidding me? It's iconic! You have two of the best killers there are. Not to mention the last scene. You think they're both dead but come on, everyone knew that was a lie. What is so iconic about the last scene is that—" He quickly reached out, covering my mouth.

"Hey, now! I haven't watched this one!" he practically whined, and I looked at him through sheepish eyes, mumbling an apology behind his hand.

He moved his hand and shook his head but couldn't help the smile that made its way onto his face. "You're something else." He stood from the bed, moved to his side, sat down, and patted the spot next to him. "Well then, let's watch it before you spoil the whole movie."

I quickly put the movie in the disc slot and ran over, jumping onto the bed next to him. His chest rumbled with laughter as I cozied up next to him.

"I could talk circles around you. Don't even get me started on slasher movies. The ones you picked are good. Actually, the best one you got is—" He quickly covered my mouth with his hand again.

"Babe, you talk too much." My tongue darted out, licking his hand. He gave me a horrified look, quickly bringing his hand away, and it was my turn to burst out laughing.

"Not funny." He mumbled, wiping his hand on his pants.

"It was your expression that was." I managed to laugh out, and he rolled his eyes.

"I hate you sometimes."

"That's a lie. You love me." I said playfully, and my heart stopped when I realized what I had just said.

"Do I now?" Mason grinned down at me.

Dammit, Octavia, you and your big mouth.

CHAPTER SIXTEEN

Octavia

My heart pounded, and my hands felt clammy. How was I supposed to come back from that? The humor in his eyes told me he didn't mind the joke but was it a joke? What did he feel exactly? What if it wasn't anything? Oh, Goddess, Octavia, why do you do this to yourself? Is it too early to love someone? Is it different for mates? Did I love him? Why is all of this just now entering my mind?

"Are you ok?" his brows furrowed at my sudden change in expression.

"Yeah… I was just joking, you know…" I trailed off.

"Hey," His pointer finger and thumb grabbed my chin, tilting my head up to him. "What's wrong?"

"Was that weird? I mean, I didn't mean to make it weird. Ok, I know, I'm making it weird now. Never mind me. I tend to overthink." I rambled on, and he leaned forward, pressing a soft kiss to my forehead.

"You're my mate. It didn't make anything weird. Are you trying to ask me how I feel about you?"

"Yes. No! Yes… ok no. I know how you feel about me. I mean," I let out a nervous laugh. "You're my mate."

He sighed, his hands moving to cup the sides of my face, his thumb rubbing small circles against my cheek, and my eyes fluttered shut. "Don't ever doubt that I don't care about you, ok?"

I couldn't help but ask. "Do you love me? I am so confused. I don't know why this just suddenly started to weigh on me, but I almost don't know if it's too early even to be asking questions like that. Goddess, I probably sound crazy."

"You don't sound crazy, babe. If I am honest, I don't think I have ever loved a partner before. I don't know exactly what I feel right now, but if it's love… then it's love. You're not the only one who's confused here. Your smile alone lights up my day. I didn't sleep a full night until you came along, and you were in my arms. At the darker times in my life, I didn't think I could love someone. I had too much anger holding me back. Now, I see that differently. Love doesn't come with a timestamp. It's different for everyone."

Love doesn't come with a timestamp. What a beautiful way to put it.

"You know, I always wanted a mate. I wanted someone to look at me like… I was the most beautiful thing they had ever laid eyes on. I wanted someone to treat me like a queen. I thought that was love, but since I met you, that's not all that love is. I love teasing you and getting you riled up. I love when you hold me at night, and I feel safe and secure.

"My heart flutters at the small gestures you do. Maybe for mates, it *is* different. Maybe with our bond, it speeds up the process because I do know you're my other half. Yeah, we don't know what we feel… because I have never loved a partner either, but maybe this is love? The love of the mate bond between two souls that were matched from birth."

He smiled, resting his forehead against mine. "Maybe so."

"I'm sure we'll know when the time is right." I nodded.

We stared at each other intensely before he leaned forward, pressing his lips to mine. My eyes shut, feeling him pull me onto his lap and instinctively, my arms wrapped around his neck. His hand wrapped around the back of my neck, pulling me impossibly closer.

It wasn't just a heated kiss or a lustful one. It was full of passion and want—need even. I didn't want to let him go. His hand found its way under the back of my shirt, trailing it up to my spine, sending shivers down it. A low growl rumbled through his chest as he grabbed hold of me, flipping me over as I laid on my back, looking up at him breathless.

"Tell me to stop," He nearly whispered, our movie completely forgotten. "Because if you don't, I won't be able to keep my hands off you." His head dipped, pressing a soft kiss upon my neck while my hands found their way into his hair.

I stared up at the ceiling questionably as he worked his way down to the spot where he was supposed to mark me.

"Do you want to mark me?" I asked, and he froze. His lips left my neck as he slowly lifted his head, his eyes meeting my worried ones.

"I've wanted to mark you since the day I found you."

"Then do it. Mark me." My heart thrummed in my ears.

"With pleasure," His voice was husky.

I gulped, feeling his hands trail down to the hem of my shirt. Raising my arms, I let him pull the top off of me. He leaned up, looking me over.

Suddenly, he grinned. "I'm so damn lucky." He tossed my shirt to the side before leaning back down.

Holding onto his shoulder tightly, I felt my breathing hitch as his nose trailed down my neck to that certain spot. When I felt the scrape of his canines, I closed my eyes, worried about the bite.

My wolf was howling with joy, knowing that he was about to put his claim on us. The other part of me, the part I hated, was warning for me to stop. The beast didn't want any more ties to another, but I mashed her down.

Ripping me from my thoughts, I felt his teeth sink into my skin. A gasp escaped me, my nails digging into his shoulders. The pain was terrible, but it was gone in seconds as I felt something tighten within me. It was like the imaginary string that held our bond together knotted up. I couldn't help the moan that escaped my lips, causing my cheeks to heat. Mason pulled back, moving my hair from my neck completely to get a better look.

His eyes were shining a bright red, and the look on his face showed the pride he felt. When he looked at me, the boyish grin left his face, and he almost looked confused.

"What?" I questioned, worried he screwed it up or something.

"Your eyes… never mind. I think I'm just seeing things." He mused, shaking his head.

"What? What about them?" I tried to sit up, but he gently pushed me back down.

"It's nothing. I thought they flashed red for a second. They could have though since our bond strengthened, and our minds and emotions tangled together." He waved it off.

My heart jolted in my chest, knowing what he saw was true, and I mentally scolded myself for letting that happen—I let go of control for a split second, and she already tried to break through. Though, when he grabbed the collar of his shirt, pulling it over his head, the thought soon evaporated.

"What… what are you doing?"

He smirked. "Letting you mark me."

"What? Males don't typically let a female mark them. I mean, it's happened before, but it's looked down upon. I mean, the queen was cursed to not even be able to mark her king."

He shrugged. "I'm not like the others. If you have to have my claim on your neck, it's only fair that you can do the same to me." He bundled his shirt together, bringing it to my neck and wiped it off. "We'll need to clean that properly after this," He snorted.

Shock coursed through me. I don't even know how to mark him. *I wasn't taught this.*

"Go on, babe. I want you to."

"Are you sure?" I stuttered out.

"You're mine and mine only. Just as I am yours, so go ahead."

"I don't even know what to do." He let out a small laugh at my bewildered state.

"You just give your wolf control and let her do her thing, but if you're too scared..." He trailed off and started to move away, but before he could, I grabbed hold of him, flipping him onto his back as he did to me.

He had a cocky look on his face, knowing I wouldn't give this moment up. I looked him over, loving the feeling that bubbled within me. He was astonishingly beautiful. Trailing a finger against his perfectly sculpted abdomen, up to his chest, I noticed him gulp. I gave him a devilish smile and leaned forward to place a kiss on his neck while channeling my wolf. Within seconds, she took no time sinking her teeth into his neck.

Talk about a change of events.

CHAPTER SEVENTEEN

⸻◆⸻

Mason

I woke before Octavia did. Last night after she marked me, she wouldn't let me live it down, but her giddy expression and bright eyes made it all worth it. A marking isn't as pleasurable for males since it is mostly unheard of, but I didn't care. We talked a little bit after, and before I knew it, she fell asleep with her head on my chest.

All this was so new to me. Never once did I think I'd find someone who lit up my whole world as much as she does.

After our markings last night, it became clear as day. I already loved this woman with everything I had. Love doesn't have a timestamp, I had said, and that was so true. Before, I would have laughed at someone if they told me I would love a girl in just a few months of knowing her, but the mate bond sure is something else.

I think she loved me, too, but I didn't want to scare her last night. I want her to realize it on her own and not feel pressured to say it. She said we would know when the time was right... and I did. It was just her time clock that was still ticking, and I would wait to hear those words as long as it took her to figure it out.

After all, she was my everything. I would wait until the end of time for her.

She stirred in her sleep, breaking me from my thoughts. I looked down, not being able to help the smile that crawled onto my face. Her blonde hair was all over her face, and to be honest... she kind of snores, which I usually would hate, but it didn't bother me for some reason.

I felt my phone buzz next to me, and I reached towards my nightstand to grab it.

Alaric sent me a link to an article labeled '*Crisis at the Palace*', and my brows furrowed. I clicked it, gently moving to sit up in bed without waking Octavia. The article opened, and I was quick to start reading.

"The soon-to-be Queen looks like she'll no longer be getting her title. King Christian announced not but just two days ago that he had proposed to the alleged Scarlett Madison. A day later, the church officials were seen arriving at the royal palace. Now, we're preparing for the coronation of Amanda Allister, who was supposed to take the crown before Christian had met Scarlett. It's safe to say something fishy is going on in that palace. Where is our Scarlett Madison, and why isn't she taking the throne alongside her mate?" I read, and my eyes widened.

How the hell am I just hearing about this?! I quickly dialed Christian's number, putting the phone to my ear. It rang, and soon, he picked up.

"Hello?" his gruff voice came across the line.

"Christian, what the hell is going on?"

"My life is over. That's what is happening." My brows furrowed.

"Are you drunk?"

"No. *I'm absolutely obliterated.* Scarlett left last night. There's some stuff you can't know, Mason, that I really wish I could tell you. Let's just say I hate my mother, and I hate the church officials. I'm about ready to burn this whole place down."

"Why did Scarlett leave?"

"For the sake of her people. You know how she is when it comes to the sectors. They threatened them. They threatened something I had been working hard on fixing. I just… man, I did everything right! I don't know why the Goddess is doing this to me! Why… *Why me?*" his voice cracked at the end, and I ran a hand over my face, not even knowing what to say.

"You say the word, and my men are me are there. You know my distaste for the church officials."

"I can't ask you to do that. I'll find a way to fix this and get my mate back if I have to. I love that woman. If I have to kill anyone in my path to make sure she's by my side again, I will. First, I just need to do this damn coronation to get the church officials off my back. Then I guess I'll go from there."

"Ok. Let me know if you need anything, Christian. You know I understand."

"Thanks, man," He burped, causing me to grimace at his drunken state. "Now, I'm going to finish drowning my sorrows before I have to temporarily marry the wicked witch of the west."

"Be smart and be safe."

"Always." The line went dead, and I sighed, dropping my phone onto my lap. I hated that for him, but I knew his words were true. He'd get her back no matter the cost. I know I would. If he needs me to storm the palace, I will. Until then, I'll wait for the order.

My phone rang again. Confused, I saw it was Alpha Ryker. *Great.*

"What?" I answered.

"It's quite rude to answer the phone like that. I know you have my number, Mason. We're pals, best friends even so—"

"Is there a reason you're calling? Or are you just calling to annoy me? I have more important matters to attend to."

"Buzzkill per usual," He grumbled. "But anyways, yes. What the hell is up with the royals lately? First Scarlett, now some Amanda chick?" I rolled my eyes, letting out a deep sigh.

"Christian didn't tell me much, but it doesn't sound good. The church officials had something to do with it."

He was silent for a moment. "Are we going in to raise hell? I hate those bastards with everything in me." He spoke more seriously.

"No, we'll wait for Christian to tell us to do something. For now, we wait."

"Man, I hate that for him. I couldn't imagine losing my mate."

"Your mate? What on earth do you know about having a mate?"

"Christian didn't tell you? I found my mate when I helped you two raid that party Octavia and Scarlett slipped off to."

I was shocked, to say the least, and couldn't help but let out a laugh. "Finally, someone to actually tame your ass."

"Yeah, don't remind me. She's literally the female version of me, and it's terrifying. I mean, she literally ran from me when I first met her. As if I was going to let my mate get away." He scoffed, and I chuckled, shaking my head.

"Looks like the Goddess decided it was about time for you to grow up. How nice. Tell me, does she know about your playerish ways?"

"Bye." He grumbled, hanging up the phone, and I snorted, tossing the phone next to me.

I knew that'd make him shut up.

"Who was that?" Octavia spoke, startling me.

"Sorry, babe. I didn't mean to wake you."

"It's okay. I needed to get up anyway." She yawned, stretching her arms above her head.

"It was Alpha Ryker. He was calling to ask about…" I trailed off, knowing she wasn't going to take the news well.

She raised a brow. "What? What aren't you telling me?"

"Here," I mumbled, grabbing my phone and pulling the article back up.

She took my phone with furrowed brows and started reading. A small gasp escaped her as she tossed my phone to the side and threw the covers off of her.

I closed my eyes, knowing she was going to act this way. "Octavia, what are you doing?" I asked, warning in my tone.

"What am I doing?! I'm going to shove my foot up some royal ass! I just know those church officials did this. They probably figured out she was from the sectors and looked down on her. Ugh! They're terrible." She grumbled, running towards my closet.

"Babe, you can't go down there. I'm sorry. I already talked to Christian. He has it under control for now."

Her head peaked out from the closet. "What do you mean?"

"We cannot go unless he gives us the order to do so. I'm sorry. These are the royals we're talking about. He's my king, and he pretty much told me to stand down. I'm right there with you. I wanted to go, too, but we can't. We'll only make it worse."

"Can I at least call her?"

I nodded. "Of course, she's your friend. She could probably use one right now."

She was quick to walk back over to the bed and grab her phone. She clicked her phone a few times, then put the phone to her ear.

"Scarlett? What's going on?" I looked over curiously.

"What? Who? Oh… ok… No, wait!" she pulled the phone from her ear with wide eyes. "She hung up on me!" she whined.

"What'd she say?"

"I could barely make it out because she was whispering something about Alara Lavender, and then I heard some girl tell her to crouch behind a bush. Do you think she's ok?"

Alara Lavender? I haven't heard that name in a long time.

Christian said he was trying to fix something earlier… I sat up as realization sat in. "Oh Goddess, I know what he was trying to do," I mumbled.

"What? Who's Alara Lavender? I am so confused."

"Christian was trying to make new packs." I smiled, impressed. "Alara Lavender is the last witch that is a descendant from the original witch that made our alphas. He was trying to get her to do the spell to bring up new alphas like me. That has to be it. She's the only one that could do it. Why she's with Scarlett, I have no idea, but I have a feeling she's okay." I smirked, knowing one thing: The church officials feared and hated the Lavender Coven, which means they would fear Alara.

"Did Scarlett sound scared or anything?"

"Not really. She just sounded like she was in a rush."

"I think we need to wait a few hours and then check the news. Christian said there are things he wishes he could tell me, but he can't.

I think it has to do something with Scarlett and Alara. I don't know why else they would be together, and I damn well know if Alara was still a threat, Christian would have her locked up." I stated, knowing something big was about to happen.

"Alara used to be a threat?"

"A big one. She was mated to Alpha Evan of the Malevolent Pack if you remember those stories."

She gasped. "That's who Scarlett is with?! She's crazy!"

"As I said, let's give it a few. If Scarlett didn't sound scared, I don't think we need to worry. Plus, Alara has been in a facility to get black magic out of her that originally corrupted her. Maybe she's better now. If she was in danger, I don't think she'd be answering a phone call either."

Octavia scoffed. "Do you know Scarlett?"

"Touché, but trust me on this. I've been alpha for many years."

"Fine, but if anything happens to her because of that crazy witch, it's on you, and I'll never be able to forgive myself for being a bystander."

I shook my head, opening my arms. "Can you just get back in bed? This has already been a stressful morning, and I would like to relax before all hell breaks loose again."

Reluctantly, she walked over and crawled back in beside me. I wrapped my arms around her, placing a kiss on her forehead. "Good morning," I smiled down at her.

She flashed me a bright smile. "Good morning."

"What would you like for breakfast?" I asked, and her eyes lit up.

CHAPTER EIGHTEEN

———◆◇◆———

Octavia

"Is there any progress in the war I need to know about?" I asked, munching on the pancakes Mason had made.

He wiped his mouth with a napkin. "Same old news. We get one step ahead, and then we're two steps back. Alpha Jackson keeps making tabs on where they are hiding and camping, and then we send our men there to stop them. On the war fronts, where human territory meets wolf territory, we're not gaining anything. It hasn't moved for a few weeks. We hoped that going in and smothering them from the inside out they would surrender, but we can't even get past them. They're strong. I'll give them that."

"Do you really think trying to invade human territory is a good move? I mean, we kind of took their land beforehand and what they have left is small enough. You're just giving them an excuse to join the hunters and make their numbers bigger. They see the hunters as their protectors just as we see your army and Christian's army as ours." I pointed out.

He thought about it, sitting back in his chair. "What would you suggest?"

I cleared my throat, surprised he would ask my opinion on the matter. Sitting my fork down, I thought about it for a moment.

"Um, well, I don't think that invading their territory is going to help you win the war. Stop your men from trying to enter and just station guards by our border to make sure nothing gets past them." I suggested.

"I don't know… the hunters will still try to get into our territory. How is that fair? How are we to get to them without getting into human territory? That's the hard part."

"Show the humans we don't mean any harm. We just want to stop the people who are hurting innocents. Get a broadcast out to them or send flyers. It doesn't matter, but apologize and state how your intentions were not to harm them but to stop the people they think are protecting them. Wolves haven't bothered humans in years, and we haven't tried to enter and conquer their land until the hunters tried messing with us. The people they think are protecting them are really just putting them in danger. One wrong move on our part by entering their territory, and we're done for."

"So, we need to show the humans that their so-called protectors are really the ones putting them in danger?"

I nodded. "I think so. Then the wolves can bring the hunters to them. Alpha Jackson can make a better plan than I could but bring them to our territory. Let them in but make it a setup. Let them think they have pulled ahead but hit them when they are least expecting it. They'll camp out, Alpha Jackson will find them, and then you go in and put an end to this once and for all. Most importantly, if you can get Megan, you end it all. Cut off the head of the leader, weaken them, and then finish them. Easier said than done, I know, but that's my take on it."

He nodded, looking pleased and slightly proud. "I think you're getting somewhere. I think you're right. We're just pushing and pushing and getting nowhere, but if the humans can turn on their own kind… that gives us an advantage. The humans won't want them in their land if it is bringing danger to them. I could have Alpha Ryker place a protective hold on them. We reverse the situation at hand." He smirked.

"A protective hold? What's that?"

"When a pack declares allegiance with another when they are weak. They protect them. They give them anything they need. Men to guard them, food to feed them, anything really that helps them get back on their feet. Alpha Ryker has to do it because he's the Alpha of Power.

"Alpha Ryker made peace with the humans not too long ago before all this started again. He even has clubs there, as you know. If he swears to protect them as long as they place their allegiance with us, the hunters have lost their biggest advantage. Now, I don't know if it would work, but it's definitely worth a shot. I'll need to speak with Alpha Jackson about it."

I sat back with a content look. "Wow, I just helped you with war stuff. How exciting." I teased.

"You know, you could sit in on more of my meetings if you would become Luna. You have a different outlook on the way we alphas see things. We need that. Maybe force isn't the way to go about this war."

I shook my head. "It's not. Also, are you suggesting you accept me into the pack as Luna?"

He bit his lip, trying to hold back a smile. "I am. If you're ready to take on the title, of course?"

I spoke eagerly. "Yes! Please. I would like to be in the loop of things."

"Then it's settled. Tomorrow I will officially introduce you to the pack and swear you in as Luna."

Excitement filled me, and I couldn't help but hop up from my seat at the kitchen table and run over to him. Our laughter bounced off the walls as I leaped into his lap, throwing my arms around his neck.

"Alpha Mason and Luna Octavia." I mocked in an announcer's voice. "I like it." I winked.

His arms circled me and he mirrored my smile. "It sounds nice."

I went to speak up but heard footsteps approaching. Our heads snapped to the side as Alaric practically ran into the room with a huge smile, holding up his phone. "Sorry to interrupt, but she did it! That woman is… wow!" he spoke, nearly out of breath, causing us to give him a confused look.

"What are you going on about?" Mason mused.

"Right, sorry, you don't know yet. Let me read this article out loud." He cleared his throat, pulling his phone up.

"This morning, we received great news. Scarlett Madison, the former mate to King Christian, stormed the castle with an unknown person to stop the coronation of King Christian and Amanda Allister. Not only did she get her mate back, but she terrified the church officials and crowned herself as Queen Scarlett Spur. It's safe to say, our new queen is quite powerful. Though we don't know just how much, we do know that we are proud to call her our queen. Kneel before your queen, wolves. Times are about to change." He finished it and looked up with a giddy smile.

My jaw practically dropped to the floor. I jolted up from my chair. "That's my best friend! Whoop, whoop!" I started doing a victory dance causing Mason and Alaric to burst out with laughter. "Yeah, Scarlett, keep your foot up their ass!" I yelled, doing a victorious wolf howl.

The men laughed but couldn't help but join in, letting out a howl of their own in honor of our new Queen.

"Mason, you know what this means..." Alaric stated, and Mason grinned, nodding.

"What?" I questioned, looking at their excited faces.

Mason stood from his chair, offering a hand to me. "It's time for the whole pack to honor our new queen. Come on. Alaric, mindlink the pack to get ready."

I eagerly let Mason lead me outside. People were already start gathering by the gates in front of his house. Mason looked back at me and smirked.

"Shift."

"What? Now?"

He nodded, pulling his shirt off, and before I knew it, his large black wolf stood in his place. I quickly did the same and shifted into my wolf, standing next to him closely. When I looked back towards the gate, people were shifting into their wolves as well.

"It's time to honor our new queen, War Pack! She stood up to some nasty people today and showed you just how admirable she truly is. She will lead with respect, and she will care for each and every one of you. Let's let everyone hear our support!" Mason started pacing back and forth in front of me as he talked, and I was so glad I could hear his mindlinks now.

The wolves snarled in excitement, and Mason finally tilted his head back, letting out a roar so loud, it shook the trees around him. Tilting my head back as well, I let my wolf let out a howl along with the other wolves. Our howls together were loud and made a statement.

Scarlett was our queen, and no one could say any different.

CHAPTER NINETEEN

·◇·

Octavia

I looked at my reflection in the mirror with a bright smile. There were no longer dark bags under my eyes, and I looked happy. *I was so happy.* It was a beautiful sight to see. No longer was the girl staring back at me in misery. She was in her own little fairy-tale.

The red sundress that I had on was beautiful and held such an important meaning. I was wearing my new pack's colors. Today I would be labeled the Luna of The War Pack. Today, everything changed. It was nerve-wracking, but I couldn't help but feel giddy inside.

"Nervous?" Mason's arms wrapped around me from behind, his chin resting on my shoulder.

I smiled, laying my hands across his as I leaned into him. "A little, but who could blame me? Today is a big day."

"Indeed, it is." He placed a small kiss on my mark, causing shivers to dance down my spine.

"Did you inform Christian why we couldn't come to their celebration?" I turned in his arms, wrapping mine around his neck.

"I did, and he totally understood. He told me to tell you congratulations and that Scarlett will be incredibly proud."

I bit my lip, trying to hold back a smile. "Did you tell him what I said to tell her?"

"About keeping a foot up the church officials' ass? Yes, I did. He laughed and said he would… do his best to get your meaning across."

I rolled my eyes. "Him and his posh ways." I joked.

Mason snickered, releasing me. "I came to say that it is time and the pack is very excited to formally meet you."

I let out a deep breath of air. "I'm ready." I nodded.

I looked him over, seeing his elegant suit. He was a sight to see—one that I could barely take my eyes off of.

"If you keep looking at me like that, there won't be a Luna ceremony today." He raised a brow, and my cheeks heated.

"My apologies," I took a step towards him with a devilish smile. "You do look rather ravishing, though." I winked.

A low growl rumbled within his chest as he shook his head. "Stop it. I'm not trying to be late, and if you keep it up… we will be."

I held my hands up in defense. "No more comments."

He nodded, satisfied and turned to walk out of the bathroom. I followed after him with a small smirk. "Only if he knew what I was wearing under this dress," I whispered, knowing damn well his wolf hearing would pick up on it.

He halted, snapping his head in my direction. "You like to play games, huh?" I watched as his eyes danced back and forth from red to brown.

I flashed him a toothy grin, brushing past him. "I just like getting you worked up, honestly."

I reached for the door, but a yelp escaped me as his hand gently, but still had a tight grip, wrapped around the back of my neck, jerking me back to him. My heart beat frantically from the scare, my eyes wide as his chest was pressed against my back. His mouth lowered next to my ear.

"Just wait until we get back here tonight." With that, he nipped at my ear and let go of me.

My jaw remained dropped as he mocked my movements earlier with the same grin, walking past me to open the door and exited the room.

Breathless, I followed after him like a lost puppy.

It wasn't long before we were in the car and headed towards the building that held all the packs' ceremonies. Mason told me it was where he was introduced as the new alpha, and the passing of titles was given.

When the car stopped in front of the building, there were already hundreds of people lining the gates, cheering as we stepped out of the car. I looked over, seeing Mason shift into alpha mode. His face looked stern, but it held a small, appreciative smile as he waved to the people of his pack. My nerves were officially wrecked as I saw how many people were gathered here. He held out a hand to me, which I graciously took as he led me inside.

I walked in to see Alaric, Braelyn, and a few others standing around with proud smiles. Mason placed his hand on the small of my back, leading me forward. Braelyn walked up, throwing her arms around me.

"I'm so happy for the both of you. I'm proud to call you my Luna." She whispered.

"Thank you, Braelyn. That means the world to me." I let go, turning to Alaric.

He opened his arms with a grin. "I'm excited to see you sitting in our meetings. I've heard some input you gave Mason. Even Alpha Jackson liked the idea of it. I think this title is going to be perfect for you. I'm glad to call you my Luna, Octavia. You're going to be one hell of a good one." I walked into his open arms, pride filling my chest at his confession.

I was ready for this title, I was ready to be a part of this war, and most importantly, I was ready to help end it.

"Thanks, Alaric."

I looked back to Mason, where a young woman stood next to him. Her eyes were a golden color, but not like those of a royal. It was… brighter—enchanting almost.

"I hope you don't mind, but an old friend reached out to me recently. This is Lyra. She is what we call a speaker of death. She can connect to those who we have lost. She called me in a frantic state, saying she needed to speak to you. Well, *someone* needed to speak to you."

My hands grew clammy as I looked at her. I gulped, nodding at her, and she smiled, walking forward.

"I don't get this much attention from someone usually, but for some reason, this person was rather persistent. She had to say a few things to you."

"S-she?" I croaked out, knowing just who she was talking about.

"I believe an old friend would like to talk to you. Are you ok with that?"

I quickly nodded, and she slowly raised her hands, placing them on the sides of my head. "It will go dark for a moment, but then everything should come clear." She explained.

Once she closed her eyes and mumbled something under her breath, everything went black. For a moment, I stared into nothing, but soon I heard a small voice.

"So, you just leave me and become some badass Luna? How unfair." I quickly turned around, seeing the one and only. Tears brimmed my eyes, and I wondered if this was even real. She looked the same as the last time I saw her. Dark complected, curly hair and beautiful brown eyes that made any man swoon.

"Liza," I sobbed.

She smiled, walking over to me. "It's me, babe."

"H-how is this possible? How did you… is this real?"

She looked around. "Not the best place to do this. It's quite dark in this woman's mind, but I had to see you. It's very real. I tried many other people with the same gift as her, but none knew how to reach Alpha Mason. Each one told me the same thing: find Lyra. She once helped him talk to his family that passed away. She was hellbent on keeping me away, saying she doesn't do that anymore, but I'm quite persistent, as you know."

I let out a strangled laugh, trying to keep my tears at bay. "Goddess, I've missed you."

She gave me a pitiful look. "I've missed you too, 'Tavia."

"What did you need to tell me?"

"Uh? How freaking proud of you I am! Look at you! You got over Josh, met your mate, are about to become a Luna, *and* you're about to help assist in the war. Octavia, you're a badass."

I giggled, throwing myself into her arms. "Thank you. I'm so sorry I didn't tell you sooner or that I didn't come to visit you or—"

"Octavia! Stop it. I'm ok. I'm happy. Truly, I am. Yeah, it sucked having to go so soon, but I learned to look at the positive side of things. You were busy, and no one knew this was going to happen. Life has unexpected twists and turns, and sadly, it took me for one, but it's time to move on and live your life to the fullest. Just know I'm happy, and I'm so proud to call you my best friend. Forever and always, I promise."

Another sob escaped me. "Forever and always." I agreed.

She turned her head to the side with a sigh. "The woman is growing weak. Her link between us is breaking. I need to hurry. Look, I know you want to get revenge for my death, but don't. Don't let that beast out. You locked her away for a reason. I've seen how this plays out, and I get the justice I deserve but don't put yourself through that. Promise me, Octavia."

"You knew?"

She giggled. "I'm dead. I know everything now, and I know what I saw when you stared in that mirror. You were going to let her win, but you can't. Not yet. The right time will come for that, but you can't do it because of me. So, promise me."

"I… I promise."

"Good, now, go get sworn in as Luna. I love you. Make me proud." She winked.

"I love you too, Liza."

We had our last hug, and I cried out, not wanting to let her go. When I opened my eyes again, I could feel my wet cheeks. Everyone gave me a pitied look, and I quickly wiped my tears.

"Thank you, I really needed that," I told Lyra, who placed her small, delicate hand on my cheek.

"You are very welcome, dear. Now, she is yelling for you to go out there and show everyone just who you are."

I sniffled, a small laugh following shortly after. "I think I will."

I turned to Mason, who quickly engulfed me in a hug. I held onto him tightly. "Thank you," I whispered.

Wordlessly, he kissed my forehead and gave me a small nod.

I turned, wiping my hands on my dress and nodded. "Let's do this."

Mason took hold of my hands, leading me towards a door. "This will walk you out onto a stage. Everyone has filed in and is patiently waiting. He nodded to Alaric and Braelyn, who opened the two, mahogany doors and then cheers flooded my ears.

Mason wrapped his arm around my waist as we walked out. Once Mason held his hand up, the hundreds of people went silent.

"I would just like to say thank you before we start. Thank you for standing by us in a time of doubt, a time of fear, and a time of worry. This war has been brutal so far, but that doesn't mean we accept defeat. We will get our victory. My heart goes out to the families who might have lost someone so far. They gave their life saving us, and that was one hell of a way to go out, so thank you all." Mason expressed his love and gratitude, something I haven't seen him do with his pack yet, and I could see why they loved him so much as they cheered and clapped.

I smiled up at him, my hand reaching out to grab his, giving it a small squeeze. He smiled down at me and raised our joined hands, pressing a small kiss upon mine before looking back to his people.

"As you might already know, a while back, I found my mate, Octavia. It is my great honor to accept her into our pack tonight and give her the title as your Luna." People whistled and cheered at his words.

I watched as someone walked up to him and handed him a bowl and two knives. I hated this part. I knew what was to come, the bonding of blood. Once my blood met his, they would become one and I, not only would be a part of his pack but would also obtain the same rank as him with the connection to all of the people within his pack.

"By cutting our palms, we will link together by blood. Do you accept the title as Luna of The War Pack?"

"I do," I answered, trying to keep my voice steady.

He smirked as he brought the knife down the center of his palm and handed another one to me. I gulped, taking it and watched as he held his dripping palm over the golden bowl.

"I've been shot twice. What's another wound to add onto that list." I mumbled, and people chuckled, clearly hearing me, causing my cheeks to heat. I quickly sliced my hand and winced as I held it over the bowl.

In seconds I felt a power surge through me, and I looked up at Mason, shocked. Our cuts easily healed, and Mason grasped my forearms, making sure I was steady as I took it all in.

"You ok?" he murmured, and I nodded.

"Just a lot to take in."

It was an out-of-this-world feeling. I could feel all the different links within the pack. My wolf even sensed Mason as her equal now. It was new, but I loved it.

"Your new Luna!" he called out, and I watched as people tilted their heads back, howling. Mason wrapped his arm around my shoulder, pulling me to his side, and I looked around, feeling content.

"Your parents would be proud." He told me, and I rolled my eyes.

"Oh, I'm sure they would. I managed to get a hold of the big bad alpha." I joked, causing him to scoff, but he couldn't help the grin that crawled onto his face.

"Let's go meet some people."

CHAPTER TWENTY

◆◇◆

Octavia

Meeting everyone was nice. The people of his pack were so kind and welcoming, unlike the stories I was told as a kid. It's crazy how life works. Sometimes, it makes you see that the world around you isn't as bad as you first made it out to be. Maybe you just needed a push in the right direction. Maybe that's exactly what I had needed. If none of this happened, I would still be that same depressed girl from The Power Pack.

"Your pack is something else." I giggled, walking into our room.

"*Our* pack." He corrected, "And trust me, I know." I smiled, and he walked over to me.

"Close your eyes." He ordered, and I sighed doing so.

"Why?"

I felt him cover my eyes with his hands just in case and guided me through the room to the door, and I couldn't help but laugh as I kept stumbling.

"Where are you taking me?" I giggled.

I heard him open a door, and soon, his hands left. I looked around, feeling my heart speed up. His arms wrapped around my waist from behind as he sat his head on my shoulder.

"My mom had this made before she passed. I was just becoming alpha before her death, and she was so excited for me to find someone to start a family with and keep the Cage name going."

"Mason..." My eyes stung, trying to blink away the tears.

"I know it's kind of fast, but it is our future after all. I would wait a bit, but I couldn't help it when you agreed to be accepted as Luna. I know it's not mating tradition to marry since we're already stuck together for life, but if you want to, I'm completely ok with that. This, though, comes with all of that. Our future, you being Luna, and it was burning a hole in the back of my mind knowing you hadn't seen it yet. I wish my mom was here to meet you. I know she would have loved you." He mumbled, and I smiled, looking around the small nursery.

One of the last things he had from his mother was staring me right in the face, and I so desperately wish she was here to experience this moment with us.

"It's beautiful, Mason." I smiled, turning in his arms, staring up at him with a curious expression. "So, you want kids then?"

"I do... if you do." He spoke almost hesitantly, and I nodded quickly.

"I love it." I turned, looking around the nursery once more. "She has very good taste."

"It's gender-neutral, so when the time comes... we'll be ready."

When the time comes... wow. We were really going to have a family of our own one day. The thought alone excited me.

"I love you," I finally admitted.

When the time was right, we would know, I had once said. At this moment, I knew I loved this man with everything in me.

Mason quickly let go of me, walking in front of me with a goofy smile. "Took you long enough." He chuckled.

My eyes widened slightly. "What?"

He bit his lip, trying to hide his smile. "I've known for a while that I loved you."

I laughed in disbelief. "You never said anything!"

"Yeah, because I didn't want to scare you."

"I was scared of scaring you!"

We both laughed, shaking our heads at one another. "We are something else," I groaned, falling against his chest as I rested my head there.

I looked up at him, trying my best to fight down a smile. "Hey,"

He looked down at me, raising a brow. "Hey."

"I love you," I repeated.

His smile was breathtaking. "And I love you. With my whole heart, you cheesy woman." As he leaned in, my eyes shut, welcoming the kiss eagerly.

It was soft—gentle even. It was full of pure love, something new to me. His lips pressed harder into mine, and I opened my mouth as his tongue met mine. Goddess, I loved this man.

He pulled back a bit, an evil glint in his eyes. "So about earlier…" He reminded me, and my eyes widened.

I pulled away, taking a wary step backward. "Uh…"

"Oh, no, you don't. You're not getting off the hook that easily." He taunted.

I belched out a laugh, spinning on my heels and darted out of the nursery. Our laughter bounced off the walls as he chased after me.

Excitement filled me as I took a sharp turn, darting down another hall in his huge mansion, getting lost in the laughter that escaped him.

"You can run, but you can't hide!" he called out.

"I can try!"

Just as I leaped through the door of our room and slammed it behind me, I felt him hit it with a thud. I held my stomach, losing it in laughter, barely managing to lock the door. He patiently knocked.

"I'd rather not break down our bedroom door. I think you know how capable I am of that."

I bit my lip. "Technically, all my stuff still hasn't moved up here yet. I only have a few things up here, so if you would like to break down *your* bedroom door, knock yourself out. I have a room with a perfectly attached door that I can sleep in tonight."

Teasing him would only get him riled up, but I loved it too much to stop now.

"Mhm, I see."

I shook my head, knowing he wasn't going to break down his own bedroom door. Then, I heard the click of the lock. My eyes nearly left my head as it opened, and he leaned against the doorframe, keys dangling from his finger.

"Dammit," I grumbled.

"You tried; I'll give you credit for that." He mused, entering the room, kicking the door shut behind him.

I staggered back as he stalked toward me, seeing the look in his eyes. It was like I was his prey. Maybe I was.

He pointed to a window, and I looked out, seeing the moon shining brightly. "Another bad heat will be coming soon. I'm sure you wouldn't like that." He tossed his keys to the side, shrugging off the jacket to his suit, causing me to gulp.

Heat indeed was something I did not want to happen. Ever again. The episodes weren't fun.

"That is... very true."

"So, I think it's safe to say... we both know where this will be going tonight."

I shook my head at him. "Enlighten me."

"With pleasure." He jerked me to him, smashing his lips onto mine.

I was quick to move my hands to the buttons of his shirt, quickly trying to undo them. Once I finally got them undone, he moved back, letting me push it off his shoulders. In seconds his lips were back on mine as he grabbed the hem of my dress, pulling it over my head. He reached down, grabbing the back of my legs and swept me up, wrapping my legs around his waist. Our kiss grew hungry as I ran my fingers through his hair, tugging every so often.

Before I knew it, my back was against the bed as he hovered over me, and he leaned back, looking me over. "Well, I'm seeing what was under your dress you mentioned earlier." He tilted his head to the side. "Not that impressed."

I gasped, swatting at his chest. He laughed, grabbing hold of my hands and pinned them above my head as he leaned back down, his lips just a hair's breadth above mine. "I lied. You're a damn Goddess, Octavia. Don't ever forget that."

Closing the gap before us, my legs were quick to wrap around his waist, tightening my hold around him, bringing him closer to me. I let my head fall to the side, allowing his lips to travel down my neck as he placed tortuous kisses upon it. He stopped on my mark, working his lips in a way that made my toes curl and sparks dance down my body.

He moved down, trailing wet kisses down the valley of my breasts, making my eyes snap shut, my grip on him tightening as his kisses got lower and lower. Suddenly, he stopped. I looked down at him with wide eyes, seeing him give me yet another wicked grin. He moved back up, pressing a soft kiss on my lips.

"Are you sure you want to do this?"

"Positive. Now shut up and get back to doing what you were." I grumbled out, agitated.

He let out a husky chuckle. "*So demanding.*"

I let out a huff, leaning forward and grabbed hold of his belt, yanking him to me while my fingers worked quickly trying to unbuckle it. He sat back, watching me amused. "Who has gotten you all worked up?" he teased as I pulled it from the loops of his pants.

"Shut. Up."

I reached for the button of his slacks, but he stopped me, pressing me back on the bed. "We'll work on you first. Seems like you need it."

I went to curse him, but as his fingers grabbed ahold of one of the last pieces of clothing on my body, pulling it down, everything left my mind.

And I was on cloud nine for quite a bit.

CHAPTER TWENTY-ONE

Octavia

"Dad, please, stop," I begged, sobbing as I pulled on the ropes that were tying me to the chair.

He gave me a sad look, shaking his head. "You need to learn, Octavia. Learn to fight your own battles without letting her do them for you." I snarled at him, the ropes digging into my wrist.

"You don't think I've tried?"

"Obviously not enough. I see her now. She's staring at me through your eyes with those bright red and bloody ones of her own. You're keeping her at bay, so that's progress. Learn to mash her down and keep your control. As your father, I simply cannot let you leave and socialize with people until you learn." He walked closer, resting a hand on my cheek. "My sweet daughter, I hope you know I'm doing this for you. I only want the best for you. You could hurt someone."

"I've been at this for months. She hasn't shown. Please, Dad, just let me go."

"*I'm training you just like I would any of my warriors. Learn, Octavia. Get yourself free. I'm not helping today.*" With that, he reached over, grabbing a mask, and I cried out, frantically thrashing in my seat as he slowly put it on me.

"*You have twenty minutes before the gas takes you. Don't let it get that far.*" He mumbled, turning and headed towards the steps, leaving the basement along with his own daughter in a world of pain.

I tried my best to hold my breath, but it wasn't helping. The gas kicked on, slowly starting to invade my senses. *People like you don't survive, Octavia,* my father would tell me. I shook my head, trying to get his words out. *You need to learn to protect yourself because they will come for you.* I growled out, trying to mash the tight pain in my chest down. She begged for me to let her loose, to save us both.

Black veins crawled up my arms, and I whimpered, watching them grow higher and higher. She was too strong. I could never truly keep her at bay, no matter how much he tried to train me to do so. I wasn't some warrior. I was a girl alone in a world where people saw her as a weapon, not a human being. My genes were unheard of, and because of that... this is what my life has come to.

I gulped, starting to feel dizzy. Snapping my eyes shut, I tried to calm my mind, as well as trying to mash her back down. When my eyes snapped back open, I started to rock the chair back and forth, but I was too weak to knock it completely over. Though, when the ringing broke out in my head, I screamed in pain, knowing what she was doing. She was using my own pain against me to break the mental hold I had on her.

Then, I was cast to the back of my mind, seeing out of my own eyes but not being able to do a damn thing about it. *Father is going to kill me!*

She looked around, taking in our environment. Slowly, she raised one arm, ripping the ropes right off her. The wolfsbane that soaked them didn't *even phase her. She quickly pulled the mask off, throwing it to the side. Undoing the other side of the ropes, she let out a huff, standing up. Slowly, she stalked towards the gas tank my father kept down here to torture us both. With a simple kick, it flew into the wall, bursting into flames.*

She looked into the mirror next to us, and I saw the red eyes staring back at me. She raised a brow as if saying, I told you so.

"Please don't hurt him! Don't do it." *I cried out to her. She cracked her neck to the side, a humorless laugh escaping her.*

"I won't kill that pathetic excuse that you call a father, but I will be putting him in his place along with the others who tried to experiment on us. Don't you see, Octavia? He's not training you to mash me down! He's training you to get you angry enough to let me out. If they want to see what I can do, I will give them my all." She spat out, but the voice didn't sound like my own.

As she stalked up the stairs, leaving the basement, I called out to the Goddess. Because the beast within me was about to release hell on earth, for I had finally let her out for the first time in years.

I gasped, jumping up, looking around as my heart beat frantically. Sweat dripped down my forehead, my body soaked with it. I looked next to me, noticing the bed was empty. The sun was shining brightly behind the curtains. When the bathroom door opened, I looked over to see Mason walking out with a towel around his waist, steam rolling off him.

"Good morning, beautiful." He smiled.

Shakily, I sported a half-smile, running my hand through my hair. "Morning,"

"Hey, you ok?"

I pursed my lips, thinking my answer over. "Bad dream."

"Do you want to talk about it?" he asked, sitting on the bed next to me with worried eyes.

I shook my head. "No, no… I'm fine."

It seemed so real. It was as if I was really there in that basement again.

Mason reached over, grabbing my hand and brought it to his lip, placing a delicate kiss upon it.

"How are you feeling this morning?" his worried looked morphed into a cocky one.

I raised a brow. "Great, and you?"

He hummed, faking a thinking face. "I'm decent."

I scoffed, swatting at his arm. "I think you're more than decent if what I saw last night was correct."

His chest vibrated with laughter. "It was amazing, Octavia. Have you noticed the difference yet?"

I narrowed my eyes. "What do you mean?"

He got up, squatting in front of me. "Our scents are different and my favorite part…" He reached out, placing a hand on the side of my cheek.

The normal sparks were gone, but I couldn't help but lean into his hand, my eyes fluttering shut. Content. That was the feeling I got from just one touch.

"That's different." I giggled, opening my eyes.

"I have a feeling this bond is about to be very new to us since everything is officially completed."

I fell back on the bed, letting out a content sigh. "No more heat."

"No more heat," He agreed.

"How lovely." I turned my head, looking back at him.

His eyes showed the love he felt for me, which warmed my heart. However, I was afraid that my subconscious was wracked with too much guilt with us growing so close. The guilt of lying to him about who I truly was. I wasn't just some wolf from The Power Pack. I was so much more—a destroyer of packs, they used to say.

What happens if he finds out? He's opened himself up to me completely, yet I haven't even begun to let him see the real me. I had blood on my hands and a lot of it. It wasn't something I was proud of, but I couldn't help but think that what I did to those people... they deserved every second of it.

After what I did and what she showed them she could, my father left us alone. I was able to socialize with people again and somewhat return to a normal life. After that, I learned to keep her locked away, which she hated me for. I could still hear the screams of the men that tortured me for so many years as she ripped them apart, making my father sit and watch.

After that, I went numb for a while. She was content for the time being, and my father and I lost any relationship we once had. When my mother learned about what he was truly training me to do, she was distraught and almost left him, telling him I couldn't help how I was born and that I was no weapon to be used.

It wasn't until recently, when I came to The War Pack, that she became active again within my mind, which confused me. I didn't understand why.

"I have a meeting with Alpha Jackson today. Would you like to join?" my eyes lit up at the thought.

"Really?!"

"Yes," He chuckled. "You're Luna now, Octavia. You can sit in whenever you like. Although I hope it's every meeting, the choice is yours."

"I'd love to. Let me shower and get dressed. I'll meet you in your office."

"Perfect." He leaned over, pressing a kiss on the top of my head. "See you in a few."

I got up, brushing past him into the bathroom. I showered as quickly as I could, eager to get to the meeting and actually participate as Luna for the first time.

Minutes later, I was combing my wet hair, looking in the mirror with a bright smile. I looked… different. Maybe it was the completion of the mate bond, or maybe it was the fact that I finally felt like I belonged somewhere—that I had a purpose for once that was actually in my best interest.

It wasn't long before I walked into Mason's office, seeing him sitting across from the one and only Alpha Jackson. He was a man to admire. Being the Alpha of The Intelligence Pack, it was safe to say Alpha Jackson fit the part. They say his mind works like no others. He was a calm and collected man, but that doesn't mean you want to make an enemy out of him. They also say you'd never see him coming. He was well respected in our nation.

His appearance was less formal than Mason's. He wore boots, jeans, and a flannel with a white tee underneath. His hair was a mess on the top of his head, a slight stubble growing on his face. He was the complete opposite compared to the other alphas, but I respected him for that. He didn't care what anyone thought.

"Good morning, Octavia. It's been a minute." Jackson spoke with a southern drawl you couldn't miss.

"Good morning. Yes, it has, thankfully you're not here to find me at a party." I joked, making my way over to Mason and took a seat next to him on a vacant chair.

He let out a soft laugh. "Thank the Goddess for that. Congratulations, by the way. Being a Luna looks good on you. Just don't screw it up." He teased me.

I shook my head. "Thank you. I'll try my best not to."

We both looked over to Mason as he cleared his throat, sitting forward. "So, Jackson, what did you want to talk about today? Anything new with the war?"

Jackson grabbed some papers, handing one to Mason and one to me. I looked it over, my head tilting slightly.

"These numbers have increased by hundreds," I spoke, gulping.

"Yeah. It's not looking too good for the wolves. Deaths are rising, and the number of injured is even more. I've never seen some of the things they're using. I mean… you have the normal silver bullets, but now it's wolfsbane bullets that break apart in the wolf's skin. It's almost impossible to get all the fragments out, and half the time, a small, laced fragment is missed, and the wolf dies."

My eyes widened, a tight knot forming in my stomach. "So… what is the next step?"

I glanced over at Mason, who was looking at me proudly. "Jackson, would you like to tell her?"

"Mason informed me of your… idea. About pulling our men back and trying to gain the human's trust first. I thought it was completely idiotic at first." He shrugged, and I pursed my lips, not used to his bluntness. "But after Mason explained your reasoning, I warmed to it."

I let out a breath of air I didn't know I was holding. "Ok, and?"

"But I tweaked it a little. We'll have Alpha Ryker order a protective hold. We'll send humans word of it and explain how we are not their enemy. As part of my idea goes… we're going to trick them. I know you have the best intentions, but a soft heart will not win you a war."

"Wait… what? How is that going to gain their trust?"

"Because they won't know any different. When we pull our men back, and hopefully when they kick the hunters out, we'll come back. The protective hold won't just be our word— It will be our men. We won't invade their lands, but we will station around their borders. We'll fake a hunter attack against them to make them believe their own kind turned their backs on them.

"No one will be harmed; we'll just enter their territory. We come in, saving the day, and their trust will be ours completely. We'll offer them a chance to join us, and we'll send them to the hunters as… spies, you could say. Then we'll lead the hunters right to us… or I guess I should say they lead us to them, unknowingly, of course."

"And if that doesn't work?" I questioned, raising a brow.

"We bring in the big guns. We'll join people we absolutely despise to defeat a common enemy." He shrugged. "I personally hate the idea, but you have to do what you have to do. These hunters think they're winning. And while they might be winning the battles, we're going to win the war. I'm certain of that."

"Join who exactly?" I nervously asked, the thought already in my mind.

"Do you know the creatures that live in Italy? We banished them there years back." He smirked, and my eyes widened.

"You can't be serious."

"We have connections. Ryker is already contacting them as we speak."

"You're wanting to join arms with vampires… *freaking vampires.* The same creatures that nearly wiped the humans off the map just years ago! If you do that, you can forget the human's trust."

"Don't worry. The borders are still closed to vampires, and they are not allowed on our territory AKA the states. But—"

"Then how the hell do you plan to work with them? Sneak them in?"

"As I was saying before, you rudely cut me off," He snickered, a playful look in his eyes. "There is one group we let stay. Not many know of them, and the reason we let them stay is not my story to tell, but let's just say Alpha Ryker knows them well. They're called the McKinley Crew. They're a group of vampires created by the first vampire ever created, the vampire king that goes by Dante. He rules over the vampires in Italy and does one hell of a good job at it."

So, the stories are true. *There is a vampire king.*

"I know this is a lot to take in, Octavia, but we believe there are some vampires that snuck over the borders. We had a few border guards killed, and it looked like a vampire attack. They've been working with the hunters and are a common enemy of The McKinley Crew. It is the only reason the McKinleys will join us." Mason explained, and my head hurt at the thought of it all.

How did Alpha Ryker know these people? And why were they able to stay? I was always taught vampires were our enemies, even if I hadn't even seen one before. Wolves knew this. The fact we were going to work with them made my stomach turn.

Mason reached out, placing a hand on my own. "The humans will not be harmed; you have my word… just as they will. I know it's not the best thing to do, trick them, I mean, but we have to do something that will make them join us. As far as the vampires go, it will be our last option. Don't stress too much just yet."

I nodded, still not liking the idea.

The end of the war was going to be brutal; I know that much.

CHAPTER TWENTY-TWO

———◆◇◆———

Octavia

After our talk with Alpha Jackson, the next few weeks flew by. Everything went into effect. The humans got our message, and Ryker offered his hand in protection. It was almost unbelievable when the humans were quick to agree. The hunters fled from the human territory, which Jackson stated was in a distraught manner. We were slowly gaining the upper hand, but the hunters were pissed. The next move they pulled shook us to our cores.

"What do you mean a gas form of wolfsbane?" I yelled as Mason quickly packed a bag.

"I had a meeting with Christian and Jackson, and it's dire that I leave now. I have to help my people. Christian is going as well. It takes us longer to be taken down."

"You're going to get yourself killed!"

He threw his hands up angrily. "No, I won't! Octavia, I have to go! This is what the Alpha of War looks like. You know this. I don't just order the wars to start, I join them and help when I am needed, and that's now. We've spoken to Alara Lavender. She's going to put a protection spell on us… one that keeps us from dying, but I have to leave now. Christian is waiting for me." He pulled the duffle bag over his shoulder, shooting me one last pleading look.

Why the hell they all trusted Alara Lavender was beyond me. Over the past few weeks, that's all I've heard: Alara Lavender. Scarlett contacted me, explaining everything. I almost didn't believe it at first, but when the sectors were officially destroyed, and they brought up new alphas for new packs, I knew it was true. Still, that woman caused chaos and destruction years ago—something that is almost unredeemable.

"Don't worry about me. I'll be fine. You need to stay here with the pack. They're going to feel the snap." He mumbled, his eyes leaving mine as he nervously looked away.

"What do you mean they will 'feel the snap'?" I asked, taking a threatening step towards him, a growl rumbling in my chest.

"It's a gas wolfsbane, Octavia. I can stay up long enough to get to the building with the supplies they need to make it and help destroy it, but I won't last much longer after that. I will die, but with Alara's spell, death will be short-lived. You'll feel the bond snap, but when I come to, everything will return to normal, I promise. Now, I've got to go. I'm already running late." He rushed over to me, pressing a hard kiss to my forehead.

My eyes closed, tears brimming my eyes at the thought. I don't want to go through this. Even if it was temporary, my wolf would feel his death.

"Promise me you'll explain this all to the pack and keep them calm. They'll feel their alpha die, and they will be distraught and will need someone to look to. That is you, Octavia. You're Luna now. You can do this."

Numbly, I nodded. "I promise. Please come back to me."

The side of his mouth lifted some. "I will."

With that, he turned and walked to the door. When it shut behind him, I brought a shaky hand to my mouth. My idea that Jackson tweaked worked, but it created something ten times worse. It made the hunters more motivated than ever to harm us, so was this all my fault?

"Attention, War Pack members, please meet at the church for a pack meeting. There is a lot you need to know, and there is a lot that we will be experiencing together in the next few hours. Please hurry. As your Luna, I'm deeming this mandatory, and you are not to miss it. I will see you in a few." I mindlinked the pack.

There was a knock on the door shortly after. "Come in," I wiped my sweaty palms on my jeans, seeing Alaric peak his head through the door.

"I'm here to escort you to the church, Luna." He half-smiled. "I also thought you could use some company."

I tried to muster up a smile. "I would appreciate that, thank you. I'm assuming Mason told you everything?"

"Yeah... he did."

"Well, let's get going then."

When we reached the church, a lump formed in my throat. I didn't know how this would go, but I hoped it would go better than my mind was thinking it would.

I walked through the church to the front as people were talking to one another. The chatter quieted down as I stood in front of them, worried looks on their faces.

"I've called you here today to explain some things to you that are… concerning. Though, I ask you to remain calm and let me explain everything before you say anything." My voice shook.

I was used to Mason standing beside me, doing all the talking. Without Mason here, they knew something was up.

I explained what was happening with the gas form and why Mason had to leave. Gasps left everyone at the news. Though, when I stated that Mason and Christian would not leave the field alive, cries erupted all around. Alaric was quick to quiet them, begging for them to let me finish.

"As you know, Alara Lavender has resurfaced, leaving the facility she once stayed at to get help. She has made a deal with the Alpha King, Christian. She has placed a protection spell on them, and their death will only be temporary. I gathered you here today because we will feel it all happen. Bonds will break, and we need to be united so we can get through this together. We're waiting for the cue of when they reach the war front where the gas is being held. Everyone, I ask you to join hands."

I watched with a warm heart as my pack members linked their hands together without a second thought, squeezing each other's hands tightly. I reached out, offering a hand to Alaric and one to Braelyn, who had joined us moments before.

I watched as Alaric's eyes glazed over. "They're there." He called out.

I gulped. Braelyn's eyes snapped shut, tightly squeezing my hand. It felt like an eternity as we all stood, waiting for something to happen. Braelyn moved, resting her head on my shoulder. I locked eyes with Alaric, and he gave me a small nod as if saying, you'll be ok.

"May the Goddess be with us," I whispered.

Maybe twenty minutes went by before I felt it—the snap that caused us all to gasp out in pain. People cried at the feeling of losing their alpha while I stood frozen. I could feel the link that felt as if it was slowly shredding piece by piece—the mate bond. It knocked the breath out of me, causing my eyes to glisten with tears as I dropped to my knees. I tried to hold it back but failed as the loud, crying sob ripped through my chest.

Alaric was quick to squat down to grab me, but Braelyn pushed him away harshly. "Your touch will hurt her. Her wolf thinks she lost her mate, and your touch will be like a scorching fire since you're a male with a wolf of his own. I got this." She mumbled, pulling me to her chest as I cried out in pain, clawing at her shirt.

"Women of The War Pack, you may approach!" Alaric called out.

I heard the shuffling of feet across the church floors, and before I knew it, I felt gentle hands being placed on my back. I numbly looked up, seeing women of all ages standing around Braelyn and me. The ones with their hands on me had women standing behind them with their own hands placed on their backs as well. It was a rippling effect. Their eyes were closed—praying.

"They're praying to the Goddess to come through them all to give you comfort," Braelyn spoke in awe, and sure enough, I felt at ease, letting out a breath of air I didn't know I was holding.

I couldn't help the tears that leaked down my face at the caring women of this pack. They were experiencing their own pain yet taking all mine with the help of the Goddess to ease my own.

I glanced up at Braelyn, who still held me, a small smile on her face as she wiped the tears from my face. "Your mark is still there." She smiled brightly, sniffling.

"Is it?"

She nodded. "It worked. He's alive."

A happy sob escaped me as I curled further into her. *Thank the Goddess.*

"Let's get you home. You need to rest," She mumbled, starting to move.

The women of the pack helped me to my feet. They looked at me questionably, and I finally smiled... a real smile.

"Thank you all for your kindness today. I am truly blessed to be a Luna of this pack." I confessed, watching their faces light up at my statement. One by one, I moved, hugging them each.

My heart still hurt, so desperately needing to be in Mason's arms, but I pushed it away to give my own comfort to the people who needed it now. They each hugged me tightly as if I would leave this world any minute. It was so odd to see people look at me like they do the alphas— with a look of admiration and love.

After the hugs and sweet nothings were said, Alaric and Braelyn escorted me back to the comforts of my room. I knew some of Mason's men that survived the battle today were bringing him back, but I couldn't help but feel empty. He literally died. We all felt it. The horrid, gut-wrenching pain nearly snapped us in half. I can't take that again. I knew, in my heart, I'd take a bullet to the skull for that man. I will not let him get hurt in this war. No matter what it took. No matter what I had to do... *or what I let out.*

I patiently waited on the edge of the bed, biting my fingernails anxiously. My wolf whimpered within me. She was confused—so damn confused. She knew she felt his wolf die along with him, but there also was that small incredibly thin string that was barely holding itself together. I guess the spell that was cast on him held it together. Thank the Goddess for that. I guess Alara Lavender was more trustworthy than I thought, but that doesn't mean she one hundred percent has my trust just yet.

My door abruptly opened, Alaric rushing through. "He's here."

I jumped up, rushing past him as he called out, informing me he was in the infirmary. I quickly made my way there, my heart thumping in my chest. When I walked through the door, I halted. He wasn't awake yet. The doctor was looking him over, a confused look on his face. I opened my mouth to speak, but nothing came out. What is wrong with him? When the doctor noticed me standing by the door, he smiled, motioning me over.

"He's ok. I thought he would wake by now, but the king hasn't woken either. It will probably take a few for the spell to work its course. In the meantime, you can sit with him if you'd like."

Nervously, I stepped forward and took a seat beside him. He looked pale and lifeless. I looked away, fighting down my tears. He's ok. He's ok. He's ok, Octavia. Stop worrying. He will wake up. I kept repeating this in my mind, hoping the Goddess was on my side. As I sat there, staring at his lifeless form, my sadness turned to anger. *Those damn hunters.* I growled, my breathing becoming harsh. *I will release hell on earth for them.* Looking at the black, taunting veins starting to crawl up my arms, I sighed.

"Mason, you need to wake up." I gritted out. "You need to wake up, or I'm going to do something completely stupid and reckless." I looked at him, mentally pleading with him to open his eyes, show me some sign he was coming back.

I looked behind me and saw no one around, so I leaned closer. "I will make them pay. You're a good man, Mason, for what you did for the wolf kind today. But I am not a good woman. I have never been." I whispered out, the voice almost not sounding like my own.

I gulped, rubbing my hands together anxiously. She tapped at my mind, asking for the release she so desperately wanted. She could cause them pain. Hell, she could probably kill them all without batting an eye. I knew Mason was coming back to me. I could feel it in my bones, but what about the other lives the hunters took? Liza. Our men and women. The hostage wolves. They don't deserve to get away with this.

"Forgive me for what I'm about to do," I closed my eyes, a stray tear dripping down my cheek.

I stood, letting out a deep breath of air. I put my arms out in front of me, digging deep within my mind to find her. The veins started to crawl higher, and I felt my wolf side whimper, hiding deep within my mind as my other side came forward. The mental hold on her shattered, and I could feel her true emotions rush through me. My fists clenched as my senses grew stronger, my eyesight clearer and my body felt stronger. I held her back slightly, starting to walk towards the door.

I almost let her have the reins until a hoarse voice called out, "Octavia?"

My body froze at the sound of my mate's voice, and my eyes grew wide. "No," I whispered.

It may be too late.

She's freed.

CHAPTER TWENTY-THREE

Octavia

My body didn't move as I stared forward, the taunting voice in my head telling me to run. I looked down at my arms, seeing the black, horrid veins still prominent. I dug into my mind, trying to pull her in, but she wouldn't budge. Instead of fighting her, I begged for her just to hide until I figured out my next move. Eventually, the veins faded away.

"Octavia?" Mason called out once more.

I turned, plastering a smile on my face. "I'm glad you're awake." I made my way toward him, sitting back in the chair beside the bed.

"Are you okay?" he asked, the question tugging at my heart.

I raised a brow. "I am now, but shouldn't I be asking you that?"

He looked me over, a confused look on his face. "I just..." He shook his head. "Never mind. I'm still loopy, I guess."

Did he see the veins?

"Probably," I placed my hand on his forearm. "Do you want me to get the doctor?"

"Yeah, just to make sure all is well."

I couldn't help but notice the wary look he gave me, making my heartbeat quicken. He knew something was up. I could feel it. *Goddess, Octavia, what have you done?*

I hurried out of the room in search of his doctor. Once I found him, I informed him of Mason's state. The doctor was quick to rush off, and as I watched his retreating figure, I felt the pull in my mind. *She wasn't going to be hidden for much longer.* I went to head back towards the room Mason was held in, but I felt a horrible ringing in my head. Crying out in pain, I stumbled forward, clutching the sides of my head. A maid walked by, a small gasp leaving her.

"Luna? Are you alright? Do I need to—" I quickly stepped away from her.

"Don't touch me. I..." The room became dizzy, the ringing sound piercing my ears only getting louder with each passing second. "I can't..." I stumbled forward, trying to grasp the small table against the wall but missed. My hands knocked off the lamp on the table, making it tip over and shatter against the floor.

Eyes wide, I looked around. "I need to go... I have to..."

Without looking back, I rushed outside. Once the cold air kissed my cheeks, I fell to my knees, gasping for air. I haven't felt so much pain before—at least not from her. She was making me feel each and every ounce of pain I caused her, and she loved every second of it.

"Stop, please stop!" I screamed. "I'm sorry! I'm so sorry, you win! You're free. Just stop!"

"**Then get up and shift!**" She yelled back at me through our new link. "**You're pathetic. I could have given you everything, yet you let me suffer in a black pit within your mind.**" She reminded me.

I sat back on my knees, her wrath slowly lifting from my mind. Over and over again, she yelled at me to shift. The voice echoed in my mind, reminding me of all the horrid memories of my childhood. She was always taunting me from a young age. *Hurt them. Kill them. Completely destroy those who go against you*—it was never-ending.

"I don't want to shift. Please don't make me." I whispered out, completely numb. Hot tears glided down my face as my bottom lip trembled. Shifting to her form was not like a normal wolf shift that I'm prone to. She was a different breed. A different type of beast.

"*Ramani*, I'm begging you." Her name hadn't left my mouth in years. It not only surprised me but her as well. She went silent, shock coursing through her.

My body went slack as she gave me back control, and a breath of air I didn't know I was holding left me. Relief flooded through me, and I fell onto my back, staring at the stars above me.

"**At least you have the courage to acknowledge me now.**" She whispered as she retreated deep into my mind. My chest shook, sobs escaping me as I realized what I have caused.

I can't stay here. I can't stay here with her free, knowing what she is capable of. What if she hurts Mason? Alaric? Braelyn? My pack? Why the hell did I think this would be a good idea?!

"Octavia!" my eyes snapped open.

Mason appeared over me, looking down at me with an unreadable expression. "What is wrong with you?"

I gave him a weak shrug, turning my head to the side. I couldn't look at him knowing what I had done. If I tell him, everything ends. Maybe I should. Maybe I should let him know all my deep, dark secrets. Maybe then it would scare him away, and he'd let me go so I could try to run and escape my past. He's my mate, after all. If I die, he will too. He wouldn't deem me to the death I deserve, would he? He wouldn't.

Mason squatted next to me. "Octavia, you're worrying me."

I sat up, letting him pull me into his arms. "Just hold me. Please." I croaked out.

His embrace was warm, and as I laid my head against his chest, I never wanted him to let go.

I clutched his shirt in my hands, closing my eyes as I mumbled, "I screwed up, Mason. I really screwed up." My voice gave out at the end.

"What do you mean? What did you do?"

"I don't want to tell you. If I tell you, everything is over. You'll hate me."

"You're scaring me, Octavia."

"I'm scared of myself, Mason."

"What is so bad that you can't tell me? You can trust me, and we'll figure out what to do next, ok? You know this."

I lifted my head, craning my neck to look up at him. "Can I just tell you tomorrow? Please, I just want to spend one more peaceful night with you before this all comes out, and everything goes to hell."

"No, I don't think that is a good idea. Just tell me now."

"Mason," Tears glistened my eyes again. "I'm begging you. Just one more night."

He went to protest, but when he saw the stray tear leak down my cheek, his features softened.

He stood up, offering me a hand. "What would you like to do to get your mind off things?"

"Anything." I took his hand, standing to my feet.

"Well, my wolf needs a good run. He went through a lot today and needs to blow off some steam. Would you like to join me?"

Shifting into my wolf form scared me, with Ramani lurking in my mind, but I nodded. "Sounds nice." I'd do anything to spend one last peaceful night with him.

"Ok. Let's go."

I followed after him as we headed to the nearby woods. We neared the edge, and he stopped, pulling his shirt over his head. "Through here is a trail alongside a small river. We'll run for a few, and then we can stop for some water."

It had been a while since I let my wolf out, and she was bursting at the seams with excitement. It was the first time I felt her presence since Ramani emerged. Maybe that was a good sign.

As we changed out of our clothes, I asked, "Are you ok? Really? I've been selfish. I mean, you just literally died, and I wasn't exactly there to comfort you through the waking up process." I tossed my shirt to the side.

He pulled the belt from his pants, nodding. "It's ok. The doctor said everything was fine and that I probably needed to let my wolf out for a few so he could energize again. He went through a lot. Though, I heard what you did for the pack, so thank you. They were lucky to have you there."

I let out a small laugh. "I think I'm the one that should be lucky to have them. I got the worst of it, but they put their pain aside to help me get through my own. They are good people, Mason."

"That they are."

We stood, fully unclothed. Usually, Mason would crack some dirty joke, but nothing came. It was tense between us, and I knew he desperately wanted to know what I had to tell, but he refrained. Our shifts came quickly, and when I looked through my wolf's eyes, it was like a breath of fresh air. Shaking her fur, she stretched out, loving the feeling of being let out again. Mason's large, black wolf towered mine, per usual. His head nudged my side, meaning to start moving, and my wolf took off. He followed behind, almost protectively, as we ran through the forest.

My wolf felt giddy as she let out a howl, prancing around, looking at the beautiful sights circling her. The moon was high in the sky, sending a beautiful stream of light over the river next to us. Getting an idea, I halted, letting Mason catch up with me. He tilted his head to the side.

"What?" his mind-link ran through.

"Catch me if you can." I teased, jumping forward to nip at his ear before shooting off.

A husky chuckle drifted through the mindlink. **"Game on."**

I felt him nip at my tail, causing me to force my wolf to run faster. Her paws smacked the ground as she rounded a tree and took off in a completely different direction. I looked back, letting out a snort as he almost smacked into the tree.

My wolf loved the chase. Taking another sharp turn to try and throw him off, she ran as if her life depended on it. I thought Mason was purposely letting us win the chase, but seconds later, we were knocked down and pinned to the ground. Mason towered me, a playful growl rumbling in his chest.

As I looked up at him, I never wanted this night to end.

"So close yet so far," Mason teased through our link, letting me roll out from underneath him.

"Maybe I wasn't trying." I lied as my wolf shook her fur. I walked towards the river, Mason following at my heels. "It's beautiful out here."

"I know. We're getting more to the outskirts of the pack. It's more free and open. It's kind of like a big park for wolves." He joked.

"I like it." I replied, leaning down to let my wolf slurp up as much water as she needed. "Do you always come out here for a run?" I asked once she was done.

"Usually. I just like the calmness of it all."

"That's understandable." Something caught my eye, causing my wolf's ears to perk up. "Is that a cliff?"

"It is, and it comes with an amazing view. Come on." I followed after him, jumping over a broken tree to get to where the edge was.

"Oh wow." It was indeed an amazing view.

"That looks into no man's land. It's quite beautiful. Sadly, some of the worst wolves live there." Under the glow of the moon, I could see the wolves trotting in the distance below us.

"Is that where Derek will be relocated to after you're done with him?" I asked, suddenly remembering the man I was responsible for getting banished.

"Actually, he's already there now." Mason sighed.

"What? I thought he had to stay here first?"

"I told him he'd stay here until I decided his sentencing, which I did. I don't like the kid, but he doesn't deserve to rot away in a pack cell. Even though he should. Being drunk at a party is never good. I'm not excusing his actions, trust me, but they lost him a lot. The least I could do was let him be a rogue since Christian deemed him as one. It's almost just as bad as a cell, but you're free in a way. Just no pack or family."

"I still feel bad. I mean, if we would have never gone to that stupid party, he'd still have a life." I sighed, not liking the guilt that filled me.

"Don't be. He could have left you two girls alone. Instead, he shoved Scarlett to the ground and acted as if he would do much worse. He threatened the Queen and my mate, two things I refuse to tolerate. He's not your concern anymore. He got what he deserved."

Maybe he did, but I still couldn't help but feel guilty.

"Are you ready to head back?" he asked, and I nodded.

On the way, our wolves darted through the forest carefree. I loved it. The wind on my fur, the hooting of the owls in the distance, or even the crickets chirping. It was a feeling a wolf desired.

We slowed down, trotting side by side. Mason seemed to be in thought, and I wondered what was going through that head of his. Maybe the war... It was hard to tell. He was good at hiding his emotions, but I didn't want to use the bond against him and figure it out. He'd tell me if he wanted to.

Mason froze, his head snapping up, sending my wolf into alert.

"What is it?" I asked, following him as he started walking to his right, sniffing the ground.

"I smell... stop walking!" he yelled, about to charge at me, but he was too late as I heard the click and completely froze.

The trap caught onto my front leg, latching tightly, and my wolf dropped to the ground, yelping in pain. In my mind, I was screaming. It felt as if my leg was on fire and someone was digging a blade through it. Mason immediately shifted back to human form, cursing as he looked at the death trap laid out for me.

His hands were quick to grab the trap, frantically pulling at it. His face scrunched up as a hiss left him, and he snatched his hands away.

Realization sank in as he stared at his bleeding hands that weren't healing. I whimpered, trying to move closer to him, but he shook his head at me.

"I can't break it off. It's silver! Damn them, hunters!" he cursed, his hands shaking. "I also think it's the only thing stopping you from bleeding out, Octavia. Silver is deadly to us wolves." I whimpered, fear seeping through me like hot lava.

"I'm sorry. Just... hold on, I have an idea." He looked in thought before his eyes glazed over, mind-linking someone. "Ok, babe. I need you to hold on. Help is on the way."

Today was just not my day. If this trap didn't come off soon, I knew someone would surface and get it off herself: *Ramani.* I could feel my body going into shock, sending her into alert as my wolf howled in pain. She was ready to come forward, but I begged her to stay down. Not yet.

It felt like hours had passed before someone finally showed up.

"A little birdie said you needed help." A voice spoke, and through my blurred vision, I could see a man emerge from the shadows. From what I could tell, he was a tall, dark-haired man—the scent on him reeked.

"I asked for Raven. Can Ryker not follow one certain task?!" Mason growled out, and the guy shrugged.

I could barely keep my eyes open as the two discussed non-important things. *Just break the trap already*, I wanted to scream.

"Well, you got me." The man replied and walked over, crouching down beside me and let out a whistle. "That's a bad injury you got there. It's cutting right into the bone." He mused.

"My mate is dying. This is no time for jokes. Help her, please, Grayson." Mason said, and the man, now known as Grayson, sighed, finally taking things seriously.

"She needs to lay fully on the ground. It'll be easier for me to break the trap off without causing her too much pain. Make sure she does not shift back yet. It won't end well for her. After I get it off, then she can shift, and she'll need to do it quickly." Mason nodded, helping me lay fully on the ground. My wolf whined in protest from the movement.

"I'm sorry, 'Tavia. It will be over soon," Mason cooed.

"Ready?" Grayson asked, and Mason nodded, moving next to me as he waited for him to break it off so I could shift.

Grayson grabbed hold of the trap, his teeth grinding as he used all his strength to break it in half. When I felt the pressure release from my leg, I slouched against the ground, panting. Grayson took the trap, throwing it away from us with a disgusted look. When he looked back at me, he told me to be quick with my shift. I did so, hoping the pain would quickly end.

Grayson bit into his wrist and held it near my mouth. "Drink. No buts or questions just yet." Not even caring to question it, I latched onto his wrist, greedily drinking.

When I let go, Mason let out a sigh of relief as he stared at the wound. I could feel it quickly healing, faster than my wolf ever could, and the bone snapped back together. I knew what Grayson was, but I was too tired to talk about it. Even though I hated his kind, I was grateful.

Vampire.

Grayson pulled his shirt over his head, handing it to Mason. "I'm not always a dick." Mason let out a snort at the comment, thanking him.

"Sit up, Octavia. I know you're tired, but I need to put this on you."

"Ok." I gritted out, wincing as I moved to let him put it on me. Once the shirt was over me, Mason sat back, looking in thought.

"What are you going to do now?" Grayson asked, addressing the previous situation.

"Now it's personal," Mason growled.

CHAPTER TWENTY-FOUR

◆◇◆

Mason

"Uh, is she okay?" Grayson skeptically raised a brow, looking out the window of my house at my mate.

"Oh, yeah." I bit my lip to hold back my laughter at the scene. She was outside, staring up at the sky, waving her arms frantically as if she was in a heated discussion. *She definitely was.*

"She said she had some words to say to the moon Goddess about something with always getting her in *bloody* situations, and there she is." I motioned to the lovely scene ahead.

"Interesting mate you have there. I feel as if I need some popcorn." Grayson mused.

"Something like that."

Grayson went silent, shifting his weight from one foot to the other awkwardly. I knew what he was thinking, and I knew his stupid mouth would open any second to mention it.

"Look, I know I haven't seen you since Vivian, but—" I held my hand up, cutting him off. *I knew he'd bring it up.*

"Don't start this. Please, Grayson. It's been a long day."

"She was dying, Mason. We had to help her." He said, and I rolled my eyes.

"I need to go check on Octavia." I said, ignoring him and walking outside, shutting the door behind me.

Vivian was a memory I'd rather not dig up. It pained me to even think about her. To think about her joining the McKinley Crew. Though, with the McKinleys now lurking around, I'm sure my past was going to resurface quicker than I thought.

"First Ramani, then a wolfsbane bullet, then another bullet, and now a freaking bear trap! Oh, let's not forget fifth grade either!" Octavia screeched, still looking upwards.

"Better watch out. She may strike lightning down on you." I joked, catching her attention.

"Yet another one of her deadly situations for me. This is what I say," She made an angry face and turned, putting both middle fingers up to the sky. "Screw off!"

"A bit harsh…"

"Sorry." She readjusted her shirt and smoothed it out. "You were saying?"

I couldn't help but laugh. "It's not funny. I know I shouldn't be laughing. I just can't help it. I'm sorry." Her glare didn't falter as she folded her arms.

"She wants me dead! How is that funny?!" she nearly yelled.

"I think you're being a bit dramatic." She shook her head.

"I disagree. I'm being perfectly reasonable. Why am I always in these situations?"

"Oh, I don't know... maybe because you get yourself into them?" I asked, and she scoffed.

"I got myself into one of them, thank you very much."

"The first bullet, yes. The second one, not so much. Bear trap... definitely not. You may have a point, but... you said Ramani? Who's that?"

She almost paled. "An old friend. She was... mean."

I frowned. "I'm sorry to hear that."

"Look, that trap tonight... it was obviously laid by hunters."

"I know. I have no idea how they got past the border nor my wolves patrolling, but you can believe me when I say I'll be talking with the guards on perimeter watch."

"Oh, I believe you alright." She walked forward, wrapping her arms around my neck. "Thank you for helping me out there tonight." I smiled, placing a kiss on her forehead, a newfound habit of mine.

Wrapping my arms around her waist, I whispered, "I'd give my life for you." She playfully smacked my chest, causing me to laugh.

"Don't even mention that around me. I can't picture losing you."

I raised a hand to cup her cheek. "I love you." I kissed the tip of her nose, and she gave me a goofy smile.

"And I love you." She quickly brought her lips to mine, and I let out a playful growl kissing her back with just as much force.

Eventually, she pulled back, much to my dismay. "We need to talk about why you called for a vampire to help me, though."

"I knew they were at Ryker's and could get here quickly and heal you just as quick." Her expression furrowed.

"Why are they at Ryker's?"

"Remember how I said we'd bring in the McKinley Crew as a last resort?" she nodded. "Well, we did. I know I should have told you sooner, but I didn't want to freak you out. You were already worried enough when Jackson told you. Ryker has connections to this crew, and he trusts them. They're powerful and some of the best of the best. They are the only vampires allowed on werewolf territory, as you've been told."

"But how? Please, just tell me. I know it's Ryker's story to tell, but you have to give me something."

"Let's just say… Ryker is related to one of them." Her mouth dropped in shock.

"No way. How is that possible?"

"Because she was dying, and he couldn't let her. So, he called me to ask a very powerful man to turn her. This man gave her his blood. Technically she did die, but she woke up as one of us. Ryker would rather turn her into the thing he hated the most than let her die." A voice spoke, and we turned to see Grayson making his way towards us.

"It doesn't make sense, though. She was a wolf. You can't be a wolf then suddenly a vampire." Said Octavia, shaking her head in confusion.

"You can if you demolish the link with your wolf," Grayson explained, and Octavia's expression turned to a look of disgust.

"You killed her wolf?"

"It was the only way. It was hard, but we got it done." I could feel the disgust radiating from her.

"Tell me she's at least happy," Octavia mumbled.

"Quite. Jared is quite the charmer." Winked Grayson.

"Raven is with… Jared?" I asked, genuinely surprised.

"Who?" Octavia questioned, and Grayson chuckled.

"You'll meet everyone in due time. Don't worry your little blonde head." He teased.

Jared was a part of their crew. He was one man you didn't want to mess with. Calm, but deadly. He was also someone I deeply respected, despite his supernatural side.

I saw Octavia yawn, and I sighed.

"Grayson, will you run the perimeter with me? Make sure there aren't any more traps?" I asked, and he nodded.

"For sure."

I looked at Octavia and smiled. "You go get rest. I'll be up soon." She nodded, pecking me on my lips.

"Thank you, Grayson." She spoke softly, resting a hand on his shoulder as she brushed past him, walking off to the house.

"You are one lucky man," Grayson whistled, watching her retreating figure.

"Indeed I am."

"Now, let's get to looking for these traps. Those hunters are seriously pissing me off. I'll have you know; I was about to head on a nice, long vacation before we got called in by Ryker."

"How sad for you." I mocked.

"Tell me about it," He placed his hands on his hips. "They're working with vampires, as I'm sure you know, and I think we know who they are. Dante is pissed."

My eyes narrowed. "Who?"

"It's what us vampires call a clan. There are hundreds of them, and it's led by a vampire that we despise. He never follows the rules, and he ruins everything for us. He's part of the reason we have such a bad reputation. I mean, he got his people banned for causing killing sprees in the states. He couldn't stick to blood banks or animals." Grayson let out a humorless laugh. "I want to rip his head clean from his shoulders."

"What's his name?"

"Marion. He's one sick bastard too."

"And how is Dante handling this?"

Grayson pursed his lips, looking away as if he should tread carefully. "Um… you're not going to like it."

"Grayson," My tone had a warning to it. "What is happening?"

"Dante was permitted to enter the states by Ryker."

"What?!"

"Look, he has rules to follow, and he isn't going to do anything bad… I hope. You know why he's here."

"Lachlan?" Grayson nodded, confirming my question.

"Ryker threatened her. We all know Ryker won't lay a finger on her pretty little head, but Dante doesn't know that. Dante has hated Ryker since Ryker banished him and all vampires from the states completely, and he had to leave Lachlan behind—his beloved. A beloved is just like a mate to you wolves. You, of all people, should know that someone threatening your soulmate will get you to do anything."

I ran a hand through my hair. "You're right about that, but Lachlan just let this happen? I'm confused. I thought she hated Dante."

Grayson snorted. "They confuse the hell out of me. In her eyes, he betrayed her by leaving and not taking her with him. In his eyes, she wouldn't leave the McKinley Crew. It's a bunch of miscommunications to me, but oh well. Not my problem. Just know that Dante is here to help because he doesn't want Lachlan getting hurt, and he knows this clan can be powerful. With Dante *and us* on your side, you've already won the war. I can promise you that."

"I don't doubt it. When will Dante be here?"

"Soon. Now, let's go. I'm hungry and ready to get back to The Power Pack to piss off Ryker some more. He hates me."

I chuckled. "Piss him off for me, too, while you're at it."

"Oh, I will."

It took about an hour to make sure there were no more traps laid out. We found a few at first, which Grayson easily disarmed in seconds and crushed them to pieces. My blood boiled at the thought of hunters getting onto my territory—entering my pack. It made no sense to me. Why would they lay out some bullshit trap?

"Grayson?" I called out as we reached back home.

"Hm?"

"Why would hunters just place random traps out in my pack? They know that it was risky even to enter and place them. It's almost as if—" My eyes widened, and I glanced over at Grayson, whose mouth formed an "o".

"It wasn't a trap."

"It was a distraction." He grumbled, looking around.

"Grayson, you're faster than me. Get inside now and check on Octavia!" I yelled, seeing something flash to my right.

Grayson sped off just as I reached out, catching an arrow that flew towards me. I snapped it in half, a growl escaping me.

"Show yourself, cowards!" I yelled.

I stepped forward, but Grayson was back by my side in seconds, a worried look on his face. "I'll take care of them. You go inside. She's gone, Mason."

My heart dropped, and I took off inside the house, completely forgetting the hunters in the shadows outside.

No! Goddess, don't do this to me.

CHAPTER TWENTY-FIVE

———◆◇◆———

Octavia

Head throbbing, I groaned in pain. I moved my neck side to side, trying to work out the crick in it. When my eyes fluttered open, a thick lump formed in my throat as I took in my surroundings. I looked around the dingy room with wide eyes. When my head turned to the left, I noticed a table of knives and other torturing tools winking under the light that hung above me. Panicking, I tugged on the chains that were wrapped tightly around my wrist, pinning me to the metal chair. My wrist stung at the bite the chains gave, making me realize they were pure silver.

Memories erupted in my head, and my pulse quickened. I remembered walking into my room, and then a hand covered my mouth as everything went black. Someone took me. Oh, Goddess. Why is all of this happening to me? Is this my punishment for my past?

"Help!" I screamed and tried pulling again, but it only made it burn more.

I sobbed out, hating the memories all this gave me. My father... the basement... Ramani. Oh, Goddess, Ramani! Where was she now? I called out to her, but nothing came.

"Quiet down, will you?" A man spoke as the door was thrown open, hitting the wall with a crack.

"Who are you?" I spat.

"A man with good intentions. I need you to answer a few questions about Mason and this war. You're now Luna, no?" I let out a snarl, and he laughed.

"Octavia, isn't it?" I didn't answer, and he snickered once more. "We could make this easy, or we could make it hard. Which do you prefer?" Once again, I didn't answer, and he nodded.

"Fine. We shall see how long this tough girl act stands." He rolled his eyes and grabbed a knife off the table next to me, twirling it around. "Silver... hurts like a bitch, doesn't it? Did you like the gift we left you? It's quite funny, actually. We knew Mason would leave you alone to look for more traps. Stupid decision, really. The man he was with him, who is that?"

I remained silent, mentally cursing Mason and me for being so clueless. I would not give up Grayson's name. If I did, they would know the McKinley Crew had joined us. If that happened, our element of surprise would be gone.

"Look. I'm trying to be the good guy here. If you answer my questions now, you won't have to live through the consequences. I recommend you answer them now because if you don't, Megan will drive here herself and get them out of you and let me tell you... it will not be pleasant."

I threw my head back, letting out devilish laughter. "Of course, that bitch is behind this. She's just so *obsessed* with my mate. Tell me, is she jealous?" I raised a brow, taunting him. His jaw tightened, and in seconds, the knife was at my throat.

I gulped, bravely saying, "Let her come."

"You won't survive if you don't cooperate." He pointed out, agitated.

"If she thinks she can crack me. She is mistaken. I'll say it once more for you. Let. Her. Come. I'd enjoy ripping her limb from limb."

"You're one idiotic girl, Octavia."

I winked. "And don't you forget it."

He gritted his teeth together, bringing the knife away from my neck and flipped it in his hand, swinging it down slamming it into my forearm. I screamed out, the burning pain flaring through my body. I panted, trying to control my breathing. For once, I thanked my father. He was right. People would come for me. It just wasn't the ones he had thought.

Come on, Ramani, it's your time to shine! I called out to her again, but nothing came. My brows furrowed, and I tried to reach my wolf, but nothing came from her either.

The man removed the knife from my arm and did it as slowly as he could. I clenched my jaw, trying not to show any more pain. I wouldn't give him that satisfaction.

He smirked. "Trying to connect to your wolf? Yeah, we blocked that. There's this little drug swimming through your system right now. You won't be in contact with her for a few days." He faked a thinking face. "Or maybe ever again. Who knows? Megan can get quite creative, and she really doesn't like you or Mason."

I will kill them all.

"Come on in, boys!" he yelled. The door opened again, and two men walked in. One grabbed my head, thrusting it back, and the other put a cloth over my face.

"Just tell us who is working with the wolves, how to successfully breach your pack, and what spies Mason sent our way, and no harm will come to you." The first man demanded.

"Ok! I will! Please, just stop!" I yelled.

The cloth was ripped from my face, and his eyes lit up. "I knew you'd come around."

I smirked. "Actually, I lied. I just wanted to see your face as I told you to burn in hell, you sick bitch." His face twisted in anger as the men aggressively yanked my head back again, covering my face, pouring water over it.

I coughed, kicking and scrambling as the water started to drown my senses. It went through my nose, my mouth—everywhere. My father's voice ripped through my head. *Hold your breath, Octavia!*

The old waterboarding lesson resurfaced, and I calmed down, stopped my breathing, and went slack. The cloth slowly moved from my face, and I could feel the uneasiness of the men around me.

"Did she pass out?" one questioned.

I felt a hand in front of my face to see if I was breathing. I jolted forward, biting into the man's hand. He cursed, ripping it away, and I let out a wicked laugh, blood dripping from my mouth.

"You all suck at this."

The head man in charge shook his head. "Knock her out. I'm done with this. Megan can have at her. I'll kill this whore myself if I stay any longer." I let out a grunt as his right arm snaked out in a quick hit, cracking into the side of my jaw.

I closed my eyes, taking in a deep breath. "You call that a right hook? A five-year-old hits harder than you." I teased.

He lunged for me, but the other two men caught him, whispering something in his ear. He sighed, relaxing before they released him. One man left the room for a minute, but a familiar gas tank was rolled into the room when he returned. At the sight of it, my body felt paralyzed, and my smirk was quick to leave me.

"Night, night." He waved.

When one of the men grabbed the mask, I thrashed in my seat. Mental pain surfaced at the horrid memories it brought back for me.

"Mason will come for you!" I screamed. "He'll kill you all!"

"It'll be too late for him to get you, darling. You know, you could have just answered my questions. I only want the best for you. After all, you'd make a great team with Megan. You could have joined us—joined the winning side." When the words left his mouth, my body went numb.

My sweet daughter, I hope you know I'm doing this for you. I only want the best for you. You could hurt someone. My father's words rang loud and clear.

I will not let another man torture me. *We* will not let another man torture *us*.

My body started shaking with anger, my fever spiked, and my wounds healed within seconds. Suddenly, *I felt her presence.* I don't know how she did it, but she'd overcome the drug in my body, letting me know she was here and ready. Black veins shot up my arm, and I suddenly didn't care anymore. *I really didn't.*

"You've really pissed off the wrong woman..." I growled and felt a surge of energy hit me as I raised my arm, breaking the chain of my wrist, and the men's eyes widened.

"And..." I started, popping the other one off. "Today, I feel like causing some chaos." My body was up in a flash, and the men staggered back in shock.

"Chaos that will destroy you all." A voice echoed in the room, but it wasn't my own.

"Your eyes... they're red." Said the man.

"Because Octavia's pushed back for a bit," Ramani spoke, and the men shivered, darting from the room.

She let out a snicker, sauntering towards the open door. "One, two, how many bones are in you?" she creepily sang out, leaving the room as she looked for the men. "Three, four, I've counted before." She narrowed her hearing to one nearby heartbeat. "Five, six, I'll use 'em like a toothpick." She used her stealth, inching closer. "Seven, eight, don't underestimate." Our hands twitched as she neared a wall. "Nine, ten... *Ramani kills again.*" Her arm smashed into the wall, breaking her arm through the other side. She grabbed hold of a man's throat, yanking him back through it effortlessly. Drywall flew everywhere as we heard the bones of the man cracking.

Looking at us through weak eyes, the man began to cry.

"*Boo.*"

CHAPTER TWENTY-SIX

◆◇◆

Mason

I snarled, pushing everything off my desk. My heart beat in my chest furiously, and my wolf was so angered he was ready to tear anything that dared stand in his way.

"Mason, calm down. We'll find her. This isn't the time to let your wolf out, ok?" Ryker's voice came through the phone line, and I shook my head.

"Don't tell me to calm down," I growled out, reaching over to end the call.

"Mason," The soft voice spoke up, and I looked over at Scarlett.

"If there is one thing I know about Octavia, it's that she is a fighter. We will find her." She encouraged, and Christian nodded, putting his arm around her.

"I promise. We won't stop until she is back in your arms." Christian added.

I had called everyone here the moment I knew she was missing. Jackson and Christian could make it, but Ryker said he was dealing with some stuff and would only be able to make the conference call, to which he was no help.

I looked to Jackson, who looked in thought before he asked, "Where was she taken from?"

"Our bedroom, I believe. Why?"

He stood from the couch. "Take me there." I was quick to nod, leading him out of my office and down the hall. Once we walked in, he started looking over my room.

"Let him work, Mason." Christian rested a hand on my shoulder, holding me back from entering as Jackson crouched down near the bed.

"She was knocked out with a drug. Probably chloroform. You can pick up that dense but sweet smell it carries right by the bed. There are minor scuff marks on the floor from the attacker's shoes. She put up a fight." Jackson said before making his way back over to us.

"You think so?"

"I know so. I need to go to your office and be alone, so I can think. I need to lay out possible places they could take her. Get someone to give me a map of your pack. This wasn't an outside job. She could still be in your pack. I looked at the gates before I came in—I even looked at the visitor logs. Those gates were closed around the time before she was taken and all the way up until we showed. They couldn't have malfunctioned nor been broken through. Perimeters have certain alarms for prisoners escaping we made a while back."

"I know, but those traps that were—"

"Trust me. It would have gone off the moment someone stepped over the line. Only me and you know about that, and I know it works because

I designed it. She's still in the pack. They're just waiting for the right time to get her out. That is most likely the case. They want you to think she's outside of the pack." He went to walk off but stopped, turning his head to the side. "You have a traitor amongst you. Think wisely before you talk to your people." He added and left.

I stood shocked at his words. Was she really still in our pack? Did I really have a mole betraying me?

"I don't know how he does it," I mumbled, and Christian shook his head.

"He's the Alpha of Intelligence for a reason. Nothing goes unnoticed by him. We can't do anything while he is thinking all this over. I'll go find Alaric to send Jackson that map. Stay, and I don't know... take a moment to relax and clear your mind, at least. Don't let this cloud your judgment. You're the Alpha of War. You don't accept defeat." Christian reminded me before he walked off.

"I can sit with you if you'd like?" Scarlett asked, and I gave her a faint smile and a nod.

"You really think she's ok?" I asked, and she gave me a sad smile.

"Come on," She mumbled, walking into the room. Sitting down, she patted the spot on the couch beside her. Reluctantly, I went and sat.

"The day I met Octavia, I knew she was a strong and fiery woman. She doesn't go down without a fight. She probably has them shaking in their boots. The one thing I do know is that she will find her way back to you. She loves you, Mason."

I sported a fake smile, nodding at her words. No matter how kind they were, it was hard not to think the worst.

"Can I ask a favor?" Scarlett shot me a nervous look.

I raised a brow. "Of course."

"I need you to accept my sister to transfer here from The Royal Pack." She nearly whispered.

"Why would she want to do that?"

"In short, my sister was rejected. I see her stare at him all the time and can practically feel her hurting. I can't see it anymore, Mason. He marked and mated someone else before meeting her. That is why he rejected her. I just want her to be happy. I promised her I'd get her into a new pack because she doesn't want to hurt anymore. Luckily, she accepted his rejection, so she didn't go into heat or anything like that... but I was hoping you would transfer her so Octavia can keep an eye on her for me." Said Scarlett with a solemn look.

"If that's what she wants, it'd be my honor." Her eyes lit up.

"Thank you so much, Mason."

"Of course, Scarlett," I added. I went to ask her more about her sister but froze as I felt it. *The bond was hitting me in waves*. She was channeling me, and she didn't even know it. I heard the door bang open, snatching me from my thoughts, and turned to see Jackson and Christian rushing through.

"We think we found three locations as to where she could be," Jackson said, and I sprung from my seat.

"Well, let's narrow them down." I walked forward but staggered back as energy drained from me.

"Are you ok?" Jackson put his hands out as if I'd fall over at any second.

"She's channeling me. Unknowingly, of course." I confessed, and their eyes widened.

"But that can only happen if..." Christian trailed off.

"If we marked each other. I let her mark me." I answered confidently, revealing the mark, to which Jackson smirked.

"She has you whipped."

"Shut it," I growled.

"This is good, though. If they drugged her wolf, your energy surging through her would make her wolf side be able to overcome it. It most likely happened out of fear. It's the mate bond working. It knows she's weak and in distress and that you're not near. Since you both marked each other, it acted for her... letting her wolf come forward. You won't be able to mindlink her until the drug fully wears off, but it should be enough to get her up and going." Jackson explained.

My brows furrowed, and I grew dizzy again. "I knew that was always possible, but it isn't supposed to drain this much energy from me. How is her wolf that strong? Usually, that energy being taken from me would be some to fuel an alpha..." I asked, and Jackson locked eyes with me at the information.

He warily glanced at Christian and Scarlett, who were just as confused as I was, but when Jackson locked eyes with me again, he had a knowing look, and my eyes widened.

"Christian, will you go get that map, please? Scarlett, will you go into the closet and get one of Octavia's shirts for her scent."

I knew what he sent them to do was busy work and pointless, but they scattered off quickly. Jackson pulled me out into the hallway, looking at me with wide eyes.

"How well do you know your mate, Mason?"

"What are you talking about? Well, obviously."

"Mason, it shouldn't have nearly drained you for her to get some energy back to her. You looked as if you were about to faint. That's no normal wolf coming forward. You of all people should know that."

I leaned closer to him, whispering, "I haven't sensed anything else from her, though."

"Has she sensed anything from you? Exactly. There's a way of locking sides like that away to make them pretty much non-existent. If she was struggling with keeping a side like that at bay, she just took enough energy from you to completely be reborn. Energy that would let her completely take over Octavia's body. Do you know what this means?"

"We share the same energy… the same side that we wished stayed locked away." I gulped.

"I kept your secret, but it's about to get out, Mason. Christian is here. When we find her, there's no telling what's going to happen. *She's like you.* You're the only one that's going to understand her."

As it finally set in, I felt as if everything was about to go to hell. "That's what she was trying to tell me last night. She's different. Little does she know… I'm different too." I cursed, shaking my head. "I should have told her! We… we could have gone through this together."

"It's too late for that. Now we need to stop her before she hurts an innocent."

We heard footsteps approaching and looked over at Christian, who held the map up. "Let's go."

"Here!" Scarlett rushed out of my room, a shirt in her hands.

"Thanks," Jackson mumbled, taking it from her.

"What do we need a shirt for? We're wolves. We can easily sniff her out." Christian spoke up.

Jackson scratched the back of his neck awkwardly, looking at the shirt. "Oh, you know… the uh… channeling of the mate bond needs physical touch for Mason. So… this is the closest thing." Jackson lied—terribly, might I add.

Christian nodded, though frowned slightly, and turned to Scarlett. "We'll be back." he placed a kiss on her forehead.

"I can help, Christian."

"I know, but we can't risk anything right now with you." He placed a hand on her rounded belly. "You're pregnant, and I can't have you going into a line of fire."

She frowned, nodding. "I understand. Bring her back to me safely, ok?"

I smiled. "Will do."

Us three alphas were quick to hurry out of the house. Looking over the map, Jackson explained the locations where she could be kept. They were old, abandoned houses deep within the woods, right by perimeter borders. There were three. It wasn't long until we scoped out two of the houses, but she wasn't there. I grew worried, starting to believe that for once in his life, Jackson was wrong.

"The last house is this way," Jackson pointed, making his way through the woods.

"I'm tearing these houses down after this," I growled out, walking behind him.

"It would probably be for the best. Why did you keep them around, to begin with?" Christian asked.

"There were some wolves that used to live in the pack that were recluse. My father, when he was alpha, built the houses for them. They had a lot of PTSD from previous missions he had sent them on. He did his best to keep them as comfortable as possible, but that was many years ago, and they are no longer living."

"I'm sorry to hear that."

I shrugged. "I wasn't that close with them, but I admired my father for doing it."

"Speaking of parents, when are you going to formally meet Octavia's parents?" Christian mused. "I remember when I met Scarlett's. They were quite funny."

"No idea. Octavia doesn't have the best relationship with her parents. It's almost as if she'd be embarrassed for me to meet them. I wouldn't mind, though."

Jackson held his hand up in a fist, causing Christian and I to halt. He pointed to his ear. We narrowed our hearing and heard faint yelling and grunting. I took off, running towards the house that was now coming into sight. I could smell her scent. *She was near.* As I neared the house, my body halted as someone grabbed me from behind.

"Jackson," I growled. "Let me go before my wolf rips you to shreds."

"Mason! Look, dammit." My eyes snapped up, and I watched as many hunters ran out of the house, turning back to face it with guns.

"I have to help her!" I pleaded.

I struggled once more to move, but Christian joined Jackson to hold me still. "We have to be smart about this." Jackson rushed out.

"I command you to stand down!" Christian ordered, and my body froze, the command wracking over my body, forcing me to stop my thrashing.

I hated his title sometimes.

I watched, paralyzed by his command in utter distress. My heart jumped when the house's door flew off its hinges, and a body flew through it, wiping the hunters outside off their feet. We all three staggered back in shock as we watched the hunters groan as they pushed a lifeless body off them.

Slowly, my blonde-haired beauty waltzed out the front door... *covered in blood.*

"Holy shit." Christian stammered out.

CHAPTER TWENTY-SEVEN

◆◇◆

Octavia

My body hummed to life as blood splattered against my face. Ramani was thriving as she beat each hunter to a pulp. Each punch, kick, or claw, she was smiling with glee. One hunter was running from her, but she loved the chase. She let him gain some ground, only to speed up to mess with him as his screams bounced off the wall. Finally, she stopped, letting him run into a room. I was confused as to why she just didn't end it right then and there.

"And we wait," She whispered.

When the door shut and locked, we heard the dialing of a phone. *Smart.*

"Megan, I'm telling you, we're all going to die! I... I haven't seen anything like this before. She... she has the eye color of alpha Mason. How is that possible?" the man panicked.

Megan. I'd like to chat with her.

"Me too," Ramani spoke, bringing her leg up, forcing it against the door. The door kicked open with ease, and she sauntered through, staring at the wide-eyed hunter.

"Playtime is over," She said, sticking out her bottom lip in mock-sadness.

In a flash, she was in front of him, her hand through his chest. She grabbed hold of his still-beating heart and grinned at his shocked state. His mouth was wide open as his eyes rolled into the back of his head. With her free hand, she reached over and grabbed the phone out of his clenched one.

Putting it to her ear, she licked her lips greedily.

"Hello, Megan."

"Octavia... don't make this personal."

Ramani laughed. "This isn't Octavia, but before you speak with her, I have a few words to say. If you ever try to come after me and or anyone I care about again, I will rip your head from your body, and I will enjoy every second of it. Actually, no... I'm going to do that anyway. I will find you... and I will kill you in the slowest, most torturous way I can. Hold, please." Ramani mused, and then I was forced back into control.

I let out a breath of relief. My hand tightened around the phone.

"Haven't you done enough already? Just give up, Megan. You're not going to win."

"Not enough, apparently." She sighed. "But that's where you're wrong, Octavia. I already have. You wolves are done for. It is *you* who should bend the knee." My blood boiled at the sound of her voice.

"I won't let Ramani kill you." I gritted my teeth.

"How nice of you."

"I'm going to let Mason. No one will bring you as much pain as he will. Typically, this is where I would feel sorry for someone in your shoes, but today... I'm out of remorse. You're dead already." I let out a humorless laugh. "Here's a reminder that you're not unstoppable, and your reign is coming to an end." I lowered the phone, ripping my hand from the man's body, his heart coming with it as he let out one final breath of life.

"Goodbye, Megan."

I let the phone drop to the ground and crushed it under my foot. Letting the heart fall from my hands, Ramani resurfaced and grabbed hold of the body. "Didn't know you had it in you, kid."

"Shut it," I growled back.

She effortlessly lifted the body from the ground and started walking with it. As she left the room, she saw the rest of the hunters left running out the front door. She chuckled, picking up her pace. With as much force as she could muster, she tightened her grip and threw it at the door. The body broke through like a baseball through a glass window. She grinned at the sound of grunts, her aim having met its targets.

She made her way outside, her smirk widening when she saw the hunters wiped out by the flying body. Ramani walked down the steps of the old, crumbling house one by one, watching the men's fear grow. *She could smell it in the air.*

They raised their guns, shooting, but she dodged each one, running at them as they stumbled to their feet. She jumped up, grabbing a man by the head, snapping it sideways. He dropped to the ground as she turned, sending a kick to another. Spinning on her heels, she leaned backward, watching a bullet fly past her face. She gained her footing easily and swiped her leg out, knocking the shooter off balance. One man boldly ran towards her, but she side-stepped him, watching him fly past her. Spinning around, she grabbed his head from behind, twisting it.

I winced at the sickening crack. *She was here for blood and nothing else.*

Ramani breathed harshly, turning to the last three that remained. Shakily, they lifted their hands, their guns falling from their hands, and dropped to their knees.

"Please, spare us." One begged.

"Were you going to spare me when you were pouring water over my face?" she teased sweetly. "I didn't think so." She dove forward into a roll as the men scrambled for their guns again. She snatched one before they could reach them.

One by one, she fired a bullet straight into each head.

She threw the gun to the side, letting out a harsh snarl. "Not particularly my style, but it seemed fitting," She mumbled, dusting her hands off.

"Octavia?" a voice called out, and she froze.

Turning slowly, she thrust me back into control when the realization hit.

"Mason?" I mumbled, my bottom lip quivering.

We met halfway as we ran to one another. I jumped into his arms, holding him tightly.

"I was so worried." He whispered.

I looked up, seeing King Christian and Jackson walk up behind him. Jackson looked over at me slowly after Mason let go but covered up his curiosity with a small smile.

"I'm glad you're ok." He nodded at me.

"Thanks for coming to look for me. It means a lot."

"Well, it seems as if you didn't need our help." Christian mused. "But I'm glad you're ok. Scarlett is at the house, and I'm sure she'll be happy to see you. It's been a while."

I nodded. "I would like that."

"Octavia? How did you do… that?" Jackson asked.

"I was trained at a young age," I confessed.

"I see… Well, are you ready to head back?"

Slowly, I shook my head no. "I need a minute."

"I know, babe. I'm so sorry you had to do this." Mason mumbled, pulling me back into his arms. "It was you or them."

I shook my head. "But I didn't do it." I cried out. "I… I mean, I did… but I didn't. Those men surrendered yet she…"

"She?" Christian piped up, his eyes narrowed. "Your wolf, you mean?"

I bit my lip, looking at Mason with worried eyes. "No. My father calls her a beast. She's a killer, and she loves it. She's… she's out again, and there's nothing I can do to stop her."

"What do you mean? Your wolf? Is she different? Likes to make you kill?"

"It's hard to explain." I stammered, wiping my sweating palms onto my bloody pants.

"Everyone has different wolves. Some simply live more on the animalistic side rather than human, but some simply merge into… another side of them with no control. Her instinct is to kill as any other normal wolf would… but you're not just any normal wolf. So, Octavia… get on with it." Jackson spoke.

"As a kid, I was always different. I had anger issues to the extreme. You could simply tell me no, and I would destroy my whole room at the age of five. As I got older, it progressed into something much more dangerous.

I almost killed a girl one day at my school that I simply got into an argument with. That same day, I got my wolf. I was ten." Christian's eyes widened while Jackson and Mason glanced at each other.

"And?" Christian urged.

"I didn't want to hurt the girl, but this voice... I didn't know what it was. My parents told me I just imagined things."

"But it wasn't just a voice... she can talk to you," Jackson suggested, and I reluctantly nodded. "It's like a voice whispering nothing good into your ear. Coercing you into doing horrible, horrible things. Right, Octavia?" I nodded once more, unable to speak. He knew.

"Wait, what does this have to do with her getting her wolf at ten? Don't you shift for the first time at sixteen?" Asked Christian, and we nodded.

"Yes, for wolves, you shift at sixteen," Jackson confirmed.

"For wolves? You're saying she's..." Christian trailed off, his eyes snapping to meet mine, his jaw tightening.

"Greek," Jackson randomly spit out, and my heart sped up. *He definitely knew.*

"Oh, Goddess," Christian mumbled, a hand wiping over his face.

"Ancestors. The theory is that many were Greek. I said the simple word, and her heart sped up. So, you know about it? How?" I sighed, gritting my teeth.

"My father is a head gamma for The Power Pack. He trains the fighters there. I was strong, well my *other side* was, and he wanted me to... I don't know... for her to teach them how to fight. He stayed up countless nights just wondering how this happened, how it worked, how he could control her, and one night he found something. And when he did, he called the church officials."

"How did they react to the news?" Jackson questioned.

"They experimented on me for days. Just hearing Greek words... It terrifies me. My father used to say all of it was to teach me to keep her locked away, but she informed me it was a lie one day. He wanted to use her. Locking her up mentally angered her, so she always forced herself to take control. No matter what the situation was."

"They could speak to her through Greek, couldn't they?" Jackson asked, and I nodded.

"It took her a while, but she learned our language easily, and she didn't need Greek to talk to them. One day, my father locked me in a basement. One of his torture sessions is what it was. I was nearing death. He knew she'd save me... and she did."

"Did she retaliate?"

"Yes. After, she went and found some of the people that had hurt us. She tied my father up, and she made him watch as she slaughtered them all. He didn't bother us after that. She made my father lie to the church officials to say I went missing so they wouldn't come after me. She had finally mastered how to take control of my body that day. That's when I knew I had to learn to mash her down and lock her away."

"So how did this happen? How does this connect to you?" Christian asked, and I looked at Jackson, who nodded, basically saying it was ok to tell them.

"It comes through my mother's side. She... has a powerful line of ancestors. Ancestors that you seem to already know about. My mother didn't get the gene." I mumbled, looking at the ground.

"Lycanthropes. Many get them confused with werewolves and put them both into the same category, but that's not the case. They are completely different." Jackson delved further, and Christian sighed, looking away. I looked over at Mason, who had yet to say a word. He looked deep in thought.

"I'm what many would call a half Lycan. I could somewhat control her when she surfaced before I locked her away. When I did, I could shift like a normal wolf some days, and she would cooperate like she didn't care, but at times that I couldn't control her she..." I trailed off and looked to Jackson for help.

"She shifts like a Lycan. She can stand on her hind legs and walk like we would in human form. Her Lycan would stand roughly six feet tall and look like a terrifying beast. They used to call them destroyers of packs. One Lycan alone could wipe out a wolf pack within an hour. They are indestructible in Lycan form and power-hungry. Nothing can kill them other than another Lycan."

"What would make her resurface if you had her locked away?" Christian asked, and I shrugged.

"It didn't happen until I moved here. I don't know what could have made her so worried that she forced herself out of my mind. It was mentally exhausting to fight her, and I eventually gave in. Maybe it's the war?"

Jackson groaned. "Mason, you fool." He nearly whispered.

I looked at Mason with worried eyes. What did he have to do with it?

"I know," Mason spoke up. "I know, Jackson."

"Then tell her," Jackson spoke softly, and my heart sped up. "Tell her now and get this over with. Everyone is going to know at some point. You know why her Lycan resurfaced. You can trust us." Christian raised a hand to rebuttal, but Jackson shot him a look that basically said to shut up.

Christian shrugged. "Yeah… yeah. You have my trust. No harm will come to her. If you need to tell her something that could help her figure this all out, then do it."

"Say it," Mason gritted out, looking at Jackson, who sighed, shaking his head.

"You will create something nasty if you do. I don't want to be in the same room when it happens. So... I'm saying no. Just be a normal, smart person and tell her. You know... with *words,* not actions." Jackson disagreed, and I looked at Mason confused.

"Then leave after you do. She should see for herself. They both need to know." Mason added. *They? As in Ramani and me?* "Say the words, Jackson. You'll have to since they've been locked away for so long."

Jackson let out a small annoyed growl and looked at a confused Christian. "On my cue, you run like hell," Jackson told Christian.

"To hell with it. I'm so confused that if it gives me answers, fine with me, I'll do whatever." Christian nodded.

Jackson took in a deep breath, getting into a running stance, and the words rolled off his tongue as if he had known the language his whole life. I gasped, immediately turning on my heels to run, but cried in pain as ringing happened in my ears.

He spoke Greek. He told her to come forward, but not just through me—*but her actual form.*

Jackson quickly turned on his heels, grabbing hold of Christian's shirt collar, sprinting for the forest with a quick *'see ya'* with Christian staggering closely behind.

When I felt the familiar snap within me, I could curse Jackson. In seconds, I was forced to the back of my mind. Her true side came forward, excitement rippling through our body.

"I haven't been in this form in ages." She taunted, cockiness in her tone.

I could feel her powerful shift. All the clothes started ripping from my body, and my bones snapped in every which way. This was no normal werewolf shift. *She had been kept in for too long.*

When the cracking of bones was over and fur grew to cover our arms, our form grew inches taller. A few blinks later, I saw through her crystal-clear eyes. She could smell the deer from miles away, she could hear the commotion from the city, and I could feel the power radiating off her. She was in her actual form. The all-mighty Ramani was fully back.

My secret was finally let out.

However, her cockiness left her, and anger surged through us. Her head snapped to the side, a familiar scent entering her nose. A similar beast stood just feet away. Another Lycan.

Mason.

As Ramani snarled, I could tell they were communicating with each other, but she wouldn't let me into her thoughts. Though, when they both charged at each other, my heart dropped. I knew the stories. I know how each and every Lycan is power-hungry. I was always taught one thing: There's only one survivor at the end of a Lycan fight.

CHAPTER TWENTY-EIGHT

◆—◇—◆

Octavia

I gasped when I felt her take the hit. Mason's Lycan instantly knocked Ramani to the ground, causing them to both plummet towards the earth's hard surface. She effortlessly rolled into a crouched position and snarled at him, but she slipped up when she let her guard down—I was finally let into their conversation.

"You do not want to go against me. Stand down now!" His Lycan's deep voice yelled through their link.

"I am hundreds of years old. Do you really think you stand a chance?" She snarled, standing back to her full height as they circled each other.

"Ramani, you may be strong, but you have no ranking like me. You do not want to challenge me. Our vessels may be mates, but I do not have a problem taking care of a threat." His Lycan snarled.

It all made sense. The times I wondered how my Lycan was so experienced. The myths I heard were true. Lycan spirits pass on when their vessel dies and into a new one of heredity. They were indeed hundreds of years old.

"Orion, I was known as alpha during my time. My rank matches yours. Don't try to belittle me. I may be a woman, but I can still rip your heart out. After all, it was *you* who was channeling *me*. I felt your power. That is the worst thing to do for a Lycan— help them by channeling, I mean. Now I want your power, and I *will* have it." She snarled and charged at him. She easily ducked under the swing of his claws, turning on her heels to drag her own down his back.

Orion roared, making the trees shudder from their roots around us. He was too late to turn, though, as she delivered a right hook to his jaw, causing him to fly back into a tree behind him.

She watched, amused as he made his way back to his feet, brushing parts of the broken tree off him. Orion growled, his eyes shining a bright red. She flashed him her own color of red. It wasn't a threat... It was a promise. *She wasn't scared of him nor his authority.* In seconds he had already advanced back at her. She went to dodge the swing of his claws again, but he faked the swing, bringing one around back to slice down the side of her ribs.

Ramani yelped, hunching over to grab her bleeding side. One hit to her jaw, another to her stomach, and one knee driving into her chin sent her crumbling to the ground. Orion towered over her.

"I was trying to go easy on you, but I'm not here to play childish games. You should be thanking me for saving your pathetic excuse of a life. I didn't have to channel you, I didn't have to go through mental torture to breech the hold Mason put on me so many years ago, but I did. I did it because my vessel cares about yours, and if she dies, Mason dies. Stop acting power-hungry and put that annoying stereotype of Lycans behind us. We have bigger problems now. I quite like my vessel, and I don't wish to return to the ancestor realm. I don't suppose you do, either."

Ramani went silent, listening closely to how true his words were. No matter how much she said she despised me, she didn't want to leave my vessel either. If she were to kill Orion, it would kill Mason, which would lead to my own death. If I died, she would be sent back to the ancestor realm, where she would have to wait years for another vessel with Lycan genes to merge with.

"Ramani, please just stop all this. You've won." I pleaded out to her.

Finally, she got up off the ground as Orion gave her a wary glance. She popped her neck to the side, letting out a puff of air. She stared at him for a moment, then began to shake her head slowly.

"Unlike you, I despise this vessel. Who cares?" She mumbled, watching Orion's eyes widen as she lunged for him again.

Hit after hit, he let her do it. She clawed, kicked, punched, but he took it all. I was screaming for her to stop, but she didn't listen as she continued to beat him to a pulp. Orion looked up at her through weak eyes as she sat him up, holding him by the throat.

"Why aren't you fighting back?"

"Because Mason asked me not to. You're too lost in a world of selfish revenge to even think about how we messed up their lives the day we entered them. I don't blame Mason for locking me away. I was power-hungry, and I convinced him to try and do terrible things, but being locked up wasn't years of planning my revenge. It was years of realizing how I screwed up and how I'm lucky to at least have a vessel. So, when I finally was let out again, I wanted him to know he could trust me. This is how. I'm not going to fight you any longer, Ramani. Do as you please."

She let out an angered cry, pulling her hand back, and I sobbed out, knowing what move she was going for—she was going to rip his heart out, but her arm didn't move as she shakily watched him, her decision starting to falter by the second. Her fingers twitched, itching to rip through his chest.

"Ramani, please don't do this. You can be better." I sobbed out through our mind-link.

She let out a shaky breath, her grip not loosening on him. **"I do not take orders. Especially not from him."** She replied back to me.

"That man that Orion is controlling is my mate, and I love him. I know you feel something for him, too, just as he does for you. He's literally laying his life down for you. He's telling you there's still time to change. Please, prove me wrong after all these years. Do something good with your time with me! Don't do this, or I swear to the Goddess that I will find a way to end you before I die. I can promise you that. Haven't you done enough?!"

She went silent for a moment.

"I did it all for you. Everything I have done was for you, Octavia! I protected you! I didn't kill that pathetic excuse of a father for you even though he tested you the moment he knew you were different. He used you *and* me, but I knew even after all that you still cared about him. Why, I never knew, but I didn't kill him because it would have hurt you. The people he sent to test us, I slaughtered them, and yes, I enjoyed it because I was protecting you. I was getting justice for *you!*" she let out a humorless laugh.

"Ramani I—"

She snarled through our link, shutting me up instantly. **"Before, I'd risk getting myself killed if that meant I died protecting you. Us**

Lycans do what is best for our vessel, and how did you repay me? You pushed me down like I'm some monster! I wanted to hate you so much. I cursed myself for choosing this damn vessel every day I sat in that corner pushed away, but I couldn't hate you. I can't explain why I don't, but I wish I could. I really do." She completed, and I sighed.

"I mashed you down because you threatened the people I loved. I was scared. At the age of fifteen, you were telling me to kill my father. To hurt people. Do you know how much that screwed with me? People thought I was crazy! No one believed me, and every day you made it worse."

I wracked my brain to explain to her how wrong she truly was.

"You may or may not hate me, but guess what? I hated myself too. I hated myself so much, to the fact I didn't care if I lived or died. Now? Now... I want to—no, I *need* to be here. Because I have a man who loves me just as much as I love him! Don't you think it's time to start something new and see this as a second chance to do what's right?"

After a minute of deliberation, she spoke. "You won't mash me down anymore?"

"Not if you cooperate with me. I'll treat you the same just as I would treat my wolf. No more controlling me, coercing me, or speaking for me."

"Fine."

"Are you serious? Or are you playing with me?"

"If this will give me my freedom, then yes. If you truly saw me like that, then I am sorry. We have two different viewpoints and apparently a lot of miscommunication. It seems we both unintentionally made our lives hell."

"**Then, thank you. Now, please let him go.**"

She looked back down at Orion, anger still bubbling within her. "**I'll let him go, but one last thing... you're an alpha, you have my genes. Act like it.**"

Ramani let go of Orion, letting him fall to the ground and gave one last final growl before I felt the shift happen. I was surprised. I thought it was going to take a lot more convincing, or worse... that she wouldn't listen at all. As I stood on my own two feet again, a breath of relief left me. Awkwardly, I covered myself the best I could, looking away from Mason's Lycan. I winced as I moved my arms, my side flexing. Looking down, I saw the claw marks from Orion against the side of my ribs. They were red and bloody.

With the sound of heavy footsteps approaching, I quickly looked up to see Orion walking my way. I gulped, taking a wary step backward. I didn't know if he was staying true to his word or not now that I was now in human form. After all, Lycans are sneaky.

"**He can sense your fear. Calm down.**" Ramani reminded me, freely using our mind-link with her newfound freedom. I could cry in relief now that there wasn't any pain from her forcefully coming forward to speak to me.

"**Be confident... you're his mate.**" She added.

I tensed as he reached me, and his arm raised, gently grasping my arm. He lifted it and looked over the claw marks. I craned my neck up to look at his Lycan's face. He had many scars and looked quite terrifying. Orion let out a puff of air, shaking his head. Reluctantly he dropped to one knee, bowing his head.

"**He's apologizing for the wound,**" Ramani explained.

"It's ok," I told him, shifting from one foot to the other nervously. "Could I... talk to Mason, please?"

His eyes met my own and softened, nodding. I heard the familiar snapping of bones, causing me to look away as he let Mason shift back to human form. Seconds later, I felt his hand glide across my cheek, cupping it gently. He turned my head, a frown upon his lips.

"I'm sorry you had to go through that, and I'm sorry I didn't tell you about my other side sooner."

"Mason, I'm in the same boat. You have nothing to apologize for. I should have done the same thing, but Lycans aren't really liked. They're actually hated. Goddess knows what Christian thinks of me now. The Royals hate us the most."

"The church officials hate you the most," Mason corrected. "Christian stays true to his word. No harm will come to you, and your secret is safe with him, but maybe we shouldn't keep this a secret."

My brows furrowed. "What do you mean?"

"If we come out as being half Lycans, it will no longer be a secret. We could use our Lycans in the war. Nothing can harm a Lycan other than another Lycan. We can't be killed by bullets, gases, or any of that."

"If that's true, why haven't you tried that sooner? Especially when that gas form of wolfsbane was created?"

"Because, like you, I was afraid of the consequences. But now Christian knows, and it's finally off my chest. I have nothing to fear anymore. The church officials are terrified of Scarlett and Alara, and we both know Scarlett won't let anything happen to us. Christian and Scarlett are pretty much the head of the church right now. It's finally our time to be free and for our Lycans to do something good for us wolves."

Mason was right. We had been living our whole lives in fear, and I was sick and tired of it. Who knows, maybe there are other half Lycans out there that could come forward. We deserved this. We could do this.

"Fine. Let's do it. We can send our story to a news outlet or something. Screw it." I let out a nervous laugh, and he grinned, a huge smile on his face.

"Oh, we are going to own this war." He pulled me to him, and my cheeks warmed at our bare touch.

"Are you seriously embarrassed right now?" his brows rose.

"A little! I have no clothes, and neither do you, and we're just hugging in the middle of nowhere."

He pulled back, giving me a toothy grin. "You're a werewolf, and you're embarrassed by nudity? Not like you haven't seen all this before."

I rolled my eyes, playfully shoving him away. "I'm so over this. Can we go now?"

"Yes, but you probably need to shift into your wolf. Your wound is pretty bad, and she can help speed up the process and get you home quicker. It'll take a few days to heal since it was a Lycan's doing, though."

"Aye aye, captain." I saluted, turning to shift but halted. "Wait, where did Grayson go?"

"After we realized you were gone, he went searching the woods, but I forgot about these houses or I would have told him to come this way. Eventually, Ryker told him to head back because something happened he needed his help with. Grayson left once he knew I had Christian and Jackson coming to help."

"You know… he actually seems like a nice person. It's not what I'd expect from a vampire."

Mason nodded. "He's a nice guy. He can be a sarcastic asshole sometimes, but he always does what's right."

"When will we all meet the rest of them?"

"Soon," Mason replied, a wary look on his face. "It shall be interesting."

CHAPTER TWENTY-NINE

$$\diamond$$

Octavia

I walked out of the bathroom towel drying my hair. I felt relieved that I was now clean and refreshed. My head hurt just thinking about what I had gone through in the past twenty-four hours. Never in my life would I have thought that Mason was a half Lycan as well. It all seemed surreal to me.

I winced as I pulled on a shirt over my head. My side was radiating hot pain, and I knew it would take a bit for the claw marks to heal. Mason was with Jackson and Christian, explaining everything thoroughly to Christian. I was glad that I didn't have to hide anymore, it was freeing, to say the least. I was more than lucky to have a mate like Mason.

A soft knock sounded on the door, and I called out to let them come in once I was done changing. The door to the bedroom opened, and I smiled as Scarlett walked through.

"It's so good to see you." She beamed, and I smiled, embracing her with a hug.

"Look at you, Scarlett. You're glowing!" We pulled back, and she smiled, placing a hand on her belly.

"I can't control my emotions, I want to eat any food in sight, I apparently like pickles now, I have to pee every fifteen minutes, and my back constantly hurts, so I better get some relief by looking good from this." She joked, earning a laugh from me.

"It'll be worth it after it's all over and you're holding your baby." I countered, and her facial expression softened, her eyes already filled with so much joy.

"I can't wait to hold them." She mumbled, and my eyes widened.

"Them?"

"You didn't hear? They're twins! A boy and a girl!" She took a seat on the side of the bed, and I quickly walked over to sit next to her.

"No way. Have you decided on names?" I asked, and she grinned, nodding.

"Prince Eligh Alexander Spur and Princess Rosemarie Elizabeth Spur." She gushed out.

"Those names are perfect," I replied, a small smile on my lips. "I'm so happy for you."

"Thank you, Octavia. It took a lot of arguing to compromise." I giggled, shaking my head.

"I don't doubt it."

She looked me over for a moment, a small frown appeared on her lips before she asked, "What's wrong?"

"What do you mean?"

"You don't seem like the Octavia I know. There isn't that normal spark in your eye. So what's up?" I sighed, looking down as I fiddled my thumbs.

"You're going to hear a lot about me soon, and I hope that it won't change how you see me. I wish I had more time to tell you everything, but that would take days." I bit my lip, glancing over at her.

She frowned and pulled me into a hug. "Everything will be ok. Nothing you could do would make me see you any different. I promise. Hell, I told you months ago about being a half-witch and that I was working with Alara Lavender. You didn't bat an eye."

I smiled, nodding. "True."

"So yeah... your story isn't going to change how I think of you, Octavia. I promise. When you want to tell me...just know I'm a call or drive away. No pressure." She leaned in one more time, hugging me tightly.

"Thank you, Scarlett. I promise you'll be one of the first to know. Though, Christian may just tell you it all anyways. He kind of witnessed it all. The part he's going to tell you... just know that there is more of a story to tell from my childhood, and it's a painful one, so when I finally can separate my emotions... I'll tell you it all."

Rubbing my back, she offered me a warm smile. "And I'll be all ears when that time comes. In the meantime, just know that I am always here to support you. Just like you have been there when I needed it."

"You're too good to me."

She shrugged. "It's what friends are for." She went to stand, and I quickly got up, helping her do so.

"Anyways. I came to say goodbye. Christian and I are heading out soon, and I couldn't leave without checking on you."

"I'll miss you." I frowned, and she grinned.

"I'm sure when these two are born, and the war is over, you'll be up to convincing me to do nothing good." She winked, and I couldn't help but laugh.

"I'm a little scared of Christian and Mason to attempt that again."

Chuckling, she tapped on her temple. "Chris just linked me. We're heading out. Bye, 'Tavia." She headed towards the door but stopped and turned to face me. "Congrats on the marking and mating." She winked, giggling as she walked out the door.

***

Days went by, and news broke out about Mason and me I. Scarlett had texted me, stating that she indeed didn't think any different of me and, in a way, she thought I seemed badass. It gave me a little comfort knowing her and Christian were ok with it. Though, I'm sure the hunters now knew that two Lycans were a threat to them.

Leaving my thoughts, I walked into the kitchen, grabbing a drink from the fridge. Mason sat at the kitchen bar, fooling around with some laid out papers in front of him.

"What are you reading?" I asked.

"New advances for the war Jackson gave me. He's narrowed down the hunter's main location to two spots now. This is good. We have more to work with than we thought. The fronts are holding up well, but at the same time, the hunters haven't been as aggressive. Jackson thinks they're planning something big. I believe his direct words were, *shit's about to go down, man.*" I let out a small laugh, and Mason gave me a confused look.

"Sorry. I can't take him that seriously sometimes. He acts serious, but some days he just says the funniest of things." Mason shook his head with a small grin, and looked back at the papers.

"Dinner is on the stove if you're hungry," He pointed out. I grinned, looking back at some lasagna that sat there, the steam still rolling off it.

"You cooked?"

His brow raised. "Surprised?"

I bit my lip to hold back a giggle. "No, just... didn't expect it tonight." I grabbed a plate, cutting myself a slice. "Why haven't you eaten?"

He sighed, running a hand through his messy dark locks. "Too stressed."

I rolled my eyes, fixing another plate. Carrying the two back to the counter, I placed one next to him.

"You need to eat. You'll think better on a full stomach." He didn't reply, his eyes still locked on his papers. I huffed, leaning over and grabbed them, causing him to let out a sound of protest.

"Babe," His voice was clipped as I moved them away. "I need to look over those."

"Sue me for wanting to have an hour with my mate that doesn't involve this mess. It's been a very long week. Relax in this small moment with me before something else happens. You have the rest of the night to look them over, I promise. Staring at them is going to get you nowhere. Take a break with me, please." His features softened at my response, and he grabbed my hand, lacing our fingers.

"You're right. I'm sorry. I've barely seen you all day. I promise, work will wait." He smiled. "How's your side?"

I couldn't help but smile. He'd changed so much over the past months. Times had been tough, but he'd been better about keeping me in the loop of things as well as acknowledging me. It was nice. For once, I didn't fear the future because at this exact moment, it was just us.

"My side is getting better. The wound is almost completely healed, so hopefully, the aching will stop soon."

He grabbed his fork, cutting into his food. "I'm glad. Orion has felt like crap ever since that day."

"Well, at least he realized what happened and tried to stop it. He's not the only one to blame. Ramani was out of control too."

"True, but it doesn't make him feel any less bad about the whole matter. Has Ramani spoken to you lately?"

I shook my head. "She's actually been pretty chill. No snarky comments, no trying to overpower me, and no mind games. I think she's finally content with me."

"True," Her voice flooded through my mind, and I belched out a laugh.

"Now you show."

"Heard my name." She teased.

"Ramani?" Mason questioned, and I nodded.

"She agrees with me."

"Well, that's nice."

"I guess so. Anyway, is there anything exciting I need to know about?" I asked, and he started to shake his head no, but his eyes seemed hesitant.

"I honestly forgot to tell you. Between you and me, Scarlett asked me to let her sister transfer here." I gave him a confused look.

"What happened?"

"Her mate rejected her. Apparently, he was a royal guard there, and Scarlett was tired of seeing her sister so down all the time. I accepted. She's actually arriving today some time. Scarlett called me this morning that Ashlee was heading over to her new pack."

"Poor girl," I mumbled. No one deserves that. "That was nice of you. I'm sure she needs it."

"I'd want a chance to get away from everyday torture if I was her. It's the least I could do. Who knows, maybe she'll really like it here. Scarlett wants you to keep an eye on her, though. Just to make sure she's holding up ok."

Wiping my mouth with a napkin, I nodded. "Of course."

We finished the rest of our dinner talking about anything and everything. It was nice to have a stress-free night. We haven't had much of that lately. To actually see Mason laugh and smile warmed my heart. I think he needed a break just as much as I did, even if it just was for an hour or so.

"So, I meant to talk to you about... future plans. Would you like to—" Mason jumped at the sound of the kitchen door flying open.

Elizabeth, Mason's head of staff, walked through with a stressed look. Her breathing was harsh as if she had sprinted the whole way here.

"Alpha, sorry to interrupt, but Miss Ashlee Madison is here, and beta Alaric is... having a meltdown." She rushed out, and Mason looked at me confused before glancing back at her.

"Why?"

"He's claiming she's his mate." She explained, and our jaws dropped. "And she denies it. It's safe to say the foyer is a mess."

Mason was quick to stand up, but I placed a hand on his shoulder. "Wait a second... Ashlee already found her mate. Is it possible for second chance mates?"

"It is if you were rejected..." Mason replied, giving me a knowing look.

"Shit," We muttered, darting from our spots and out the door, leaving Elizabeth stunned in her tracks.

CHAPTER THIRTY

◆—◇—◆

Octavia

My heart pounded as I followed behind Mason. If this was true, if Ashlee was actually given a second chance, this was such a huge deal. Maybe she was in denial. I mean, she just had to leave somewhere she considered a pack because of being rejected by her mate. Though, the Moon Goddess works in mysterious ways. Maybe she was doing all of this for a reason.

"What are you going to do?" I asked Mason once we neared the shouting from the main foyer.

"Whatever I have to," He grumbled, rounding the corner.

Once we took a look at the situation, I covered my mouth in shock. Ashlee was cowered away toward the door as Alaric angrily paced around the destroyed room. Tears glistened in her eyes. What the hell?

"I don't understand!" he nearly yelled, pulling at his hair in frustration.

"I told you, Alaric. I already have a mate." Ashlee responded, her voice quivering.

"I am your mate!" Alaric yelled back.

"No, you're not!" she defended.

"Enough!" Mason's powerful voice bounced off the walls, stilling the two and bringing them to silence.

"What in the hell is going on?" Mason snarled.

"I'm her mate, but she denies it." Alaric stated, turning his back to us.

"Alaric, you're terrifying the poor girl! I wouldn't want to be your mate either." I snapped, causing his head to snap to the side, glancing back at me with angry eyes.

"This isn't your problem." My eyes widened from his reply.

In a flash, Mason stood before him, his head tilting to the side in a taunting way.

"Say it again. You're in my house, speaking to my mate—your Luna… so please use that tone with her again. I dare you." His chest rumbled, holding back a snarl.

"Mason, stop. It's fine." I rolled my eyes, placing my hands on my hips. Glancing over at Ashlee, who was practically clinging to the door in fear, I opened my arms, waving her over, and she was quick to rush to my side. I pulled her into my grasp, wrapping a protective arm around her.

"He's crazy, Luna Octavia." She nearly whispered.

"I got you," I mumbled. "It's going to be ok. He's just an overprotective male who's upset." I tried to comfort her.

Alaric assessed the situation, and his features softened. "Luna, I apologize. Ashlee, I'm sorry as well. My intention was not to scare you."

Mason let out a content hum, moving away from Alaric and walked back to us, taking a protective stance in front of us. "Now, are you calm, or am I going to have to guard these women against my own beta?"

He bowed his head, ashamed. "I'm calm, Alpha. Again, I'm sorry."

Mason turned towards Ashlee, trying his best to manage a kind smile. "Hello, Ashlee. I'm sorry your arrival at my pack happened to be this way. I assure you, it is not like that here. You're safe, and we'll do our best to get you accommodated. Your sister is a great friend of ours. Now, would you like to explain to Alaric why you already have a mate?"

She glanced up at me, and I nodded at her, shooting her a small wink. "It's ok."

"How did you know?" she asked.

"Scarlett," I smiled, reaching out to wipe away a stray tear from her cheek. "You're in good hands, I swear. You can tell him."

"This is your second chance. Take advantage of it." Mason encouraged, and her eyes glossed over again. I frowned, giving her a small hug. Poor thing. I hated this for her.

"I was rejected." She croaked out. "He may not technically still be my mate, but I did already have one. I don't want to go through that again."

Alaric's mouth opened a little, shock wracking over him. "That's what you're scared of?" he asked, and she shrugged her shoulders in response.

"Well, that and the fact you destroyed this room when I told you otherwise. You're quite temperamental. Not a good look." I had to look away and hide my snicker.

"I'm sorry. My wolf just… he didn't like the sound of his mate denying the bond. I may not be your first mate, but you're mine. We're really mates, Ashlee. There's no denying it. Let your wolf feel the connection trying to take between us. Second chance mates are a real thing. It's rare, even more rare than finding a mate to begin with… but it has happened before. It's not unheard of. Maybe the Goddess blessed you with another chance because she saw you hurting. Let me prove to you that all us mates aren't bad. I'm not going to reject you, not unless you want me to. But I'd like the chance to at least try and show you what the bond is really all about."

If I weren't still angry at him for acting like an ass, his words would have touched my heart. Ashlee looked down, moving out of my grasp as the nervousness left her. She seemed to be thinking her words over as her hands trembled ever so lightly.

"I feel it." She confirmed. "I guess I just didn't want to believe it. If I did, then that's when all the hard stuff comes into play. You're really not going to reject me?" she looked up at him with hopeful eyes.

"Goddess no," He took a step toward her. "I know I scared you earlier, but as I said… that was not me or my intention. It was my wolf. He was mad, but I promise neither of us would ever hurt you." She couldn't help but smile, slowly nodding.

"You're my second chance, mate." She mumbled, finally accepting it.

Alaric walked over, gently tilting her chin up to where she would look at him. "I am. I promise I'll give you the whole world if you let me."

The anger had left me, and I glanced up at Mason as a smile tugged at his lips. Alaric could finally be happy, Ashlee could finally be happy, so maybe in the dark times around us, there was still light to guide us through.

"I think we should go," I whispered to Mason.

He looked at the two, who were now smiling at one another, pure adoration in Alaric's eyes.

"Yeah." He agreed, grasping my hand.

He guided me out of the room as the two started talking to one another, and I laughed, shaking my head as we headed down the hall.

"I did not expect that."

"Me either." Mason let out a breath of air. "I think we need to inform Scarlett."

"Let Ashlee do that. It's her big news to tell, not ours." I reminded him.

He pursed his lips and nodded. "True… very true."

A sudden thought crossed my mind, causing me to halt in my steps. "Isn't Ashlee like… sixteen?"

Mason shook his head. "On her papers, it said she turned seventeen a few weeks ago. Alaric is only a few years older. He's her mate, after all. It's not like it's a bad thing. If her parents approve, it doesn't matter. A mate bond is… well, the mate bond. There's really no going against it."

I couldn't disagree with that. I let Mason lead me upstairs to our room. I was tired and wanted nothing more than to curl up in bed with him, but I knew he had more paperwork to do. Bummed, I let his hand slip from mine.

"I'll see you later?"

He gave me a confused look. "No?"

"I thought you had to get back to your paperwork?"

Closing the door behind him, he waved me off. "It can wait. After all that, I just want to spend time with you. You never know what the Moon Goddess is going to throw at you."

Grinning, I stepped closer to him, placing my hands on his chest. "And what did you have in mind?" I teased, all the exhaustion suddenly leaving me.

He let out a playful growl as he rested his hands on my hips. "As much as I would love to do unimaginable things to you… you have open wounds on your side." He smirked, playfully pushing me away as he walked toward the closet.

I scoffed, folding my arms. "They're almost healed."

"Keyword: *almost*. With the stuff happening around us, we need you at your best. I'm not risking anything. Especially not you." He shrugged.

"There's nothing I could do to make you change your mind? I mean, for once… There is nothing bad happening around us. The fires have been put out for now, but I could ignite another one if you'd like." I smirked.

He belched out a laugh. "You're incurable." He walked into the closet, grabbing some clothes and walked back out. "I'm going to shower, and before you ask… no. You may not join. I'm not letting you change my mind on this."

My jaw dropped, and, at that moment, I wanted to stomp my foot like a child. "Fine," I replied, knowing I would make his life hell after these damn wounds were healed. "I'll remember that."

His eyes narrowed. "What sick plan are you brewing in that twisted little head of yours?"

"Me? Nothing. I would never," The devilish look in my eyes said otherwise.

I waited for a snarky response from him, but nothing came. He stared at me with an odd look. It was as if he was rethinking everything but was having an internal battle within himself. Feeling smug, I waltzed past him into the closet to retrieve my own clothes.

"I'll shower next door then," I mocked sadness, brushing past him. I bumped into him just enough for the tingles to shoot up our arms from the bond.

I was only a few feet away when I was jerked back to his chest. A low growl rumbled within his chest as he lowered his mouth next to my ear. "Sometimes I don't know whether to pin you against a wall to shut you up or just give in to your ways," He hummed, nipping at my ear.

I pressed back against him, craning my neck to the side to get a good look at him. "I've heard it's best to just cooperate with me."

"Mhm, is that so?"

"Indeed, it is." As the words left my mouth, he spun me around with a heated gaze.

He leaned in, causing me to stand on my toes as if I was in a trance. Just as his lips started to brush against mine, he paused. "Not going to happen, babe." He whispered.

I growled, pushing him away. "I'm actually starting to hate you."

Placing a hand over his heart, he pouted his bottom lip. "You wound me."

"I'm *so* walking around the house in nothing but a towel." I challenged, turning my back to him.

"Do as you please. My claim is upon your neck now, so I'm not worried about any mateless wolf looking at you as anything other than his Luna." He shot back.

I spun around to shoot him the bird, but he was already walking into the bathroom. I could curse him and his new personality. I should be flattered he was thinking about my health, but to hell with that! It was finally a peaceful night, and I was left hot and bothered. *Males*, I inwardly grumbled.

I left the room, walking next door to the guest one to take a shower. I should be in our shower with the nice jets, but no, Mason's too paranoid I'll start something. True, but damn him.

Turning on the shower, I stripped my clothing and got in. The hot water was refreshing, and it soothed my aching side. I glanced down at the wounds, seeing they were almost healed completely. Due to my quick Lycan healing, they wouldn't leave any scars.

I scrubbed some shampoo into my hair as I thought about the last few weeks. I would have never thought I'd be out as a Lycan nor having a mate just like me. Weeks ago, I feared that my secret would bring me a swift death. Instead, I was using it to my advantage in the war. Things were about to change. I knew that much.

As I washed my body, I felt a pull from Ramani as she suddenly went alert. Confused, I quickly washed off and tried reaching out to her.

"What is it?"

There came no response, scaring me. Why was she alert and not saying anything? Turning off the shower, I got out to dry myself off.

"Ramani?"

"Quiet. I'm trying to listen." She growled.

I went silent, my brows furrowing. Throwing on my clothes, I went to reach for the bathroom doorknob but groaned as she forcefully came forward.

"Don't fight me, and it won't hurt, Octavia. We talked about this." She mumbled softly, and I realized that out of instinct, I was trying to push her down. I quickly gave control as I was thrown to the back of my mind. For once, the process was painless.

She walked us back to our room and threw open our bedroom door. I still heard the shower running, and she huffed, walking over to a nearby window. Pulling the curtains back slowly, she peeked out the crack, looking over the backyard.

"I caught a scent. One that I haven't recognized before, and my hearing picked up the cock of a gun." She explained to me, assessing the situation at hand.

"I forget how good your hearing and smell is."

"It's a blessing and a curse." She replied, her tone confused. **"I don't see anyone..."** she looked back toward the bathroom and shook her head. **"How the hell Orion isn't alert is beyond me."**

The shower turned off, and she froze, snapping her attention back to the window. It suddenly felt like a terrible idea to be standing in front of a wall of pure windows. The bathroom door opened, and when Mason walked out, he raised a brow. When he saw Ramani's red eyes, his instantly shifted to the same color.

"What is it?" Orion walked over, looking out towards the same spot Ramani had been looking at.

"How the hell have you not been paying attention? I heard the cock of a gun and caught an odd scent." She questioned.

"Unlike you, I'm not on guard twenty-four-seven. I haven't been free in his mind in a long time. It's hard to balance our two worlds after a while. You grew up trying to protect her, so you're used to being on guard." He pointed out.

Closing his eyes, he looked to be focusing his hearing. His nose crinkled, and his eyes shot open. "The scent... that's a vampire scent."

"I thought so. It reminded me of when Grayson helped Octavia and Mason, but it's not him. In fact, it's almost foreign to me."

"I agree."

"Wait... do you smell that?" she asked, and he sniffed, his eyes widening a little.

"Humans."

"Hunters." She corrected. "They're here."

"We need to hurry before they hurt someone." He stressed.

A crack against the window startled them. Orion pulled the curtain back more and saw a bullet lodged in the window. Thank the Goddess for Mason bulletproofing them. Growling, Orion shot Ramani a knowing look.

"Do you think we can break a bulletproof window?"

"Absolutely. As a Lycan, of course." She shot back.

They closed their eyes, growls rumbling in their chests as they channeled a shift. Soon, we stood taller, looking through crystal clear eyes. Ramani pulled her elbow back, thrusting it forward. The glass shattered and she snarled, looking at him.

With a nod of approval from Orion, she leaped from it.

CHAPTER THIRTY-ONE

◆◇◆

Octavia

The minute our feet touched the ground, our Lycans dashed across the backyard towards the forest line. As we did, arrows flew from the darkness of the tree line. Our Lycans dodged them easily, not missing a beat as they forced themselves to run quicker. Orion let out a roar—a signal. The moment he did, alarms broke out from near lamp posts, signaling we were under attack.

Out of nowhere, wolves darted from around the front of the house, darting past us. Snarls, cries, and grunts were heard as they entered the tree line. As we neared the darkness, the hunters rushed out by the second. I watched from the small corner she held me in as our wolves and guards from the pack charged at them.

She moved swiftly around stray bullets and arrows. Seeing two men pointing their guns at a nearby wolf, Ramani darted in front of them, taking each bullet they fired. She snarled as she grabbed their throats in each hand and simply squeezed their necks, tossing them aside after a satisfying crack. Digging into her shoulder, she picked out the bullets one by one, flicking them away from her. I guess it was true when they said Lycans were indestructible in Lycan form. The wounds instantly healed.

Mason's Lycan was killing so quickly and effortlessly that it was terrifying. I saw a flash of white dart from the tree line, heading right toward Orion. Before I could recognize what it was, Ramani had already headed to it.

She ran, our heart thumping in our chest at the thought of it getting to Mason before she could. I knew the scent... it was a vampire. She reached Orion first and jumped, pushing off Orion's back and tackled the vampire before he had a chance to grab Mason's Lycan.

By the time our feet hit the ground again, she had already effortlessly decapitated him as his head went flying in one direction and his body in another.

I winced as something hit her back, only angering her. She turned, narrowing her eyes on her target and found a man with a gun. Moving instantly, she had him by the throat.

"How pathetic. I hate people who hide behind a gun." She told me before smashing her hand through his chest, ripping his heart out—a terrible habit of hers.

I felt sick at all the blood coating us.

"They really think they can control us? Beat us? They're mistaken." She humorlessly laughed out, and I felt it go through to Orion's link.

"These hunters are a disgrace to humankind." He responded.

As they stood side by side, they let out a ferocious roar, rattling the trees around us. The vampires halted, only yards away. Knowing they were outnumbered and didn't stand a chance against us, they fled along with the other hunters.

How stupid could you be to enter The War Pack with an open attack?

***

After getting everything back under control, we checked our wolves to make sure none were seriously hurt, and thankfully, just a few had minor injuries. It boiled my blood to know that the hunters were getting so brave to start crossing onto wolf territory. I didn't understand why they thought they'd win that fight. We were in our home base—a complete advantage.

It wasn't long before we were sitting in Mason's office, discussing all that had just happened with Christian and the other alphas on a video call.

"You and I both know that they had some other motive to try and ransack the place," Christian stated, running a hand over his face.

Alaric walked in, grabbing all our attention. "Because it was a coverup—a distraction. A prisoner broke out. One that we definitely didn't want getting into the wrong hands." He explained, his jaw tight.

"Please don't tell me it's who I think it was." Christian gritted out.

Alaric gave Mason a knowing look causing him to curse, slamming his hand onto the table. "How was that possible?! He was in the most locked up cell ever created!"

"So, my assumptions were right. It was Martial." Christian growled, letting out a string of curses shortly after.

"Find him, or we're screwed." Was all he said and hung up, leaving the conference.

"Have you located his tracking chip?" Jackson spoke, his face popping up onto the screen.

"It was the first thing I went to check on until I found it in a chunk of skin on his cell floor," Alaric replied.

"Well, there goes our advantage." He mumbled, shoulders slumping.

"I can send one of my vamps there, let them get a scent and see if they can track him?" Ryker asked.

"That's the thing. He doesn't have one. His scent automatically blends in with anything around him."

"Ok, can someone please explain to me who the hell this man is?!" I questioned, fear lacing my tone.

"An experiment gone wrong." Mason spat, leaning against his desk with his arms crossed.

"Patient zero, AKA our first and only trial that successfully succeeded the main tests without having to move on to other people. He was a trained killer. Didn't think twice before following an order. He was done within seconds, and he didn't look back nor leave any evidence. On the last trial, we put a serum in his body that basically enhanced his werewolf genes. It was to make him faster, stronger, and even smarter." Jackson started explaining.

"The serum seemed to work at first, but in seconds he started screaming. I had never seen the man in so much pain. He was one to keep it locked away; no emotions whatsoever. When I watched the video, after I was informed of what happened, his skin started to just... boil from the inside out. He tried to shift to maintain the pain. After the shift, he couldn't shift back." Mason added.

"We tried everything. Some of his fur was burned off, his nails long and sharp. He was part wolf, part human. He was thirsty for our blood for doing this to him. Over the years, he gave into his wolf and honestly? He's the thing kids fear in the dark. He's a monster." I stared agape at Mason, processing the new information Jackson gave.

"Please tell me he signed up for this, and you didn't force him."

"Of course he signed up for it. He knew the risks, and he still didn't care. He wanted power... well, he got it. It just wasn't what any of us, including him, were expecting."

"And... they broke him out? How?"

"Well, once they opened the room he was contained in, it wasn't hard for them to get him out. He slaughtered all the guards on that block. He's loyal to the hunters now, considering they broke him out—helped him. It's an animal instinct to stand by those who helped you when in need. We just kept him locked away." Mason confessed, and I felt disgusted. This was terrible.

"Do you have anyone else like him? How did they even know about him?" I asked.

"No, he was the first and last we experimented on, and I don't know how. Jackson once said we have a mole, and obviously, we do. I've been looking into it, but we haven't gotten anywhere. Our circle is now just us Alphas and Lunas. It's going to be hard to find this mole, but I promise you we will."

Who would betray their own kind?

"How do we stop him?" I gulped.

"There's only one thing to do, and that's to put a bullet in his head. I hate to do it, but we have no other choice. All these years, I kept him alive in hopes that we could fix him, but everything we tried kept failing. No matter how many times we tried to explain we were trying to help him, he didn't care. Now, I'm going after them with all we got. Once we locate their main headquarters, we're going to end this all. I'll have snipers ready on the field. It'll be their mission to take him down, and if they can't... we do." He clarified, and I looked down.

"You mean our Lycans." He nodded.

"This is the final straw. I won't sleep until I have their main headquarters in sight. Hopefully, the spies we sent will get that information soon, but it's taking longer than we hoped. Alpha Jackson is getting help from a friend of Ryker's, so maybe they can find the location. Once they do, it will be time for us to take them down. They wanted this war. They got it. It's just not what they hoped for. I'm now declaring no mercy. We'll end them all." He growled, and I could tell the anger was taking over as his eyes flashed blood red.

"Alphas, I'll be in touch later. I need to go." Mason replied and ended the video call. He spun around, headed towards the door, and my brows furrowed.

"Where are you going?" I asked, standing from the couch I was perched on.

"I need to sink my teeth into something. I'm going for a run. Alaric, go back to the cells and check for anything to give us more clues." He answered and closed the door behind him and Alaric.

I sighed, shaking my head. Looking over at Mason's desk, I saw his computer was still on. I went and sat down to call Jackson back. I had too many unanswered questions. On the third ring, he picked up. When he saw it was me who had called, he raised a brow.

"What?"

"This Martial guy. Something doesn't add up about it to me. You mean to tell me this perfect killing monster is created, and everything you tried to do to fix him failed?"

Jackson sighed. "That wasn't all. The doctor that was on the project played us pretty much. He wanted to create this beast, and he did. I can send you all the files if you'd like to see for yourself. You're the Luna now. You deserve to know what goes on inside your pack. We banned any more trials, so you have nothing to worry about, but the files would answer a lot of your questions. When Mason found out about this doctor betraying him, he nearly killed him. Though, instead, Mason showed mercy and got him banned as a rogue. Little did we know he'd join the hunters. He's helping them, and I'm sure that's why they wanted Martial so bad."

"I want to see them for myself. Maybe if we can capture this doctor, we can help this man."

"Octavia, that's very kind of you to think, but he's no longer a man. When you see him in person during this final battle, you'll understand. He can't speak, he can't feel emotion, he only takes orders. He'll kill us all if we try. I'm sorry. Now, I've got to meet Grayson to try and narrow down their headquarters. I'll see you around, and I'll send over those files."

"Goodbye," I nearly whispered, my heart heavy.

That poor man. After the call ended, it wasn't long before the computer dinged, signaling Jackson had sent the files over. I opened the message, clicking the folder. I skimmed over a few documents, but my mind got the best of me when I saw a video file. Feeling uneasy, I clicked on it. Once it started playing, I couldn't contain the gasp that left me. It was Martial and the doctors. He looked normal, a serious look on his face as he talked with the doctors.

"Ok, Martial. Today is your very last treatment day. Are you ready?" the doctor questioned.

Martial nodded. "Completely. Let's do this." The doctor started reading off some potential side effects, but I knew those were all a lie now. That doctor knew exactly what he was creating.

"The serum has now been injected into the patient. Now we wait for it to travel through the bloodstream. Nurse, please monitor his vitals." He commanded, leaving the room.

I watched in horror as the nurse remained locked in the room. Covering my mouth at his sudden gasps for air, I almost had to turn it off when the screams started.

"Please! Something isn't..." He stopped talking, letting out a bone-chilling scream. "It hurts, please!"

His skin started to turn red before it quite literally started to burn off his body, leaving nothing but a black color underneath. "Shift! Shift now! It should stop." The doctor yelled, and Martial did, but he only managed a partial shift.

I jumped at the sudden roar that left him, tears brimming my eyes from his pain. How on earth could someone think this was ok? Martial fell to the ground, snarling as he scratched at his skin, more black showing through. The nurse screamed, banging on the door for them to let her out, but no one came to her aid. In a flash, Martial was up and charged at her.

I yelped, smashing my hand on the spacebar to pause the video. I didn't want to know what happened next. Though, looking at the paused screen, I bit my trembling lip. He indeed looked like a monster. There was no doubt that all his skin was gone by now, and he was completely charred black from the burns. Spots of fur were already breaking through in some spots.

I clicked off the video. It would fill my nightmares tonight. I started reading reports and more files on Martial. It was all pretty much what I already knew, but when I saw the most recent picture of him just months ago, I got chills. He looked like a demon mixed with a wolf and a human.

His skin was covered in black fur, while his eyes were near black and his nails and teeth were long and sharp. He was almost like a smaller version of a Lycan, just more terrifying... if that was even possible.

It felt like hours had passed as I kept reading and looking before Mason's office door opened. Mason's head peaked through, and he gave me a curious look as I sat behind his desk.

"What are you doing?"

I gulped, closing out of the files. "I... I had Jackson send me some more stuff on Martial. I thought maybe I could figure out a way to help him, but I think you're right. He might just be unsavable."

"Oh, Octavia." His eyes shut and he rested his head against the door. "I didn't want you seeing all that. It's too much."

"I see that now. That video..." His eyes snapped open at my comment, walking farther into the room and shut the door behind him.

"You watched it?!"

"Yes. I didn't know it would be... like that. Mason, what that doctor did to him was terrible." I croaked out.

He quickly made his way over to me and pulled me up from the chair, wrapping me in his embrace. "I'm sorry you had to see that. I could barely watch it myself after I was told what had happened. It's sickening. That's why I banished the doctor, but I seemed to have made the wrong choice." He rubbed soothing circles on my back, and I tightened my grip on his chest, resting my head against him.

"Do you think he can be saved? If we were to capture the doctor and redo what he did?"

"No. I tried that before I removed the doctor from the pack. Plus, he's so deformed now, I don't think there's any coming back from that."

I gave a subtle nod, wishing differently.

"Now, I know you had to shift into Lycan form, so how is your side?"

I lifted the side of my shirt, revealing the pink wounds. "Seemed to heal some more, so I guess that's good."

"It is. Your Lycan form probably helped speed up the process for a few. I don't know about you, but I'm exhausted."

"Me too, but I'm sweaty and need another shower." I yawned, more than ready to crawl into bed.

"No snarky remarks about letting me join you?" he teased, and one side of my lips lifted.

"I'm too tired to even try."

"Good, let's go shower then."

CHAPTER THIRTY-TWO

◆◇◆

Octavia

The next day was a busy one. Mason was hellbent on finding the mole, and I couldn't blame him. We were up early as Mason and Alaric questioned each prison guard that Martial was kept in. Well, he questioned the ones that Martial hadn't slaughtered. Each story was the same—*we don't know how they got in, but we didn't see anything out of the ordinary.*

Mason grew agitated every time, feeling more and more defeated as the hours flew by. Each guard that used their key card to get into that prison seemed to be telling the truth, and their story checked out.

"I'm starting to think that whoever this mole was, was a guard for sure. I just think that he was killed by the hunters that he helped or Martial himself. I mean, why would hunters leave any loose ends after pulling off such a huge stunt? It's the only logical thing at the moment, and until I find out otherwise, I have to focus back on the problem at hand, which is finding where they're stationed at." Mason suggested, and Alaric nodded in agreement.

"It would make sense. If that's true, though, I just wonder what the hunters offered him in return? What would make someone turn on their own kind… especially to help hunters." Alaric shuttered in disgust.

"Pull up the key card log again. See what cards were swiped around the time he was let out." Mason motioned to me, and I looked back at the computer, pulling the list back up.

"Two people. Arnold Osland and Richard Krater." Mason nodded.

"Both are dead," Alaric added. "That could very well be it."

"Or is someone trying to make us think that they were killed off? That would be the smarter play here." I mentioned, only adding to Mason's stress level as he let out an exaggerated groan, his head falling backward.

"Ok. Then who knew either man to get them alone and not alert them something was off? I mean, I trained these men myself. They know exactly what to look for. To leave their station or to hand over a keycard to the building, they would have to trust someone high up." Mason threw the idea out there. "It just doesn't make sense to me."

"The only high-up titles to have that kind of access or authority are you, Octavia, me, and Gamma Peter."

Mason shook his head. "Well, it obviously isn't Octavia or me, and you were with Ashlee."

"And Gamma Peter always has training days for our men on Thursday nights, so it wasn't him, but I can look into it to confirm?" Alaric asked.

"Just for safe measures, check where he was and check the men that were training that night to back his story up."

"Will do. Would you like me to go now?" he asked, and Mason nodded, waving him off.

After the door shut behind Alaric, Mason pinched the bridge of his nose. "I have a massive headache."

"Would you like me to get some medicine?" I offered.

"No, thank you. I'm just ready for all of this to be over."

"Me too." I closed the laptop, walking over to him as he opened his arms to me.

He pulled me onto his lap, wrapping his arms around my waist. "I promise when this is over, I'm taking you on a getaway." He confirmed, and I grinned, wrapping my arms around his neck.

I raised my eyebrows. "A getaway, huh? What do you have in mind?"

He smiled up at me. "Anything you want. A beach vacation, Italy, anything, I don't care. We desperately need it."

I leaned down, placing a soft kiss on his lips. "We really do. Wow, a week of no interruptions or drama. I'd love that."

He let out a playful growl, squeezing my hips. "Absolutely no interruptions. More us time than anything."

Letting out a small laugh, I leaned closer to him. "I like the sound of that."

"Mhm, me too." He closed the gap, giving me a hungry kiss.

My hands found their way into his hair, and he shifted me to where I was straddling him. As his tongue met mine, his chest rumbled in satisfaction. Lost in the moment, his mouth left mine, his teeth deliciously dragging down my neck to my mark. The minute his tongue swept over it, a gasp escaped me. Shocks trailed down my spine, a delicious shiver wracking over my body.

Grabbing a handful of his hair, I pulled his head back, my mouth smashing against his. Mocking his movements from before, I found my mouth against his own mark, a sound of approval ripping through him. I pulled back slightly, seeing his eyes blood red. Smirking, I removed myself from his lap. I stood as he watched me questionably. As I squatted to my knees, his eyes widened slightly.

"I could easily help that headache." I teased, and he ran his tongue over his bottom lip, a dark laugh leaving him.

"I swear if this is you about to show me some lesson from yesterday…" He trailed off, and I raised a brow, my hands resting against his thighs.

"Do you think that low of me, Alpha?" he gulped, and I almost wanted to laugh.

I was *so* going to show him a lesson. *Being hot and bothered is not fun.* But before I could make another move, the door to his office swung open, and Mason stood abruptly, a yelp leaving me as I fell backward and my head smacked against his desk.

One hand flew up, covering Mason's mouth as he tried not to laugh. I laid on the floor, groaning as I stared up at him. *I actually hate my life.*

Suddenly, Grayson's head appeared above me, a toothy grin on his face. "Well, well, well, what do we have here?"

Mason snickered, shoving him away and offered me a hand. Embarrassed and angered, I smacked it away. "You have terrible timing, Grayson!" I complained, getting myself up.

"Apparently, I have impeccable timing because if I had walked in any later, I would've had to have Jackson gouge my eyes out."

Once I was fully standing, I looked at an amused Jackson leaning against the doorframe to Mason's office. "Good evening, Octavia." He smirked.

"Shut up," I growled out, taking Mason's seat as I folded my arms like a five-year-old.

Instinctively, I rubbed the back of my head, causing another laugh to leave Grayson.

"Ok, leave my poor mate alone. What's up? What do you two need?" Mason mused, leaning against the side of his desk.

Jackson held up a piece of paper, a proud look on his face. "We found it."

Mason flew off the desk, walking over to snatch the paper from him. Looking it over, his eyes closed in relief. "Praise the Goddess. Are these the coordinates to their head base?"

"Yep. We came as soon as we found it. We literally roamed no man's land since the call last night. It was the last place we hadn't looked. It took hours, and Grayson may or may not have had to rough up some rogues, but that's where it is. I always thought it was near human territory, but it was right under our noses the whole time. It's an old building on no man's land that I thought to have been flooded with rogues, but I was wrong. I saw the hunters entering and leaving. And guess who I saw getting out of an SUV…"

"Who?"

"Megan herself. That's how I knew it was the main base. It's also why hunters have been getting into your territory so easily. They are literally stationed next to your border. They kill or severely injure your guards and roam right through. They obviously can't now since you've doubled your men, but it's time, Mason. We need to act fast before they try to move or find out that we know."

"Wait, what if it's a trap?" I asked, and Mason quickly shook his head.

"It's not. If Megan's there… That's their main base. It's where she's protected the most. Goddess, I can't wait to kill her."

"I was thinking about that, actually. When we capture her, I don't think she should be killed by your hands. I think she deserves a death far worse." Jackson grinned.

Grayson rubbed his hands together wickedly. "I loved this idea."

"And what's that?" asked Mason.

"Death by your secret execution weapons. The things that terrify any supernatural beings. The things that are currently residing in a pit deep within your pack." He pointed out. I glanced at Mason as a slow smirk crawled its way onto his face.

"Now that... *that* is a wonderful idea."

"I thought you would think so."

Mason turned to look at me. "Octavia, there's something I think you should know. I'm not the Alpha of War for just any old reason. I have some of the most powerful weapons at my disposal. I've had them for a long time, long before I was alpha. My father used to control them before he transitioned his power over to me. They were only used to execute the worst of the worst, and I believe Megan falls under that category..."

I grew nervous by the wicked faces of the men before me as I asked, "Well, what is it?"

"It's not an *it*." Jackson shot back. "It's a *them*."

"Hellhounds," Mason smirked. "I have four hellhounds in my execution chamber."

My jaw dropped, my eyes wide. "H-hellhounds?! I thought they were a myth!"

"Nope. They're quite real. When I became their alpha, it was a great day."

"Mason, if that's true and it's not a myth... you do realize they were originally created to kill Lycans and drag them to hell? At least, that's the stories people used to tell."

"I'm quite aware of the story, and it is a very true one. They were originally werewolves, but a witch cursed them into being a hellhound to drag Lycan souls to hell. The witch's family was killed by a Lycan, which sparked her revenge. The first alpha that was a half Lycan faced them. He showed them just who truly was their alpha, and it wasn't some witch. They have been loyal to the Alphas of War ever since." I gulped, not knowing if I should be proud or *terrified*.

CHAPTER THIRTY-THREE

———— ◆◇◆ ————

Octavia

There were so many new things that I learned when I entered this pack. I never knew what really went on in packs or what the alphas and lunas went through, but now I did, all too well. It was a lot to take in. When I lived in Alpha Ryker's pack, I always saw a corny and snarky side to him. I always thought that Alphas were just the face of a pack and lived a nice life without any worries. Clearly, I was wrong. There never seemed to be a peaceful time in their lives, from what I've gathered.

I wondered what the other alphas had kept secret from the outside world. What did they know that the normal, everyday wolf didn't? Ryker knows vampires, Mason has hellhounds, Christian's mate is a powerful witch who knows another powerful witch, so did Jackson have anything up his sleeve aside from his intelligence?

I shook the thoughts out of my head, staring out the window as rain poured down outside. I was still in Mason's office while they got the word out to the other alphas that it was time to take the final battle to the hunters. Mason immediately wanted everyone to head over to our pack to train for the next two days, and then we would attack. As far as I knew, our allies were on their way here the minute Mason sent word. I was nervous. We were going to lose good men and women to this battle.

For months, wolves had been going into war fronts in small numbers, but now it was all in. *We were all going.* One could only hope we all made it back alive.

The door creaked open, and I turned to see Alpha Jackson walk in. He ignored me, walking to Mason's desk, a map in his grasp. As he sat in Mason's chair, he squinted his eyes while smoothing out the map in front of him. I could tell he was trying to think of every possible outcome of our attack.

"Stop staring at me; it's weird." I heard him mutter, and I quickly looked away.

"What are you doing?" I questioned, looking back out the window.

"Work." I rolled my eyes, letting out an annoyed sigh from his bluntness. He was just like Mason when we first met.

"Are all alphas here?"

"Soon. Ryker and Christian are on their way. The new alphas Christian and Scarlett made are coming as well. Evan, Oliver, and Adrian will take a little longer to get here." He replied, going back to his work. Wow, the new alphas are coming here, too? That made me even more nervous.

"Where is Mason?" I asked yet another question, and Jackson groaned, covering his face.

"I came in here to think quietly away from the commotion. You are not helping the situation. He's at the training grounds." He looked back at the map as he grabbed a pen to write something down.

"In the rain?" With one last look at me, Jackson dropped his pen as he abruptly stood, grabbed the map, and walked out. *Well then.*

Looking back out the window, I knew I was nothing but useless, just sitting here worrying about the inevitable battle. Instead, I got up and headed off to find Mason. When I neared the training grounds, I saw him standing with his hands on his hips, the rain misting over him.

"Again!" Mason yelled. He surveyed their every move, shaking his head in disbelief as they did so. "You call that sparring?! You look pathetic!" he growled out.

Sighing, I walked up beside him, resting my hand on his shoulder. "Hey," I mumbled, looking at the field of wolves. The rain had let up some, but everyone was still soaked.

"You go for the neck!" he yelled, "You had the perfect opportunity, and you screwed it up!" The tone of his voice made me flinch.

"They need a break. You've been at this all morning." I tried to reason with him, but he shook his head to disagree.

"No. We need to practice. Megan could catch wind of our plan and attack any time. I need them prepared in case she comes for us first. " Running a hand through his hair, he let out a frustrated sound as he faced his wolves again. "Again!" I heard the small whimpers of protest, causing me to grit my teeth.

"Everyone, take ten!" I called out, and Mason quickly looked at me with a heated glare while everyone froze, not knowing what to do.

"Now!" I added with a more authoritative voice, and they scattered off.

"What the hell was that?" he snapped.

"Watch your tone." I snapped back and faced him. "You need a set of wolves going into battle ready—not tired. If you keep working them like this, you'll be lucky if they don't fall asleep on the field." I snapped, earning a growl to rumble within his chest. "I know this is a lot for you lately, and you can let all your anger out by killing as many deer and animals as you can. You can work your wolves to death, which will be a loss for you, but do *not* get smart with me." I challenged.

From the pressure building within my head, I knew Ramani was getting pissed from his disrespect. Telling her to stand down, I looked up at him with a raised brow watching as his eyes flashed red. Not liking the small threat, I let Ramani seep through just enough for my eyes to change to the same threatening color.

"Do you really want to do this here? I'm sure everyone would love a good fight." He snarled out. It was his Lycan talking, no doubt, but I wouldn't back down that easily. I am his equal and nothing less. Letting go of the reins, the pressure released.

"Try me." The voice didn't belong to me as Ramani emerged. Tilting our head to the side, she gave him a taunting smirk. "Equals, remember?"

"Now, girls, let's not do this here." I heard and turned to see Alpha Ryker, a small smirk on his face. He stood in front of a group of people, and by their smell, I knew they were vampires. I saw Grayson towards the back, and he shot me a knowing grin. I remembered Mason and Grayson telling me about their crew. They were the McKinley Crew.

Mason's eyes flashed to his normal brown ones, finally calming down. "I thought you got Dante on board?" Mason narrowed his eyes.

I knew the vampires were joining us, but the vampire king himself was coming? That was a terrifying thought.

Ryker smirked. "Trust me, I did. He'll be here for the big fight. They don't need practice. Grayson and these guys here are to help your wolves prepare for the vamps that will be on the field tomorrow." Mason nodded, seeming to like the idea.

I looked over to the group standing behind Ryker. They were beautiful, and it looked as if they didn't have one flaw to them. There were nine of them. Four men and five women. Giving them a small wave, I started to introduce myself.

"It's nice to meet you all. I'm Octavia, Mason's mate." I spoke. I couldn't help but notice the girls glance at one girl in particular who looked down at the comment.

"It's nice to meet you, Octavia." Grayson mused, causing me to roll my eyes.

"To be serious," A man spoke, shooting a glare at Grayson. "It is an honor." He smiled, "I'm Jared. This is Raven, Ashlynn, Vivian, Lachlan, Grayson, as you know, Julian, and Jax." he motioned to each of them, who each gave a small wave.

The girl, who seemed affected by my introduction as Mason's mate earlier, now had a name. Vivian. Who was she?

Though there was a wolf scent among the group, and Jared didn't state her name. I locked eyes with one girl with long, brown hair. She gave me a knowing look, taking a step forward.

"I'm not a vampire." She grinned, confirming my suspicion. "Strong nose you got there," She added.

I shrugged. "It's useful when needed."

Ryker walked over to her, placing his arm around her waist. "Everyone, this is Madeline... my mate," Ryker stated. I blinked. Once. Twice. Then I couldn't help but burst out laughing. Everyone gave me a confused look, and I covered my mouth, embarrassed.

"What?" Ryker's eyes narrowed.

"You have a mate?" I managed to get out. His expression went from amused to serious.

"Har har." He scoffed, waving me off.

Grayson and Mason snickered at my comment. I grinned at Grayson, trying to hold back my laughter as he gave me a subtle thumbs up. Who would have thought the playboy himself would get a mate?!

"Let's get started, shall we?" Ryker asked, rolling his eyes.

"It's nice to meet you," I said to Madeline as she watched everyone get ready to practice.

"Likewise. You seem to have some funny comments."

"Well, I never thought Ryker would get a mate, honestly. Good for him, though." I said, and she scoffed.

"He's a sarcastic bastard. Sometimes I'd like to punch his face in, but sometimes I could kiss the hell out of him. There is no in-between. I guess the Goddess saw me as the only one fitting enough to tame the beast." She snorted, and I looked at her, amused.

"I can relate to you on a spiritual level. We're going to be great friends." I joked, causing her to let out a small laugh.

"I hope so. I need some Luna friends, but sadly I need to go practice." She frowned.

"Me too. Don't have too much fun out there."

"Oh, trust me, I won't." She plastered a fake smile on her face, causing me to bite my lip to hold back another laugh. We walked back over to where everyone gathered to see who was sparring with who.

"So, Mason, who are you sparring with?" Ryker asked.

"Octavia," Mason stated, pulling his shirt over his head.

"What?" Ryker asked, quite confused.

"I'm sure you've all heard the news about our other sides. Now, you get to see it in person." Mason smirked and walked to where I stood but kept a distance of a few feet. "You ready?" I nodded.

"As I'll ever be. Be ready to get your ass handed to you." I replied, and the guys howled in surprise, covering their mouths.

"Jackson! Would you like to do the honor of giving our other side a grand entrance?" Mason yelled, and I looked at Jackson, who sat under a tree a few feet away. Is he even going to practice? I wonder if he could even fight. He had the physical build for it. I've just never once seen him lose control—not even an eye color change to his wolf's.

The Greek words rolled off Jackson's tongue effortlessly. Not once did he look up from his papers as our shifts ripped through us. It was easy to shift into our Lycan forms without Greek words now but doing it this way made it seem so much more badass. *I guess Mason is just as extra as me sometimes.* When our shifts were complete, I stared down at the people around me. They gawked at us, clearly not expecting us to look the way we did.

"Well, I'll be damned," Ryker mumbled.

CHAPTER THIRTY-FOUR

$\blacklozenge\!-\!\lozenge\!-\!\blacklozenge$

Octavia

A grunt left us as Orion threw us aside, letting out a taunting snarl as he did so. Ramani rolled over in a flash to dodge his quick kick. Making her way to her feet, she ducked to miss a swing of his and spun on her heels, a punch going right to the center of Orion's back. He grunted, tripping forward from the impact. Ramani huffed, kicking her leg out to swipe his legs out from under him. Satisfied when she saw him crash into the ground, she leaped for him. Though, he was quick with his movements and caught her by the throat, tossing her aside once again.

The others watched in awe as we battled back and forth. It seemed always to be one step forward and two steps back as we fought each other. There was no winning unless we gave them full control, which was a dangerous move. As they circled each other once more, Ramani grew bored with the pointless sparring. She was itching for a real fight but knew Orion would not give her the satisfaction of one.

"Can we end this already? This is quite boring. I think we'll do perfectly fine on the field. That is unless you would like to *really* fight." She mind-linked him.

Orion relaxed, giving her a sharp nod. I could tell he was growing bored with this whole sparring thing too. I almost wanted to spar in wolf form, but considering we were using our Lycans on the field, it was pointless to do so. She walked away, grabbing a spare set of clothes off a nearby bench and moved out of eyesight so I could change properly after the shift.

Though, with how calm Ramani has been lately, as well as Orion, it was odd to me. They were too quiet, in my opinion. It was like they were saving everything they could for the big battle.

After I was fully changed, I walked back out with a small grin on my face. "So, Ryker... want to spar?"

He raised a brow, amused. "In wolf form, sure. You know... to make it fair and all."

"Where's the fun in that?" I taunted, and his eyes narrowed.

"Are you secretly out to kill me?" I shrugged a shoulder in response as Mason walked up to us.

At that, he took a wary step closer to Mason. "Your mate is crazy," He whispered, causing Mason to belch out a laugh.

"That she is."

The others snickered as my eyes drifted to Alpha Jackson, who remained in the same spot as before. With a pen in his mouth, he stared down at a map with narrowed eyes.

"Does he ever fight with you all?"

"He's a very controlled man, but don't let that fool you. He's too smart for his own good, and that makes him more dangerous than you could imagine." Ryker replied, and Mason nodded in agreement.

"I'm going to go get some water. Anyone want some?" Mason asked, and we shook our heads no as he walked off. The others got into smaller groups, starting their own sparring matches. Ryker remained beside me, watching his mate spar with Grayson, a proud smile on his face.

"You know, as much as I like to tease you, I'm happy you found your mate. It's a blessing." I spoke, grabbing his attention.

"Indeed, it is. When I first met her, I didn't know if I'd be able to do it. She is... something else—someone I'm not used to being with."

"You mean someone that doesn't let you get your way all the time?" I teased.

He pursed his lips. "Yep, pretty much."

Chuckling, I looked over at Mason, who was now talking to Vivian. He didn't look happy, and neither did she. I could listen in on their conversation, but I didn't want to make Mason upset. Looking back at Ryker, I nodded my head towards them.

"What's the deal with them? She's been off ever since she got here. I'm not getting a good vibe."

"Vivian is a nice person, I promise. She's also with Jax, so you have nothing to worry about if that's what you're getting at. As for why they seem to hate each other, it's not for me to tell, and as much as I love pissing Mason off, I'd rather not die." He explained, causing me to scoff.

"That makes me even more curious."

"Just ask him about her." Was his response as he walked off towards the alpha under the tree.

"Jackson!" He called out. I held back a laugh as Jackson let out an annoyed sigh, lifting his eyes to him.

"For Goddess' sake, what?"

"Are you sparring with Mason or Christian when he gets here?" My eyes widened as Jackson stood to his feet. Oh, my Goddess, am I actually going to see him fight today?

"I guess I will spar with Mason considering I need to get back to my papers." He replied, shrugging off his flannel. I couldn't help but notice how all the girls turned their heads to look at him when he reached to pull his shirt over his head. I have to admit; he had a nice body. Battle scars were scattered across his chest and back, which showed he had been in countless fights. I guess he was a fighter, after all.

"Mason! Come on," He motioned, pulling Mason from his conversation with Vivian. He looked more than pleased to be dragged away from her.

"Start in human form?" Jackson asked, and Mason nodded, a smirk crawling onto his face.

Mason took a swing for Jackson, but he easily maneuvered around it. I watched as Jackson watched Mason's movements, and my jaw dropped slightly. Each time Mason swung, Jackson ducked. Jackson easily studied Mason, getting an idea of his slight triggers to signal his next move. *He isn't the Alpha of Intelligence for nothing.*

"You see..." Jackson spoke up as he dodged another hit. "If you would throw your arm a little to the left more, you'd actually hit me." Jackson mused, and as soon as the words left his mouth, Mason's arm swung out, his fist making contact with Jackson's jaw.

"Like that?" Mason asked, smirking as Ryker and I let out a small laugh.

"I see what you're doing," Jackson growled out, ramming his fist into Mason's nose. "You want him, you got him." I watched in shock as his eye color shifted his wolf's blue, and my mouth dropped fully.

He moved quickly and effortlessly around Mason. They both got a few good hits in before I saw Jackson deliver a swift kick to the right side of Mason's chest. The impact sent him flying backward, but he shifted midair before he hit the ground, landing on all fours.

His wolf was as beautiful as the last time I saw it. His midnight-black wolf stood tall as authority swarmed him. Mason's two front paws raised, slamming back into the ground one by one as he let out a snarl getting into an attack position.

Jackson grinned, a devilish look in his eyes, and took a couple of steps back. My eyes nearly left my head as Mason charged at him, but Jackson ran at him, still in human form. Right before Mason reached him, Jackson jumped, shifting and tackled Mason swiftly. It was hard to tell the two apart considering they were both around the same size, but Jackson's fur was a dark brown instead of black. Without the sun out, it was hard to tell.

Their snarls grew louder, and I saw Ryker sigh, shaking his head. "This is why we don't let them spar; they'll kill each other." Ryker shrugged the jacket to his suit off and tossed it to the side, and walked out of view behind a tree. Before I knew it, a tanned wolf was darting at the two.

He tackled Jackson before he charged back at Mason. Regaining his ground, Ryker stood in-between the two snarling. After a minute, they backed away. I learned one thing from today: Don't screw around with Jackson because he'll hand you your ass.

As the three separated, heading to change, I looked back at the field of other wolves and vampires fighting. The vampires were helping some wolves learn to withstand a vampire attack, which I appreciated. Vampires are deadly to wolves if they get their hold on them. My attention shifted back to the three wolves who were no longer in sight. Soon they walked back out dressed. I couldn't help but listen in on their conversation.

"Screw off," Mason said to Ryker, who was laughing. Jackson, for once, looked amused by the whole situation.

"Hm, just like you said to Vivian." Jackson joked, and my brows furrowed as Mason rolled his eyes.

"She's dead to me. Quite literally." Mason replied as the two other males chuckled, leaving his side.

Brows furrowed, I walked over to Jackson as he took his spot beneath the one tree. If there was one person who would give me the answers I needed without any care in the world, it was him.

"So, how has your day been?" I shifted from one foot to the other awkwardly. Not the best way to start a conversation with the man, but it'll have to do. Jackson sighed, sitting papers back onto his lap.

"Besides being surrounded by stupid people all day... It's great." He answered, a smug look on his face.

"I see. So, what are you—"

"What do you want, Octavia? Ask away." He cut me off, looking back up at me with annoyed eyes.

I bit my lip then decided just to rip the band-aid off. "What do you know about Vivian? Who is she to Mason?"

There was no hesitancy as he said, "Vivian was Mason's first mate." He tossed some papers to the side. "She left him a few years back to join the McKinleys."

And just like that, I felt like my whole world had been shattered.

CHAPTER THIRTY-FIVE

─◆◇◆─

Octavia

My hands shook as I angrily left Jackson. I didn't know what to think. Did I have the right to be mad at Mason? It was before we met, but the fact he never bothered to tell me he had another mate made me sick to my stomach. What else hasn't he told me? For Goddess' sake, she's a freaking vampire! Was she one when they met? I paused, my eyes moving to look at Vivian. She laughed as she and Grayson messed around, teasing one another. She looked like the definition of perfect. My wolf whimpered at the thought; we were the second choice.

Turning, I shook my head, walking toward the house. I needed to think—maybe kick something, I didn't know. Before I reached the back door, I heard Mason call out to me.

"Babe! Where are you going? We still have to practice!" he ran up to me, a confused look on his face.

"Not now, Mason." I grabbed the door handle, pulling it open, but his hand shot out, closing it again.

"What's wrong?"

"What's wrong? Why don't you go ask Vivian." I snarled out, and he immediately looked at me with realization.

"Who told you?" his chest rumbled with a growl.

"It doesn't matter. Just... forget about it. We'll talk about it later." I murmured, trying to pull on the door once more, but he stopped me from doing so yet again.

"Yes, it does. *Who told you?*" I furiously turned to face him, knowing my eyes were shining a bright red.

"What? Are you upset because someone else did your job before you could? Don't worry. I feel the same way." With that, I shoved his hand away from the door and made my way inside.

As I made my way down the hall, I didn't know where I was going or what I was going to do. I just knew that I needed to get away from him before I punched him in the face. Turning a corner, I bumped into someone.

"Why, hello there." Braelyn smiled, but her smile quickly faltered once she noticed my state. "What's wrong?"

"I just found out about Vivian."

Her jaw dropped slightly. "Oh... Mason told you?"

"That's the thing... he didn't. Jackson told me."

"I see..." She awkwardly looked away. "What did he tell you exactly?"

"Just that she was his first mate." I sighed, running a hand through my hair. "So, you know as well?"

"Well, Octavia, I'm his sister. I lived through it as well. Though, you should get the full story first. She was his choice mate, not his real mate. His real mate is you and only you."

Confusion sat in. "So, he marked and mated her as a choice. There was no original mate bond?"

"No. It's a long story, and it happened not too long after our parents and brother died. That's why you should probably talk to him about it. He was going through a lot, and I think he saw it as something to numb his pain, to fill that void in his chest. Though, obviously, it didn't work out."

Did that make me feel slightly better? Yes. Did having to find out about it from someone else? No. Braelyn reached out and pulled me into a hug.

"I'm sorry you had to find out from someone else, but don't let this make you think any less of him. You're his whole world, and I'm sure he didn't think he'd have to see her again. I'm not excusing his actions of not telling you. I'm just saying that it is a very touchy subject for him. I'm sure he was going to tell you when he thought the time was right." She pulled back, patting my cheek with an amused smile. "Give him hell, though. He deserves it for not telling you the moment he knew she was coming."

I couldn't help but let out a small laugh. "Don't worry. I'm planning my argument as we speak." I teased.

"Everyone meet in my office. Christian and Scarlett are here." Mason's mind-link ran through my mind.

Noticing my glossed-over eyes, Braelyn raised a brow. "Duties await you?"

I nodded. "Christian and Scarlett are here. I guess we're having a quick meeting."

"Well, have fun. Don't stress too much, ok? It'll all work out. I promise." She finished, brushing past me. I watched her retreating figure feeling a little better. I'm glad I have her in my life.

It wasn't long before we were all filing into Mason's office. I took a seat on a couch as everyone stood around, waiting for Mason to speak. The room was filled with tension, and I couldn't help but feel claustrophobic amongst all the people in here. The McKinleys stuck to one side of the room near Ryker and Madeline. Mason and Jackson were leaning against Mason's desk, and Christian and Scarlett were standing near the door. Alaric was casually leaned up against a far wall.

"As you all know, we have found the spot where their main headquarters are. Jackson and Grayson saw Megan entering the place on no man's land. To be certain, we sent one man to confirm it." Mason spoke, looking over to Ryker.

"Dante has entered the states." Ryker declared, and I could see everyone tense up at his name. "Dante is a man of many gifts, and staying unseen is one of them. He surveyed the premises and agreed with us. It's where we need to attack."

"And where is Dante now?" Christian asked, folding his arms, a look of distaste on his face.

"Dante will come when needed. We can promise you that. He doesn't like the whole... planning thing. He just does." One of the McKinleys spoke up. Jared, I believe.

"How comforting," Scarlett mumbled.

"So, what is our exact plan of attack? Surprise?" I asked, and Jackson nodded.

"Yes. We'll enter from the east side. Any other way will be seen easily. The east side is guarded more by forest. According to Dante," Jackson walked over to a map that was taped to a board. "They have snipers sitting here, here, and here high up in the trees." He pointed to three red circles. "McKinleys, you'll take them out first. From there, Mason and

Octavia will shift to Lycan form. We hoped to have our own snipers to take down Martial, but we won't have time. It's up to Mason and Octavia to deal with him. All other alphas will follow behind the Lycans and then our pack armies." Jackson completed.

"Where are my new alphas?" Christian asked.

"Alpha Oliver is here. He is doing some quick training since he got here late. Alpha Adrian is coming from farther away, so he'll be here by tonight. Evan is supposed to be arriving anytime. Though, he's not one to ever be on time." Mason mused.

"Will Alara be with Evan?" Ryker asked Scarlett, and she nodded.

"She will be taking my spot since I won't be able to fight." She clarified, placing a hand on her belly.

"And she'll listen to you? Doesn't she hate Christian?" Ryker questioned.

"I'm her leader, so she will do as I say. I know most of you only know bits and pieces of my alliance with her, but that is one of them. You can trust her." She answered, and Christian nodded in agreement.

"You? Their leader?" Ryker snorted, letting out a laugh. "I never saw that coming." Scarlett squinted her eyes, quickly waving her hand, foreign words leaving her mouth as she did so. Ryker dropped to the floor, knocked out cold.

Jackson jumped away from Ryker's unconscious body. "What the hell?"

"I just put him asleep for a few minutes. He just doesn't know when to shut up." She grumbled.

"That was gold." I snickered, and she laughed, shooting me a wink.

"I'm rethinking having you all on the field," Jackson muttered while still looking at Ryker. "So childish sometimes."

"Don't worry. I actually tolerate you. Plus, I won't be there." Scarlett grinned at Jackson, who looked at her skeptically.

"I can't say the same for all of you." He shrugged, moving to sit behind Mason's desk.

"Dude, you're in my chair." Mason raised a brow, to which Jackson looked at him like he was dumb.

"And?"

I smothered my laugh just thinking about how easily we get off task with our bickering. Abruptly, the office door swung open, and by the authority and power that filled the room, we all knew who it was.

"You asked me to come. I'm here, so what's the plan?" a deep voice asked. I turned, eager to see him in the flesh. With the stories I've heard, you would never think he was the one behind them. Alpha Evan, the alpha of The Malevolent pack, stood smugly. He had on a black leather jacket with a white t-shirt underneath and a simple pair of jeans. He has a casual look to him, but that wasn't fooling anyone.

I watched as he looked over to Ryker's unconscious body on the floor, and he smirked, giving a knowing look to Scarlett. "You're doing, I assume?"

She shrugged. "Someone had to shut him up."

Mason was quick to fill Evan in on everything, and Evan took in the information carefully. It was odd to see him go from smug and carefree to alpha mode so easily.

"That seems easy enough. No rules for me? I can do as I please during this battle?" Evan asked.

The alphas all shared wary looks. "To our enemies, yes, but this is your only time you are granted it," Christian replied, a cold tone to his voice.

"Christian, you lost your trust in me, I get it, but I promised no more black magic. What controlled Alara and me is no longer within us. We're different now. Our bad years are behind us, and I hope everyone can come to that conclusion. I'm here to help. The old me could kill everyone in here within a blink of an eye and not give two shits after, but here I stand in the same place—unbothered and harmless. That's no longer me, and I gave you my word. I don't break that. Ever." Evan said, addressing everyone's concerns.

I heard a groan and turned to look at a now waking Ryker. "Scarlett you bi-" He stopped when his eyes landed on Alpha Evan. "You've got to be shitting me." He groaned, and Evan smirked.

"Miss me?"

Ryker scoffed. "Hardly." He stood to his feet and shot a glare at Scarlett, who gave him a teasing wave.

Mason pushed himself off his desk. "I'll inform Alpha Oliver and Adrian later. Evan, where is Alara?"

"She'll be here for the fight. Doing all this makes her a little uneasy. She stayed back to prepare herself and her mental state. You have to think, using her magic after all these years against something so big is nerve-wracking. Using small spells here and there isn't a big deal to her, but going into *war*… It makes her nervous."

"That's understandable," Scarlett mumbled, placing her hand on his forearm in a comforting way, earning a small smile from him.

"Ok then. Everyone, get ready. Soon we're off to battle. We will strike tomorrow night." Mason stated, clapping his hands together.

I hung back, letting everyone leave the room. Mason shut the door behind them, turning to face me with a serious look. "Can we talk?"

I pressed my lips together and nodded. "Yeah. I think we need to."

"What do you want to know?" he asked, sitting next to me on the couch.

"Everything. Start from the very beginning."

"Well, Vivian wasn't my actual mate. She was my choice mate. A stupid decision I made as a new alpha and teenager. She was actually a human when we met. One of my wolves was on a run one night. She was driving, and he ran out in front of her. Her car flipped, and it was so bad she could have died." He grimaced, reliving the memories in his head. "I couldn't have her death on my hands after just losing my parents and my brother."

I reached out, taking one of his hands in mine. "We don't have to do this today, Mason. I know I was mad earlier, but I was just in shock. I know a lot is going on, and I'm not trying to remake you live all this before we go into battle. I didn't know this was around the time your parents passed."

He shook his head. "No. You deserve to know."

"Ok. Only if you want to."

"After we found her, I took her back to the pack house. I got her fixed up with medicine humans hadn't even got their hands on yet. It was medicine that did wonders for wolves but was unimaginable for humans. When she woke, she figured out she was in my pack—something most humans don't ever get to witness. After we just got close. I let her stay as long as she needed, and it turned into something more between us. She wanted me to mark her, and I was young and reckless, so I did. Though, she never became Luna. Shortly after her marking, we found out she had cancer."

Guilt flooded through me. "I'm sorry you had to go through that."

He shrugged. "It's what happens when you start a relationship with a human. Humans get diseases. They're not like us wolves. I should have known, honestly. She didn't want to die, and I hated seeing her in so much pain. So, we agreed to do something… I despised." He spat it out with so much distaste I could tell it still bothered him.

"She wanted to be turned into a vampire," I mumbled.

"I hated the thought of it, but I couldn't let her die. I couldn't let her die in my arms, knowing there was a way I could save her, so I called Grayson for help. I had a witch sever our link in the bond, and then Grayson got everything set up, and she was turned. Dante added another McKinley to his crew. When she arrived here today, it was the first time I saw her since she changed. You have to believe me when I say that I never thought I'd find my mate. Now you know why I first said that everyone that gets close to me dies. I felt like I was always losing someone. Until you. You pulled me from my darkness—you were my light." He reached out, placing a hand against my cheek.

"I'm so sorry, Mason."

"You have nothing, and I mean *nothing* to apologize for. I kept saying we'd stop keeping secrets and be honest with one another, and I was lying straight through my teeth. It is me who should be apologizing. I love you and *only* you. You have to believe me." He pleaded.

"I believe you, Mason. I never thought you didn't. I was just upset you kept something so big from me. I should have handled myself better earlier. I didn't know the full story." I sighed, leaning into his touch.

He leaned in, pressing a soft kiss to my lips. My eyes fluttered shut, completely content with the man before me. We all have our pasts. Who am I to judge? Mason pulled back, the corner of his lips lifting up.

He went to speak, but his office door flew open. Alpha Jackson burst into the room, breathing heavily.

"We have to go, now!" he yelled, motioning for us to get up.

"What?! Why?" Mason snapped into alpha mode, rising to his feet.

"Because Ryker sent two of the McKinleys out to keep an eye on the hunters. Mason, they're loading up. They know we're onto them. It's now or never."

Mason looked at me, and I nodded, my heart racing.

It was time.

CHAPTER THIRTY-SIX

◆◇◆

Octavia

Nauseous. Terrified. Confused. I didn't know what my body was trying to tell me I felt as we dashed through the forest. Our armies snarled in anticipation as we ran towards no man's land. Thoughts flooded my mind of who our mole was. That was the obvious reason the hunters knew we were on to them. Was it an Alpha? Beta? Who could it be? Our circle was already small enough. I didn't know who to trust.

I gulped, fearing what was to come once we crossed onto their land. Ramani was silent, and that scared me more than one realized. A silent Lycan is a dangerous one. I prayed to the Goddess she'd keep us all safe, but I knew that we would be losing people tonight.

"Get ready! We're nearing their location!" Christian mind-linked everyone, even those not in his pack—perks of being the king.

Our paws hit the ground harder as we forced our wolves beyond their limits. They were ready for blood. Being in wolf form was odd, but our

Lycans wouldn't emerge until the real battle begins. We crossed over a hill but skidded to a stop once we saw lines of hunters armed and ready.

"The mole told them we were coming. They are beyond prepared. They were never leaving." Mason snarled.

"I'm tired of this damn rat!" Christian snarled back.

We looked around, waiting for anything from the hunters, but they remained still. I prayed the vampires would make their appearance soon. They are our element of surprise, after all. Without them, we're doomed.

"Hello, Mason!" A voice called out. A tall man walked out in front of the hunters, a shotgun in his hands.

Mason took a step forward, a threatening growl ripping through his wolf.

The man laughed in response, shaking his head. "You wolves think you can take on us hunters and our vampires? You're clearly delusional. Do us a favor and just wave the white flag already. You're outnumbered and weaker than we are. Our bullets will kill you, and our vampires will slaughter you." He threatened as many people suddenly appeared beside him, pale-skinned. His vampires took a protective stance on either side of him, giving us a taunting smirk.

Mason glanced back at me, and I shook my head. He needed to wait. He couldn't attack until our own vampires showed.

"Nothing to say? How about you stop being a coward and shift back and talk to me like a man, Mason." He snapped, but right as the words left his mouth, bodies fell from the trees, their heads rolling away from them and their guns falling beside them. *Their snipers were dead.* The man staggered back, a worried look creeping onto his face.

Figures dropped to the ground from the trees, and I almost cried in relief as Ryker's vampires walked into sight, fresh blood dripping from their mouths.

"You see... they're not alone." Grayson stated, and Christian shifted back to his human form, a devilish look on his face.

"You're going to wish you never started this." He snapped, his eyes shining a bright gold.

"So what? You think we're scared of a couple of vampires? We have over fifty compared to what... eight?" The man asked.

"Make that eight... nine." A thick accented voice called out. We looked over to see a man walking from the shadows. He was tall with dark, black hair. His eyes shined a golden color of his own, a scowl plastered on his face.

King Dante.

"You see... some of my own people left me to help *you?*" Dante called out, a brow raised. The vampires next to the hunters noticeably gulped at the sight of their king. "And speaking as I'm more fearful than some pathetic old hunters, *that was a low blow.*" He added as his eyes darkened.

"Dante..." One of his rival vamps began to speak, but Dante dashed to a tree before anymore words were spoken. He grabbed a limb and ripped it off, throwing it with such great force it effortlessly glided across the field and into the heart of the hunter that had been speaking to us.

When the man fell to the ground, Dante raised his arms. "Let the games begin." He mused, and the hunters quickly raised their guns. Though they didn't fire. Instead, a ferocious roar was heard. A beast-like creature emerged from the crowd, roaring once more as his sight locked on us. My body started to shake as Ramani became aware of who he was. *It was Martial.*

Ramani forcefully took control, making me shift from my wolf to her Lycan form. When we were many feet taller, she threw her arms to the side as her claws extended and let out a roar just as powerful. It wasn't long before Mason's Lycan took over, and he did the same, walking beside us.

With one last glance at one another, we charged toward Martial. With that, the other alphas took off after us, signaling our army to do the same. Thunder rumbled above us as the winds picked up, and I wanted to shout with relief as Alara ran into view.

The hunter's vampires immediately charged for Mason and me, trying to take us down first before we did the most damage. They met us, grabbing onto us, trying to hold us back as we snarled. Ramani kicked and punched her way through them the best she could, but they were overpowering us by their numbers. They couldn't kill us, but they could definitely slow us down.

Ramani growled, grabbing hold of one with her one free arm and crushed the vampire's neck, tossing him aside. She looked over at Orion, who finally got a free arm, and he threw it toward her. She grabbed it, letting him use his strength to jerk her free. We flew towards him out of the vampire's grasp, and she spun on her heels, jabbing both arms out. Each arm crushed through the chests of two vampires, and she ripped their hearts out, roaring. She grabbed two more vampires holding Orion back and threw them aside.

Though, it didn't slow more vampires from coming at us. She got ready for another attack as one charged at her but halted as a figure darted in front of her. Dante caught the vampire by the neck and easily decapitated him. He spun, sprinting toward the others. Ramani turned, locking her eyes on Martial, who was tearing a wolf apart. My heart clenched at the sight. Her eyes didn't leave him as she pushed forward, ready to end him.

"Ramani, what if he could be saved?!" I cried out to her.

"Did you see what he did to that poor wolf?! He is beyond saving!" she snarled back through our link, throwing a hunter aside that got in her path toward him.

"You can at least try!" I screamed. **"What if that was you?! Wouldn't you want at least someone to fight for you?"**

She continued her killing spree, destroying anything that got in her way. **"You're trying to save a murderer."**

"And what are you doing, Ramani? He's fighting for the side that saved him, just like you are." I replied, and she went silent.

Soon, there was no one between them. Orion was still a few feet back, trying to catch up with us. Martial locked eyes with her, and it was like time slowed. She sniffed the air, confusion washing over her.

"He has Lycan DNA. I can sense it. They put Lycan DNA in him." She mumbled, a slight tinge of fear filling her for once.

"Which means he could kill us," I whispered.

"Octavia, I will try my best, but if he tries to hurt us. I *will* kill him." With that, she took off.

She dodged a hit from him, trying to put her arms out in front of her to signal she meant no harm, but he ignored her, leaping for her once more. She moved swiftly again, growing agitated. Repeating her motions from before, she tried to signal to him once more. He froze as if he realized what she was trying to do. Gulping, she took a step forward and shook her head, motioning between the two of them. Tilting his head to the side some, he seemed just as confused as she felt. She didn't know how to communicate with him without a link.

Suddenly she balled her fist up, bringing it to her chest and rubbed it in a clockwise motion. It was an easy sign many people knew. *I'm sorry.*

Martial's head dropped as if he was hurt and actually understood her. She relaxed some, walking closer. Placing a hand on his shoulder, his head snapped up. She looked at his eyes but soon realized they held no hurt as a wicked look crawled onto his face. Her heart jumped in her chest as she tried to move backward, but he already grabbed hold of her. His claws ripped out, slicing into our stomach before he dug deeper, looking at us with evil eyes.

She yelped, grabbing her stomach as blood spewed when he ripped his claws out. He raised his claws once more to deliver the final blow, but a flash of black appeared beside him. Orion's hand ripped through Martial's chest, and out came his heart.

Orion angrily threw Martial's heart to the side as he crumbled to the ground. **"How stupid could you be?!"** Orion snarled to Ramani.

"We thought we could help him, but he fooled us."

Orion looked around, making sure no one was coming toward us as he extended his hand, helping her to her feet. **"Well, it was a stupid thought. Can you fight?"**

"I'll manage." She huffed, still holding her stomach.

His eyes softened, and he saw the blood spewing around her hand. **"You need to get out of here. You're hurt."**

"I'll be fine. I'm already healing." She lied. **"Just go! We're standing around like idiots."** She growled. With one final sigh, Orion took off.

With the strength she could manage, she charged for a nearby hunter. Looking through her eyes, I saw Alpha Jackson rip a vampire's head from its body. Jackson looked up to see Alpha Ryker being held down by two vampires. Jackson snarled and took off. He grabbed hold of one, latching his jaws onto its shoulder. Ryker maneuvered and turned, killing the other swiftly. They nodded to one another and took off for their next target.

I felt a shot enter my Lycan's thigh, and she looked down at it with a growl. She dug into her thigh and pulled the bullet out. Looking up, Ramani locked eyes with the man who fired it. With a great force, she threw it back, watching as it spun through the air and entered right between the hunter's eyes.

Ramani seemed to be communicating with Orion from across the field, and before I knew it, they were running towards each other just as Alara ran towards them as well.

Right as they met, Alara met them too. Both grabbed hold of her and threw her incredibly high, and then backed away. I watched in amazement as Alara came down, slamming her fist onto the ground. The ground rumbled beneath us, and I watched as vines shot up from the ground, wrapping around the hunters and left-over vampires.

"Now!" She yelled to The McKinleys, who took off, killing them with glee in their eyes. Our army wolves went around, taking down hunters easily now that their vampires were done for.

We turned, looking toward the building that we finally were nearing. Megan was in there somewhere. *I couldn't wait for Mason to end her.* New hunters ran out of the building just as the alphas met up with our Lycans as we ran to meet the pathetic humans.

"We have to get into that building now!" Christian's voice drifted through all of our heads.

"What's wrong?" Ramani asked.

"Jackson can smell his mate in there. We have to save her before they kill her! He just mind-linked me."

Our Lycans glanced over at Jackson, who let out a whimper at the thought. Determination suddenly filled Ramani.

"We got this. We can get him there."

"The McKinley's will finish the rest off. Dante will make sure of it. Let's go." Ryker replied.

"We'll clear a path. Alphas follow behind." Orion ordered.

We all fought to the best of our abilities, killing left and right. We will not let another wolf die because of these hunters. Especially not a potential Luna. The number of hunters quickly limited, and Ramani went to take another step forward but stumbled, her vision going blurry.

"Ramani? Are you ok?" Orion asked, turning to face her.

"I'm fine. The rest of the hunters are inside. Go. I'll be ok." She replied, waving them off.

Orion looked as if he didn't want to leave, but he had to go with them as the alphas ran into the building.

Ramani looked down at her stomach as blood continued to gush out of it. She fell to one knee as she became dizzy, and the wound started to burn.

"Ramani, what's happening?"

"I... I don't know. I've never felt this way before." She spoke softly, her voice quivering.

"Ramani, I'm so sorry!" I cried out.

This was all my fault!

She let out a small laugh. **"It's ok, kid. You did the right thing. At least you tried to save him. There are not many people like you left."**

"I really thought we could. I... I didn't think this would happen."

"Don't fret it. Thank you, Octavia. Thank you for showing me a new side to life. A good one... a happier one." She let out a breath of air, falling backward. **"We did good, kid."**

"Ramani?" I called out, but slowly I felt my body shifting.

I felt empty—numb even.

Seconds later, I was in human form, staring at the sky above me. *I couldn't feel her.* A crying scream left me. My fists smacked the ground next to me as I angrily gasped for air, my heart clenching in my chest. *It was all my fault.*

"No, no, *no*! Please, Goddess, bring her back!" I screamed.

I looked around worriedly, seeing our vampires killing in the distance.

"Help! Someone plea—" I couldn't get my words out as I started coughing. I felt something come up my throat, and I coughed once more, watching red splatters of blood fly from my mouth.

I heard shouting in the distance. Turning my head to the side, I saw Mason running from the building. He was screaming something, but I couldn't hear him. A tear leaked down my cheek as I weakly raised my hand, reaching out to him. When my eyes grew weak, I didn't know if he had reached me or not.

Darkness swallowed me.

CHAPTER THIRTY-SEVEN

***

Mason

I growled, shoving the man against the wall, my hand clenched tightly around his throat. He stared back at me with wide eyes, trembling beneath my grasp. Orion was ready to rip him to shreds, and I was ready to let him. My wolf was whimpering through my mind, feeling lost and hopeless. Octavia didn't deserve this.

"You *will* fix her," I snarled, my hold tightening on his neck. I felt satisfied as his face started turning red as he clawed at my hand.

"Mason! There will be no one to fix her if you kill him. Release him now!" Christian ordered.

I dropped the doctor to the floor. To think I had let this man live was beyond me.

The doctor coughed, holding onto his neck as he tried to gather air back in his lungs. "I... I don't know what he did. I can't fix her."

"Liar!" I roared, charging for him once more, but Jackson and Evan grabbed me, holding me back as I thrashed wildly in their arms.

Christian calmly walked in front of me, squatting down to where he was at eye level with the man. "You created Martial, so I know you know everything you can about him. What caused Octavia to lose her Lycan? What caused her to have whatever deteriorating thing that is killing her?"

"I don't know! I'm telling you the truth. In the serum I made, I did put Lycan DNA in it, so that may be the reason, but I don't know what it's doing to her physically. I—" Christian snarled, grabbing the doctor by the collar of his lab coat.

"Well, you better get damn well thinking because if that woman dies because of the monster you created, I will hand you over to Alpha Evan himself. He will rip you apart piece by piece and put you back together, only to do it all over again. You will be living in your own earthly hell—it will be worse than the death you're expecting."

Evan growled greedily in response. He released me, walking over to the doctor. Evan's eyes shifted to the threatening grayish-black his enemies feared. "Anything come to mind yet?" he asked, tilting his head to the side.

The doctor paled. "I... I can look her over and see if I can figure out what caused it. I was banished before I learned anything else about Martial. During the time he was with me and the hunters, I only learned a little about him. There are so many DNA strands that merged with his own that I would have to assess her to figure out what hurt her the most. He has many abilities because those DNA strands are from different supernatural creatures."

"Jackson, Evan, take him to where Octavia is. Do not let your eyes off him. Make sure he gets the job done." Christian ordered, shoving the doctor away. They both followed his command, grabbing his arms and dragging him out of the room.

I didn't know what to do or think. When I heard Octavia's scream, I got to her as quickly as I could, but she was already unconscious and covered in her own blood. Orion couldn't sense Ramani, and it was like she was just a vessel with no life in her. Her wounds on her stomach... Goddess, they were black and veiny. It was a terrifying sight. Orion was so distraught I hadn't heard from him since we found her.

"Mason, I don't want to upset you by saying this, but have you thought about the future? About if whatever is doing this to her... takes her from us?"

I gulped, my eyes stinging with unshed tears. "No, I can't. I won't. She's going to be ok. She always is. She's been through a lot, and she always pulls through."

"Mason, if she dies, you will die. You need to make plans so that won't happen. You're already growing weak because her life is leaving her. She doesn't have much time left. She wouldn't want this for you. You know that. You need to sever the link between your wolves. Alara or Scarlett can do it for you."

"Stop! I'm not severing our bond."

"Mason, you're the Alpha of War! We need you. Look, I couldn't imagine losing Scarlett, but I know if I was in your situation, she'd want me to do this and continue on." I went silent, not even bothering to reply.

He sighed, placing a hand on my shoulder. "I know it's a lot to take in, but as I said before... She doesn't have much time left. You need to be making a decision soon." He didn't say anything else as he left the room, leaving me alone in my office.

I turned, facing my desk. Growling, I leaned forward, pushing everything off it. I didn't realize what I was doing before the desk was flipped over, and I was crashing anything I could get a hold of.

Arms wrapped around me from behind, struggling to hold me in place. "Mason, quit!" I heard Ryker's voice yell.

I spun, shoving him away. He went flying to the ground, groaning as he smacked the hardwood. "Get the hell out of my office." I snarled, turning my back to him.

"Mason! I know I'm the last person you want in here right now, but you have to stop this. Destroying your office won't make her better. Getting angry only makes matters worse. You're better than this. Mason, you need to go be with her. She needs you right now."

I shook my head, glancing back at him. "I can't even look at her. All I see is Martial nearly killing her right there on the field and that I let her go alone to face him. I could have gotten there in time, but I didn't."

"First, you weren't in control. Orion was. Second, you were getting attacked left and right by vampires, so it's not yours or Orion's fault you got held back. It's just war, Mason. You, of all people, should know that. People get hurt. At least there's still hope for her. Some people didn't even get that tonight. If you can't sit by her side at her worst, why should you get to her best? That's not a mate." His words stung. Mainly because of how right he was.

I fell back onto the couch, slumping in defeat. "I'm scared. I'm so damn scared."

He sighed, pulling himself up off the floor and walked over, taking a seat beside me. "We all are when it comes to our mates, but that doesn't make us weak. It makes us strong. Fear only wins when you let it. Let the fear of losing her motivate you to do anything and everything you can to keep her alive. You and I both know that death is not always permanent in this day." He mumbled, and I gritted my teeth together.

"What are you getting at?"

He sighed, knowing I already knew what he was thinking. "I was coming in here to tell you that I spoke to Dante. Dante is willing to change her if you want him to. He somewhat relates to losing the love of your life, so he will do it. It would be the last option sort of thing, of course, but he said it would work."

"She'd kill me if I did that." I let out a humorless laugh, shaking my head.

"Would she, though? You would still be able to live a happy life together."

"Happy life? Ryker, she wants kids—a family. If I let him change her, she would never get any of those things!"

"There are many kids that would love to be adopted, Mason." He countered, and I groaned, standing from the couch and shaking my head furiously.

"I can't think about this right now. I just can't."

"Well, Dante and I will stay here until you decide what you're going to do. Alara and Scarlett did a reading on Octavia before I came in here. Alara said her life force maybe has another day or two. Scarlett is staying here as well, so if you decide to do it... She can demolish your mate bond link."

I nodded. "Ok."

The door opened, and we turned, seeing Braelyn walk in. At the sight of her, my heart clenched. Her bottom lip quivered, and I opened my arms, letting her run right into them. I wrapped my arms around her, holding her as if I'd lose her at any second.

"I'm so sorry, Mason!" she cried.

I rested my chin on the top of her head as she buried her face in my chest. "It's going to be ok," I mumbled, rubbing her back. "I'm going to figure this out."

***

I walked into the room Octavia was in. Wires were everywhere, she was pale, and looked as if she was already dead. Jackson and Evan were watching the doctor work before they realized I was in the room. Clearing his throat, Jackson stood straighter, walking over to me.

"He's not finding out much," He muttered. "I think he's a lost cause, Mason. He was just some terrible man playing with stuff he didn't know anything about."

"You say the word," Evan grumbled, his eyes not leaving the doctor. "And I'll take him off your hands."

I looked at Octavia once more, realizing that I couldn't live without her. If she were to die today, I wouldn't make it.

"Jackson, go be with your mate. She needs you. Evan, take the doctor away. He is of no use to me anymore."

They both looked surprised and a little confused. Nonetheless, they listened to me. I walked over to Octavia, a deep sigh leaving me. I gently took her hand in mine, biting my lip as I realized what I was about to do.

"I'm sorry, Octavia. I hope you won't despise me for what's about to happen. I guess bad habits still stay within me," I whispered and leaned down to place one last kiss on her forehead.

Her hand fell from mine as I backed away, mind-linking Alaric, **"Send me Dante. I'm with Octavia."**

As I waited, I paced the room, my heart feeling as if it was about to burst out of my chest. If I did this, I didn't know what the future would hold. What scared me the most was the thought of it *not* working. Either way, I could be on a path toward destruction. Whether that be Octavia's or mine... I didn't know.

"So, you took up my offer, I hear," Dante finally made his entrance, leaning up against the doorframe.

"Old habits die hard with me apparently," I mumbled, turning to face Octavia once more.

"You may or may not know, but I can read minds. It's part of the many gifts we elders have. That doctor of yours had no idea what he was doing. He was telling the truth when he said he didn't really know what Martial could do. He knew she was going to die, but he did try to save her for the most part—probably because of the eternal hell with Evan."

"I got that much. I'm just pissed I let this happen."

"It's just war, my friend. It takes those we love too often." He sighed, placing a hand on my shoulder. "At least you're blessed to be surrounded by people who could potentially save them. I know you hate yourself for what happened with Vivian, but you did the right thing." He brushed past me, looking over Octavia.

Ignoring his comment, I asked, "You swear this will work?"

"I'm not saying it's one hundred percent certain, but it's your last shot. Anytime one kills a wolf and then turns them, you never know for sure what the outcome would be. I've successfully done it before, as you know with Raven, but I've never tried to turn a half Lycan."

"Wouldn't it be just like killing her wolf? I mean, I believe her Lycan has already died."

"No. We don't know if her Lycan really died or not. She's vanished, sure, but that doesn't mean she won't return. It depends if whatever Martial did to her *really* killed her Lycan or merely sent it back to the ancestor realm."

"So, the ancestor realm is actually a place," I mumbled, my eyes wide. The ancestor realm is where all Lycan souls go as they wait to merge with a new soul to carry their gene.

"It is very real. If her Lycan soul was sent back to the ancestor realm, there's a chance it can find Octavia again or choose someone else. Typically, they choose someone else—a child they can grow with and teach."

"And since her Lycan is gone, she's what? Dying because of that?"

"No. This is solely down to what Martial did. I gave her my blood earlier when Alara was doing a reading. Her body accepted it, which is good. It slowed the wound from getting worse. My thoughts? Martial's claws had a serious venom in them. Anytime the claws strike its victim, the venom will slowly crawl into the skin and then into the body to eat it apart until it kills the host. It is irreversible. I know the creature that does that, and us vampires call them *Snake Eaters*." He let out a humorless laugh.

"Snake Eaters?" I raised my eyebrows.

"Back in the day, we used to think they'd eat snakes for their venom to make them stronger. They're these scaly reptile-looking creatures that reside in swampy areas of the world. Obviously, they didn't really eat snakes, but I've always wondered how they came to be. Vampires don't mess with them because their venom can even kill us. Everyone knows it's hard to kill a vampire if you don't go for the heart or head. Imagine one swipe of claws. You'd be surprised how many supernatural creatures are out there. Your doctor seemed to know as well. I don't know how he'd get the DNA of a Snake Eater, but that wound is exactly like one they'd cause."

"How will you change her if it is causing that much damage?"

Dante shrugged. "Death is death when it comes to turning someone. She'll need to die anyway. I'm just going to put her out of her misery a little earlier. Call Scarlett to come and demolish the wolf link, and we'll start. This needs—" He stopped talking when Octavia suddenly started seizing.

I sprung forward, grabbing ahold of her. "Doctors!" I yelled, my hands shaking as Dante shoved me out of the way, rolling her on her side, trying to hold her still.

"I'm sorry, Mason, but I can't wait for Scarlett!" Dante gritted out as we saw black blood foam from her mouth. "She's about to die. *Permanently.*"

"If you don't demolish her wolf link, then—"

"You'll die too." He growled, cursing at the thought.

The doctors rushed in the room, taking over as Dante moved out of the way, thinking about his next move. I mind-linked for Christian to send Scarlett my way and to get here as fast as she could. Praying to the Goddess, I hoped we weren't too late.

Suddenly, Dante bit his wrist again, feeding her his blood. The seizing stopped, and he reared his head back, cringing as he threw his head forward and bit into her neck. My eyes nearly left my head at the sight.

"What are you doing?!" I roared.

He didn't reply as he shed the first drop of blood. Dante sucked in a mouth full before releasing her and turned his head, spitting it on the ground before returning to her neck. I watched, terrified, not knowing what to do. Wolf blood was absolutely terrible to vampires. I could see the physical and mental pain he was in as he forced himself to do so over and over again. Eventually, he unlatched his teeth, sitting back on a nearby chair breathless.

"That was disgusting." He shot daggers at me. "You owe me after this."

"What did you do?"

"The venom seeps into the blood—that's what spreads it. I just drained her of most of it to allow Scarlett to get here and do whatever she needs to. It's no fix, and I feel like I'm going to throw up, but it will work for now." He cringed, wiping his mouth with the sleeve of his shirt.

As if she heard her name, Scarlett ran in, her breathing out of control as she held her stomach and back. I quickly stepped forward, steadying her.

"Are you ok?"

She waved me off. "Never mind me. What do I need to do?" she rushed out, waddling over to Octavia.

Dante looked Scarlett over with a raised brow. "Should have called Alara. Poor thing looks like she's about to pass out,"

"I'm pregnant, asshole. I got here as quickly as I could." She snapped back, and he grinned at her tone.

"Enough of the banter. Scarlett, demolish her wolf's link and please do it quickly."

Her head snapped to the side. "*What?* You can't be serious, Mason."

"We're losing time, and this is the only way to save her! She's going to die regardless, Scarlett. I am begging you to just do—"

Before I could say anymore, we heard bones cracking. Slowly, we all three turned to see Octavia's body spasm slightly.

"What the hell is happening?" Scarlett whispered as she took a wary step away from her.

"I don't know…" I mumbled, and Dante stood by the door in a flash.

"Get away from her!" he called out, and we listened to the order, running next to him.

Bone by bone, her body started cracking as if she was transitioning into a wolf for the first time.

"Dante… care to explain?"

"I… I just felt immense power radiate from her. I've only felt that once in my lifetimes."

"I feel it too," Scarlett confirmed, visible goosebumps rising on her arms.

"Did her Lycan come back? I don't feel anything that you're talking about."

Dante gulped, his eyes slowly moving to meet mine. "That's no half Lycan."

CHAPTER THIRTY-EIGHT

───────◆◇◆───────

Mason

I didn't understand any of what Dante was trying to tell me. I was too focused on my mate, the love of my life, whose every bone seemed to be breaking in front of my eyes. Was she shifting into her Lycan form? Was her wolf form trying to save her? What if her body was trying to turn into something like Martial? And why the hell was I just standing there, watching it happen like a coward?

"Mason, are you listening to anything that I've been saying?!" Dante yelled, grabbing my attention.

"Not really. If you haven't noticed, my mate looks as if she's been ripped right out of a horror movie." I grimaced, watching her arm snap in half, one that reminded me of a Lycan transition.

"What is inside her is deadly. It's a full Lycan! A Lycan that *doesn't* have a wolf side. It is *purely* a Lycan. It will *only* shift into Lycan form. It is one of the most powerful supernatural beings ever created." he said, pointing to her breaking form. "It's trying to save her, but that thing is rerouting her whole body as we speak."

"Full Lycans are unheard of. Not one has been documented in years. There's no way. This has to be something else. A full Lycan doesn't have an ancestor soul merged with their own. They are solely born like that. They are what creates an ancestor's soul when they die. There's no way a full Lycan soul went into her." I countered.

"My point. They are *born* that way. She's pregnant, Mason. Sadly, for you two, your kid won't be a half Lycan. Your two half Lycan genes merged into one and created a full Lycan baby. I cannot be in the same room as a full Lycan—that is how much they scare me, *a king*. I have to go. She will be fine, and you won't have to hate yourself for turning her now." With that, Dante spun on his heels and vanished from the room.

Locking eyes with Scarlett, I raised my brow. "She's not pregnant. The doctors would have seen that. If she were, the baby would have died from the venom. What is he going on about?"

"I... I did some research on Lycans when I found out about you and Octavia. A full Lycan is a natural-born leader. It is something that half Lycans bow down to. They are blessed with such abilities from the minute their embryo forms that no one could possibly know what they are capable of. They even have witch-like abilities. If she is pregnant, the baby could have unknowingly hidden itself from us as a form of safety—like a witch's cloaking spell. It's an instinct for full Lycans. They're protective and unpredictable."

"First, they said she had about two days left, Dante thought she was just about to die, and now she's suddenly ok? This doesn't make any sense. That venom from Martial is killing her, and we're sitting around doing nothing."

"You can't do anything until every bone in her body is done breaking into place. The venom kills everything in the host. It probably ate at her bones too. That is why your child is healing her. It's not for Octavia's benefit... it's for their own. A full Lycan needs a strong host to survive."

Craning my neck to the side, Octavia suddenly went still. It was an odd sight. She looked as if she hadn't broken one bone, let alone all of them. It was as if the bones broke and went right back into place. It made some sense to me. If she broke every bone in her body like a wolf transition, her healing process speeds up. If her healing process speeds up, it slows the venom from spreading. If she truly is pregnant with a full Lycan baby, then it knew to break every bone in her body, so her healing process would be tremendously fast, which was terrifying. *It's a baby.*

"How do I know she's truly going to be ok, Scarlett?"

Placing a hand on my shoulder, she looked at Octavia warily. "Because she's pregnant with a full Lycan. The grace of their own hand can only kill full Lycans. By the looks of it, that baby isn't going to let that happen. Thankfully, Dante drained a lot of her blood, so the baby is strong enough to slow down the rest of the venom. It will be out of her system in no time. We don't have to worry about her passing any longer."

The thought alone was a breath of fresh air. I didn't have to lose her— not to death or immortality. What did scare me was the fact that she may really be pregnant. If she made it past the next few hours, I was certain that she was. I knew the myth of full Lycans, but it had been so long since one had ever been documented. Most Lycans were killed or went into hiding once they got a bad name for themselves.

"I'll go fetch some doctors and inform them of what we've learned. There are ways of doctors seeing the baby through certain ultrasounds if so. It may cloak itself, but the doctors will find it once they know what they're looking for." Scarlett explained, her hand dropping from my shoulder as she left the room.

Nervously, I walked over and grabbed hold of Octavia's hand and gave it a small squeeze. Dante acted like the kid was going to be born evil, but I believe nothing is born evil. It's just a baby. Our baby. Regardless of what Dante or anyone else thought about our child, I would love it with everything in me.

Being a father terrified me, especially after witnessing what happened to my father after he got on the wrong side of someone. I'm the Alpha of War. I had enemies. The thought alone of someone coming after me or my child terrified me.

"You believe she's pregnant?" a voice called out.

I glanced over at the doctor who once helped me after being temporarily killed from the wolfsbane gas. He was someone I trusted—like family. He was growing old, but he had been here since I was a teen.

"Gregory, I believe so. At least, Dante and Scarlett do. If you would have just witnessed what we did, I think you'd agree. Dante and Scarlett felt immense power. I didn't, though, which I find odd. They think the baby is full Lycan." I mumbled, and his eyes widened slightly.

"If Dante was scared off, I think you all may be correct. I've read a lot about Lycans—dealt with quite a few before as well. I always knew that Lycans ran in your family after your father."

My eyes widened slightly. "My father was a Lycan?"

He nodded. "Yes. A half Lycan, much like yourself. Why do you think all Alphas of The War Pack had red eyes? It wasn't just a witch's spell that created that. It ran in the war family and was passed on for generations."

He walked over, folding his arms as he looked at my mate. "The reason you didn't sense the surge of power is that the baby doesn't sense you as a threat. He or she knows that its host is weak. With others in the room, the baby unknowingly surged energy through Octavia, not only to save her but to ward any enemies away. A full Lycan trait, I'm afraid."

"You keep saying host? She's not a host. She's the baby's mother!" I felt disgusted by the word. "And why do you seem so... disturbed that it could be full Lycan?"

"Mason, full Lycan births usually kill the mother. That is why it treats your mate as if she is nothing but a host. It will keep her alive... until the time of its birth. Full Lycans are strong—so strong they scare even the vampire king himself. They are unstoppable. I've heard they have abilities to control the mind and so much more. Why do you think it's already so powerful just from being in the womb? They're a weapon of destruction. My suggestion? Get that thing out of her while you can. I love you like a son, Mason... but this will kill your mate."

A growl ripped through me as I took a threatening step towards him. "I will *not* get rid of my own child. We're in a different time with different means of protecting a mother and child at birth. We have allies of some of the most powerful supernatural beings. We will figure this out, but I am not losing either of them. I won't. I can't let her be saved now, only to die again later. Run the tests you need to so you can confirm this but leave after that. I won't have you looking at my mate or child like they are some abomination." I turned my back to him, my body shaking with anger.

He let out a sigh, brushing past me to check on her. "I'm sorry, Mason." He nearly whispered a frown upon his face.

I reached out, brushing a strand of hair from her face. She was pale—so pale it nearly killed me just looking at her. I just needed to hear her voice, even if it was scolding me or teasing me. I just needed something. I needed a sign that she would be ok. I didn't know if Ramani was dead or if she would ever make her way back to Octavia, but I hope she did. Maybe then, Octavia would be able to have more knowledge of the baby and what to do.

CHAPTER THIRTY-NINE

$\diamond$

Octavia

I giggled, following after Liza as she ran toward the house party we'd been invited to. Her curly, brown hair bounced with every step, shining in the sun beating down over us. I envied her energetic side and how all the boys gawked after her. Each boy we passed didn't take his eyes off her. I couldn't blame them, though. Her tanned skin, perfect hair, gorgeous hazel eyes, and curvy body were to die for.

"This is going to be so much fun! When was the last time we went to a party that wasn't after lights out?!" she beamed, looking around.

The music boomed, bouncing off the walls. People were scattered about, drinking and dancing as red solo cups littered the floor.

"You say that until we get busted again, and Alpha Ryker scorns everyone here. The last time we had a day party, it kind of went to crap." I reminded, walking with her to a bar full of delicious liquors.

"Well, that wasn't our fault. That kid was dumb enough to drive home drunk and wrecked into a lamppost. Luckily, he wasn't hurt, and he didn't hurt anyone else." She sighed, flicking the cap off of a bottle of tequila.

"Still, I've never really liked partying during the day. I feel like it leads to nothing good." I took the cup she offered me watching her roll her eyes.

"People are going to make stupid decisions whether it be during the day or at night, Octavia. We just have to make sure we're not one of those people."

I raised my cup. "That is very true."

She giggled, tapping her cup against mine and turned to look at the crowd before her. "Have you seen Josh?"

Scanning the room, I shook my head. "Not once. He said he didn't know if he'd be coming today or not."

"He's such a party pooper. I don't know how you've dated him for so long."

I bumped my shoulder with hers. "Wait until you get a boyfriend of your own."

She made a disgusted face. "Not my thing. I like being single."

"Yeah, yeah… whatever." I tipped back my drink, letting it drain down my throat. I placed my cup on the bar and grinned at her. "Come on!"

She smirked as I grabbed her hand and let me pull her into the crowd of people. We started dancing, letting our worries vanish with every shake of our hips. A few of our friends met up with us once they arrived, joining us on the dance floor. It was so peaceful to just let loose every once in a while. We just finished college last year, and it was a breath of fresh air, not having to worry about school or anything. Though soon it would be time for my big girl life to start, and I hated the idea of it.

As I spun around to head back to the bar to get us some more drinks, I saw a girl leaning up next to it, her eyes locked on me. She seemed a little older than me, but she was absolutely stunning. Her blonde hair flowed in beautiful waves that stopped a little past her shoulder. She was tall and looked as if she was a trained warrior at the scar that trailed from her neck under the collar of her black tee. Her sapphire eyes stared back at me with curiosity. Who was she?

Looking away from her, I walked up to the bar, trying my best to ignore her. I grabbed some fresh cups, pouring a drink into them. As I reached for a vial of wolf's venom, a hand shot out, stopping me. My head snapped to the side as I narrowed my eyes at the girl.

"Can I help you?" I couldn't help but snap.

She let out a humorless laugh. "You're still snarky, even in a dream world." She mumbled, shaking her head.

"I'm sorry?"

"Hello, Octavia. We need to talk." she cleared her throat and nodded her head towards the front door.

"I'm sorry, but that won't be happening. I don't know you."

"Yes, you do, and I won't ask twice. This conversation needs to happen. It was hell getting here, and you're going to listen."

"What's your name then? If I apparently know you."

Her eyes squinted. "Ramani. Does that name ring a bell?"

For some reason, it did. It was odd. I was so certain I'd never seen this woman in my life, yet a part of me felt like I had known her for all of it just by hearing her name. Raising a brow, she nodded her head towards the front door. She pushed off the wall, walking towards it. I bit my lip, wondering if this was some prank. Though, my curiosity got the best of me. Forgetting about the drinks, I placed the cups down and went after her.

Once we were outside, she glanced around as if she was looking for prying eyes. Once she saw no one, she went over to lean against a pillar on the front porch. Folding her arms, she cocked her head to the side.

"You really don't remember anything?"

"You act as if I know what you're talking about."

An annoyed sound ripped through her as she threw her arms up. "This isn't real, Octavia!"

"What isn't?"

She flailed her arms around. "All of it! This day, this party, your friends. *Liza*, especially." She gritted out.

I let out a snort, turning my back to her. This woman was crazy. Before I could reach for the door handle, she grabbed my arm and jerked me back to her. Anger spiked within me, and I snarled, my eyes shining a bright yellow of my wolf's color.

"Don't touch me."

She grinned, her eyes shining a bright red. "The dream world erased me, but this should jog your memory a bit."

Staring at her blood red eyes, my heart jumped a beat. I've never seen anything like it. Only… only Alpha Mason had red eyes. At the thought of his name, I felt a tug on my heart.

"What's going on?" I mumbled.

"You were hurt. Well, we were." She raised her pointer finger, tapping on my temple. "I used to be in here. After the war, Martial hurt us pretty damn badly. I was sent back to the ancestor realm. I thought for sure he had killed me, but it turns out he just exiled me from your body—the venom he infused into you, I guess."

"You're making no sense." I shook my head.

She growled, her head dropping in defeat. "This is going to be harder than expected. Short story short, you are mated to Alpha Mason. You're both half Lycans. I've been with you since birth, trapped within your mind. You used to hate me, but we got over it. We went to war, and we won it. But I vanished from your body when we got hurt. I don't have much more time to explain, but wake the hell up, Octavia. You're just in some coma that is holding you here. It's a safe spot for you—something you're familiar with. It blocked all the negative things from your life."

I belched out a laugh. "Lady, are you on crack or something? None of that is true. I'm sorry to inform you. You have the wrong girl."

She reached in her pocket, grabbed a paper and shoved it into my hands. Glancing down at it, my heart stopped. It was a picture. I was locked hands with a man, Alpha Mason to be exact, as we waved at people. We had huge smiles on our faces, but what confused me the most was how Alpha Mason stared down at me, pure adoration in his eyes. This was impossible.

"That was when you became Luna of The War Pack. I'm not so crazy after all, am I?"

My hands trembled as I stared at the thin picture in my hands. Covering my mouth in shock, I looked back up at Ramani.

"Why can't I remember this?"

"I don't know. I thought by now it would have all come back to you. Try to remember. Remember the war. Remember Martial and the horrible things that happened to him. We tried to save him. He seemed like he was going to let us until he played us. He clawed our stomach, nearly ripping our insides out, but we continued the fight after Orion, Mason's Lycan, killed him. We went to help Alpha Jackson get to his mate once he sensed her, but we didn't make it inside the building before we collapsed."

Suddenly, a burning pain happened in my stomach, causing me to clutch it.

Ramani's eyes widened. "You're remembering. Keep it going!"

One by one, memories started slamming into me. The first time I met Mason, our first kiss, our first time together. I saw Scarlett, the alphas, all of it. Then I remembered the war. *Oh, the pain that coursed through me.*

With wet eyes, I looked up at Ramani. "I remember."

As the words left my mouth, the world around me grew dim, and the setting changed. I heard gasping for air and turned my head, seeing Ramani lying in Lycan form on the ground right outside of the hunter's main building. My eyes stung as I watched the scene play out in front of me. My body shifted, and I cried out, trying to reach Ramani. I coughed up blood, raising a weak hand. At what, I didn't know, but it fell to the ground as I slipped unconscious.

Turning to face the real Ramani, I gulped. "How are you here?"

She smiled in relief as everything resonated with me. "I tried to reconnect with your body. This was the first step at a positive sign after leaving the ancestor realm, but something has changed. I thought by remembering, it would all snap back into place." She looked down at her hands. "I haven't been in this form in a long time."

"Is this what you looked like back with your time on earth?"

"Indeed, it is."

"You're beautiful." I smiled.

"Thank you. I'd like to think so." She teased.

A small laugh escaped me. "So, what now?"

"Now you go back to the real world. Not this one."

"You're not coming with me?"

She shook her head. "As I said, something has changed. Something won't let me merge with you again. At least, not for now. Typically, once a Lycan soul gets sent back to the ancestor realm, we search for a new vessel, but I couldn't leave you just yet. We still had unfinished business together, and I hoped for many more years with you."

My bottom lip trembled, knowing this may be our last moments with one another. "You tried, though? To merge with me again? After the way I treated you?"

She shrugged. "I did. I care more about you than I let on, Octavia. I have a feeling I know what's not letting me merge with you anymore, but that's for you to find out on your own. You have a little guardian angel protecting you from everything and anyone I believe."

I raised a brow. "What's that supposed to mean?"

"As I said, you'll find out when you wake, I'm sure. For now, we shall depart. Thank you for giving me a second chance, Octavia. If this is our final time together, just know that the next vessel I choose, I will uphold the lessons you taught me. Times have changed, and I am a new person now. I'm not in this for power anymore… just a companion on my journey."

I couldn't help but reach out and pull her into a hug. "I'm so sorry, Ramani."

Reluctantly, she wrapped her arms around me, squeezing tight. "Don't be. I love ya, kid." she rubbed my back once more and pulled back. "See you around," She winked.

With that, she vanished.

CHAPTER FORTY

◇

Mason

There had been a lot that happened recently, and all of it was nothing but a massive headache. Before I knew Octavia was really hurt, we entered that building not only to end the rest of the hunters, but we captured Megan and saved Jackson's mate. That was a win, I guess. Though, my mate lying in a hospital bed ruined it for me. The last thing I needed to finish was finding that damn mole. I had a bad feeling in my gut I knew who it was, but I didn't want to assume just because of his past.

"Now our circle is down to two. I don't like keeping the alphas out of this, but better safe than sorry." Alpha Jackson mumbled, rubbing a hand over his face.

It had been three days since what happened with Octavia, and Alpha Jackson was at my house once again. I respected the man and how he dedicated his time to helping me this past year. He didn't let that stop after the war was over either.

"I appreciate your help, man. I don't know what I'd do without you, honestly."

He cracked a small smile. "You know I have your back. You're like a brother to me."

It was true. I had known the man since I was a mere child. Jackson had a tough life growing up, and I watched him grow from an immature teen to an honorable man—despite his bluntness at times. I never knew life had all this in store for us, however. Perhaps our tough childhoods and being thrown into our titles at a young age bettered us. We weren't superheroes; we were simply survivors.

"So, you said that you had a feeling you know who the mole is?" he asked.

I nodded, explaining my reasoning and who I thought it might be. Shock washed over him when I finished. Slowly, I saw the gears turning in his head.

"It's possible." he pursed his lips. "I mean, it would make sense. The person who would have authority to access to the cells, who people would fear, plus he's a torture machine for prisoners. At least, that's what Alpha Evan's title used to be."

"What shall we do?"

"I don't know. We can reprimand him right away, but then there's his mate who could possibly get in the way. We have to be smart about this, and we have to get more evidence before doing so. In the meantime, we'll put eyes on him twenty-four-seven. If it is him, there's something fishy to it. Why would he risk all of this after everything he's been through? Especially after getting his mate and risking his title?"

"I agree. At least the war is over, and Megan is under our control. He has nothing to mess with as of right now. Speaking of Megan, I have scheduled her execution by the hellhounds tomorrow night. After that, I can finally live in peace without the fear of her lurking around."

"I'm happy for you, Mason. I'll see you tomorrow then. I'm definitely not going to miss that." He grinned, standing to his feet.

We shook hands and parted ways. As I started signing off on some papers, my office door flew open, hitting the wall with a crack.

Eyes wide, Braelyn panted. "She's awake! Octavia is awake!"

I went to run past her, but she grabbed my arms. "Mason, you need to prepare yourself for when you walk in. She's... she doesn't look the same."

"What do you mean?"

"It's something you need to see for yourself. I was placing some flowers in her room when she woke up. She flew up out of bed, and it was a scary sight. It took her a minute to realize where she was, but the weird part is... she's completely healed. Not a wound in sight. How is that even possible?"

I knew the answer to that, but I needed to speak to my mate before others knew what was currently residing in her stomach. "I'll explain later."

I rushed to see Octavia, fearing what I would stumble upon once I entered her room. I neared her room of the infirmary, seeing doctors walking in and out. Confused, I walked in. Gregory was shining a light in her eyes.

At first glance, she seemed fine. However, when she sensed my presence, her head snapped to the side. Blood red eyes stared back at me, and I stepped farther into the room, confused.

"Ramani?" I spoke warily.

She sighed. "Not Ramani."

Not caring what was happening, I made my way to her, wrapping her in my embrace. She looked completely healed and even glowing. I guess I had our kid to thank for that. Octavia squeezed me tightly as if she never wanted to let go.

"She's gone, Mason." She whimpered. "Ramani is gone. For good, I believe."

I rubbed her back, feeling Orion's mood suddenly dampened. He had grown to love Ramani just as much as I loved Octavia. "I'm so sorry."

"It was all my fault. I was so stupid thinking I could save that man."

"Shh, no, it wasn't. Your heart was in the right place. He was just too far gone to accept any help from us."

She pulled back, and I raised my hand to wipe a stray tear from her cheek. "Did the doctors tell you the news?"

I smiled, nodding. "They did."

"I'm pregnant. They told me everything before you got here. How the baby... saved me. But Gregory also told me what the baby was and what it could do to me. That's why my eyes are a Lycan red, Mason. They won't change until the baby's birth. It's... feeding off me." She whispered, her eyes full of fear.

I shot daggers to Gregory, who was standing by the door, a solemn look on his face. Looking back to Octavia, I plastered the best fake smile I could manage.

"It's all going to be ok. We'll figure it out. Just as I told him, we're in a different era. We have new means of protecting both of you. The baby is just super strong, and it needs your body to help it continue to grow just like any other baby would. It's just a Lycan baby and not a normal one." I lied, praying to the Goddess we could truly figure this out.

She looked down, placing a hand on her stomach as she let out a shaky breath. "He said I needed to get rid of it, or it's going to kill me."

My heart dropped in my stomach as a growl ripped through me. I spun on my heels to charge at Gregory, but Octavia reached out with unbelievable force and yanked me back to her.

"Stop. He did nothing wrong. He was just telling me my options, Mason. We have to be logical about this. I'm growing a human being inside me. One that could potentially kill me. We needed to know that."

"So, what… you want to abort it?" I spat, disgusted.

Her eyes met mine, and she pulled me down to eye level, placing a soft hand on my cheek. "Of course not. I've been near death many times; this one doesn't scare me if I know that my baby will at least be okay. I'm keeping it just as I told Gregory, and no one will change my mind, but regardless of what research or help you're going to get, we need to get a plan prepared. If I can't be here to raise this child, you have to. Promise me that."

I shook my head. "We're doing this together, babe. You're going to be fine, and when the time comes, then we'll work it all out. I know—"

"Mason! Just promise me."

I flinched from her tone of voice. "I promise."

"Gregory, tell him the rest." She mumbled.

Turning to face him, I clenched my jaw. What else did he have to say to make matters worse? I respected the man, but recently, I wanted nothing more than to rid him of my presence. He was being too negative for my own liking.

"A full Lycan pregnancy only lasts six months. By the looks of it, she's already a month gone. It's not a normal pregnancy, as I've said. It matures quicker than the average wolf or human. It doesn't take nine months."

Looking down at Octavia, she gripped my hand tightly. "We have five months to get this all figured out. During the last month, he can come at any time, so we need to prepare."

My jaw dropped slightly. "He? *You said he.*"

She bit her lip. "They develop quicker. It's a boy. You have a male heir to your title now."

I sat down on the bed next to her, shock coursing through my veins. This was real. This was happening. I was having a son. I ran a hand over my face, cursing the moon goddess. Just when something goes well for me, there is always another problem around the corner. Now I had to prepare yet again for the potential death of my mate if we can't figure out a loophole to this.

"The Goddess is out to get us," I murmured.

Octavia snorted, patting my shoulder. "I've been telling you that since day one, babe. I don't think she likes me very well." She joked, but I couldn't find it in me to even crack a smile.

Looking back at her, I asked, "What was it like? Being out for so long, I mean."

She sat back, a sad look in her eyes. "Well, let me tell you about it."

CHAPTER FORTY-ONE

◆◇◆

Octavia

I stared at my reflection in the mirror, confused at how I didn't have a single mark on me. Glancing at my blood red eyes, a shiver ran down my spine. It was like I was staring back into someone else's eyes. I blinked. Once. Twice. Leaning in closer, they twinkled from the ceiling light above me. Five months. They will be like this for five months. There was no hiding the secret behind them anymore. People will know soon enough.

I stepped back, turning to the side. Running a hand over my stomach, I could tell I gained a little weight. The baby was growing tremendously fast. I knew nothing about being a mother, and that terrified me. It was times like this when I wish my mother were around, but she hadn't bothered reaching out to me once since I left with alpha Mason. I guess I didn't have much room to talk. I hadn't tried reaching out either. I know she and my father got the news that Mason and I had come out as half Lycans, and that may have been part of the reason for her silence.

My mother never hated me, but she wasn't a fan of Ramani. She despised my father for a while, of course, after discovering what he was doing to me. However, I still think he weaseled his way into her mind, convincing her that I would be nothing but a killer.

Arms wrapped around me from behind, pulling me from my thoughts. Mason rested his head on my shoulder, looking at me in the mirror. He smiled, running a hand over my stomach. "How was your morning?"

"It was ok. The doctor said I just needed to rest for a bit after he let me leave, but you and I both know that is not in my vocabulary. I'm too stressed to lay around and do nothing. I feel great physically, but I can't help but feel drained mentally. With all the recent events, my head is nothing but constantly aching. A lifelong headache, perhaps."

He spun me around, placing a soft kiss on my forehead. He placed a finger under my chin, tilting my head up. "We'll get through this. It will take a few to get adjusted to the new changes, but we will come out on top. We always do." He encouraged me.

Although I loved his optimism, I didn't see it that way. It seemed as though we were never going to get a break. I'd do my best to be strong these last few months, but I had an eerie feeling that I wouldn't be leaving that hospital once the baby was born. Flashing him a fake smile, I nodded. Leaving his grasp, I walked out of the bathroom and into our bedroom.

"I wrote down some names this morning while you were having your conference call with the alphas. What do you think?" I grabbed the piece of paper off the nightstand, handing it to him.

He skimmed over the names, the corner of his lips turning up. "Heath? After your favorite candy bar?" he snickered. I growled, going to snatch the paper from him, but he pushed away my hands with a laugh. "I'm still reading!"

His laughter quieted down as he looked at the paper closely. Curious as to which name he kept staring at, I peered over at the paper. He pointed to a name that was one of my favorites and raised a brow. "Is this named after...?"

I nodded. "Mathias. After the all-powerful warrior that aided the moon goddess in wars. It seemed fitting," I let out a small laugh. "I know it's just a made-up story, but I love the name."

"I love it." He smirked, placing the paper back on the nightstand.

"You do? I thought if you did like it we could nickname him Matt or Matthew for short. Who knows if he'll want to be named after some warrior with how everyone already sees him?"

"I like it. Mathias Cage." The name rolled off his tongue as if it had already been written in stone.

I felt a sharp kick in my stomach, causing a gasp to leave me. "Whoa, I didn't know he'd be moving this soon. Seems like he likes the name." I giggled, and Mason's eyes widened as he quickly placed a hand on my stomach. Not a second later, there was another kick.

"We seem to have a soccer player on our hands," He joked.

I bit my lip, trying to contain my smile. "Maybe so."

Mason's eyes glazed over as he got a mindlink. Pulling back, a sigh left him. "I hate to ruin the moment, but everything is ready. It's time for Megan's execution. We need to go." He went to walk off but halted. "If you want to come, of course. You don't have to."

If I were honest. I didn't like the idea of watching some getting ripped to shreds, but I knew this was a big moment for Mason. He was finally getting justice for his family that died at the hands of Megan herself. I shook my head, lacing our hands together.

"We're in this together, remember?" With that, we headed off to where the execution would be held.

***

This was no normal execution chamber. It looked like a stadium similar to the ones that they used for football. People of The War Pack were filling the stadium as they laughed, cheered, and howled with excitement. How anyone could be excited about seeing a woman get mauled to death is beyond me. Mason explained this place as the hounds' war grounds. It is where the worst of the worst were brought. Rarely did the hounds get to make their grand appearance, and when they did, no one wanted to miss out.

Mason stood tense beside me. We were on the ground floor, sitting in the throne-like chairs designated for the Alpha and Luna. On either side of our chairs smaller ones were made for other alphas that wished to join these executions. Looking high up, a boxed-off room away from pack members sat surrounded by guards. It was like club seating. It was also made for the King and Queen. From behind the plexiglass, King Christian sat alone. I guess Scarlett didn't wish to see this either.

Looking next to Mason, Alpha Jackson sat with his chin high. He seemed more than ready for this execution. On the other side of me, Alpha Ryker sat looking rather bored. The only other alphas that showed were the news ones: Alpha Oliver and Alpha Adrian.

Craning my head to my far right, I heard the knocking of chains. Guards walked out of a gate that was on the field, bringing the prisoner into our eyesight. I leaned forward, expecting a warrior of a woman.

Instead, a fragile-looking one was walking before us. She was tall but little compared in muscle size to the men holding her. To be powerful, you don't always have to have physical strength; just a strong mind can make the biggest fall. That was Megan.

She was caked in dried blood and looked as if she could barely stand up. Open wounds were present on her thighs, and her eyes looked burned around them.

"Goddess, what happened to her?" I mumbled.

Mason couldn't help but smirk as Jackson grinned, leaning closer to us. "That was the doing of my mate, Aurora. She was the missing wolf from Mason's pack. Looks like she had enough of Megan's shit. Before we got to her, she had already wounded Megan and had her ready for Mason to take." He explained, and my eyes widened slightly as I looked back at Megan, who was forced to her knees.

Goddess, I didn't want to ever be on Aurora's bad side.

The guards took the chain that was around her wrist, jerking her arm up as they latched it on a wooden post to her right and repeated it once again with the other. She was in the center of the ring, on display for all to see. *Just how she liked it.* Mason stood up and everyone fell silent. Megan didn't bother to look up as her head hung low. She had accepted defeat. *She knew a painful death was coming.*

"Years I have waited for this moment!" Mason yelled to the people of his pack. "Years I have dealt with deaths in my own family because of this very woman. A woman who is nothing without her army doing her bidding." The wolves of our pack snarled with agreement.

Finally, Megan lifted her head. Her near-black hair moved from her face as she shot daggers toward Mason. Even though I knew she was in excruciating pain, she didn't show it. Her throat bobbed as she tried her best to hold her chin high, taking in each word Mason threw at her.

"Megan, your reign has come to an end. Do you have any final words?"

Her body shook as she laughed, causing the chains that wrapped around her wrist to jingle. "You are pathetic." She gritted out, "You claim you waited years for this, but that is what is so funny to me. You could *never* kill me. You claim I hid behind my army, yet you did just the same. After all, that is the reason you finally caught me. Is it not?" She grinned as Mason's nostrils flared in anger.

"I guess I took a play from your book," He replied.

She snickered. "Maybe so. To each their own, right? I never killed you because I wanted you to suffer. I wanted you to think I was lurking in the dark, waiting for my final moment to strike. To kill your sister, your mate, *you*. I didn't, though. It was too much fun seeing you squirm. So, get on with it Mason, you won after all. Chop my head off, beat me until my head is smashed in. I don't care. Just do it already."

Her comment set me off. I stood to my feet, my anger spiking— unbelievable anger that I've never felt before. *Courtesy of Mathias, I assume.*

"You may have your own mind games and secrets," I spoke, watching her dark eyes focus on me. "But so do we. You don't deserve a quick death. No, you… you deserve much, *much* worse." A bone chilling howl was heard at my last words, causing me to grin as confusion washed over her.

I don't know why my mood suddenly changed. One moment I didn't even want to be here, and the next, I was ready to watch her get ripped to shreds.

"You people are nothing but the devil!" She yelled, yanking on the chains as fear finally set within her.

"Didn't you know? The devil takes people to hell, and darling, I'm planning on giving it to you." Mason smirked, a wicked look crawling onto his face.

She glanced around nervously, not knowing which beasts were going to tear her apart. It wouldn't be the ones she despised, though. It was something much worse.

"Let's see if you are deemed worthy of being on this earth. Though, I'm not the deciding factor. I have beasts to do that for me."

Alarms broke out as a huge gate yards behind her started rising. It looked like nothing but a black pit as fog emerged from it. Megan turned her head, trying her best to see what was happening behind her. Nothing happened for a minute, but finally, four sets of orange eyes appeared through the blanket of darkness.

"Let it begin!" He yelled. Mason lifted his hand to his mouth, whistling so loud it rang my ears.

The people of the pack started cheering, beating on the railings before them and stomping their feet to rile up the beasts that had yet to emerge. I narrowed my eyes, waiting for the hellhounds to run out, but they waited as if they were assessing the situation, letting everyone see nothing but the color of their eyes. Eventually, one gigantic paw stepped out, and everyone went silent.

My jaw dropped slightly as the four hounds made their way out of the pit. They were huge—bigger than even Mason's wolf. They walked out slowly, power radiating off them. At the sight of the beasts, Megan choked out a cry, yanking on the chains that imprisoned her.

"Please!" She pleaded out to us. "Octavia, please!"

When she made eye contact with me, my eyes didn't leave hers. I once promised I wouldn't kill her or let Ramani kill her. It would all be

Mason's doing. She seemed to be remembering that conversation as she paled, knowing all hope for her had gone.

The hounds started to circle the ring, all going in different directions. She stood paralyzed in fear as one left the circle, walking up to her. The hound leaned closer to her, growling as her jaw dropped slightly as she looked into its eyes. She seemed to be in a trace as her screams seized, and she went silent. After a moment, the hound stepped back, and she broke free from her trance, gasping for air. The hound tilted its head back, letting out a piercing roar.

"She was deemed unworthy," Jackson mumbled, gripping the arms of his chair tightly in anticipation.

"I knew she would be." Mason grinned, taking a seat. I sat beside him, watching as the other three hounds ran up beside the other.

As if asking permission, each of the four hounds looked back to Mason. He gave them a sharp nod, and then they leaped.

Growls and screams mixed together. I had to look away as I saw blood splatter. Megan's screams suddenly stopped as a sickening crack rang out. My mind got the best of me as I glanced over. Just as my eyes locked on the sight, a hound yanked its head back forcefully, the head of Megan latched in its jaw.

A hand covered my mouth as the hound dropped her head, blood dripping from its mouth as it dived back toward the other parts of her body the others were tearing into. Nausea washed over me, and I placed my hand on my stomach. Before I knew it, I turned to the side, throwing up.

"Octavia, are you ok?" Mason asked, and I pushed his hands away as I wiped my mouth with the back of my hand.

I barely heard what he was saying over the cheering of our pack and the victorious roars from the hounds. Looking back up at him through wet eyes, I shook my head.

"I need to get out of here. Now." The smell of blood hit my nose, and I clutched my stomach again, turning to the side as my stomach emptied its contents once more.

"I'm sorry, I shouldn't have let you come to this." He tried to speak over all the commotion.

Regaining control, I sat up. "Don't be. You did what you had to do. I'm sorry I can't sit here with you. I don't have the stomach for it." I told him, resting a hand on his cheek.

"I'll have someone escort you back." I quickly nodded, and he placed a kiss on my forehead, and motioned a guard over.

I followed the guard out of the stadium but halted as my name was called. Alaric was running toward us, a worried look on his face. "Are you ok?"

"Just sick. I don't have the stomach for this." I explained, and he nodded.

"Me either. I got her." He told the guard, putting a hand on the small of my back, a frown upon his face.

"Let's get you home."

CHAPTER FORTY-TWO

—◆◇◆—

Octavia

"Will you be alright?" Alaric asked as I sat on the edge of the bed.

"Yes. Thank you, Alaric. Just too much for this momma to witness." I reassured him.

He smiled, glancing at my stomach. "Odd to see you as a mom, but I think it suits you well. Mind link me if you need anything. I'll be right down the hall."

"Thank you." He nodded and left me in the confinements of my room.

I didn't think this pregnancy was going to be in my favor. If my stomach was betraying me this early, Goddess only knows what was next. I was just glad Dr. Gregory got in touch with an OB-GYN here for me. I had an appointment that was bright and early tomorrow.

Shuffling into the bathroom, I quickly brushed my teeth to get the nasty taste from my mouth and stripped to take a much-needed shower.

After a few moments of washing off, I rested my head against the tiled wall as the hot water poured over me.

I'm not mad. How could I be? He got something he had wanted for years. He needed this. He needed to know that it was over, and he could finally breathe. I did feel bad for the way she left this world, but maybe all the years she terrified innocent people for her own game, it came back around to bite her. Quite literally.

Megan killed everyone important to him. His mother, father, even his little brother. She had me kidnapped. She experimented on innocent wolves. Why should I even feel the slightest bit bad for her?

She did deserve it.

***

My shower was nice, but as I got ready for bed, I couldn't help but stress about where Mason was. It had been hours since the execution, and he had yet to return home or reply to my text or mindlinks.

I pulled the covers over me, and as if the Goddess finally answered a prayer of mine, the door to our bedroom opened as Mason stumbled into the bedroom. I looked over his wobbling figure with a concerned expression. He nearly fell over, trying to kick off his shoes.

"Are you… drunk?"

This was odd. It was usually the other way around.

"No," he pointed a finger at me. "I'm shit-faced."

He let out a childish laugh, stumbling to the bed. I jumped when he tripped over his own feet and nearly plummeted to the ground but grabbed onto the bed to catch himself.

"Oh, you reek of tequila," I complained as I helped him crawl into bed.

"You were right-" he paused, trying to think his words over, "Tequila helps a lot. With just a tiny, tiny drop of wolf's venom."

"Yeah, and you'll feel like crap tomorrow." I teased as I pushed the hair back from his forehead, running a hand through it. He was in desperate need of a haircut. His usually cropped black hair had grown out, curling just a bit at the ends. His stubble had grown out more as if he hadn't shaved in days, and he looked exhausted.

Was I too focused on myself these past months to see my own mate was withering away in front of me? He had to seem strong. He was the alpha after all, but these past months had worn him down.

"You act as if I've never been drunk before." Mason scoffed.

"I'm sure you have, but that isn't important right now." I leaned against him as he tossed an arm around my shoulder. "Talk to me."

He pulled me closer to him, letting out a breath of relief. "It's done."

"What is?"

"My pain. It's done. Every day I felt pain knowing she was still alive. Knowing that she... she got away with what she did. That I failed my parents. But I got the justice they deserved tonight." He whispered, his eyes fixed to the ceiling.

"Hey, look at me," He reluctantly did. "You never failed anyone. Not your mom, not your dad, not your brother, not your sister, not me. No one. What happened was out of your control. You tried to save them, and they know that. That's all you need to know. You can live in peace now."

"You say that, but I don't feel any different." He grumbled. "That ache... it's still there. The pain may be gone, but that ache will never go away, will it?" The way he looked at me nearly broke me.

Resting a hand on his cheek, I shook my head. "It takes time, and now that you've gotten that closure, you can go beyond this. My mom used to tell me that the comeback is always stronger than the setback. You'll get through this. I will help you just like you did me with me, Mason."

"I just miss them." He closed his eyes, but I saw the tears leak down his cheeks.

"I know." My voice quivered as I wiped his tears away, just as he once did for me.

"I was afraid." He admitted, "I was afraid we weren't going to win that war. That she was going to get away once more. That she'd take you from me, or she'd come after my sister to finish what she started. I thought... Goddess, I thought I'd lose it all." His eyes remained closed, but the pain was still etched across his face.

"Hey, we're not going anywhere. We're safe now. She can't get to us. Not ever again."

"I'm still scared, Octavia. I, The Alpha of War, am afraid. I'm afraid I can't be that person you need—that I will screw everything up. I worry about what will happen when Mathias is born. I'm afraid I won't be a good father. I'm afraid someone will try and take him from me. I can't lose my own flesh and blood, Octavia. I just can't."

His words tugged on my heart as my own tears betrayed me. I sniffled, for once not knowing what to say—to express how wrong he was. He already *is* everything I need. He *will* be an amazing father, and he is *not* going to lose Mathias. But fate works against us sometimes. Who's to say what the future held? At the sounds of my sniffles, his eyes snapped open. In seconds, he wrapped me in his embrace, holding me tightly.

"I didn't mean to make you cry."

"Don't worry about me," I managed a smile. "Blame it on the hormones." I lied.

"With you, I always worry. You know I love you. Right?"

"I know, Mason. I love you too. I love you so much it hurts."

He didn't reply. Instead, he gave me a small squeeze as we sat in silence. He understood what I meant. I snuggled up closer to him and closed my eyes as sleep overcame me.

CHAPTER FORTY-THREE

◆◇◆

Octavia

I sat on the edge of the bed, kicking my feet nervously. The doctor I was seeing was known for her knowledge of Lycan births. I had been waiting in this examination room for almost an hour, and I was growing impatient.

"Would you stop that?" Mason yell whispered.

I scoffed, glaring at him. "I can't help it. I'm fidgety."

"Well, you're making me even more nervous with all your moving." He mumbled, rubbing his temples.

"Don't blame me for your hangover." I shot back, folding my arms stubbornly.

"Never did."

"Stop being grouchy. Today is a good day! We get to see Mathias, we can get even more news, and maybe this doctor can give us some clarity on the whole birth to relax us a bit."

"Maybe she'll give me something for this headache while she's at it. Goddess, my head is throbbing." Mason complained.

I quickly pointed to the door. "Out!" I growled, and his eyes widened at my tone of voice.

"I'm sorry?"

"If you're going to complain this whole time because of problems you could have avoided by not downing tequila, then leave."

"Goddess, you're already moody." He sighed, not moving from his chair.

When he noticed the daggers that were shot his way, he slouched in his chair, mumbling an apology. Satisfied, my expression calmed. *That's what I thought.*

"I am so sorry for your wait, Luna!" a voice called out as the examination room's door opened. "A little one decided to come a day early, and I had to deliver her." She smiled, shutting the door behind her.

"It's no problem." I waved her off, my heart jumping in my chest nervously.

She looked up from her clipboard, her brows raising in surprise. "And hello to you, Alpha. I hope you two are having a fantastic morning." She chirped, rolling over a chair for her to sit on.

"Just peachy," Mason mumbled, earning a kick in his direction from me. He plastered on a fake smile. "Long night, as I'm sure you're aware." He added, trying to make his tone better. *Hungover asshole.*

The doctor quickly nodded. "I had to miss the execution because I was on call, but I did hear a lot about it. I'm glad that woman is finally out of our lives." She sighed. "Anyways, as you may already know, I'm Dr. Asher, and I am very excited to be helping you two on this beautiful journey of yours." She beamed.

I had to force a smile. The journey? Maybe. The ending? Questionable. "Thank you for doing so. I hear you are very booked and squeezed us in. I really appreciate it."

"Of course! You are my Luna. It is my honor. Now, I've looked at the tests that Dr. Gregory ran while you were under his care and the others just came back that you took when you first got here. Everything looks great. You have a strong baby boy!"

I let out a breath of relief. "That's good to hear."

Her excitement faltered as she thought her next words over. "Now, I know that Dr. Gregory informed you that Mathias is a full Lycan. I can also confirm this. And I know that his testament of the birth has probably scared you both tremendously. I've done a lot of research on Lycans and full Lycans as well as the pregnancies that can come with each. I'm here to say that it was very long ago when the last full Lycan was born. Times have changed."

Mason perked up at her news. "That's what I've been saying!"

She let out a small laugh, nodding. "Although a full Lycan baby is energy-draining and a handful, I can assure you that it does not mean death for either of you. It has been almost fifty years since the last full Lycan was documented before he died. Do you two know a lot about full Lycans?"

I shook my head. "Honestly? Not much."

"Let me explain it to you. A full Lycan means it has no other sides. That part is pretty self-explanatory. Full Lycans are what creates Lycan spirits. They do not have an ancestor soul within them. It's a good thing. They don't have anyone trying to convince them to do certain things from a young age. When a full Lycan grows old and dies, their soul will be sent to the ancestor realm for them to merge with someone who has the Lycan gene later on."

It made sense. How else would Lycan spirits have been created? I remember seeing Ramani in my dream state. She used to be a normal person before she died, and her soul moved on to the ancestor realm. It was an interesting thought. Full Lycans were somewhat immortal, which means Mathias would one day merge with someone else if he chose to.

"As many know, Lycans were hunted and killed because people feared them, so many went into hiding. I cannot confirm that there are any other full Lycans due to that, but I don't think there is. If that is the case, it will bring many other Lycans out of hiding when your son is born. He will be the alpha of all Lycans, which sounds crazy considering he will just be a baby. This is simply because full Lycans are so powerful that even half Lycans will bow to them. They have unique abilities that one can barely comprehend. I, still to this day, don't know what all the abilities are. No one does."

"So, he didn't get the werewolf gene at all?" Mason asked, and Dr. Asher nodded.

"He will only be a Lycan, nothing more. The full Lycan trait is stronger than any other for some reason."

"So, when he healed me, did he know what he was doing? Or was that just instinct?" I asked, eagerly leaning forward.

"Pure instinct. The protective animal instinct took over because when you weakened, so did he. He needs you to survive and make him strong. If you're not strong, he can't be either."

"Is he the reason Ramani can't merge with me anymore? She mentioned that once. It's a long story." I let out a nervous laugh, fidgeting with my hands.

"I'm assuming Ramani is your Lycan half?" She asked, and I nodded. "Then yes. Mathias is unknowingly blocking her merge. I'm very sorry you had to lose her. I know that must be a toll on you, but maybe once he is born, she'll come back to you."

"It is hard, but I'm coping with it. I think she has moved on, sadly."

"I'm sorry to hear that. Mathias doesn't mean any harm by it; he just doesn't know her, and she is very powerful too. Any Lycan soul is. An alpha doesn't share his title, to put it short. He's unknowingly making a point of his status."

"How, though? He's just a baby. It just doesn't make sense to me." Mason piped up, a confused look on his face.

"As I said, it's just instinct. When Mathias is born, he'll have no recollection when he grows up of the things he did while in the womb. What he can do, though, is simply just keep you safe. He'll know if you're hurt, and he'll heal you and so on. He can't physically take over like your Lycan used to. He's much too small for that." She mused.

"And back to the birth, how will it go? Dr. Gregory made it seem like there was no other way around it." Asked Mason.

"It will be hard and brutal; I'm not going to lie. When you're in labor, all of your energy will be drained and, not to scare you, but he will basically strip the life force out of you. That is why most believe the mother dies giving birth. She gives her lifeforce to the baby."

"And I'm supposed to survive that how?" I choked out.

"My recommendation would be to get Alara Lavender to put a spell on you beforehand. A protection spell from death. It will help in case things don't go our way. I strongly believe that you can get through it, though. By glancing at both of your necks, I can see you've marked each other. When giving birth, you'll need to channel Mason. This is something many mothers didn't have, which played a part in their death. Channeling a mate is powerful."

I glanced over at Mason, who seemed to be thinking it over. Slowly, his eyes met mine. "It'll work. When you were taken from me, and the hunters drugged you, you unknowingly channeled me. Well, Ramani did, at least, but it's easy enough to learn. It helped her overcome the drugs in your system for her to emerge and protect you. It drained me of almost all my energy, but if it will help you, then of course. I'll do it."

Dr. Asher smiled, standing from her chair. "Then it's settled. Mason will teach you to channel him, and then you'll be ready when the time comes. Octavia, I know it's hard not to stress, but I promise you that you will be leaving that room with your son in your arms, ok?"

"Ok." I bit my lip, feeling tremendously better.

I'm going to make it.

"Now, do you two want to see the little guy? If he'll allow me." She grinned.

We both nodded eagerly.

"Well, then lay back and let's get this show on the road!"

***

I walked into our room and sat my purse on the bed, running a hand through my hair as Mason babbled to me.

"Did you see him?! He's so tiny but already so powerful. He is literally going to be a baby, and powerful half Lycans will bow to him—a baby! Wow, my son is a badass." His smile was so big. I couldn't help but laugh.

"Yes, he is."

Mason proudly put his hands on his hips, grinning at nothing. I walked over, wrapping my arms around him, looking up at him with a smile just as big. "I love seeing you like this."

He looked down at me, wrapping an arm around my waist. "I'm just so relieved. Everything is going in our favor for once." He placed a soft kiss on my lips.

My eyes fluttered shut as I responded, loving the feeling of relief and nothing to worry us. His kiss was hard but full of love. I nipped his bottom lip, causing a growl of satisfaction to rip through him. In a swift movement, his arms moved from my waist and to the back of my thighs. I let out a yelp as he hoisted me up. Wrapping my legs around his waist and my arms around his neck, he looked at me through lustful eyes.

"Care to show me how this happened in the first place?"

With a raised brow, I mocked his famous words, saying, "With pleasure."

CHAPTER FORTY-FOUR

◆◇◆

Octavia

"I just don't understand why you can't tell me." I groaned, following Mason into his office.

He didn't reply as he walked around his desk, shuffling through the papers scattered across it. He cursed, his fist slamming down on it in a short burst of rage. I jumped from the action, a small yelp escaping me.

"What is your deal?" I snapped, frowning at his behavior. He had been on edge all morning.

"I can't tell you who the mole is solely because there are eyes everywhere. Jackson is the only person who knows. It's not that I don't trust you. It's just that I can't put you in the line of fire in case they act out. We don't have solid proof yet, but I have my suspicions."

"You mean to tell me they're still walking free?!" I stressed.

"Yes. Because of his title, without proof, it could end up a mess. I have to have solid evidence. I have no security footage—nothing. As for why I'm pissed, I have misplaced some important papers."

He pushed through the mess on his desk once more, tossing packets of papers out of his way. I pursed my lips. *Because of his title*? That limited the number of people it could be. It was a male with an important title. Was it alpha Evan? No. It couldn't be. Christian still has a hold on him, and he knows he can't risk anything, or he will lose everything again. Another alpha? One of the new ones, perhaps?

"I'm just saying that this mole has been a problem for months. If you and Jackson believe it is this person, then put him away! Hell, Jackson is the Alpha of Intelligence. The man is never wrong. What if he strikes again?"

"Then I will deal with it. We can't risk anything, and we definitely can't risk him catching wind and running. I have more important things to attend to today, like making a statement for the grieving families who lost their loved ones in the fight against the hunters. I've been busy the past few weeks with everything that happened with you and the doctor appointments that I haven't been formal about this whole thing, which looks bad on me as an alpha. I'm disappointed in myself. They deserve better." He grumbled, finally snatching a few papers with a satisfied look.

"Don't I need to come with you then? Are those the papers you needed?"

"Should you? Probably, but the choice is yours. I know that you've been tired lately from Mathias, and the pack knows about the pregnancy now, so no one will hold it against you if choose to stay home. As for the papers, yes. It is the number of wolves we lost and each of their names.

I will be sending letters and some care packages to the families this week after I make my statement today."

I waved him off. "I'm coming. I may be a little tired, but that is no excuse. I am their Luna. As for the packages, that's very kind of you. I'm sure they will be very grateful."

"I sure hope so. It's the least I can do. These families know what their loved ones signed up for, so it was always possible to lose them to the fight. At least they know they died saving their country."

"Agreed. When are we doing the statement?"

"I'll mind-link everyone to come to the church tonight, and we'll do it then. I have made preparations for a pack dinner in honor of our fallen after our speeches." he glanced at his watch. "We have a few hours until then. I am going to meet with Braelyn for lunch. I haven't spent much time with her lately, so I'd like to catch up with her. You're free to join us if you'd like, of course."

"Thank you for the offer, but I think she needs some time alone with her big brother." I smiled, walking over to him. I placed a kiss on his cheek. "I'll see you after. In the meantime, I am going to have Alaric order me the biggest burger he can find. Mathias is demanding food right now."

Mason chuckled, placing a kiss on the top of my head. "Feed the poor boy. He's growing too quickly."

"Oh, I am! I might get a huge milkshake while I'm at it." I winked, walking over to the door. "Bye, babe. I love you." I called out, leaving his office.

Placing a hand on my stomach, I groaned as it grumbled once more, and I felt Mathias move around. "I'm going, I'm going!"

"Alaric?" I mind-linked.

"Yes, Octavia?" He mused. "**What can I order for you today?**"

I giggled, biting my lip. Poor thing. "**How'd you know?**"

"**For the past three days that's all you mind-link me for.**"

"**Well you're the one that knows all the good spots to eat at.**"

"**True. What are you in the mood for today?**"

"**A huge burger and a chocolate milkshake just as big.**"

"**On it, boss. I know just the place. Meet you in the kitchen?**"

I walked down the stairs, holding my aching back as I did. It had been about two weeks since my last doctor's appointment, and my stomach seemed as if it had inflated overnight. I didn't doubt the six-month pregnancy anymore. *Three and a half more months to go.*

I walked into the kitchen and took a seat at the kitchen bar. I saw one of Mason's guards standing by the staircase that led upstairs, and I sighed. Ever since Mason and Jackson figured out the mole, Mason had put guards all over the house and pack grounds. It worried me, and people were catching on, but I couldn't blame him. It made no sense to me that they just wouldn't go ahead and take him in, though. Title or not, he's a threat that needs to be taken care of. I'd rather be safe than sorry.

It wasn't long before Alaric made his appearance. He waved at me, holding his phone up. "The best burger is on its way here now. I got us both something to eat. Andrew's diner has the tastiest burgers, and I couldn't resist."

"Thank Goddess. Mathias is getting hangry, I believe."

"Hm, just like his mother, then."

"Rude. I do not get hangry!"

"You nearly bit my head off Monday during a meeting because I asked a question, and the meeting ran over. All because you were hungry. Matter of fact, I think you scared everyone in that meeting."

I stuck my tongue out at him in response.

"Child." He mumbled.

"Asshat." I threw back.

"You can be a real pain in the ass, Octavia."

"Thank you, captain obvious."

He gave me a salute. "No problem, Sargent sarcasm."

"I hate you." We both mumbled at the same time. Slowly, we looked at each other with annoyed eyes but couldn't contain ourselves as we burst out laughing. *Goddess, we're like bickering siblings.*

Alaric leaned against the kitchen bar, cocking his head to the side. "So, did Mason ever let you in on the mole situation? He is leaving me completely out of it, and I hate it. I'm his beta! These guards give me the creeps. They're everywhere." He grumbled, eyeing the one near us with an annoyed look.

I threw my hands up. "No! It's driving me insane. Every time I ask, he either ignores me or says the normal 'I can't tell you, I'm sorry.'" I mocked, shaking my head in disbelief. "And I agree. I feel these guards are stalking me." I groaned, my head falling onto the bar.

"I can't imagine who it could be. I thought it might be Alpha Evan, but I don't think he's that stupid."

"I thought that, too, but I have to agree. He's too scared of Christian to try anything like that. Plus, I really do think he's changed." I leaned forward, whispering, "Do you think it's an alpha or someone within the pack?"

"I think it's someone within the pack. No alpha could get in here without Mason knowing. I check the logs every day as well. It's not possible. It has to be an inside job. Plus, why would Mason have all these guards around?"

I sat back, slumping in my chair. "True."

Thinking his words over, my eyes narrowed. The day I was caught in the trap and taken, I was taken in my own room. It definitely had to be an inside job. Who could get into the alpha's house himself? Plus, if it were an alpha, they would have to be logged in, and Jackson said no one— I quickly looked up at Alaric, my heart lurching within my chest.

Oh, my goddess. Alaric is responsible for checking the logs…

When he caught my gaze, he raised a brow. "What?"

"Nothing. I just thought of something."

"Like?"

"If the mole is within the pack, he has to be able to get into the alpha's house. When I was taken, you know?" I asked, hoping to see some emotion from him, but nothing came.

"Yeah, I'd assume." He responded, looking down at his phone as it dinged.

He didn't look as if he guessed I was onto him, nor did he seem to get worried about it. If he were the mole, it would make sense as to why Mason had so many guards in his own house. Then again, Mason didn't seem concerned I was meeting Alaric to get me food. Maybe I'm overthinking.

"The food is here." he grinned, pushing off the bar. "Be right back."

I watched his retreating figure with an eerie feeling. Something wasn't right. My gut was telling me he was the mole and to get the hell out of here. I stood from the bar, heading toward the guard with worried eyes. Though, before I could reach him, I heard someone clear their throat.

"What are you doing?"

Slowly turning around, I saw Alaric leaning against the kitchen doorframe. I nodded toward the stairs. "I'm going to go pee." I lied, cursing myself for such a stupid reply. Patting my stomach, I gave him a weak smile. "Pregnancy problems."

He walked further into the kitchen, tossing the carryout bag onto the bar and placed my milkshake down rather harshly. "Are you sure about that? You look pretty sketched out."

I gulped, feeling as if I was in an interrogation. "No?"

To play it off, I walked over to the bar. I reached for the food, trying my best to stop my hands from shaking. I could practically hear my heartbeat in my ears. "But the smell of this food is a game-changer. My bladder will have to wait." I let out a small laugh.

Looking back at Alaric, his eyes look like they'd darkened. My eyes darted to the kitchen knives that sat on the counter next to the fridge. I grabbed my food out of the to-go sack and placed it before me.

"Want anything to drink?" I asked as I maneuvered around the bar and made my way to the fridge.

"Water is fine."

I grabbed two bottles from the fridge. As I shut the door, the bottles dropped from my hands as I lunged towards the knives. My fingertips barely grasped them before I felt his hand grab the back of my hair, yanking me back. I yelped, thrashing as he tried to hold me in place.

Out of the corner of my eye, I saw the guard kick into gear as he ran toward Alaric. Alaric pushed me forward, causing me to smack into the counter. My eyes stung as I held my throbbing stomach from the impact. He easily caught the guard, holding him in a headlock. I ripped a knife from its holder and faced him, holding it in front of me.

"Stay back! Let him go!" I warned him.

Alaric snickered in response as the guard's face turned red, then blue seconds later. Fear wracked my body as the guard dropped to the floor, unconscious.

"Mason, please get home now! I know who the mole is." I cried through our link.

Alaric looked me over, surveying my worried state. "You know, I'd be a little more scared of you if you weren't pregnant and lycanless." He grinned.

In a flash, *he lunged for me.*

CHAPTER FORTY-FIVE

———◆◇◆———

Octavia

I jumped back, swinging the knife toward him. It slashed across his forearm, drawing blood as he snarled in pain. I stared in horror as the wound healed in seconds, much too quick for his own wolf's healing. *Oh, Goddess, you're really testing me lately!*

"Help!" I screamed out.

I dodged another hit and so desperately wanted to shift into my wolf, but I had no idea how doing so would affect Mathias. *Oh, how I miss my Lycan side.*

"Put the knife down, Octavia!"

"Not in a million years!"

He reached out with one arm and caught the knife in his hand, surely slicing through it. With his other, it snaked out and grabbed me by the throat. I coughed, kicking my legs as he effortlessly raised me off my feet. When I looked into his eyes, they held no emotion nor life. It was like it wasn't even him. He ripped the knife from my hand as he tossed to the ground beside him and brought his other free hand to join his other around my throat.

I raised my arms, grabbing at what I could. I reached his face, digging my thumbs into his eyes as he cried out in pain and dropped me from his grasp. As I hit the floor with a thud, I felt a crack and gasped out, feeling breathless. As I looked up through teary eyes, Alaric had his eyes covered, cursing to himself. My back hurt terribly, but when I felt movement in my stomach, I immediately came to. My body started shaking with anger at the thought of him hurting Mathias.

A snarl ripped through me as I quickly got to my feet. Alaric tried to lunge for me once more, but I ducked, kicking my leg out and struck him in the side. Ducking low, I swung my leg out once again. When he wiped out, a breath of relief left me as I whipped around. I darted for the stairs but slowed as I was drained for a split second. I froze, feeling a painful surge through my body.

"I got it from here, little one." A voice whispered within my mind.

I raised a shaky hand only to see black veins crawl up my arm. My body immediately stopped aching and was replaced by frantic energy. Instinctively, I let go of control as I was pushed to the back of my mind. My body spun around, my arm snapping out in front of me. My hand was clenched around a knife in front of my face that was, no doubt, intended to be planted deep within my back.

Ramani? Can it be?

"You see, you don't mess with Lycan spirits. We've never really liked wolves because we are superior to you—*especially when you mess with our damn vessels.*" Ramani snarled, throwing the knife in a sharp motion. It struck Alaric in the shoulder as she sauntered toward him.

He let out a strangled cry as he jerked the embedded knife from him and tossed it aside. She ran toward him but leaned back with bent knees as he swung an arm out. One hand touched the ground as she did so, but she pushed off and turned to the side, kicking her leg out. Our foot made contact with his jaw and sent him stumbling backward. She flew upright, seeing him regain his footing. He advanced toward us once more, only angering her at his relentlessness.

"Oh, give up already. You're not going to win this!" She ordered, delivering a right hook.

"That's all you got?" He growled, raising his fists out in front of him. I was ready for her to pounce, but she cocked her head to the side as power seeped through to her, Mathias moving around within my stomach.

"Oh, I like the feeling of that power! Shall we use it?" she asked herself out loud. "I understand what you're getting at, little one. I used to be a full Lycan after all." She slowly raised her arm, but as she did so, Alaric rose with the motion. He clawed at this throat from the invisible hold on him.

"Goddess, you are stupid to go after not only your Luna but a mother with a powerful child who wishes nothing more than to protect her. Mathias sends his regards." She smiled, throwing her arm to the side. Alaric flew into a nearby wall at her motion but stayed pinned against it as she kept her arm out. "How does it feel to be powerless, Alaric?"

"What the hell?!" A voice spoke.

Ramani turned, looking at Mason and Braelyn, both standing in the doorway of the kitchen. "Mason, how nice of you to join us! You've missed the party."

Guards flooded in behind them and ran into the room, grabbing hold of Alaric as Ramani released her hold on him. Alaric shook his head, his eyes going back to their normal hue.

"What happened?" He groaned. "What's going on?"

***

As I spoke with Mason, I watched the guards handcuff Alaric with a sad look. I knew whatever was wrong with him was not his doing. The eyes that stared at me when he had been choking me were not his.

"So, you believe that he was under some sort of spell or something?" Mason asked, folding his arms.

"I'm not sure. I just know that wasn't Alaric. I know Alaric, and he would never dare hurt us."

"Agreed. He's like a brother to me. I don't see him doing something so traitorous."

The guards pushed him in front of them, motioning for him to walk. Alaric glanced at us, a pleading look in his eyes.

I heard running footsteps only to see Ashlee barge into the room, tears immediately flooding her eyes at the sight before her. "What are you doing with him?!"

"Look at me," I spoke, earning her attention. "He's going to be ok. We're taking him to a safe room until someone gets here to see what's been happening to him." I said, and she gave me a confused look.

"What do you mean?"

"He's the mole, but it didn't seem like he was in control over his body."

"No... it can't be." She spoke sadly.

"It's true, but I promise you everything will be okay." I said softly, managing a small smile.

Ashlee gave me a slow nod, fear present in her eyes. I hated seeing her hurt like this. She'd finally got a real mate and now had to deal with the idea of potentially losing him. With one last glance, I followed Mason and the guards.

I walked into the room, wincing as the guards aggressively chained him to a chair. He thrashed, confused about why he was being treated like this.

"Mason, you have to believe me." Alaric pleaded.

"I don't know what to believe! You put the woman I love in danger countless times!" He seethed, and I sighed, walking over and laid a hand on his shoulder.

"Let's just wait for her," I mumbled.

Mason visibly relaxed at my touch. He was hurt. I know he didn't want to see Alaric in a bad light, but the idea of Mathias and me almost getting hurt once again because of him didn't sit well with him.

"Her?" Alaric spoke, and I looked over to meet his eyes.

"Have you been losing your memory lately? Just bits and pieces of time that have seemed to vanish?" I questioned him, and he looked shocked by my words.

"At times… yeah. I didn't think about it. I had been drinking a bit. I just thought it was due to that." He mumbled, looking at his feet.

"I called Scarlett. I feel something has its hold on you. Your eyes clouded over like you just lost control. It was frightening. She called Alara Lavender. She's going to come do a reading on you to see if we're right." Alaric stiffened at the name.

"And if you're wrong? If she can't find anything, then what's next?"

"You're taken to the pack cells." Mason declared, avoiding Alaric's eyes.

We waited for what seemed like hours until we heard the rumbling of thunder. Alara was here. I tensed, praying to the Goddess she could fix him and that we weren't wrong. Chilling authority wrapped around us as the door opened, revealing none other than Alara Lavender herself.

"I was told to come here. Where is he?" We moved aside, letting Alaric come into view.

Her brows furrowed as she neared him, holding her palm out flat in front of his face. "I can already feel the hold on him."

"Can you see what it is?" Mason asked.

"Yes, but the way I have to do it is going to hurt like a bitch." She gave no one time to speak as she grabbed the sides of his head, and Alaric let out a groan of pain and clenched his teeth together.

Alara's head fell backward, and she started mumbling to herself. Her eyes rolled in the back of her head as she mumbled words in a foreign language. When her words grew louder, Alaric screamed out in pain, causing me to grab ahold of Mason, burying my face into his chest. The screams were terrifying.

"I said reveal yourself, now!" she yelled out. "Fine, I'll do it myself!"

Eventually, the room went silent. I turned slightly, seeing Alara jerk away from Alaric. She stared at him with wide eyes, her hands trembling slightly, and she looked pale as a ghost. Alaric's head fell forward, unconscious.

Mason took a wary step towards them. "What is it? What did you see?"

Alara gulped, her eyes not leaving Alaric's body. "I broke the hold that was on him. Whatever it was, it's gone." She reluctantly turned around, looking as if she didn't know what to do. "I need to speak with Scarlett."

"Do you know what did this to him? You can't leave until we know." Mason snapped.

"I dug through his memories. He wasn't technically your mole; it was someone else using him as a ... spy, you could say. I commanded them to reveal themselves, and they wouldn't, so I seeped deeper into his mind to find them for myself. I have never felt so much power before besides Scarlett or me. When I broke the link that tied whoever was doing this and him together, it revealed who it was. My brother." My jaw dropped at the newfound information.

"I thought only you and Scarlett were living from the coven?"

"I did too. It's not possible for him to be alive." She mumbled.

"Why?"

"Because I killed him." She declared, raising her chin. "He came after my mother. He was a lunatic, Mason. I watched him kill her and take her power, and one day, I just snapped. I couldn't let him hurt any more people I loved."

"If you killed him, is it possible for him to be alive again?"

"No. That's why I feel it's a very dark being."

I raised a brow. "And what's that?"

"They call themselves shifters. They can peak into your mind and find your worst fear, and they use it to their advantage. That is probably how they got their hooks in your friend here, but it's gone now."

"Thank you, Alara," I mumbled, and she gave me a small nod.

"Whoever they were, they were working with the hunters, and I have a feeling the shifter isn't done yet. They would have left your friend if it was done since the war is over with. It didn't." She added and looked at Mason. "Does Octavia have any enemies?"

"I'm the alpha of war. We have many."

"Well, I wouldn't worry about them right now. Now that I got a glimpse at who they really are, they ran for the hills." She informed me, placing a comforting hand on my shoulder. "And they seemed to be frightened at how Ramani took over your body and merged back with you." She added.

"Well, good. It was a scary moment for me too." I placed a hand on my stomach, and she stared longingly at it but quickly cleared her throat.

"The shifter knows you're well protected from all sides no matter what. If you're wondering why Ramani was able to merge back with you, it was because Mathias sensed your fear and knew he had to do something to protect you." She explained.

Ramani hadn't spoken a word since she'd merged back.

"Besides, they know I'm coming for them. And I'm going to make it painful." She gritted out, stomping over to the door. She opened it, turning her head. "He should wake in a few hours." With that, she fled from the room.

"Goddess, this is a relief," Mason mumbled, running a hand over his face.

"It is. Can I ask you something?"

"Of course."

"Why did you let me go meet Alaric for lunch? If you knew that he was the mole, why let me ever be alone around him?" I couldn't help but feel slightly angry.

"Octavia... I never suspected it was Alaric. I was too blinded by his loyalty to me to even assume. We thought it was Alpha Evan. He had enough authority to do what Alaric did. We thought he was out for revenge. I guess... we were wrong to assume the worst in him. The minute I got your mind-link, I felt sick. I'm just glad Ramani came back and that Alara could help us too."

Glancing back at the door Alara left from, I sighed. "I'll be right back. We'll talk about this later." I made my way out of the room to run after Alara hoping she wasn't gone yet.

However, when I entered the hall, I halted. I saw her figure stopped a few feet away from the room. She had a hand against the wall with her other covering her mouth as she shook lightly. *She was crying.*

"Alara?" I called out.

She stiffened, turning her back fully to me. "Yes?" She croaked out.

"Are you okay?"

Slowly, she turned to face me. The cold-hearted witch everyone knew was gone, and in her place stood a teary blue-eyed beauty. I never knew she could grasp such emotions from the stories I had heard. Though, maybe I needed to stop listening to the lies people spoke and instead focus on the truth in front of my eyes. She was just like the rest of us—human and burdened by the horrors of her past.

"Yes. Just shaken up after seeing such a face I buried from so long ago." She admitted and quickly wiped her face.

"What did he do to you, Alara? Besides what happened with your mother, what did he do to cause you so much pain?"

Her eyes flooded with tears again. "He made me a barren woman. He cast a spell on me when I found my mate, Evan. He hated Evan so much because he was a wolf. He thought I was turning on my own kind by loving the wolves. I was going to run back to Evan's pack with him, but my brother caught wind of my departure. He thought I betrayed him and created the spell. Only he could break it, and I killed him before he could." My chest ached at her response.

I couldn't imagine not being able to conceive a child and what that could do to one mentally. No wonder she is like she is. The world constantly turned against her, even her own brother.

"I'm so sorry, Alara."

She sniffled, wiping her face once more. "It's whatever. There's nothing I can do now. Cherish your baby, Octavia. Some people aren't as lucky. I got your message about doing the protection spell on you for the birth. It would be my honor. You will hold your baby and walk out of that room. I'll see you around."

As I watched her walk down the hall, I could only want to know more about her.

CHAPTER FORTY-SIX

$\bullet\!-\!\diamond\!-\!\bullet$

Octavia

Months flew by like a breeze. Alaric was fine and back in the arms of his mate. Mason and I gave our speeches to the people of our pack to honor their loved ones who sacrificed their lives to save our people. Mathias was growing like a weed, and we were just a week out from my due date. I learned to channel Mason and was doing a good job at it. Scarlett gave birth to two beautiful twins. The other alphas were doing great, and Ramani was fully back as well. She explained everything that had happened when the shifter controlled Alaric.

Just as Alara had said, Mathias felt my fear and knew I was in danger. He let Ramani merge with me in hopes of saving me. Now, she gets to stay. She can also use his gifts while he's still in the womb, hence how she picked Alaric up without even touching him. She can even speak to him, which amazes me. Apparently, his own Lycan spirit is developing quickly.

It's not full conversations, she said, but she can grasp his emotions well. Everything was going well—for at least a few more minutes, that is.

"I can't believe we're doing this," I grumbled, smoothing out my hair.

"Octavia, it has been almost a year since you've seen your parents. This needs to happen. I know a lot has been drugged up from your past recently, and that's taken a toll on you, but at least for your mother's sake, please do this."

"We're having dinner with my mother and father. It's going to end in a mess. My father knows we have come out as Lycans, which he despises. There's no telling what Ramani will do either when she sees him. I'm genuinely concerned for him."

When my mother had reached out, asking to see me when she caught wind of my pregnancy, I didn't know whether to be grateful or mad. I did miss her, she's my mother after all, but it took me getting pregnant for her wanting to see me again?

"I will be there to be the mediator then." Mason grinned, wrapping his arms around me.

I looked up at him with a sigh. "This might put me into labor. I'm already stressed just thinking about it."

He chuckled. "Well, at least Alara went ahead and put the protection spell on you already. We are more than prepared. Honestly, I think this dinner will be good for you. It might give you the closure you need. Ramani, too."

"Maybe so." Mason placed a kiss on my forehead and pulled back as his eyes clouded over.

"Alaric just mind-linked me. Your parents have arrived."

"Lovely," I grumbled.

I pulled away from his grasp and stepped back, doing a small twirl. "How do I look?"

"Like a Goddess." He replied, looking me over.

I had on a simple red sundress. It was honestly the only nice thing I had that fit my rounded belly. I ran my hand over my stomach and held the clothing tight underneath it as I turned to the side.

"Am I glowing?" I teased.

Mason chuckled, reaching out to run a hand over my stomach. "Indeed, you are. Now, I believe we best be on our way since our guests are waiting."

I frowned, not wanting to do this. Reluctantly, I followed him out of our room. We reached the dining room shortly after, and I took a deep breath. I can do this. My father will not dictate my life any longer.

Mason laced our fingers together and gave my hand a small, encouraging squeeze. I let him guide me into the room, and when I laid eyes on my parents, my heart skipped a beat. My mom gasped, covering her mouth when she saw me.

"Oh, Octavia! You're glowing!" she gushed, nearly running over to me.

I let out a small laugh, looking down at my stomach. "He has grown so quickly."

"He has! Wow. It's such a beautiful sight. What are you naming him?"

"Mathias Cage." I grinned, rubbing my stomach as he eagerly kicked around.

"I like it." My father spoke up. My eyes slowly moved to meet his. "A warrior of a name. Just like his mother and father."

I bit my tongue and managed a smile. He was being nice, Octavia, act right.

"Of course, he'd like the name of a warrior." Ramani scoffed.

Not now, Ramani, not now.

"It's nice to meet you two officially. Mason Cage," Mason spoke up, holding his hand out.

"It's nice to meet you as well. I'm Chelsey, and this is my husband, Keaton." My mother shook his hand respectfully, and my father followed shortly after.

"I do apologize for not having you over sooner. The day I met Octavia, I had a lot on my plate. The weeks after didn't slow down either. As I'm sure you know, the war was very rough on us."

"Understandable. We are just as at fault. I should have called sooner." Mother replied, glancing at me with regretful eyes.

"Shall we sit?" Mason asked, and I was more than happy to scurry over to my seat, plopping down at the table.

"So, the red eyes? Lycan thing?" My father asked, clearing his throat.

I nodded. "Mathias is a full Lycan. Until he is born, my eyes will remain red. I guess it's a warning type of thing. He's very protective already." I explained.

I watched my father try not to cringe at hearing his grandson would be a full Lycan. I knew he was trying his best and, for that, I had to give him credit.

"Interesting." My mother cooed, leaning forward eagerly. "Tell me all about it!"

So, I did. I explained what had happened to me during the war and how I had lost Ramani temporarily. Then Mathias saved my life. I went more into detail about the birth and how Mathias would be special with his abilities. My mother seemed to be in awe of her grandson, but my father was the opposite. He sat silent, not speaking once.

"I hope you all are hungry. I had the chef make us some Italian for dinner. We have fettuccine alfredo amongst other things." Mason changed the subject, sensing my father's growing irritation. As if hearing Mason, the servers walked out with plates of food.

We sat in silence for a few moments as we ate. It was annoyingly awkward with pent-up emotions no one wanted to speak on. Ramani's anger bubbled by the second, trying to remain calm as she stared at the man who caused her so much pain all those years ago. I looked up, catching my father's gaze. We shared unspoken words. He was disappointed. I could tell.

"Something on your mind?" I asked, biting into a piece of garlic bread.

"I just have one question." He blurted out, dropping his fork onto his plate.

I sighed, grabbing my napkin, and wiped my mouth before tossing it on the table and folded my arms. Here we go. "And that is?"

"Why come out as Lycans? You could be in danger, Octavia. You should know better than anyone that the church despises Lycans."

"The church fears our good friends. We have no worries." Mason all but snapped.

"You say that, yet many people would like to see you dead." He shot back.

"They've tried." I sneered. "Yet they failed again and again. You should know that, *Father*."

"Octavia, I just want what's—"

I was forced out of control. "Best for us?!" Ramani snarled. "You never wanted anything but to use me as a weapon. What, Keaton, mad that you can't control us anymore? Shut your mouth before I finish what I should have had many years ago."

"Ramani, enough." Orion snapped, taking control of Mason.

"Oh, look, now we have both Lycans out." Dad laughed humorlessly. "How lovely. Chelsey, we should have never come."

"You're finally right about something," Ramani growled as Father stood from his seat. His movement set her off as she flew up from our seat as well, giving him a challenging look.

"Enough! I'm so sick of this!" My mother screamed, causing even Ramani to wince. "Keaton, sit the hell down! Now!" she ordered.

"I don't want to be here. I didn't want to come to this! I don't give a damn about her anymore! She's chosen her people, and that's not us." He snarled.

My chest ached as Ramani threw me back into control. She finally got the words she wanted to hear—wanted me to hear. Stop trying with him, she had once told me. Even though I expected such harsh words from him, I didn't know it'd hurt me that much. Tears brimmed my eyes as I stared at the horrible excuse of a father.

"Then get the hell out of here." Mother snapped. "I'm sick of being in the middle of all this. I can't take it anymore. Each day my daughter was away from me, my heart ached. I love her, and you should, too! You're her father, Keaton. Shame on you. I wanted to reach out so many times to her, but you always talked me out of it. You made me think that she didn't want us anymore, and I believed you. I'm done with your manipulative ways. I gave you a second chance once, and I'm out of those now. Leave. I am done."

"Chelsey, don't do this—"

"No! You made your choice with those hateful words you just spoke about her. Yes, she's different, but that shouldn't matter. Ramani has protected her more than either of us ever has. Be grateful. She may have chosen her people, but I have, too. I want a life with my daughter in it and my grandson, so leave. I can be happy without you."

"Chelsey—"

"You heard the woman. Leave. Now, before I make you." Mason gritted out.

I quickly wiped away a stray tear as my father angrily fled from the room. Looking up at my mother, she held an apologetic look.

"I am so sorry, Octavia. If you want me to leave as well, I will. I haven't been a good mother, and, for that, I'll never be able to forgive myself. I love you with everything in me as well as Ramani. I thank her for protecting you these past few years. It doesn't matter what you are or what your son will be. I will love you both unconditionally." She went to stand from the table, but I stopped her.

"No, please stay. I… I need you, Mom." I choked out. "I'm at fault, too. I associate you with Dad so much, and I didn't even bother to hear your side. I'm so sorry." I cried.

"Oh, my baby." She rushed around the table and wrapped her arms around me. "I will always be here for you."

My chest shook with heavy sobs. All the sadness and anger finally left my body as we cried together. Even Ramani wept as I felt her sadness wash over me. My mother's words affected us both more than she knew. When I pulled back, she smiled, wiping my tears.

"You are such a beautiful and strong woman. Never *ever* see yourself differently. It is me, after all, who carried the ancestor gene in the family for the Lycans. Your father can't hate you without hating me as well. We're a team now. I'm not going anywhere."

"Chelsey, you are more than welcome to stay here as long as you need. If you'd like, I'll even send someone for your belongings and get you a place within our pack. I'll talk to Alpha Ryker and get you transferred as a War Pack member. You just say the words." Mason stated.

"I'd appreciate that very much. I can no longer be with a man like that. I just can't. Not after what he's done to our family."

"Then consider it done. Welcome to The War Pack."

CHAPTER FORTY-SEVEN

—◆—

Octavia

I cried out at the pain that wracked my body.

"In and out like I taught you!" My mother reminded me, showing me the breaths to do. I mocked her motions, trying my best to get through these contractions.

"Mason, hurry up!" I yelled.

"I'm driving as fast as I can!" He stressed, whipping into the parking lot of the hospital.

As I looked out the window, I saw all the nurses and doctors waiting outside for our arrival. Mathias had decided to come a day early, which I was more than pleased about. News had broken out that their Luna was in labor, and by the looks of it, many people had gathered at the hospital to show their support.

I was glad that I had a week with my mother to prepare me for this moment. She had taught me everything she knew and what helped her best through her birthing experience with me. It was safe to say that she had been my rock this past week.

It was a blur as I was helped out of the car and into the hospital. I probably looked like a lunatic as I was rolled in. I had black veins crawling up all parts of my body. Ramani was doing her best to help me with the pain, but Mathias was quite literally draining any energy I had. He was ready to enter this world, and he was coming quicker than we thought. I cried out in pain, squeezing Mason's hand tightly. He looked pale as we rushed down the hallways to our room. I think he was more nervous than I was.

"You can do this!" He encouraged me, but I groaned in pain, questioning whether that was true or not.

"You're getting fixed after this!" I sneered, squeezing his hand. "I'm never doing this again!"

He dared to laugh. "We'll discuss that later."

Dr. Asher made her way into my room, gowning and gloving up. "This baby is coming now. Full Lycans don't waste time." She spoke up, her team following in after her.

"Mason, sit down. She needs to start channeling you now!"

My eyes nearly left my head as he dropped my hand, walking to a chair next to my bed. "No! I need you next to me!" I cried out, holding my hand back up.

"He has to sit, Octavia. We can't have him passing out during this." Dr. Asher reminded me.

"I got you, baby girl." My mom rushed out, running to my side. She grabbed my hand, squeezing it tightly. "Squeeze as hard as you can, all right?"

I nodded, taking in a sharp breath. "I can do this."

Dr. Asher walked over, helping me get set up. Glancing at me, she nodded. "It's time. Push, Octavia."

I closed my eyes, channeling Mason as he had taught me to. The minute I felt myself grow stronger, I screamed in pain, listening to Dr. Asher's orders. This was brutal.

Everything around me blurred and clashed together. I heard yelling and things clattering. Turning my head to the side with weak eyes, I met Mason's worried ones. He didn't have the energy to move as he stared at me. Black veins were swarming his body up to his neck. Dr. Asher yelled something at me once more, but I grew terribly weak. I had to do this.

With as much strength that I could gather, an ear-piercing scream left me—then that's when I heard it. A baby's cry. My mother let out a happy sob as she stared at Dr. Asher. I released my link with Mason, coming to. My body instantly surged with energy, which I'm assuming was my Lycan healing kicking into play. Dr. Asher smiled at me, holding Mathias in her arms. She turned to the side, showing me him.

"Say hello to momma, Mathias." She cooed.

Mason stumbled to his feet, walking over to our son. Tears filled his eyes as he looked him over with nothing but pure adoration. My head fell back against my pillow as I let out a breath of relief. I'm alive, Mathias is alive, Mason is alive. *We did it.*

Soon, Mason walked next to me, holding a newly wrapped up Mathias. Slowly, he placed him in my arms. My bottom lip trembled as I first made contact with him. I stared at him through tired eyes, my energy coming back slowly but surely.

"He's so beautiful." I choked up as Mason wrapped an arm around my shoulders.

"You're amazing, you know that?" Mason asked me, and I let out a small laugh in response.

"We made this." I looked up at him, astounded. It was his turn to chuckle.

"We did." We looked down, seeing Mathias suddenly open his eyes. We stared in awe as they flashed red but then went right back to his beautiful brown.

"His eyes have met mine just once, and I know I'm a goner. I'm never leaving his side." I declared.

"Me either." Mason smiled and looked down at Mathias.

"You two have a healthy baby boy *and* mother. Congratulations. I'll give you some time." Dr. Asher spoke, and I thanked her before she left the room.

"Mom, do you want to hold him?" I asked, and her eyes lit up.

She eagerly reached forward, taking him into her arms. "Hello, Mathias. Oh, I can't wait to spoil you. You'd love that, wouldn't you? Grandma giving you all sorts of treats?" Mathias let out a content sound, and we all three laughed. Goddess, I was so content at this moment.

Glancing up at Mason, I rested my head against his shoulder as he sat on the edge next to me. "I love you."

"I love you, too, Octavia."

***

I was thankful for my Lycan's healing process. It wasn't long before I was discharged from the hospital and took Mathias home. The days I spent in the hospital were blissful, and I rarely wanted to let Mathias leave my arms, but Mason informed me that I was being stingy—whatever that means, he's my child, after all.

However, when we got home, we were surprised with friends, family, and gifts. I was in awe at the thoughtfulness of Scarlett. She had put it all together.

"You're too kind." I thanked her, giving her a big hug.

"You deserve this after all you went through. Where is the little one?" she beamed.

I moved aside, letting her see Mason, who was holding Mathias. "He's sleeping," Mason whispered, moving closer to her.

Scarlett peered over at Mathias, puffing her bottom lip out. "Awe! He is the cutest!" she cooed.

"Congratulations!" Christian walked up to us.

"Congratulations to yourself. Where are your little ones?" Mason asked.

Christian pointed to Alpha Ryker and Madeline, who were each holding a baby. "Ryker is surprisingly good with children. It's very odd." He mumbled.

"Maybe it's a wake-up call for him." I teased and placed my hand on Mason's forearm. "I'm going to go and say hi and see the babies." He nodded, turning to let Christian see Mathias.

Walking over, I grinned at Madeleine as she turned to show me the baby. "All these babies are giving me baby fever." She stated.

"They are gorgeous, much like their parents," I replied. "Thank you all for coming. It means a lot."

"You're welcome! Congratulations, Octavia. You've come a long way. I'm proud. It feels like so long ago when I found you shot in my club." Ryker mused.

I snorted, shaking my head. "I'm glad those times are behind me."

Looking around, I smiled at my surroundings. I was blessed to have so many great friends and family. The alphas had come to show their support and to give their congratulations. Mason beamed as he showed Mathias to everyone, my mom was making new friends, and I was more than content. I was so lucky.

Looking back at Ryker and Madeline, I raised a brow. "You never told us how you both met."

Ryker smirked. "Well… let me be the one to tell you. It's quite the story."

ACKNOWLEDGMENTS

Wow. I cannot believe I have finished another book! This has been such an amazing journey, and I was so excited for all of you to be able to learn Octavia and Mason's story. I cannot wait for you to dive deep into book three, "The Power Bond" to see what Ryker and Madeline have in store for you. Thank you to all who made this possible.

I would like to thank my fans from Wattpad and Radish, who have supported me from day one. None of this would be possible without each and every one of you. Thank you to my family, who all supported this girl with a big dream and made it happen. Your constant love and support helped me tremendously. Thank you to my parents, who will always be my number one fans. I love you.

As always, thank you to my best friend, Emmy Parke, who has been here behind the scenes. She has helped me figure out plot lines when I get stressed and don't know where to go or whether my ideas are good or not. I will always love you and be grateful for your kindness and friendship— you're a real one. Thank you to my best friend, Taylor Vincent, who has been here since I first started writing and always said she would be the first one to buy my books when I got published—she stayed true to her word! She also helped me stay motivated to write during book two's process, and without her, I don't know if this book would have been done as quickly as it was. I love you!

Lastly, thank you to my editor, Paige Lawson, for working with me through this much longer book and helping me make this book amazing! You're the best! Thank you to Maja, my cover designer, for designing such a beautiful cover. You always amaze me.

As always, **bunches of love.**

ABOUT THE AUTHOR

KEYLEE HARGIS is currently in the midst of publishing her series "The Bond Series," with The War Bond being her second. Keylee hails from Bowling Green, Kentucky, and enjoys spending time with her friends and family. When she's not reading or writing, she enjoys videography and photography. As she furthers her career as a writer, she is excited to see what the future holds.